Why She Married Him

Why She Married Him

MYRIAM CHAPMAN

For Diana,
 Best wishes in the .
New year — Hope you enjoy
this —
 Myriam Chapman
 12/24/05

OTHER PRESS • NEW YORK

Fic
Chr

Production Editor: Robert D. Hack
Text design: Rachel Reiss
This book was set in 10 pt. Arrus by Alpha Graphics of Pittsfield, NH.

10 9 8 7 6 5 4 3 2 1

Library of Congress Cataloging-in-Publication Data

Chapman, Myriam.
  Why she married him / by Myriam Chapman.
    p. cm.
  ISBN 1-59051-175-1 (hardcover : alk. paper) 1. Jewish women–Fiction.
2. Paris (France)–Fiction. 3. Fashion illustrators–Fiction. 4. Women
immigrants–Fiction. 5. Married women–Fiction. 6. Ukraine–Fiction.
7. Tailors–Fiction. 8. Domestic fiction. lcsh 9. Jewish fiction. lcsh I. Title.
  PS3603.H374W47 2005
  813'.6–dc22

                        2004027000

For Nina's descendants and especially for
Augusta, Nora, May, and Ophelia

ACKNOWLEDGMENTS

HEARTFELT THANKS TO IRENE Bowers, Rachel Brownstein, and Susan Glendening for their steady faith in me; to Jean Ayer, Helene Campbell, Adele Glimm, Tom House, Eleanor Hyde, Elisabeth Jakab, Pat Kulleseid, Carol Pepper, Maureen Sladen, and Marcia Slatkin for their support, comments, and encouragement; to Miriam Finkelstein, whose insight and humor I miss; to Andrew and Lisa, Jon and Jennifer and the little people for their sustaining affection.

And special thanks to my agent, Elaine Koster, for her confidence in the project, and to my editor, Rosemary Ahern, for her careful, always sensitive editing.

Wedding Night

Paris
June 1912

I

A YOUNG WOMAN WEARING A blue satin suit, the same suit she was married in only the week before, sits in an armchair beside an open window. It is about ten o'clock on a mild night in June. A light breeze passes through the heavy lace curtains but does not ruffle them. The street, four stories below, is quiet, although a horse-drawn carriage occasionally clatters on the pavement, a sound the young woman doesn't hear because, like all city dwellers, she has learned to shut out city noises. Besides, she is not interested in the world outside. All her world is in this room. It is her husband's room and now it is hers too.

The young woman sits straight in the chair and crosses her feet at the ankles. The tips of her shoes are just visible under the long skirt. She wears low-heeled shoes in gray suede with blue leather trim that matches her suit. The skirt of the suit is fashionably narrow and the tunic jacket flares like a bell over the skirt, showing off her tiny, corseted waist. Her mother made the suit for her. Her mother is a fine seamstress and her father a fine tailor. That is why her wedding suit is so well made: the darts are where they should be, the seams are straight, the hem is tight. It is a good piece of work and it fits her perfectly. Wearing it, she thinks she is as well dressed as any rich, fashionable girl in Paris, although it is not what she dreamed of wearing to her wedding. Her hair, brown, abundant, shiny, the way young hair is, but too curly, almost unruly, is piled on top of her head. Her hat is on her lap, a straw hat also dyed blue with blue ostrich plumes around the brim and a veil that when pulled over her eyes, gives her, she feels, a mysterious, worldly air. The hat was created especially for the wedding by a real milliner, a friend of the family. She will not place it on the table or hang it over the back of the chair or on one of the wooden pegs that her new husband uses to hang his clothes. The hat remains on her lap where it covers her virginity. For although she has been married a week, she is still a virgin.

Her name is Nina Chaimovna Schavranski. She is twenty-two years old, not so young to be married. She is considered a pretty girl. Her mouth is small and clearly outlined as if the rim of her lips had been hemmed by a fine seamstress. Her eyes are brown and deep-set; her hands well-shaped. She is proud of her hands—her fingers are flexible; her fingertips small with rounded nails. She plays the piano. Or rather she played the piano in her parents' house in Yekaterinoslav. Since she left Russia, she has played the piano only in other people's houses. Now that she is married she doesn't know if she will ever play the piano again. There is no piano in this room and besides, her husband is tone deaf.

The room is small. There are two windows each with an iron grill surrounding a ledge just big enough for a pot of flowers—although there is none now. There is a double bed, and although Nina knows that married couples must sleep in the same bed, it bothers her that her husband, a bachelor for so long, has been sleeping in a double bed all this time. Of course, his visiting cousin Josef slept in the bed with him until yesterday. But who else? It is a thought she cannot ignore, like a tickle at the back of her throat signaling the onset of a cold, an apprehension of something unpleasant, a worry.

Her husband is also in the room. His name is Abraham Podselver. He is a young man, although not so young as she, twenty-nine, his hair already receding so that he looks older than he is. He has taken off his jacket. His shirt is clean and he has removed the cufflinks and rolled up his sleeves. He is wearing braces. His trousers are made of brown wool and there are wooden buttons along the fly front. He is on his knees. But he is not a supplicant; he is not begging her for anything. He is scrubbing the floor with a brush, sloshing soapy water on the bare wood that looks as if it has never been polished. In Yekaterinoslav, when she was a little girl, Nina was allowed to skate across the floor on old wool rags after Gascha or Rouia had spread a coat of wax on the dining-room floor. Now she wonders if she will ever know such silly, childish joys again.

Abraham sops up the dirty water with an old towel. He wrings the towel into the bucket he borrowed from the concierge. Madame Blanche neglected to clean the room today, even to make the bed— on purpose, perhaps. She is a sly old woman and she drinks.

"Let me help you," Nina says, her voice aggrieved, but not convincing. She does not want to help Abraham. She does not want to get on her knees in her wedding suit and scrub the floor with her new husband. It humiliates her to see him on his knees like a charwoman.

Her husband does not look up. He continues to slap the towel on the floor, to wring the water into the bucket. He seems, if not happy, at least content. This is what annoys Nina most. She is nothing to him at the moment; she might as well be anywhere else, in some backward town in Russia, on the moon. At least if she were far away he might yearn for her. And she for him.

Now that the wood is thoroughly wet, a faint smell of rot rises from the floor. She turns her head toward the window, but all she sees are the facades of other apartment houses like this one, three or four stories high and shuttered for the night. A street lamp gives off a dusty, not very hopeful light.

She sits, staring out of the window, stunned into silence by misgivings. How is her life going to be altered?

Just this afternoon, Abraham came to her parents' apartment and, after shaking hands with her mother and father, but without removing his hat, announced that he was taking her back to his room. Her mother had just set out the glasses for tea. The polished copper samovar they had brought from Russia glistened on the red embroidered cloth. There was a jar of raspberry jam on the table to sweeten the tea and three portions of apple tart. Oh, Nina thinks, remembering the scene, I never finished my tea, and her throat tightens with loss.

Abraham's announcement was not a surprise. They had agreed to postpone their wedding night until Abraham's cousin Josef, who was staying with Abraham for the wedding, returned to Vienna. They had counted on a week's delay, and now the week was over. A reprieve, Nina thought at the time. So it startled Nina when Abraham appeared in her parents' house, so confident, so certain of his claim on her.

When Nina's mother offered Abraham a glass of tea, he refused, saying it was getting late and that he had much work to do the following day. Her mother's face shut down and Nina sensed, once again, how disappointed she was in her daughter's marriage, because it had been Nina's choice, yes, yes, she had wanted to marry him, although everyone said he isn't good enough for you, he is a hard man, and she had said, I know, I know, but he'll change, I know he will.

"Give me something to do," she says to her husband who is washing his hands in the porcelain basin. She has finally put her hat on the table, next to her gray calfskin gloves.

"You can make the bed," he says and points to a pile of worn linen sheets on a chair.

"Are they clean?"

He gives her a dark look, but doesn't answer. She has offended him. He is always clean. His nails are clean, his shirt collars are clean, his cuffs are clean. Everything about him is clean, spotless. Why should that bother her?

She smoothes the bottom sheet over the bed, tucks it in. She slips the cases over the large square pillows as her mother taught her, turning the case inside out and shaking the pillow into it. She plumps up the neck roll. She slips the top sheet over the bottom and pulls the blanket over the sheet. As she works, she feels better, purposeful, housewifely. She knows what she is doing. Work is what will bind her to her husband.

When the bed is made, she turns to Abraham. He has slipped his arms out of his braces, undone the buttons on his trousers. He steps out of his trousers and hangs them on the peg against the wall. He removes his shirt, drapes it over the trousers. Now he is standing in his underwear, a sleeveless undershirt and cotton pants that come down past his knees. Nina has seen men's underwear before, among the piles of laundry that the laundress brings back every week, in shop windows, in the catalogue of the *Manufacture de France*, but never on a man. Her father does not appear before her in his underclothes and her younger brother affects a black silk robe whenever he is not fully dressed. So she is shocked by her husband's brazen assertion of intimacy and averts her eyes.

Abraham walks past her without a word. He climbs into the newly made bed.

"Well," he says, his voice rough, as if the words scraped his throat. "Close the shutters and come to bed."

She leans over the night table and turns down the kerosene lamp. The smoky, oily smell nauseates her. At home, her home in Paris, there is a proper toilet, running cold water. Gas has been promised soon. What has she done to her life? In the semidarkness, Nina walks to the window, and leans across the sill. The pungent smell of horse manure mingles with the delicate odor of linden trees in bloom. Nina yearns for her father to brush her hair, her mother to place a goodnight kiss on her forehead. She wants to sip tea from a glass in a filigreed silver glass holder with a spoonful of raspberry jam in her mouth.

She pulls the shutters closed and slips the metal bar across the window. Her husband is breathing heavily. Perhaps he is asleep. She wishes he were. She is apprehensive. She knows what will happen in bed, although she cannot say who told her, certainly not her mother. And she knows this is the price she has to pay for taking her place in society; her connection to Abraham is what will keep her life in place. As she stares at the shape her husband makes under the covers, she hopes this passage will not be too difficult, not too humiliating.

She begins to undress, slips off her shoes, unrolls her stockings. She unbuttons her jacket, unhooks her skirt and lets it fall to the floor. She removes her long-sleeved silk blouse. She unpins her hair; it cascades in tight curls around her shoulders. She undoes the laces of her corset. In her camisole and long slip, she feels free. She breathes in the night air and her limbs loosen. Her breath quickens; a filament of hope rises up inside her. She wants her husband to wake up and take her in his arms. She wants him to whisper "I love you," which he has not yet done this evening. She wants him to ease her into that rapturous feeling she discovered—when? Not so long ago, two years to be exact. Two years ago she wanted to be kissed and touched and loved. And she was. But not by Abraham. A flush of shame, regret, and anger covers her neck and shoulders. And Nina cannot tell if she is ashamed of what she felt or of the fact that it was not for Abraham that she felt it.

All that is over now. She slips her nightshirt over her head and in the dark, struggles to remove her combination. When she is done, she lets the nightshirt drop modestly over her legs. She fixes her hair in a thick braid. She does love Abraham, she thinks as she walks toward the bed—he is her man now.

Abraham stirs slightly as the bedspring creaks. He makes a small sound in the back of his throat—a snore, perhaps. Nina lies on her back, her heart pounding, her arms and legs tense as wires until a series of images, unbidden, disconnected, soothing, float by her mind's eye—blooming horse chestnuts in the Square d'Anvers, the endlessly sloping rue de Rochechouart at night, lilacs on the Place du Tertre, pansies shivering in their flowerbeds near the Sacré Coeur—and she falls asleep.

Sometime in the night, Abraham reaches for her and she, half asleep, lets herself be taken. When it is over and Abraham has rolled to his side of the bed, she wipes her thighs with the bottom of her nightshirt and stuffs the damp material between her legs. She lets the tears dry on her cheeks.

She is still awake when morning light filters through the slats of the shutters. She slips out of her husband's bed. If he is awake, he does not detain her. She dresses quickly in her blue satin wedding suit. Carrying her shoes, she unlatches the door with her free hand and pulls it closed behind her. She hears the latch click as it catches in the lock and her own breath seems to catch in her chest.

Madame Blanche, coming up the stairs with her early morning mop and bucket, sees her weeping on the landing and says, "Where are you going at this hour? Home to Mama already?" And perhaps because she is a little sorry for the young woman, Madame Blanche adds, "Don't make such a scene, Madame Nina. This is what comes of being too well brought up."

Courtship

Paris

1910–1912

II

ABRAHAM PODSELVER HAS NOT found the seat he wanted in the back room of the Café Charles on the Boulevard Barbès. He should have arrived at least twenty minutes earlier before all the front-row chairs were taken. Now the only available ones are in the back, and he will have to crane his neck over a sea of hats to catch a glimpse of Lunacharsky, the speaker this Saturday night at the Russian University. And so he resigns himself to waiting, arms folded across his chest, his bad left leg stretched out under the rungs of the chair in front of him, for the lecture to begin.

The room reeks of stale beer and sweat. Cigarette smoke clots the air. Gaslights flicker blue and yellow. The audience is mostly men but also some women, who greet one another loudly in Russian across the room. The windows are closed and curtained; a small wooden table and a chair have been set up in the front of the room. There is a carafe of water and a half-filled glass on the table.

Abraham jiggles his good right leg impatiently. He wears a brown wool suit, a cream-colored shirt with a stiff white collar, brown shoes, and a brown bowler, which he has placed in his lap. His clothes are well made and clean, although the fabric of the shirt is handkerchief-thin from frequent washing. His nose is large and prominent, curling dark hair recedes over a domed forehead. He sports a bushy mustache and most days a deep scowl; his eyes are brown, serious, and a little sad. He limps, the result of a badly set hip injury acquired in a Russian prison. He believes, when he thinks about what he looks like, which is not often, that he is indistinguishable from any number of young men in a big city. But that is not true. He looks like what he is, a foreigner, a Jew. In a crowd of Frenchmen, he stands out, but here in the Café Charles, he is unremarkable.

He has been in Paris for three months. Before that, he lived in Vienna, and before that he was in a prison settlement in the north of Russia, near Archangelsk. Since his arrival in Paris, he has been attending lectures at the Russian University every week. The Russian University is not a university at all, but a meeting room and lecture hall for Russian political emigrés. Famous speakers, Chernov, Lunacharsky, Trotsky himself, have lectured here to packed audiences of Social Democrats, Social Revolutionaries, terrorists, anarchists, who have come to Paris to wait for or to plot the overthrow of the Tsar and the capitalist system.

Abraham is used to attending political rallies, clandestine lectures, secret meetings. In Kovno, where he was born, he was arrested for plotting against the governor of the province and sent to the North. In 1905 he fled across the great frozen expanse in a nose-thumbing gesture of defiance to the Tsar, whose political amnesty he rejected.

Now the room is filled to capacity, there is a low anticipatory hum. Abraham spots her immediately. She is standing with her back to the wall behind a crush of men and women. He can only see her profile, hair pushed back from her forehead, neck strained slightly above a lacy collar, but he knows it is her, the same young woman he has seen at the Russian University whenever he attends the Saturday night lectures. She is sometimes there with a woman friend, sometimes with a stern-looking older woman dressed in black. As usual he registers that she is much better looking than the women around her and that she is a young lady of quality. Tonight, she wears a fash-

ionable gray hat with a quail plume and a veil tucked around the base
of the crown. Her posture—she does not appear to be leaning against
the wall, but to be standing away from it, very straight, very still—
gives her an air of dignity and reserve that reminds him of pictures
he has seen of the pretty and elegant daughters of the Tsar. That, of
course, is a very bad reason for a Socialist like Abraham to find a
woman attractive. And yet there is something regal about this young
woman that sets her apart from the crowd, a quality that he finds
compelling, in spite of his principles.

The young woman peers intently toward the front of the room. Ilya
Rubanovich, the principal organizer of the Russian University, a short
broad man with a well-trimmed beard and a hectic manner, waves his
arms to quiet the audience. The young woman turns her head and
Abraham sees another woman standing beside her. The woman is short,
blonde, curly-haired, and plump. Dear God, Fania Gomberg, here at
the Russian University, the least political person to ever cross
Abraham's path. Fania, who lives in the same building as Abraham,
whom he once thought of courting, had, in fact, made a few feeble
attempts to get to know, but the woman's manner, her silly sighs and
pouts, the way she batted her eyes at him when they met on the stairwell, repelled him. Besides, he suspects Fania is looking for a husband
and he is not about to fall into such a commonplace trap. But why is
Fania talking so earnestly to his young woman? Abraham feels irritation spread across his chest—as if he already had a claim on her, as if
just by virtue of thinking about her she belonged to him. The more
Fania chatters, the more annoyed he is. There is nothing to be done.
He will have to ask Fania to introduce him to her friend.

Having made that decision, Abraham feels steadier. He has a gift
for thinking of only one thing at a time and now he turns his attention to the front of the room. He has, after all, paid twenty-five centimes to attend the lecture, accepted the leaflet distributed by a large
and mustachioed Russian at the door, and now he is ready to hear

what Anatoly Vasilyevich Lunacharsky will say about the Russian Social Democratic Labor Party of which Abraham has been a member since he was eighteen.

A man steps up to the front of the room and accepts a hearty embrace from Rubanovich. Anatoly Vasilyevich has the deceptive air of an absent-minded professor, spectacles perched on a broad nose, hair receding from a high forehead, but he is a flamboyant speaker. Tonight he denounces the All Russian Congress for backing the Menshevik "liquidators" who use "opportunistic tactics" and want to put a stop to all underground revolutionary work. "Philosophical revisionism," Lunacharsky shouts, slapping his hand on the table in front of him. The carafe wobbles. "There is no such thing as an illegal act in the service of the revolution," he shouts.

Abraham tries to listen, yet his mind wanders. He cannot follow Lunacharsky's argument. Has he been away from Russia for too long? And then something like an itch in the middle of his back that he can't quite reach makes him turn his head to see what his young lady is doing. She is still there, squinting toward the front of the room, her head tilted thoughtfully, as if she were assessing Lunacharsky's every word. Good, he thinks, she's smart, she listens carefully.

Abraham registers a grumble of voices. The air is suddenly heavy with argument.

A young man in a Russian cap shouts, "What about the trade unions? What about the role of the trade unions in creating the proletariat?"

Abraham has trouble hearing Lunacharsky's answer above the noises of the crowd.

"What about the Jewish question?" The same young man shouts.

Lunacharsky slams his fist on the table. He yells, "There is no Jewish question. There are no Jews. The Jewish problem is a bourgeois creation. It is the result of bad thinking. All forms of national or religious identity impede the progress of socialism."

Here Abraham agrees. Long ago he shed his Jewishness like a worn, outmoded overcoat. The room is in a fury. There are angry shouts of "Bundist," and "Zionist fool" and of course, "Menshevik traitor" directed at the young man. Abraham has little sympathy for the young Bundist. When did he, Abraham, last act as a Jew? In the old synagogue in Kovno, where he said Kaddish for his mother. He long ago repudiated that lonely boy of twelve and later, as a young man, the sorrowful house where his father spat curses on him before he was taken away by the Cossacks.

All around him men have risen to their feet, fists raised, arms waving, boots stamping on the hard wood floor. Ilya Rubanovich is trying to restore calm. The young Bundist pushes his way through the crowd toward the exit, followed by three other young men, caps pulled low, shoulders hunched. Abraham follows them with his eyes. He feels distant, older. He searches for the young woman and sees her gazing gravely around the room. She looks concerned, but not alarmed and again, Abraham likes that in her.

"Good riddance to them," shouts a voice, and then another, deep and jovial, "Don't insult the boys. They have a right to their opinions. This is France, after all. What did we leave Russia for?" Someone laughs. A good-natured buzz spreads through the room. The mood has changed. Lunacharsky taps his glass with a pencil. Rubanovich says, "A little courtesy please."

The lecture is over; there is a rush of hats, caps, and shawls toward the front of the room. Anatoly Vasilyevich is shaking hands. Abraham massages his left thigh and shakes his swollen foot. She is no longer at her place against the wall. His heart takes a plunge. But then, why should he care? This is insane weakness of character in him.

As he tacks out of the back room and between the tables in the front room, he catches a glimpse of her long gray skirt and the back of her white-stockinged ankle. His cane knocks against the legs of the man in front of him. The man turns his head and glares. Abraham, scowling as is his habit, especially in a crowd, plows straight through the space the man reluctantly creates for him.

She is on the sidewalk talking to Fania. The crowd, still arguing, flows around the two women, as if around a natural obstacle. It is the perfect moment for him to approach Fania. But he cannot. He is suddenly seized with paralysis so acute he can only turn his head and stare at the first thing he sees, a horse tethered to an open wagon and calmly munching oats from its nosebag.

Someone pushes Abraham from behind. He stumbles, and when he recovers he understands that Fania has seen him and that there is nothing he can do but advance.

Fania whispers something to the young woman, who turns around and observes him with fierce concentration. Oh, she is a prize, a beauty. He cannot meet her steady gaze. He fixes his attention on Fania, who is smiling coyly behind her gloved hand.

"Fania Aronova, what a surprise to see you here." He extends his hand but does not tip his hat.

"Why wouldn't I be here, Abraham Meyerovich?" Fania says, playing with the ribbons of her cape. "I keep up with what's going on in the world. Just because I am not a revolutionary like you doesn't mean that I do not take an interest in politics."

"That is why I am here with my good friend Nina. Isn't that so, Ninotchka?" Fania smiles at the young woman who inclines her head politely. "So let me introduce you. Nina Chaimovna Schavranski, Abraham Meyerovich Podselver, another good friend of mine."

The young woman extends her hand. He shakes it and as he does so, notices that her eyes are brown.

Abraham's mouth is dry. He glares at Fania.

"I'll walk home with you," is all he can bring himself to say. "Since we live in the same district."

"But you don't know where Nina lives," Fania says in her flirty voice. "Oh, never mind. Walk with us, Abraham."

And so Abraham finds himself walking with Fania on his arm and the young woman slightly behind them on the narrow sidewalk. He can hear, or thinks he hears, the rustle of her skirt and the tap-tapping of her shoes on the pavement. It obscures all other sounds for him, just as the thought of her obscures his thoughts, ties his tongue in knots. He would like to turn around and address the young woman whose name he has in his extreme agitation, forgotten.

Fania claws at his arm. "Now Abraham, if you will permit me to say something a little bit forward. You cannot walk me home without walking my friend home first. That would not be in the least bit polite. After all, she is the one who brought me to the Russian University. And if she hadn't done that, we would not have met at all. Isn't that right, Ninotchka?"

Nina, that is her name, Nina, and he, leaning on his cane, turns toward her. She has pulled the veil of her hat over her eyes, obscuring the top portion of her face. He thinks, with relief, that she is probably a snob and not so pretty after all. He examines the points of his brown shoes in what he hopes is casual indifference.

Nina says, "Oh, I can walk home by myself. It's not so far." Her Russian is elegant, without the trace of a Jewish accent, far better than his. This he admires, then resents.

"Good night then," Nina says to Fania. "Good night," she says to Abraham and he nods.

When Nina has gone some way down the street, Fania pinches his arm and says, "Well, Abraham, you're not much of a conversationalist tonight, are you? You've hardly said a word." And he, furious with himself, lets out a loud guffaw as if what Fania has said is extraordinarily funny and thumps her bottom hard enough for Fania to cry out in surprise and then dissolve into a cascade of nervous giggles that must echo down the boulevard—right into Nina's ears.

At the door to the three-story building on the rue Rodier where both he and Fania have rooms, Abraham recovers his nerve. It has been a quiet walk home, Fania has stopped chirping and Abraham, distracted, keeps a grumpy silence. By the time they reach the door to number 37, Fania has dropped Abraham's arm and she keeps a little space between them.

Abraham knocks on the door and yells in heavily accented French, "*Cordon, s'il vous plait,*" and the concierge, from inside her ground-floor apartment, pulls on the rope, which releases the door latch that lets Abraham and Fania step into the courtyard. It is here, in the cobblestone enclosure, that Abraham manages to say, "That Nina, your friend, I would like you to arrange a meeting between us."

"Is that so?" says Fania. "What a rude man you are, Abraham Meyerovich. First you don't talk, then you punch me where no gentleman should punch a lady, now after barely saying a civil word all the way home, you want to meet my friend."

"I did not punch you," Abraham says.

"It certainly felt like a punch. Well, it doesn't matter. You are no gentleman and I'm not so sure I should encourage anything between you and Nina, who is very much a lady."

Abraham is quiet. It is difficult enough for him to ask for favors, especially this sort of favor, especially from such a silly woman as Fania. He is about to say "Never mind" when Fania, who is good-hearted and whose matchmaking instincts are well developed says, "You don't deserve her, Abraham. It breaks my heart to think she will like you, but she will. She'll like your politics, and politics means a lot to her."

Abraham is moved. Fania may be silly, but she is kind. "Thank you, Fania," and he bends awkwardly toward her. But Fania has already turned away.

THE TEA TABLE is set for four. Madame Dubreuil, Fania's landlady, has brought out her Sunday plates, although it is only Thursday, a set of Limoges tea things inherited from her mother, rosebud dessert plates with a border of gold leaf, tea cups and saucers edged with gold, and a teapot with a gold handle and a lid in the shape of an inverted rose. There are Madame Dubreuil's homemade brioches on the table and homemade jam in a porcelain jam pot. Madame Dubreuil, a woman as round as a ball and wearing a dress of the same color as her topknot of gray hair, smiles amiably at Nina and her mother.

"Where is Fania?" Nina asks after introducing her mother to Madame Dubreuil.

"Oh my dear, she told me to tell you to start tea without her. She said she might be late."

Nina casts a grave look at her mother. Alta does not go out often, although on occasion she accompanies her daughter to the Russian University lectures. But a visit to a lady who only speaks French is a trial. She has come this afternoon to please her daughter and Fania, who, bubbling with mystery and excitement, insisted she be there. Alta is a handsome woman of forty-five with a worn face, deep-set eyes like her daughter's, and a pinched mouth that no longer smiles easily.

But Fania is not there and Nina is nervous. Madame Dubreuil, whose ample shape draped in gray spills over the side of the chair like a soft pillow, pours tea. Alta sits straight-backed on one of the four wooden chairs, the tiny buttons of her black dress reaching to her chin, and occasionally casts anxious looks at her daughter.

"Don't worry, don't worry," says Madame Dubreuil. "Everything will be all right." She beams at Alta who manages a thin smile. Nina sips her tea but it is impossible to be comfortable.

"Mademoiselle Fania tells me you play the piano very well, Mademoiselle Nina." Madame Dubreuil's round face is pink with the desire to please. "There's a nice little spinet in the back room. Why don't you play for us? My daughter used to play," she says to Alta. "She was quite an accomplished pianist. Of course, now she's married, she has no time for the piano. I have three grandchildren, you know." Alta nods but the look in her eyes is uncomprehending.

"Oh, may I?" says Nina and she swoops up from her chair.

Although Madame Dubreuil's apartment is on the ground floor, the parlor is flooded with light. The late afternoon sun hovers over the courtyard and scatters sunbeams through the lace curtains. Against one wall, there is a green horsehair sofa, flanked by two velvet armchairs of a faded and indeterminate color. A flute-playing shepherd and a little shepherdess holding a staff dance on the top of a three-legged table near a tapestry-covered chair. But it is the piano that makes Nina's heart leap with pleasure, an old-fashioned, high-backed spinet that glints with sunlight and polish. The piano bench is partly stacked with music books. Nina opens one and begins to play. In Yekaterinoslav, she practiced every day. Sasha said she was good enough to be a concert pianist and Nina, blushing, had smiled back at him with hope and pleasure. She has not played in five years and her hands feel stiff. Still her fingers know the notes and she plays without thinking, allowing the music to take its shape. She plays a Chopin Nocturne, then a Mazurka, and finally her favorite, Mozart's Rondo alla Turca, but it goes badly. She cannot execute the fast notes the way she used to, her hands slip on the octaves, and so she starts again and then again until her fingers feel feathery and light. She doesn't hear the door open. It is only when she becomes aware of a shuffling and knocking behind her that she turns around and sees the man from the Russian University advancing toward the piano, leaning on his cane.

"Oh," she says. "It's you. How do you do?" Abraham nods. "Didn't I see you the other day near my house? Wasn't that you?"

"Yes," Abraham says.

Nina thinks it is probably rude to ask what he was doing there and so she waits for an explanation. Abraham lowers himself into the tapestry-covered chair. Nina glances at the closed door. "Is Fania here?"

"No," he says, his voice so gruff it seems to issue from the depth of his chest. "She changed her mind."

"What do you mean, she changed her mind? She invited us to tea."

"She's not here."

"I don't understand. I hope nothing has happened to her. Do make yourself comfortable," Nina says curtly, remembering how rude this man was at the Russian University.

Abraham extends his bad leg in front of him,

"You were playing Mozart when I came in, weren't you? My sister played that piece."

"Where can Fania have gone?" Nina says. "I didn't think she could be so thoughtless." She fingers the cameo brooch hanging from a ribbon around her neck.

"I didn't come to see her. I came to see you."

Nina widens her eyes. She is on her guard, ready to disbelieve him.

"I noticed you at the Russian University. You come every week."

"But Fania," she says. She remembers very clearly Fania's gloved hand on Abraham's arm.

Abraham shrugs. "I asked Fania to arrange a meeting. I wanted to talk to you."

Nina feels warmth spread from her face into her neck and shoulders. She looks around the room as if Fania were deliberately hiding from her. "I don't mean to be rude, but there has been a misunderstanding. I came here today because Fania insisted. She knew I would not come without my mother. But my mother doesn't speak French and she rarely goes out. It is very humiliating to have brought her here under false pretenses. Imagine playing such a joke on an innocent old lady."

"Please," Abraham says. "It was not a joke. Would you play for me again?"

Nina's voice softens a little.

"I'm not sure I should be here under these circumstances. Anyway, I have a class in an hour."

"Please play," says Abraham. And Nina relents. She plays the Rondo alla Turca again, better this time, it seems to her, her fingers stronger and swifter.

When she is done she says, "So you like music."

"I prefer Wagner to Mozart. Especially the *Ring*."

Nina looks at Abraham as if she had just noticed his presence. "I am sorry, but I'm not sure I remember your name correctly."

"I am Abraham Podselver."

"Yes, that's right. I am Nina Schavranski."

"I remember your name," says Abraham.

Nina feels rebuked. Should she have paid more attention?

"I am from Lithuania. I am a Social Democrat." Abraham says. "I have been since I was sixteen years old. I have been in prison for acts against the Tsar. I escaped and fled to Vienna. I am a Jew but it goes without saying that I am not a religious man."

A look of amusement passes across Nina's face.

"Is that the story of your life?"

"No. But I want you to know who I am."

Nina stares down at her hands. There is something about this man that she likes. He is rude, but direct, straightforward. He must have ideals, and now she thinks, he must be brave.

Abraham says. "May I take you to the lecture next week?"

"I don't know. I usually go with Fania."

"Fania doesn't care about politics."

Nina laughs. She is happier than she expected to be.

"That's true. Fania left Russia to get away from her stepmother. Not a very political reason."

"And you, why did you leave?"

Nina sighs. "So many reasons. My mother was afraid I'd be sent to Siberia. She discovered socialist leaflets under my bed. That was silly, of course." She doesn't tell Abraham about the pogrom, the days in the basement, the blood on the streets of Yekat. She wants to appear bold, unafraid in front of this fearless, politically defiant man.

"So we have things in common." Abraham leans forward, both hands on his cane. "The lecture begins at nine. I will come for you at eight-thirty."

There is a light rapping on the door. "Oh," Nina says, sliding up the sleeve of her shirtwaist to reveal the little gold watch at her wrist, a birthday gift from rich Aunt Malie in Yekaterinoslav. "I have missed my class."

She smiles at him and Abraham is aware that his heart, which as a good materialist he believes to be nothing more than a blood-pumping machine, is expanding, filling his entire chest cavity with happiness.

The door swings open. Madame Dubreuil steps aside to let Alta share the doorway with her. "You see, my dear Madame Schavranski, how nicely Mademoiselle Fania has arranged things? There they are. Don't they look happy?"

Alta, who isn't happy at all, squints at the two young people. She wishes she could tell Madame Dubreuil how distressed she is by these French manners. A young man she doesn't know has been allowed to spend an hour alone with her daughter, while she, Alta, was in the next room sipping tea and eating brioches in baffled silence. It is all so improper. She blames Fania. Still, Nina doesn't look unhappy. She has even given her mother a small smile across the room. And the young man looks respectable. Alta sighs. Something tells her that this new country is going to separate her from her children in ways she could not have imagined in Yekaterinoslav.

IT IS SEVEN O'CLOCK AND NINA IS waiting on the sidewalk for Fania to come out of the Yankelovich workshop. Fania works for the Yankelovich brothers, Isaac and Saul. She is a finisher, not as high in the hierarchy of the needle trades as the cutters who cut cloth, but not so low as the pressers who stand over the high ironing tables. She puts in the linings, finishes seams, and sews buttons. The Yankelovich brothers run a relatively enlightened shop with twelve workers on the rue des Rosiers, in the Pletzl, the Jewish section of Paris. The hours are reasonable, twelve hours a day rather than the fifteen to sixteen hours in many shops. Fania is paid regularly at the rate of four francs a day and hopes to make five francs by the end of the year. In Kiev, she was a seamstress and worked with her father. But Fania does not have anyone in Paris to protect her, and so she must earn her own living. She complains of pains in her back from bending over the sewing machine, and using the heavy foot pedal has caused a heel splint in her right foot. When she worries about her health, Fania thinks of the air in the shop filled with cloth dust and the young woman at the ironing board who coughs all day.

Nina works, too, but she is more fortunate than her friend. Two years ago, her father, Chaim, opened a tailor shop of his own on the rue Victor Massé, after three years of numbing piece work at home for the Galeries Lafayette. Fortune smiled, Chaim said, when the original owner, a Romanian Jew in bad health, sold them his shop at a loss. Alta fretted: the expense, the risk, the uncertainty. But business has been good. Chaim is a master tailor and a hard worker. Nina helps with the customers; she knows fashion. And she is a good salesgirl; she likes to match the client with the pattern, the pattern with the cloth. Just as she liked to match the customer with the right card in Etlin's card shop where she worked for the trifling sum of three francs a month. That was when the Schavranskis first came to Paris, in 1905. Now between customers and after work, she lingers over the fashion magazines, *Femina*, *La Mode*, *Le Jardin des Modes Nouvelles*, criticizing with authority the awkward drape of a suit jacket, the surfeit of trim on a skirt, the outrageous arrangement of feather or flowers on a wide-brimmed hat. Sometimes she sees a dress, so ravishing, so charming, so right for her, that she can imagine herself in it twirling with happiness. Where would she wear such a dress? Oh, it doesn't matter. To the theater, to the opera, to a ball. Why not? It would be a dress that carried in its abundance of lace and flounces, in its delicate voile bodice, its array of mother-of-pearl buttons, the promise of continuous delight. It is sad that she cannot share these moments with Fania. She had tried. But Fania, impatient, hardheaded, had scoffed.

"It's all very well," she said once after Nina and she had flipped through *La Mode Nouvelle*. "Pretty dresses for rich pretty ladies. I know how these dresses are made and it's not pretty. Anyway, who wears dresses like that? No one I know."

"Well, it's important to know what's being done in fashion," Nina said, "In our line of work."

"Your line, maybe. Not mine."

Nina understood.

Still, Nina and Fania are good friends, a commodity too precious to squander over differences.

Today, Nina has walked all the way from the rue Victor Massé to the rue des Rosiers to talk to Fania.

Visitors are not welcome to the Yankelovich's second-floor workshop. Besides, it is steamy and noisy up there. So Nina waits outside on the sidewalk until the courtyard door opens and a gaggle of young girls spills out, wrapped in their old country plaid shawls, chattering in Russian and Yiddish. The sidewalk is so narrow that Nina is forced to step off the curb and her foot drops into a stream of gutter water.

"Ninotchka," Fania shouts. "You here?"

"My shoes are all wet," says Nina, looking down at her water-spotted boots. "I hope the sole doesn't come off. I had these repaired last week."

"I've just been paid," says Fania, slipping her arm through Nina's. "Let's have tea."

The two young women cross the rue des Rosiers to a café on the corner of the rue des Hospitaliers Saint-Gervais. It is a Jewish café where neighborhood workers congregate. Here one can have really good strong Russian tea, brewed in a huge samovar, and all sorts of cakes, almond cakes and poppy seed cakes and cakes made with prunes and walnuts, Russian cakes laced with chocolate. There is also dark and light beer from Alsace, and behind the counter, the owner, a long-faced man with a drooping beard and a black skull cap, keeps schnapps and cognac and bottles of vodka, along with the staples of a French café, wine, aperitifs, anisette for the occasional Frenchman who wanders in by mistake. It is a place where respectable young women can sit and drink and talk without being mistaken for what they are not.

Fania and Nina take a table by the window. Night is just beginning to fall. The sky is a dusty blue streaked with pink.

"Now, Nina," says Fania, almost licking her lips in anticipation. "Tell me all about it."

"All about what?" says Nina, feigning innocence.

"The other day, between you and Abraham Podselver."

"Fania," says Nina, her face long and serious. "I don't understand why you did this."

"Why not?" Fania nods to the owner who is also the waiter. "He's single and you are not married. After all, let's be honest. How many unmarried men do you know in Paris? I mean men who don't pretend to be unmarried and really have a wife somewhere in Russia? Tell me how many?" Fania tucks in her plump chin and gives Nina a serious look.

"He's quite suitable you know. Perfectly respectable. Works for the Galeries Lafayette just like your father did."

"If he's so suitable, Fania, why don't you want him yourself. I thought he was after you." Nina knows she is being troublesome but she is truly troubled. The waiter brings them tea in glasses and two almond cakes.

"I think he was," Fania says, pertly. "At one time. But I discouraged him."

"Why?" Nina says.

"Oh who knows? Maybe it will turn out to be the biggest mistake of my life. But in the meantime, it's you he wants."

"But I'm not sure I want him," Nina says and all of a sudden she feels very young, very unprotected. She thinks of Sasha, sweet Sasha with his dimpled smile and lanky body. "I haven't thought about these things before," she lies.

"Then it's about time. You're twenty years old. At your age, I cannot tell you how many times I'd been in love. Not that it has done me much good. But I haven't lost hope. It's just that I'm looking for someone older these days, some one who is established, maybe even a widower with children. I'm twenty-six, after all."

"Oh, Fania." Nina imagines with distaste a fat-bellied man with a tonsure of cottony gray hair and—is that what is in store for her too?—a cohort of sour children.

"Just tell me this, Nina Schavranski. Don't you feel just the littlest bit flattered? The littlest bit interested in a man who sees you from a distance and goes to all this trouble to meet you? I would."

Nina looks down. The almond pastry lies, untouched, like a reproach on her plate. She checks an impulse to say she has been courted before, Jacob Tavrovsky wanted to marry her when she was fifteen, and there was Sasha. But she doesn't. Instead, a small smile of pleasure crosses her lips and the faintest touch of pink rises in her cheeks.

"Well, this is not about me, my dear," Fania continues. She pats the corners of her mouth with the burgundy-colored napkin that won't show stains. "Did he ask to see you again?"

"He is going to take me to Saturday's lecture."

·

Fania throws up her hands. "I can see it is not going to be a romantic courtship. I don't suppose that matters to you. You are both
such serious people."

"This is not a courtship," Nina says. "I have not committed to
anything."

"No, you haven't." Fania drops a fourth cube of brown sugar into
her tea. "But just wait and see. I have a feeling."

Nina pushes away her almond cake. Fania is right. She already
feels the burden of commitment weighing her down. How has she
come to take such a step, to make a decision without ever deciding?
She opens her purse and pushes several coins toward Fania. When
she is done, she raises her eyes to Fania's pleased little face. No, she
thinks, she will not accept anything she doesn't want of her own free
will. She is a modern, twentieth-century woman. This is France, not
Russia. She will see Abraham this time and if she doesn't like him,
she will never see him again.

III

YUDEL SCHAVRANSKI LEANS against the distempered walls of an old house on the rue de Bellefond in the ninth arrondissement, smoking a cigarette. He is fifteen years old. Although he is tall, he has no beard; pencil-fine hairs sprout above his upper lip and a flowering of red spots blooms on his nose and chin. He wears a dark gray, almost black serge suit, with narrow, tapered pants, a fitted jacket with sloping shoulders and high button fastenings. It is the uniform of the young diamond brokers who transact business at the Café Fritz on the rue LaFayette, and whose customs and costumes Yudel apes and admires. Yudel is only a jeweler's apprentice. A friend of the family, David Moisevich Epstein, has agreed to teach him the business. He is indifferent to the art of diamond-cutting, but he likes being a courier from Epstein to the Café Fritz, where, if business is slow, he can sip a beer and play a hand of bridge with the other fellows.

He takes a deep drag on his cigarette, brushes the ashes carefully off his lapels. His father made this suit for him from the finest quality serge, following his precise instructions as to the cut of the jacket and the width of the lapels. Chaim was so happy that his son was going to learn a trade. Only Alta shook her head as she snipped hanging threads off the hem of his jacket. She continues to regret that school, like an unsuccessful vaccination, has never taken with her boy.

Yudel crushes his cigarette under the heel of his shoe. It will not do to be seen smoking by anyone in the family and he has just spotted his sister Nina and the man she seems to be keeping company with turning the corner of the rue de Maubeuge into the rue de Bellefond. He is never ashamed of his well-dressed sister. But Abraham, what an odd duck, with his limp and his cane and his round, bobbing head. What does she see in this man? He is old and stiff as a board and he is losing his hair. Besides he never says anything to Yudel except "Good day" and "Good-bye." Sasha should never have gone to New York. Sasha knew how to make a fellow feel good. Suddenly Yudel does not want to talk to Abraham and Nina together. He knocks on the concierge's window and when the concierge releases the latch, steps into the interior hall. He does not climb the stairs to his parents' apartment on the second floor. Instead, he slides behind the plaster pillar and waits.

It seems a long time before he hears the latch snap. A beam of light sickles the stone floor and Nina's voice, fuller, more resonant than usual, says "Good night, Abraham, and thank you." If there is an answer from Abraham, Yudel does not hear it. When Nina's steps sound on the stone floor, he jumps out from behind the pillar, waving his arms like a prankish schoolboy.

"You scared me," Nina's hand goes to her heart. "What are you doing here?"

"Home for my free dinner."

"Where've you been?

"To the Bois de Boulogne."

Yudel hoists himself up two steps so that he can face her. He notices, with surprise, that Nina's eyes are slightly glazed and that, in the pale light of the hallway, she glistens like one of the highly polished stones in Epstein's window.

"Don't you want to know who with?" he asks. Nina smiles absently. Her eyes drift past Yudel. She stares at a thin band of light falling on the landing from the casement window behind him.

Yudel angles himself crabwise up the stairs. "So, tell me, big sister. Are you in love with that man?"

"Why, Idelka," Nina says, using the Yiddish diminutive, the name she uses when she wants to put him in his place. "What a question. I hardly know him."

"But you think you might be, don't you? That's why you have that silly look on your face."

"Don't be idiotic. Abraham is a friend."

"A friend? Really? Well, make sure he stays that way. I wouldn't want him for a brother-in-law." Yudel's eyes blink nervously, a tic he has had since he was a child.

Nina stops short, one foot above the other on the stair, one gloved hand on the banister.

"My dear little brother," she says. "When I decide to marry, it will not be to please you. And besides, nobody is talking about marriage. Certainly not Abraham. If you knew him better, you would know how laughable that is."

"Maybe. That's not how mother and father see it."

"What do you mean?" Nina's eyes narrow in a worried squint. "What have mother and father been saying about Abraham and me?"

"Oh, they talk about you all the time," Yudel grins.

"You're lying," She tosses her head and begins to climb the stairs with a determined step. "Anyway, you don't have to worry. Abraham has quite a few other female friends in Paris."

"Is that a good thing?" Yudel asks. "Don't you want to be the only one?"

Nina shrugs. But as Yudel takes the keys out of his pocket and turns the key in the keyhole, he catches a glimpse of his sister, frowning. The light has gone out of her face.

NUMBER 28, RUE DE BELLEFOND, where the Schavranskis have lived
for the past two years, is a plain stubby building on a quiet street in
the ninth arrondissement. The stairwell is dark and the wooden stairs
worn into treacherous valleys. But the building is solid, the apartment
is sunny and a plane tree blooms in the courtyard. There is running
water on every floor, a separate water closet on the landing with a
flushing mechanism that must be encouraged by pouring a pail full of
water as forcefully as possible down the toilet. In fact, the Schavranskis'
progress since arriving in Paris five years earlier can be measured by
how available water has been to them. In their first lodgings, on the
rue du Grenier Saint-Lazare in the Marais section, where Jews from
Eastern Europe already formed a tight-knit community, the pump was
in the courtyard and water had to be hauled up three flights of stairs.
Nina hated the neighborhood. She felt alien among the pious Jews in
black hats and side curls, the women in kerchiefs and plaid shawls from
the old country, the pale, sad-eyed children. She was glad to walk her
father to his job as a cloth cutter in Krasnopolsky's workshop on the
Boulevard Haussmann, away from the miasmic air of the Pletzl. When
Chaim found an apartment on the rue de Montholon, small, dark, but
not in the Marais, the family was happy to move, even Yudel who had
never like walking to school on the rue Turgot and now could practically tumble out of bed on those hated schooldays. In that apartment,
there was a cold-water tap on the landing that served all the tenants
on the same floor. Now, on the rue de Bellefond, there is running
water in each apartment, what luxury! Gas has not yet been piped
into the building, so water needs to be heated on the coal stove, but
it is always available. And the ninth arrondissement is not the sordid,
dark, and smelly Marais. The ninth is airy, the streets are cleaner,
the avenues broad enough for motorcars as well as carriages. There
is a park just below the rue de Bellefond. There are shops owned by
French people as well as Jews. There are schools and schoolchildren,
churches and church bells, handsome buildings and lively storefronts,

cafés, theaters, and a skating rink. And above the whole bustling area there are the domes of that imposing and unfinished white church, the Sacré Coeur, and the village of Montmartre where Nina and Sasha spent an afternoon that in memory causes Nina to shiver with grief.

To the Schavranskis, this apartment and Chaim's tailor shop on the rue Victor Massé mark a turn in their fortunes, the end of the strenuous and degrading poverty of their early years in Paris and the beginning of a life of laborious thriftiness.

The apartment consists of four rooms that open one into the other. The kitchen with a cooking stove, sink, and small pantry overlooks the courtyard. There is a window in each of the two bedrooms, and from the room that serves as dining room, workroom, and parlor one can see down into the rue Baudin. There is a cast-iron, coal-burning stove in the dining room–parlor to provide heat. The apartment is not so spacious as their home in Yekaterinoslav (nothing can compare with the comfortable, well-rooted existence they led there among family and friends), but there is a habitable quality to it, the even wooden floors, the practical arrangement of rooms, the reasonable kitchen, the windows that fit tightly into the window frame, doors that shut with a reassuring thwack. This is a place where people like them have lived before and to the Schavranskis, it exudes a sense of permanence and contentment.

YUDEL TURNS THE LONG METAL key in the apartment lock and steps into the narrow entrance hall. Today, he even holds the door open for his sister.

Nina unpins her hat and peels off her gloves. Yudel jams his gloves into his pocket, but he does not yet remove his hat, a small gesture of defiance. From where they stand, they can see their mother, seated at the dining-room table, a pile of sewing beside her.

"Well, did you have a good time?" Alta asks. She shoots a quick, anxious glance at her children, then dips her head back to her work. She is relieved that they are home, the habit of anxiety being hard to break even in a country that is safe for Jews.

"Both of you together," Chaim, squatting beside the dressmaker dummy, marks off the hem of a skirt with dressmaker's chalk. Although Chaim now has a shop of his own, he still brings work home with him as he did when he worked for the Galeries. He is a tall, slender man of forty-seven, with small, delicate features, a moustache that has turned gray before his hair has, and a mild, anxious expression on his face. "Maybe, Yudel, you will even stay home for dinner."

"Maybe," says Yudel. He tosses his bowler on the sideboard. Alta eyes the hat with anxiety. It wobbles, crown first, next to the samovar.

"You would make your mother very happy," Chaim says.

Alta lets out a hard sigh. She thinks, but will not say, that Yudel, her younger child, her only boy, is not much concerned with anyone's happiness but his own these days.

"Tea," Yudel says. He pours tea from the little teapot on top of the samovar.

"So where did you go with Podselver today?" Chaim asks Nina. There is chalk dust on his hands and his vest.

"We went to the Russian University to hear Victor Chernov."

"Another political lecture," Yudel says. "What fun."

"It was fun. And very interesting." Nina turns angrily to her brother. "Abraham heard Chernov speak in Vienna. Abraham has heard nearly every revolutionary thinker, including Trotsky."

"Isn't that impressive," Yudel says. There is nothing he likes better than teasing his sister. It is an old habit, from the days in Yekat when he could pinch her calves and pull her braids and make her scream. "I think our Ninotchka is in love."

"Oh stop it," says Nina. "You know nothing about it. Abraham Podselver is a new friend and that's all. I'm not like you, Yudel. I'm not in a position to meet new people every day."

"Why don't you invite him to tea, Ninotchka," Chaim pours himself a glass of tea. "Each time he comes to the house to take you out, he seems so eager to leave. A young man who spends time with a young lady should try to become acquainted with her family."

"She won't invite him because she's ashamed of him. He's ugly and he has no manners."

Now both Chaim and Alta glare at Yudel.

"It's true. You can't deny it." Yudel laughs into his tea.

"Oh, you are wrong, wrong, wrong," Nina says. She looks reproachfully at her mother and father. "Why is he doing this to me? What does he have against Abraham?"

Alta glances at Chaim. Chaim tugs at his moustache. Alta says gently, "Abraham Podselver is twenty-nine years old. Do you know what his intentions are?"

"Intentions? I have no idea. Why must he have intentions at all? Why can't we be just good friends? Like Sasha. Sasha was a good friend and nobody made fun of him. I don't understand why you are all so upset about Abraham."

"Sasha was like our own son," says Alta, in a firm voice with a trace of melancholy as if she were scolding a favorite but recalcitrant child. "His mother used to come to tea in Yekaterinoslav. Don't you remember playing the piano for Sasha when you were a little girl? He was such a sweet boy. What do we know about this Abraham Podselver? He's a Socialist. Is that enough? I know you don't believe this, my dear, but being a Socialist is not necessarily a guarantee of good character."

"Maybe he's a nice man, from a good family," says Chaim always the conciliator. "I have nothing against him. But he comes to see my daughter nearly every week and I know nothing about him. That's not right."

"And he never takes off his hat. Maybe he doesn't want to show us his bald head." Yudel jangles the keys in his pocket aggressively. "At least Sasha had a nice head of hair."

"Oh, this is too much," Nina says and flies into her bedroom, letting the door slam behind her.

"Why do you have to remind her about Sasha?" Chaim asks Yudel. "You must have a little more compassion for your sister."

"Nonsense. Do you want her to marry this Abraham Podselver, this boorish Litvak, who doesn't even speak good Russian?" Yudel blinks at his parents.

This time it is Chaim's turn to sigh. Alta bites off a piece of thread, makes a knot, and stabs her needle into the cloth.

"In Yekat it would have been easier for Nina to find a husband," she says, pulling stitches through the cloth. "In Yekat we had dancing parties for all the young folk. At Succoth and even at Chanukah we danced all night. What wonderful parties they were. You are too young to remember, Yudel. I am sorry we cannot help Nina, that she has to keep company with people who are complete strangers because we know no one here."

"Well, I hope you don't feel sorry for me, mamatchka," Yudel says. He looks up, catches his reflection in the window pane and with a flourish, passes his fingers through his black hair. "When the time comes I'll choose my own bride from among millions of beautiful French girls." He bends toward his mother and places a kiss on her forehead.

"Oh you," says Alta with an indulgent, complacent smile. "I know you'll break my heart."

In her bedroom Nina undoes the buttons of her shirtwaist, slips out of it, and passes a cotton smock over her head. When she is done, she picks up the hand mirror she keeps on the table beside her bed. She thinks she looks old, and it is true that her face has changed. It is longer and narrower. There are two faint furrows from her nose to the corners of her mouth. Her skin, which she slathers each night with old butter, is a shade less radiant, less supple than it was four years ago. Twenty is not sixteen. Abraham is not Sasha. She is a grown woman now, walking out with a man. It is exhilarating and sometimes—what is the thought that prickles at the back of her mind?—boring. She was a little girl when she frolicked with Sasha in the Square d'Anvers, and almost a woman when he left Paris, but it was never boring. Perhaps it is always a little boring to be grown up.

Nina puts the mirror down and finds she is unwilling to go to the kitchen to help her mother prepare the vegetables for the evening soup. Not yet, she thinks, my head aches. She sinks onto her bed overcome by a sudden hopelessness. She hasn't heard from Sasha in two years and she knows he could have written if he cared to. All that remains of him is his spiky Russian hand on the margins of the volume of Kropotkin's writings he gave her when he left. Even his face, when she conjures it up, evokes an odd blankness. Once she thought she would hang her life on Sasha and now she can't even call up his touch, his scent, his voice. Is that some failure on her part, some terrible disloyalty? But then, how loyal should one be to a shadow, a memory?

And here is Abraham in Paris, attentive in his own way. But even as she thinks this, she stiffens. She does not need a man to take her to lectures she used to attend on her own. She does not need a suitor, if that is what Abraham is. There are respectable professions for an independent, modern woman. She could be a schoolteacher, like Mademoiselle Chambon, a bookkeeper (she has learned to keep books at night school), or even, although she would rather not spend the rest of her life there, an assistant in her father's tailor shop. But is that what she wants? To be always looking in on other women's lives, full of spite, like Mademoiselle Chambon? Aren't marriage and children her birthright? I do not know my own mind, she thinks dispiritedly, and envies, not for the first time, those fortunate women she imagines to have made these grave decisions about their lives without anguish, without doubts.

IV

January 1911

ABRAHAM HAS FINALLY ACCEPTED the Schavranskis' invitation, through Nina, to come to tea. He sits at the round mahogany table, which is covered with a white cloth embroidered with cherries and four, no, five glasses (a glass for Yudel who is at home this Saturday afternoon) have been placed there for tea beside the white and gold saucers Alta bought at the second-hand bazaar on the Faubourg Poissonière. Since she no longer bakes at home as she did in Yekaterinoslav, she has bought fruit tarts at the Pâtisserie Alsacienne on the rue de Rochechouart. It is an expensive treat for the family, but this is a special occasion.

It is a special occasion for Abraham as well. He has removed his hat, which, at Chaim's suggestion, he reluctantly placed on the table by the window. His cane is draped over the back of his chair. He sits awkwardly, his bad leg stretched out log-like to the side. He drums his fingers on the table. Nina is awkward also, although she is pleased to have Abraham here. It has not been easy. Abraham does not like the constraints and courtesies of social life. They are antithetical to his socialist principles. Or so he says. In reality, he is shy and particularly so this afternoon, when it is clear that he is about to be appraised by Nina's parents, as if he were a piece of sewing, produced by a second-rate tailor, that may or may not fit their daughter.

"You have family in Kovno, Abraham Podselver?" Chaim asks.

Abraham shakes his head.

"Oh," Chaim looks at his daughter. Nina's face is purposefully blank. She wishes to give Abraham every chance to explain himself.

Abraham is silent.

"You are not from Kovno?"

"Yes," Abraham's fingers drum. "But I have no family there."

"Ah. Perhaps your family has left with you."

"No. My brother and sister left Kovno before me."

"They are in Paris?"

"No."

There is a silence during which Abraham glowers at his hands, and Alta, seated stiffly on the edge of her chair, sips her tea with menacing concentration. In the silence, Nina is surprised to discover how much she wants her parents to like Abraham and Abraham to make himself liked. The wish is so strong she cannot think of anything else and so she sits quiet and unsmiling. Yudel tilts his chair back.

"So you were at another inspiring lecture this evening?" Yudel blinks.

Abraham turns his head.

"I took your sister to hear Martov at the Russian University."

"Not Chernov?"

"No, Martov."

"You're sure it wasn't Chernov?"

Abraham glares at Yudel, suspecting a trap, an insult.

Nina moves her hand closer to Abraham's. She wants to give him her support. Alta notices and looks sharply at her daughter.

Yudel shrugs. "Well," he says. "I'll tell you what I did. I took Mademoiselle Ninette to the carousel on the Place Pigalle."

"You didn't!" Alta puts down her glass of tea. "You spent money on the café girl? Idelka," she says. "How could you waste your money like that?"

"It's my money," Yudel says, drawing down his mouth. He looks now like the child he was only yesterday.

Suddenly Abraham laughs. "What a little man!"

"Surely, you don't approve, Abraham Podselver," Alta glares at her guest. And the seeds of Alta's disapproval of Abraham take root deep in her soul. Abraham is smiling broadly. Nina moves her hand away.

"Chaim," Alta says, her voice full of meaning. Chaim chews his lower lip under his moustache.

"Fine," Yudel attacks the tart on his plate. "I work. I bring in money. I still can't do what I want."

"Join the Social Democratic Party," Abraham says. "I did at your age."

"No," says Alta forcefully. "That is certainly not what Yudel should do."

"I went to meetings after work. I distributed tracts. I carried messages from one cell to another. I was sixteen years old. I didn't have time to run after girls. Not then, anyway." Abraham is enjoying himself for the first time since sitting down to tea. He likes the edge of resistance, the discomfort his words produce in this bourgeois family. Surrounded by the artifacts of material success, or what appears to him to be material success, the gleaming copper samovar, the pristine tablecloth, the gold-rimmed plates, the glasses of tea in holders, the store-bought tarts, Abraham feels an itchy desire to provoke. (He is mistaken about the artifacts. The tea holders are cheap metal. The plates are second-hand. The tarts are an extravagance. He does not know, because Nina has not told him, about the years when the occasional chop went to the children and Alta stretched the evening soup with water for several days after the stringy boiled beef was gone.

The modest patina of ease is fairly recent and hard won. But he is right in one respect. Alta aspires to re-create in her Paris home the level of comfort she left behind in Yekat, and Abraham has sniffed out her bourgeois aspirations.)

"No socialism for me," Yudel says. "Thank you, Abraham Podselver. I prefer to lead my own kind of life."

"What kind of life is that?" asks Abraham.

Alta breaks in. "Perhaps my daughter did not tell you, but we endured a great deal of misery as a result of the political activities of certain people we knew well in Yekaterinoslav."

"Mama," says Nina, indignantly. "That was not why we left."

"Perhaps it wasn't the only reason. But it was an important one." Alta pats imaginary wrinkles in the tablecloth.

"How do you see yourself in ten years, Yudel, in a black suit and a black hat, a gold watch dangling from your pocket?" Abraham asks. "Is that who you want to be, a young capitalist? Living off the workers whom you have carelessly and ignorantly exploited? In Russia, we wanted to bring down the Tsar. In France, there is no Tsar, but it is a capitalist economy. Power and money are in the hands of a very few. The rest are no better than slaves, worse off than the peasants in Russia. Your sister knows this. She understands. You should know it too, Yudel. It is a fact of life, a fact of your life." Abraham leans toward Yudel. The scowl is gone. There is an exalted intensity in his eyes. When Abraham speaks like this, Nina sees a vast expanse of frozen tundra and a wooden hut sunk deep into the snow. It is there she imagines Abraham to have spent his years in prison and she feels a rush of admiration and pity for the brave young man he was. Abraham, in spite of his somber demeanor, carries about him the aura of a life lived adventurously, a rebellious yet purposeful life. And Nina, on the cusp of her own life, finds this very alluring. And she is pleased that Abraham includes her among the right-thinking people, especially in front of her parents.

"Yudel is still young," says Chaim. "He has many decisions to make about his life." He gives his son a penetrating, but not unkind look. Yudel squirms in his chair. He wishes he were far away, further than the Café Fritz, further even than the carousel where he kissed the nape of Mademoiselle Ninette's plump neck and inhaled the beery odor of her hair. Argentina, the word comes to him rich in evocative syllables. Argentina, he says to himself as he fingers the ten-franc bill lining the right-hand pocket of his trousers and that he will not give to Chaim or to Alta but will instead add to the other bills, the fruit of his bridge winnings, hidden under the insole of his best shoes.

Alta is annoyed. She is naturally a hospitable woman. In Yekaterinoslav there was always an extra setting on Friday night for any Jew without a place to celebrate the Sabbath, salesmen passing through town, soldiers billeted far from home, relatives of distant relatives who sometimes stayed with the Schavranskis for weeks until they found employment in the distilleries or the paint factories or the tailor shops of Yekat. And friends, they had many friends who enjoyed Alta's cooking and Chaim's cellar filled with pickled watermelon, herring, beer. The conversations, the laughter, the religious and political discussions, always so tolerant and open! Yet here is this Abraham Podselver, who is as immovable and as unresponsive as a boulder in a field. She wants to like him, for Nina's sake, and resents Abraham even more for not making it easier.

"Another slice of tart?" she asks Abraham and Abraham accepts the portion she slides off the serving dish and onto his plate.

"My sister would like to meet Nina," Abraham says after he has swallowed a mouthful of tart.

"That would be very nice," says Alta, smiling.

"She lives in Berlin."

"Really? And does she like living there?" Alta continues politely. "When is she coming to Paris?"

"She is not coming here. I am going there. Nina can come with me on my vacation."

Silence greets this statement. Nina tries to quiet her heart. Berlin!

"You would like Rebecca." Abraham continues. "She is an elegant woman. She is married to our cousin and she has a nice house. She will treat Nina very well."

Nina's heart pounds. To travel not to escape from history, but simply to see the world! She remembers her first sight of the church spires of Cracow from the train window, the heart-stopping elegance of the buildings in Vienna where they transferred from one Bahnhof to another. How excited she was, how full of wonder! But the anxiety, the uncertainty was always there like a bad cough that threatens to become a full-blown disease. There would be none of that now. She imagines gazing out of the window of a trolley car at the teeming street life of a city more like Paris than Yekat. A city that must be Berlin. Her head throbs with excitement.

"I'm sure your sister is very kind. But I believe, and I think my husband would agree, that Nina cannot visit your sister by herself."

"Not by herself," says Abraham. "With me."

Nina searches her mother's eyes and sees in them only the steeliest disapproval. Of course, such a trip would be unseemly, improper. It is unthinkable, although, of course, she has thought of it, envisioned it for a moment.

"Unfortunately," Alta continues, in her coldest voice. "We cannot accompany our daughter to Berlin. Much as we would like to meet your sister."

Abraham scowls. "Nina must decide for herself what she wants to do."

Nina, whose skin has paled and whose eyes have darkened with disappointment, says, "I have not been invited by your sister. I haven't even met her." Her voice rises in nervous petulance.

"Well, I shall ask her to write to you."

"No," Nina says.

"There," Alta says. "You have your answer."

"Perhaps your sister will come to Paris and we can all meet her," Chaim nods toward Abraham.

Abraham draws his chin into his chest. "If Nina doesn't want to come to Berlin, that is her business. It is a foolish decision, however."

Nina draws herself up, full of wounded dignity.

"Perhaps what is acceptable behavior in your country is not acceptable in mine. It is well known that morals in Lithuania are looser than in Russia."

"Morals," Abraham says. "What has any of this got to do with morals? I asked a question; the answer is either yes or no."

"No," says Nina firmly.

"Well," Abraham leans on his good leg and pushes himself up from the table. "I will leave now. Thank you for tea." He takes his cane, walks to the gate-legged table on which he has placed his hat and jams it on his head.

Nina remains seated at the table, color drained from her face. It is their first quarrel and it exposes a difference that at this moment appears to Nina, injured in her self-respect and torn in her loyalties, as wide as the Russian steppe and as deep as Lake Baikal.

Alta leans toward her daughter and pats her hand. "You understand, my dear," she says. She doesn't have to finish her sentence.

"Oh," Nina says with irritation. "I understand perfectly." And what she understands with bitter clarity is this: if she wants to see the world, she can travel as a daughter or as a wife. For her, there are no other choices.

V

February 1911

ABRAHAM SITS AT HIS DESK, PEN in hand, a sheet of blue paper in front of him. He is writing to his sister Rebecca in Berlin.

Liebe Rebecca, he begins. Rebecca writes to him in German and so he answers her in German, although he finds it a silly affectation. Rebecca has always been something of a snob, he thinks.

He dips his pen in the ink bottle but it remains poised over the paper. What shall he say to his younger sister? A droplet of blue trembles on the tip of the pen. He shakes the pen over the blotting paper already speckled with ink.

He stares out of the window. Rain splatters the dirty panes. It leaves streaks of clear glass through which Abraham can see the gray lowering sky above the houses. It has been raining for three days, cold wintry rain. His hat and jacket, soaked through the day before, hang on the back of a chair near the coal-burning stove. Since Abraham can only afford to keep the stove burning for a few hours when he is working, there lingers in the room the odor of wet wool and, from his shoes, also in front of the stove, the sour smell of damp leather. Abraham is wearing a sweater over his undershirt, thick socks on his feet, and the scarf Rebecca knit for him around his neck.

He sighs. His German is not very good. He has not spoken it since he left Vienna, and he never wrote it very well. So he writes an awkward mixture of German and Yiddish with a Russian word or two when only Russian will do. He does not like to write.

Liebe Rebecca, he thinks again. Yes, that's right, because she is *liebe* to him. His baby sister, five years younger and his responsibility as far back as he can remember. When their mother died, a horrible death, brain trepanation to remove a cancerous growth, Rebecca was six and he was eleven. He laced her shoes every morning, braided her unruly blonde hair with his stubby, unpracticed fingers, made sure the strap around her schoolbooks was tight and walked her to school. Their father was too busy, he sold dried fruits and nuts in a small shop in Kovno, or too undone by grief to pay much attention to them and to his other son, Herman. Abraham, as the oldest, worked long hours in his father's store and watched over the family.

He dips his pen again. I am well, he writes. The work is coming in. I am making drawings for the Galeries Lafayette as well as for our Uncle Finkelstein's fashion magazine in Vienna. Uncle has given me a new assignment, to photograph the fashionable ladies at Longchamps race-track and make drawings of their clothes. So I must buy a camera and learn to use it as soon as the weather improves and the racing season starts. I hope the camera will not be too expensive. I will have to build a darkroom to develop my photographs in my room. Madame Blanche, my concierge, might not like it, but she likes my rent so maybe I can convince her to let me do it. Otherwise, nothing new here in Paris.

Abraham stops. So far the letter has not been difficult to write. Telling Rebecca about his work is what he usually does, that, and reassuring her that he is well. But today it occurs to him that he might say something more. He might tell her about Nina. He might say that he has been walking out with a young lady for some time. That he invited her to come to Germany with him to meet Rebecca. And she refused.

He puts his pen down and pushes away the paper. The memory of Nina's refusal stings. It pinches his soul, batters his heart. And

Alta's tone, so cold and superior, how it had offended him. Wasn't he an honorable man? And hadn't he made an honorable, decent offer? To be turned down so ignominiously when he had never before wanted to introduce a woman to his family. How can he say all this to his sister? Even in conversation he never told her anything about his private life, not about Sonya Weisbrot, who introduced him to the Social Democrats in Kovno and then broke his heart, or Esfir Rouf, who turned him down in Vienna, or all the other women he had known in his life as a young ardent socialist. But of course, Nina was not like those women, it was what had drawn him to her in the first place.

He had left the Schavranski apartment that afternoon, resolved not to see Nina anymore. For several weeks he did not call on her. But yesterday, in the driving rain, as he passed the shop on the rue Victor Massé, he saw, through the glass window, Nina talking to a customer. The sight of her released a current of desire that startled him. Nina looked up; their eyes met. At that moment, he could have walked away. Instead he pushed open the door to the shop and stepped inside. The bell tinkled. The customer, a matronly looking woman in a long cape with a hood against the rain, eyed him reproachfully. He waited, aware of the water dripping from the brim of his hat, the puddle forming around the tip of his umbrella, and the glare of the customer. When she finally left, Nina said, "What do you want, Abraham?"

And suddenly, as if his mind had all this time been working independently of his senses, he remembered a notice he had seen in the Jewish paper about the coming visit of Shalom Aleichem, the famous Yiddish poet.

"He is going to read at the Jewish Union Hall Thursday," he said. "I can get tickets." Nina looked uncomfortable, cast uneasy glances toward the back room.

"My father is working in the back," she said.

"Do you want to hear Shalom Aleichem or not?"

"Yes," Nina said, after what seemed to Abraham an interminable moment. "Yes, I do."

"I will pick you up at six o'clock then. The reading starts early." Walking home, he felt lighter, more hopeful than he had in weeks.

Impossible to put all this in a letter, Abraham thinks. Nor should he. Rebecca would immediately read "marriage," between the lines, for wasn't that what all women thought. And where would that leave him? Having to explain to Rebecca that marriage was the last thing on his mind and she would say, but Abraham, if that's the case then why . . . ?

The weather is terrible, he scribbles. How is it in Berlin? I will come to visit you in August. I hope you, Josef, and the little ones are well. Your loving brother, Abraham. He blots the letter, addresses the envelope, seals and stamps it.

On the table next to the letter is a pile of half-finished drawings, women's suits, dresses, shirtwaists. Carefully, meticulously, he sets to work, tracing with black ink and a very fine brush, the outline he drew previously in pencil. He will fill in the color with a watercolor wash when the ink is dry.

Abraham works steadily. From time to time he stops to drink from a large bottle of Vittel he keeps by his side. When he works like this, he forgets about lunch.

At four o'clock, his back aches. It is impossible to ignore the rumblings of his stomach. He covers each drawing with a sheet of transparent paper, gets up, and pushes in his chair. The rain is sparser now, just a fine drizzle. Since he does not cook in his room, he will go, as he goes everyday around this time, to the café on the corner for a piece of meat and fried potatoes.

His jacket is still damp, the shoes water-logged. He retrieves a pair of ancient Russian boots from under his bed and struggles to fit his feet in heavy socks into them. He has a bulky Russian overcoat he doesn't like to wear, but it will do as an outer garment in the rain. His hat is damp too, but he cannot go out without it. He pokes the fire in the coal stove with the metal poker. Nothing but ashes, the fire has been dead a long time.

By the door, he grabs his cane, his umbrella, and the long metal key from the peg on the wall. As he is about to leave, he remembers the letter to Rebecca and stuffs it in his pocket. He is very happy all of a sudden, one of those bursts of happiness that come to him unbidden and unexamined. In one of the interior flaps of his wallet there are two tickets. Thursday night he and Nina will hear Shalom Aleichem recite in Yiddish and he knows Nina will be pleased.

VI

THE LINDEN TREES WITH their clusters of white flowers are in bloom all over Paris and the fragrance of the blossoms is so powerful that Nina, hurrying to meet Abraham, suddenly stops to sniff the sweetness in the air. It is a Sunday afternoon in early June, and she and Abraham are to take the number 26 omnibus on their way to the Buttes Chaumont Park. Abraham wants to test his new camera; Nina is happy to be going on an excursion. The Buttes are quite a long way from the rue de Bellefond, on the other side of the hill of Montmartre, past the still unfinished Basilica of the Sacré Coeur, into the eighteenth and then the nineteenth arrondissements, almost to the eastern limits of the city of Paris. Socialist friends of Abraham's who live in the working-class district of Belleville recommended the Buttes for Sunday excursions, and Abraham has convinced Alta to let her daughter spend an entire afternoon alone with him. Nina had to do some convincing, too. She told her mother that she was going to help Abraham take photographs, that he needed an assistant to handle and carry the heavy and unwieldy equipment.

"A whole day," Alta said. "Does he really need you for a whole day? And it's so far away."

"It's not so far, Mama. We'll take the omnibus. We'll be there in forty-five minutes."

Alta gasped. "The omnibus! Promise me you won't sit up on the top deck, exposed to the wind and the sun like that."

"Mama, ladies aren't even allowed on the top deck. Abraham and I will sit inside where it's safe. Besides there's no wind. It's a beautiful day. We'll be fine."

"Ninotchka, I don't like it. I'll feel better if you take Yudel with you."

"Not me and those lovebirds." Yudel appeared suddenly in the kitchen, striped tie tucked tidily into his jacket, bowler hat in hand. "Besides, I've got business of my own to take care of." He reached for an apple from the basket of fruit on the table and with a theatrical flourish, polished it on his sleeve.

"What business?" Alta lifted anxious eyes to her son. "What business do you have on Sunday?"

Yudel ignored the question. "I'm off, my darlings. Be good, big sister." He tossed the apple into the air and blew his mother a kiss.

"Where are you going, Idelka?" Alta cried, all restraint gone from her voice. But Yudel was already out the door. Alta sank back in her chair.

"Where is he going, Nina? What is he doing? He's only sixteen years old. At least when he was in school, I knew where he was all day. Now how do I know?"

"You know where he is during the week, Mama. He's working for Epstein."

"Epstein," Alta said. "I don't trust Epstein." She leaned back in her chair, exhausted by the effort to keep her children in check.

"When he was a little boy, you took such good care of him. I don't suppose you can do that now," she said almost wistfully, and Nina answered forcefully "No."

"Well, the fresh air will do you good. You need a little color in your cheeks." She passed her hand over Nina's cheek. Alta's own complexion was pale. The winter had been hard, cold and rainy, although not nearly as bad as the winter of 1910, when the Seine flooded its banks and rowboats clogged the watery streets. In the bright June sunlight streaming through the curtains, Alta looked even more strained and worn than usual.

"I wish your father were here. He could use a little fresh air too."

But Chaim was at the shop accommodating his Orthodox clients who could only come to fittings on Sunday. Because French law required closing stores on Sunday, he stood behind the front door of his shop, a ghostly figure partly hidden by the "We are closed" sign, waiting to slip a woman with a scarf on her head or an ill-fitting wig into the shop.

In the end, Alta agreed to let Nina go; she even pressed a picnic basket on her. What else could she do? Times change. Abraham, in spite of his limp, his awful manners, his politics, even his age, was not an impossible match for Nina. He appeared to be reliable, trustworthy, a sound man. Not the suitor she would have chosen for her daughter, but Nina was already twenty-one years old. So Alta did not insist. She quashed her real fear, which was that, gone for an entire afternoon so far from her parents, Nina would be compromised forever with Abraham.

Now Abraham and Nina sit next to each other on the omnibus facing the other passengers. This is not an elegant crowd. There is a young woman, hatless, wearing an apron over her skirt, a covered basket on her lap. There is a dirty-faced boy in a cap and tight jacket, two workmen in corduroy jackets and caps, a thin woman and her little girl. The lower half of the woman's face is sunken as if she had no teeth. It is impossible to tell how old she is. The little girl looks sullenly out at the world. Two housewives chatter amiably under their black straw hats.

In this public space, Nina is aware of Abraham's thigh pressing against her skirt, his shoulder and upper arm running the length of hers. The sensation is not unpleasant. It would be so simple to let her head drop on his shoulder, to openly declare this intimacy. But that would be dangerous as well as wrong. And so Nina moves her foot away when Abraham's leg shifts with the lurching of the bus. She monitors her breath. Her eyes wander to the other passengers, searching for some reflection of herself and Abraham in their eyes, but all she sees is blank indifference. No one is paying much attention to this young couple, properly hatted and gloved, although the wooden box on Abraham's lap and the folded tripod between his legs does draw every passenger's eyes at least once.

Abraham also is aware of Nina. His body is tense with the effort not to touch hers. At such close range, he can smell the rose water she has dabbed behind her ears and on her wrists. He too thinks he must keep his distance. His cane and the tripod are firmly planted between his feet, his forearms folded over the camera box on his lap and his eyes fixed straight ahead. Only the stiffness of Abraham's and Nina's attitude betrays the fact that they are together in the crowded bus.

As the bus descends the Avenue Secrétan, Nina sees the curve of the Buttes in the distance.

"Abraham," she says. "We're here."

Abraham turns his head and gazes at the expanse of green lawn, trees, and wooded hills suddenly before him. The lines of his face soften. Abraham loves things that grow, trees, flowers, vegetables, and it has been a long time, not since he tended his father's garden outside of Kovno, that he has seen anything as beautiful.

The bus lets passengers off in front of the guard's pavilion. Abraham, the camera box suspended by a leather cord around his neck, steadies the box as it bangs against his chest with one hand. With the other, he leans on his cane. Nina, just behind him, in her summer hat and summer gloves, carries the tripod and a small picnic hamper Alta has prepared for them. Passersby turn their heads and small children stare. Nina does not at all mind. She feels proud and purposeful, an emancipated woman involved in a modern project, and what could be more modern than photography?

They enter the park through the ironwork gate and immediately find themselves under a canopy of trees. Gravel paths reach in every direction.

"Which way shall we go?" Nina asks.

Abraham jerks his chin toward the right, as if he knew. He does not, but it would be unbecoming to show indecision. This afternoon means a great deal to him. Last week, he finally signed the contract with Uncle Finkelstein's *Le Grand Chic de Vienne* to photograph what women are wearing at the races at Longchamps and now he must master this camera, which he bought from a pawnshop on the rue de Maubeuge. It is not the most up-to-date camera but the only one Abraham could afford. So professionally, this is an important afternoon. But beyond that, Abraham, too, is aware of the significance of being with Nina, alone, away from the assessing eyes of friends or relations.

They walk along a path lined with silvery-leafed poplars. At the edge of a man-made lake, Abraham sets down his camera box. Nina follows with the tripod and the picnic basket. Both of them pause to look across the sun-shimmered lake at the island that rises, a vista of crags and promontories, out of the water. At the top of the island there is a round, pillared temple like the ones Nina has seen in books of Greek mythology. It is now midday and the heat has risen. The lake is quite still except for the whir of an occasional cicada. A white butterfly flutters in front of them and disappears.

Nina and Abraham stare out at the view in silence.

"Isn't it lovely," Nina says, then adds, almost apologetically, "I have been starved for beauty for years."

Abraham nods and Nina feels that he understands. She would like to touch his arm but doesn't dare.

"We should eat before we work," Abraham says and now it is Nina's turn to nod solemnly.

"Abraham," Nina looks down at the ground which is soft enough for the heels of her shoes to sink into. "I cannot sit on the grass. Should we look for a bench?"

Instead of answering, Abraham removes his jacket and spreads it on the ground at Nina's feet. It is a gesture so full of courtesy and romance and so unlike Abraham that Nina is embarrassed.

"Please don't," she says.

But Abraham has already smoothed the jacket over the lumps of earth and grass. "There," he says without meeting Nina's eyes. "We can eat here."

Nina lowers herself to the ground, adjusts Abraham's jacket underneath her, straightens the narrow skirt of her summer suit over her knees. It is not the most comfortable pose and perhaps they would have been better off on a bench, but at the moment Nina feels only the excitement that goes with the daring of her position. Abraham is in his shirtsleeves and suspenders. The sleeves of his white shirt, quite clean, Nina notes approvingly, are pushed up with arm garters.

Abraham is also excited. In front of Nina, he feels naked without his jacket. This little scene, under the acacia tree, with Alta's damask tablecloth between them, and the food Nina has laid out, the hard-boiled eggs, the salami, the bread, the pickles from Einbeinder's, and the large bottle of Vittel water, has a domesticity about it that is both comfortable and alarming.

"I love picnics," Nina says after she has torn the bread into manageable pieces. She proffers the bread to Abraham in the flat of her hands, like an offering. "Some of my best memories of Yekat are of the picnics we had at my uncle Tarnopolsky's house in the country. My uncle had seven children and we all ate on the grass while the grown-ups ate at the table. Did you have picnics in Kovno?"

Abraham, head down, slices the salami across his chest.

"No."

"I'm so sorry."

"Why should you be sorry? We didn't have time for picnics. I worked in my father's store all day. And at night I went to meetings."

"You worked very hard."

"No harder than others."

Nina sighs.

"Sometimes when we talk I feel that my life has been so privileged compared to yours. We had fun in Yekat. Did you ever have fun in Russia?"

Abraham pours Vittel water into a tumbler and takes a drink. "In Vienna. That was a wonderful time. After prison it was a paradise. I learned what freedom was in Vienna. By then I understood how often the desire for freedom is paid for with a life."

The memory of Vienna makes Abraham smile. The big house he and his brother and sister rented in Gerstoff, the ice skating on the Alte Donau, the swimming in summer, the lectures they attended, the heady feeling of release and adventure. Even the hard parts have acquired a golden patina, how he worried about money, how stressful it was to learn a new trade, to find work. I was a free man, he thinks. The future smiled on me.

When they have finished eating, Nina wraps the leftovers in the napkins and puts them back in the picnic basket. Abraham stretches out his legs and slumps down on the grass, his arms crossed over his chest and his legs crossed at the ankles. Without a word he closes his eyes.

The sight of Abraham lying stretched out in his shirtsleeves so close to her sends Nina into a mild panic. Is this proper? Should a man fall asleep next to a woman he is not engaged to? Should she wake Abraham? Should she get up and leave? But the grass is cool and the sun is warm and there is nobody around to condemn her. So she undoes the tiny buttons of her summer jacket, loosens the high collar of her shirtwaist, tucks her feet under her skirt, and gives herself over to the pleasure of a private dream. She imagines herself with someone. Is it Abraham? Maybe, maybe not. It might have been Sasha, if things had turned out otherwise. It is surely someone she loves and who loves her and they have just had lunch and now he is lying beside her, tickling her chin with a buttercup and saying how much he cares for her and he reaches for her, perhaps placing his hand on her knee. And here Nina feels heat spread up from her belly and up her chest, and although there is no one to see her, she hides her smile behind her hand.

Abraham is not asleep. He is only pretending. It would be impossible for him to sleep under these circumstances. But after the intimacy of lunch, he feels the need to make some statement about his disregard of conventions and lying on the ground is as far as he can go. But what began as a statement soon shades into pleasure. Abraham allows himself to smell the sweet grass beneath his head and to feel the mild air swirl around him.

Fifteen minutes pass. An ant climbs up Nina's white stocking. Abraham brushes a fly off his nose. He opens his eyes.

"We should work," he says. "I don't want to miss the light."

They gather the tripod, the heavy camera box, and the picnic basket and clamber back on to the path that leads to the suspension bridge over the lake. The bridge, a wrought-iron structure suspended by heavy cables, is crowded. Families cross at the same time as Nina and Abraham and parents and children eye the strange caravan with interest.

Once on the island, Abraham chooses a pretty scene to photograph, a waterfall cascading over a grotto and streaming into a little lagoon. He sets up the tripod, removes the camera from the camera box. It is an old-fashioned plate camera with leather bellows, not greatly advanced over the cameras developed fifty years earlier. At home, his hands working in the darkness provided by a thick blanket, Abraham had loaded the plates into the wooden holders that he carries in the camera box. Now he slips a black cloth over his head and over the camera and focuses the image. Nina watches him in silence.

"Come," he waves her close to the camera. "Have you ever looked into a camera?"

He holds up the black cloth as she maneuvers her head into position.

"It's upside down," she exclaims. "The waterfall is upside down."

"Well, of course. That's why you need a good eye to be a photographer. So you can visualize what the image is going to look like."

"You must be very good," Nina says, her head still under the cloth.

Abraham's voice conveys pleasure. "Oh no," he says. "I've only just started. But I'm learning. I'm learning."

Nina pulls her head away and as she does so, she brushes against Abraham's shoulder. An involuntary shiver dances along her belly. She looks up to see if Abraham has noticed but he is squinting into his camera box from which he retrieves a wooden contraption with a hole in the middle and a rubber ball attached to a tube. He brushes Nina aside and slips the odd contraption over the lens. He peers into the camera again and Nina sees that he is pressing the rubber ball. "Count to thirty," he says to her and Nina does.

"There, this camera will do six exposures. Now I want to try from another angle. Help me move the camera."

Nina and Abraham lift the tripod, which is much heavier now that the camera contains the plate and the roller blind shutter. "Put it down over here," Abraham says and they lower the tripod onto an area of level grass.

"Take the plate and put it in the box," he says. Once again he peers through the opening. Once again he asks Nina to count. When Abraham has completed three exposures, he says, "Where shall we go now? I don't want people watching me."

"It's pretty here," Nina says. "You can take the same view from different angles. And the light is different now too." She waves toward the waterfall where the sun strikes golden pellets on the water. Abraham, considering, narrows his eyes. He extracts a light meter from the box and lifts the meter to the light.

"Good," he says. "I'll take a few more pictures."

Nina is delighted. They are a team; she likes working side by side with Abraham. She takes the plate in the wooden holder from Abraham's hands.

A small boy wearing a white sailor suit and a white cap with a red pompom stares up at her. "What are you doing?" he asks. Nina smiles down at him and answers in her best schoolgirl French, "We are taking pictures of the waterfall."

"My father takes pictures too, but he doesn't use a funny camera like that."

"Well, I suppose there are many different kinds of cameras," Nina says, trying to be helpful. "This is the one we're using." She is aware of how nice it is to say "we" about herself and Abraham.

"Hah," the voice from inside the black cloth says. "Now that should be very nice."

The little boy looks puzzled. "What did the man say?'

"He said he thinks it's going to be a very nice picture."

"Oh," the child gives Nina that peculiar stare children give adults who say silly things. "How do you know what he said?"

"He was speaking Russian. I understand Russian."

"Arthur, come here." A woman's voice calls out. A family of three appears on the path, a large-bellied man with tufts of red hair escaping under his straw boater, a woman in a navy blue dress and white lace collar, and a little girl she is holding by the hand.

The family stops to observe Abraham as he holds the light meter up to the light.

"Monsieur is a photographer," the large man says approvingly. "So am I."

Abraham turns to gaze uncomprehendingly at the man.

"Yes," Nina says. "We are photographers." She gives the man a bashful smile, but her eyes sparkle with pride.

"But why is he using such an old-fashioned camera? Here, let me show you mine. It's the latest thing. Just a little box with film in it and you can take a picture of anything. It's so easy a child can use it. And besides, it costs much less than your old camera. Here," the man beckons to his wife. "Show the lady what you have in your basket, Hortense."

The lady removes a small box from the wicker basket she carries and hands it to her husband. "See," he says to Abraham. "You look through here. You press the button and you have a photograph. This little invention can take one hundred pictures. Can you do that with your old thing?"

Abraham looks at the camera from underneath scowling brows. He does not understand every word the gentleman is saying but he understands enough to know that he is being made out to be a fool. Nina senses Abraham's discomfort, and her instinct is to protect him. She glances at the man's wife for assistance. But the lady observes the two men with the placid assurance that comes from knowing that whatever her husband does is right.

"Not good camera," Abraham says in his broken French and indicating the camera in the man's hand.

"Oh yes, it's an excellent camera," the man says excitedly. "Look, I can take a picture of your little lady here. Please, Mademoiselle." He motions to Nina to stand in front of him at a place where the waterfall will frame her. Nina raises her hands and shakes them in an emphatic "no."

"Come, I'll have it developed and send it to you. It will be a nice souvenir. I don't mind at all. I do this sort of thing all the time." The man's belly seems to Abraham to advance ominously toward Nina.

"No," Nina says. "Please. No. Thank you."

Abraham's face darkens. He doesn't like the belly or the jolly smile on the man's face.

"Such a pretty lady and she doesn't want to have her picture taken. What is the world coming to?" Is the man leering at Nina or is Abraham, in his confusion, inventing things?

"Daddy, Daddy, take a picture, Daddy!" The little boy jumps up and down on the soft grass, his sailor cap in one hand. "Take a picture of me!"

The man swivels and points the camera at his son. "Hold still, you little imp!" The child beams. "There you go. Really," the man turns to Abraham again. "What a marvelous invention. So simple to use. See here," and he points to the viewfinder and the button. "Magic!"

Abraham nods. He would like to tell the man and his family to leave. They have interrupted his work, disturbed his concentration, made him appear foolish in front of Nina.

"Anatole, it's getting late," the woman says. "Let the gentleman do his work." The little girl at her side stares at her father with exasperated eyes.

"Well, think about getting a new camera. You'll thank me for it. Good afternoon." The man raises his hat and executes a bow toward Nina.

When they have gone, Nina says, "I'm sure your camera is fine, Abraham. It's all you need at the moment, isn't it?"

"I don't understand why people want to meddle in things that don't concern them," Abraham says. He is furious. He unscrews the camera from the tripod, puts it away in the camera box and snaps the box closed. Nina stands over him, eager to help. When he gets up, his eyes meet Nina's and suddenly, in one swift motion, he grabs her by the waist and kisses her full on the lips.

In ten seconds it is over. There has not been enough time for either of them to feel the pleasure of the kiss. They remain facing each other, embarrassment overcoming whatever other emotion they might have felt. Nina fingers the pearl stickpin that holds the collar of her shirtwaist closed. Abraham paddles his thighs nervously. It is the first time he has kissed her.

The wind has come up; sudden gray clouds stretch across the sky. The sound of the waterfall splashing over the rocks mingles with a solitary birdcall.

"Let's go home now," Abraham says and Nina, only just beginning to feel how shocked she is, agrees.

The walk through the park is interminable. The tripod feels heavy, the picnic basket, although lighter than it was, rubs against Nina's forearm, even through the sleeve of her jacket. Abraham's cane kicks up little clouds of dust. His feet, in their heavy leather shoes, are swollen. They cross the bridge with the other hot and tired families and noisy children making their way back to the gate before the rain begins.

As she walks slightly behind Abraham, Nina thinks how different this kiss has been from how she imagined Abraham's first kiss would be. Because she did imagine it, she did think about it. But this was so sudden, so brutal. She remembers the pressure of his lips, his body against hers. She is disappointed, but also shaken. Whatever she may have hoped for, it was not this, and yet she feels compromised. Abraham has put his mark on her.

VII

August 1911

NINA, SITTING NEXT TO YUDEL on the suburban train to Paris, nervously fingers her black string purse. She is on her way to meet Abraham at the Gare du Nord. From there they will attend an unusual afternoon lecture by Grigori Zinoviev, Vladimir Ilitch Ulyanov's right-hand man and a frequent visitor to Vladimir Ilitch in Paris. Yudel is with her to lend a veneer of respectability to an enterprise about which her parents, especially Alta, have expressed their misgivings. Of course, Yudel has no intention of attending the lecture; he will find his little friend Ninette from the Café Fritz and take her to the Gaité Rochechouart and then, who knows? If she is not there, he can always play a few hands of bridge at the café, where surely there will be some fellow like him, bored and eager for a bit of excitement.

The Schavranskis have been spending the first two weeks of August visiting Russian friends in Franconville, a village one hour north of Paris on the suburban train line. Chaim closed his shop for a full month. So has David Epstein; Yudel has no excuse not to be in the country with his parents. The Schavranskis have taken up residence in the Pension Moderne on the outskirts of town, not exactly modern, but comfortable and inexpensive. It has been a lovely time for Nina, a chance to relax among people she knows well, to take walks in the woods, to sing Russian songs in the evening. Abraham, in Berlin visiting his sister, sent her cards every day the week he was away, pictures of the city that stirred her envy and her longing and that she keeps in her little traveling case.

Upon his return from Berlin, Abraham paid the Schavranskis a visit in Franconville. Alta and Chaim were at a loss how to introduce him (was he their daughter's young man? a friend? what sort of friend?). Nina shared her walks with Abraham, her enjoyment of the butterfly-studded meadows, the fresh, sweet-smelling air, and Abraham seemed happy. He admired the well-tended vegetable gardens and said the little town was just as picturesque as the villages he had passed through in Germany. Nina felt hopeful. She would soften Abraham, civilize him. Women did that, she knew.

So now she is going to join him for an afternoon in Paris buoyed by a new confidence. The moment the train left the station, she felt altered, on the verge of a great stepping out. And she knew that even though Yudel might have the train tickets in his pocket, it was she who had decided to come to Paris, for herself.

Abraham is waiting on the platform in the great hall of the Gare du Nord. There is someone beside him. A woman, and Abraham has his arm around her shoulders. In spite of Abraham's awkward arm, this woman manages to look unattached. It's the way she stands, legs apart, hands in pockets, head tilted a little defiantly. Her appearance, black hair cut short, strong dark eyebrows that almost meet across her forehead, unfashionably voluminous skirt worn over mannish boots, shocks Nina. Even the hairs above her upper lip, a suggestion of a moustache, appear to flaunt the conventions of femininity. Nina looks from Abraham to the woman and her gaze lingers there.

"This is Rosa Maishle. She is coming to the lecture with us," Abraham says and drops his arm.

"How do you do?" says Nina in a voice as cold as a Siberian wind. "This is my brother, Yudel."

Rosa, who does not believe in wearing gloves except in cold weather, shakes Nina's gloved hand vigorously. Yudel nods.

"Would you like a cigarette?" Rosa asks. "These are quite nice. They're Turkish." She takes a black enamel case out of the pocket of her skirt, flips open the lid, and holds the case out to Nina. There are five gold-tipped cigarettes held there by a band of yellow metal.

"I don't smoke," Nina says. "Thank you."

"I'll have one." And Abraham, who as far as Nina knows never smokes, at least not in her presence, picks out a cigarette and puts it to his lips. Rosa strikes a match with practiced ease and cups her hands around Abraham's mouth. A swirl of perfumed tobacco smoke creates a little cloud above them.

"I really don't want to be late," Rosa says. "There's bound to be a crowd."

Nina is offended. Who is this woman with her brusque, officious manner? "I had no idea we were in such a hurry," she sniffs. "The train left Franconville right on time, didn't it Yudel?"

Yudel, who has barely registered Rosa and Abraham's presence, says with ill-concealed impatience. "Well, my dears, have a good lecture."

"Be here at seven, Yudel. And give me my ticket," Nina says. "In case you're late."

Yudel, annoyed, rummages through his pocket, hands Nina her ticket, tips his hat, and disappears into the crowd.

The hall of the Gare du Nord is crowded with holiday travelers. Families with picnic baskets, gentlemen in boaters, shop girls in muslin dresses and fancy hats, anxious dogs dragging their owners across the marble floor. Nina, Abraham, and Rosa step out of the great hall into the steaming rue de Dunkerque. The sun, at two o'clock, hammers the pavement. The air is heavy with moisture, and to Nina, who has just spent two weeks in the country, unbreathable.

They walk in silence up the rue de Dunkerque to the Boulevard de Rochechouart, Rosa setting the pace with her long, brisk strides, Abraham dragging his gimpy leg, Nina hobbling silently beside him in her narrow skirt. Rosa continues to smoke. Abraham takes long pulls on his cigarette. Nina opens her parasol and hopes she doesn't meet anyone she knows.

She is furious. She feels hoodwinked. A comrade in socialism, Abraham calls Rosa. Does he think she's a fool? She finds it hard to be civil. The walk is long. It is hot. Abraham wipes his forehead with his handkerchief; perspiration pearls around the base of Nina's neck and through the lace collar of her light cotton dress.

The Café Charles is crowded. As always, tables have been pushed to the side and chairs placed neatly in rows. The place smells of perfumed Russian and Turkish cigarettes, and because it is hot and there are many ladies here, of sweat mixed with lavender water. The audience mills about, voices call to one another across the room. "Sit here, Mashenka." "Volodya, we have a seat for you." "Why isn't Itzhak here?" "Late as usual."

"I don't see any empty seats," Nina says. No seats, Rosa ferreting between the aisles like a housewife looking for fresh fish. Abraham, seemingly unaware of Nina's existence, touching his hat to friends. Nina wishes she had never come.

"What a nuisance," Rosa says after she has crossed the room. "I knew we'd be too late."

The audience is settling in, chairs scrape, skirts rustle, newspapers are tucked noisily into pockets.

"Hah," Abraham says. "I see a chair over there, by the post. Come on before someone takes it." He places a hand on the small of Nina's back and pushes her forward. A field of heads, hat-covered or bare, lie between them and the empty chair. Nina's back stiffens.

"But there's only one chair. Where will you sit?"

"With you," says Abraham. "We'll sit on it together."

Nina gasps. Abraham can feel the force of her resistance against his hand.

"No," she says.

"Don't be silly. Come on. Otherwise we'll have to stand."

"Be a gentleman," says Rosa who has frayed herself a passage through the crowd. "Let the lady sit on the chair."

"And me? And my bad leg?"

"I won't sit with you on the same chair. Not in public. That's . . ." Nina hesitates. She is looking for the worst word she can find, the word that will express all the rage and disappointment she feels. "That's vulgar," she brings out in a choked voice. "It's not right. Not in public. Not even for married people."

"Married? Married?" Two heads, a man and a woman's, turn to listen. "What has marriage got to do with anything. There's a chair," Abraham says. "It's meant to be sat on. And my leg hurts."

"Then sit on it. But not with me," Nina says and adds in a low voice, "You're making a scene."

The two heads in front of them look up in amusement.

"What a silly goose," Rosa says. She has been listening, hands in her pockets. Now she gives Nina a cold, dry stare.

"Come," she says to Abraham, "I'll sit with you. But hurry. This is absurd."

She takes Abraham roughly by the elbow and pushes him to the chair.

When they have crossed the room, jostling people and tripping over chairs, Rosa says, "It's a good thing I don't care much for public opinion, otherwise I might worry about what your little friend is thinking. She seems to care a great deal." Rosa gathers up the folds of her skirt, sits down, and with one hand brushes away invisible dust on the unoccupied portion of the chair. Before slipping into the space Rosa has created for him, Abraham turns his head. Nina is standing in the back of the room, just as she had the day he met her with Fania. Her face is pinched, pale. She bites her lower lip as if there were a sore at the corner of her mouth. She does not turn her head toward him but he can feel her disapproval travel across the room. This enrages him. Why does she make things so difficult, so complicated? A chair is made to be sat on and he will not behave like a trained puppy for anyone. But then, Zinoviev begins to speak, and Abraham, with his uncanny ability to concentrate on only one thing at a time, forgets Nina, forgets Rosa, and begins mentally to refute point by point, Zinoviev's arguments in favor of the Bolshevik split in the Russian Social Democratic Worker's Party.

NINA SITS IN STONY SILENCE ON the trip back to Franconville. Yudel fidgets with his key chain, twirling it around his fingers.

"Stop that," Nina says after a while. "You're driving me crazy."

Yudel shrugs, and slips the chain into his side pocket. His sister is in a bad mood, he can see that right away. But so is he. Mademoiselle Ninette was on her day off, he lost forty francs at bridge, half the sum he keeps in the insole of his shoe.

"Thank you," Nina says and turns away. She barely registers the changing landscape, the squat, ugly houses, the low barges along the canals, the patches of sunflowers as the train leaves the city, and then the stretches of luxuriant woods between villages. She is trying to bring some order to her confused and battered feelings.

The afternoon was a disaster. She has no idea what Zinoviev said; his speech is a blur. For two hours, she tried to concentrate, but the roiling, churning inside her made it impossible. Who was this Rosa to Abraham? Why did he bring her? Not that she was jealous of Rosa, how could she be, careless, mannish Rosa, badly dressed. Careless, she repeats to herself, and then a different word, carefree. Oh, it must be nice to be Rosa, so sure of herself, so indifferent to others. Like

Abraham, she thinks with a start. Rosa and Abraham sitting on the same chair, made for each other. Disgust and something else, something more like envy, goes through her.

Because isn't that exactly what attracts her about Abraham? His defiance of conventions, the way he refuses to accept the constraints that determine her life, her behavior. She loves him, yes, yes, she has come to love him because he is not at all like her and yet she is humiliated by all the ways in which they are different.

Nina opens her string purse, takes out her handkerchief, and blows her nose. Tears gather at the corners of her eyes and trickle unbidden down her cheeks. Yudel looks up at his sister and turns his head. There is nothing he wants less than to know why Nina is crying. He slouches down on the bench, stretches his long legs as far as possible, tips his hat over his head, and pretends to go to sleep.

Nina does not want to cry, certainly not here, in public, with Yudel beside her. What had Rosa called her? A silly goose. Even now, the words cause her chest to contract with pain. Is she in fact a silly goose? Attached to an outmoded code of behavior, inherited from her parents and never to be shaken off? Nina feels a surge of resentment at the sheltering embrace she has always lived in. It has made her unfit for modern life, she thinks, for a modern attachment.

What has happened to her? In Yekat, she yearned to be like her friend Sonya, committed in her bones to the overthrow of tyrannies everywhere. Sonya thumbed her nose at the old pious and narrow world she came from. Sonya abhorred conventions; she was independent and fearless. Of course, Nina had been a child then, with a child's view of the world. But now she was no longer a child and still she was a silly goose, upset at the sight of Abraham and Rosa sitting on the same chair, when nobody cared, she knew that, nobody cared.

Yudel stirs fitfully. Nina glances down. What has he done with his afternoon? Neither Alta nor Chaim will question him; Alta will cluck and shake her head, still Yudel can do as he likes. But she will have to give an account of herself, even if she has to lie to make her parents happy.

Nina touches her eyes with the lacy edge of her handkerchief, takes in a gulp of air as if that could stop her from drowning in her tears. She will try, yes, she will try to be better. She does so want to be brave. But why should it be so difficult, when the things she wants are so ordinary, like love and happiness.

The train groans and wheezes as it pulls into Franconville. Yudel's breathing is deep and regular, perhaps he has really fallen asleep. "Wake up. We're here," Nina says and gives him a good, hard shake.

VIII

ABRAHAM LEANS AGAINST A lamppost, holding a copy of *Der Idischer Arbeiter*, a paper he has read from front to back. He is a great consumer of newsprint. He reads all the Yiddish papers published in Paris, the literary ones *Parizer Zhurnal*, *Di Moderne Tsayt*, the weekly literary review *Der Nayer Zhurnal*, as well as the leftist papers, like the *Arbeiter*. Whenever he can, he reads the Yiddish papers published in London, Warsaw, and Vilna. If there is war in the Balkans, a strike among the Jewish carpenters, trouble between the Mensheviks and Bolsheviks in Russia, he wants to know the details. Someday, he plans to read Jaurès's socialist paper, *l'Humanité*, but at the moment his French is not good enough.

He is waiting for Nina to appear at the intersection of the Avenue Trudaine and the rue de Rochechouart on her way home from night school. Nina is taking classes at the Ecole Commerciale, during the day a school for boys and young men who want to become accountants and office clerks, salesmen, and store managers, and in the evening a commercial school for women. It is not the school for foreigners she attended, insecure and yearning, when she first came to Paris. This is a respectable business school and Nina is acquiring practical skills—English, typing, bookkeeping—and Abraham approves.

He has been waiting over an hour. The sky has lost its color. It was a vivid blue streaked with orange, the memory of a sunny autumn day. Now it has faded into gray with a hint of night at the edges. His left leg, the one that is always slightly swollen, damaged by the long North Russian winters, hurts. He shifts his position and presses his back against the lamppost, stuffs the paper in a pocket, and folds his arms. The air has grown damp and the cold penetrates his clothing. His foot feels as if it has doubled in size—it is about to burst through the shoe leather. He sets his jaw; the scowl on his face deepens. A lamplighter, eyes and moustache as sadly gray as his long, narrow coat and flat cap, motions Abraham away so that he can light the gas jet with his long pole. As soon as the lamp is lit, Abraham leans against the post once again. He closes his eyes. Shards of brightness prick behind his eyelids.

He would not be here at all except that something has come up at work, an important matter concerning himself and Nina that affects his honor, his self-respect, a matter that cannot wait until tomorrow and cannot be discussed in front of Nina's parents and must therefore be thrashed out, right here on the street if necessary.

He sees Nina at the top of the hill, standing in a circle of yellow light, carrying her notebook against her chest. The skirt of her dress barely covers her little boots. The brim of her hat shades her eyes so that he cannot see the expression in them. A group of women, probably fellow students on their way home from school, stroll behind her, giggling and linking arms. He begins to walk toward her. He cannot walk fast with his bad leg, and so he is glad when she advances toward him. When he is very close, she says, "Abraham. What are you doing here?" She looks surprised, blank, as if her mind were still with her English books, the numbers in the columns of her notebook.

"I must talk to you."

"Oh," she says. "What about?"

"About your father."

"Papa?" Nina's hand flutters to her chest. "What's the matter? Is he sick? Has something happened? Oh Abraham!"

Abraham swallows hard. He has spent the past hour preparing this sentence. "Your father has behaved toward me in an underhanded and ignoble fashion."

"My father? What are you saying? My father would never behave badly toward anyone. Tell me, please, Abraham, what my father has done to you?"

"He has treated me as if I were," he fumbles for the words that will convey his outrage, his humiliation, "a criminal, a hoodlum, a leech."

"Stop, Abraham," Nina says. "Please stop."

They are standing under the street lamp. Nina's legs feel as if they were about to fold under her. Abraham chews his bottom lip. His moustache quivers. Two workmen in short coats and caps pass by. They carry clanging tin pails full of fish heads and fish entrails. The smell is nauseating.

"My father thinks very well of you." Nina presses her hands together. "Everyone in my family does."

"Really? Then why did he ask that fool I work for at the Galeries Lafayette for information about me?"

"Who do you mean? What information? I don't understand."

"Monsieur Denis. Your father went to him. He wanted to know everything about me. What I was paid for my drawings, if I finished my work on time, if Denis considered me a responsible employee. Behind my back. Without asking my permission. As if I had just been released from jail."

Nina sighs with relief. Last night, she overheard Chaim and Alta talking about Abraham. Chaim was saying what he had often said before, that he was unsure about Abraham, what he wanted, what his intentions were toward Nina. Alta had agreed with him, and Nina, secretly pleased that her parents were taking Abraham so seriously, had left the room in order not to hear the rest of the conversation.

"But Abraham," Nina says, "We have been keeping company for over a year. Don't you think it's natural for a father to want to know more about the man his daughter is walking out with?"

Abraham slams his cane against the pavement. "What business is it of his how much money I make? What right has he to ask personal questions of my employer? I am not a clerk applying for a position in his workshop."

"I know. I know. Calm yourself. He meant well."

"Meant well?" Abraham sputters. "He means to trap me into marriage. That's what he means."

Nina gasps. All color drains from her face. A scrim of tears clouds her vision. She squeezes her eyes shut then opens them.

"No one wants you to do anything you don't want to do."

But Abraham is not listening. Indignation blunts his hearing. "Have I once said I wanted to marry you? Have I asked for your hand in marriage? If you were misled, it was not by me. And I will not be trapped by your family's petty bourgeois notions of courtship. Not now. Not ever. Is that clear?"

Nina tries to swallow away the lump lodged in her throat, but it lingers there, making it hard for her to breathe. She backs away from Abraham as if he had suddenly become a danger. She cannot bear to look at him.

"Oh," she says finally. "Yes, that's perfectly clear. You've made yourself perfectly clear, Abraham. Excuse me, but I must go home now."

She turns away, clutching her notebook. She feels as if sand had been ground into her skin. The street ahead of her is deserted. Shops are closed, storefronts shuttered. Even the Gaité Rochechouart with its intricately worked facade and colorful posters of singers and musicians, is dark. Only a woman wrapped in a too brilliant cloak and feather boa, stands by the door to the café-concert, one high-heeled and booted foot resting provocatively on the front step. She watches with indifference as Nina rushes past her. Nina does not notice. She concentrates on her breathing, which is coming too fast, and on her stomach, which feels queasy and on her throbbing head. Suddenly, she is aware of a terrifying need to let go, to empty her bowels, her bladder. Please, she repeats to herself, let me get home, please.

Abraham jams his newspaper into his pocket. He follows Nina's diminishing figure down the street. I have nothing to apologize for, he thinks, I have said what I had to say. But his head hurts. He begins his walk home in the opposite direction from Nina.

As he climbs the four flights to his room, his game leg heavy and painful, Abraham is waylaid by anguish. Something is wrong. The wrongness of it clings to him like the stinking coat he wore during the many months of his Russian imprisonment, a coat in which dirt and vermin had found a permanent home. He often wanted to remove that blasted coat. But it kept him warm; it was the only covering he had for his freezing body. And now he cannot shrug off his unhappiness either. How he would like Nina to guess at his feelings, to know all the things he cannot say to her, cannot articulate, finds laughable in himself, a Socialist, a man who has no truck with foolishness, with love. But marriage, that is nothing but a trap!

When he reaches his room, on the top floor of the rooming house, he removes his jacket, rolls up the sleeves of his shirt, and washes his hands in the porcelain basin. He lights the kerosene lamp, sits down at his worktable, and begins to work on his fashion assignments for the Galeries Lafayette. He works slowly, painstakingly, drawing fashionable female figures with great care. Drawing does not come easily to him. He has no particular talent for it. In Vienna, he took art classes designed for children, humiliating classes where he was the oldest, most awkward student. But he is tenacious, and so he struggled with his large, often swollen fingers to hold the slippery pencil, to trace a silhouette, to develop an eye for fashion.

His eyes hurt, but his mind is calmer. Work always helps dispel the mantle of misery, the great gray overcoat of his turbulent feelings. He works until the early hours of the morning. Then he puts his pencils away, covers his drawing with a sheet of translucent paper, and prepares for bed. He hangs his clothes on a peg and opens wide the window. A cold wind ruffles the curtain. It stings his cheek and causes him to blink, but he does not close the window. He likes the cold. He hates the musty air of his Paris room, the smell of mildewed walls and kerosene lamps. He thinks that eventually he will live in a healthier place, in the country, where he can tend a vegetable garden as his parents did behind their house in Kovno. He sees the garden clearly in his mind's eye. There are tomato plants and pole beans and rows of leafy lettuce. There is a wisteria vine flowing over the stone wall that encloses the garden and a cherry tree that bears fruit in July. There is a ladder against the tree. And there is Nina, in a flowered gown, a basket on her arm, her brown hair tucked under her straw hat, and she is standing on the ladder, picking the cherries she and Abraham will have for dinner. And that is how Abraham recognizes that he will marry Nina, because he wants to, in spite of himself.

IX

ABRAHAM LURCHES UP THE RUE de Bellefond carrying a package wrapped in brown paper and tied with a blue ribbon. It is a tart from Chez Bourdaloux, a succulent, plum tart the woman behind the counter insisted was the best, the freshest they had, baked this very morning. He cradles the tart, steadying it from time to time with the hand that carries his cane. The tart is for Nina. It is an offering that he hopes will say all the inarticulate and half-formed thoughts he cannot put into words, cannot even think through clearly if someone were to ask him what they were. He is aware only of a desire to see Nina again and a terrible fear that he won't.

On the second floor of number 28, Abraham pauses to catch his breath. He holds the package by the ribbon with one hand and shakes the arm that has become stiff from being held so long in an awkward position. He knocks on the door and waits to hear footsteps.

Alta opens the door.

"Here," Abraham says, "this is for Nina," and thrusts the package at Alta.

"Nina is not in," Alta says. She squints suspiciously at Abraham.

"Well," he says, "Would you please give this to her. It's for you too, of course." Alta's eyes slide away from Abraham. He is sure Alta is lying, but he cannot find the words he needs. "Please, take this," he says, and Alta, afraid it will tip and fall to the floor, places her hands underneath the package and, in effect, accepts it. Abraham touches his fingers to his hat and turns on his heels.

The following Saturday, Abraham carries an apple tart from the Pâtisserie Alsacienne. This time Nina answers the door. "Abraham," she says. "I cannot accept this." She stands in the doorway, with that perfect straight-back dignity that always moves him but that today he understands as a reproach.

"Why not? It's a very good tart."

"No, thank you."

"Did you like the plum tart?"

"I didn't touch it."

Abraham feels her answer like a slap across his face. But he will ignore it. He has this gift for seeing and hearing only what he wants to see and hear, and he is determined.

"I have tickets for next Sunday, Sholem Asch, *Der Landsman*. A very modern play."

"Abraham," Nina says and purses her lips.

"Here, I am leaving the tickets with you. You can go with your mother."

His hands shake, his heart is pounding like a machine, but he has done what he intended to do. He has apologized. He has said he loves her with these gifts. What more can a man do and keep his dignity? He thrusts the envelope with the tickets into the space between Nina's clenched hands and her thigh.

NINA AND FANIA WALK ARM IN arm, like schoolgirls, along the broad sidewalk of the Avenue Trudaine. Nina suggested this walk. She appeared at the door to the Yankelovich workshop as the workday came to an end and Fania, who had been feeling that her friendship with Nina had come undone, like broken laces on a favorite pair of boots now that Nina had a young man of her own, allowed her loyalty and affection to overcome whatever resentment she may have been feeling toward her friend.

Nina squeezes Fania's arm. "I have missed you," she says.

"Why is it," Fania asks with a touch of bitterness in her voice as she adjusts her shawl over her shoulders, "that we women give up our friends when men enter our lives?"

"I didn't give you up," Nina says, although she recognizes that what she is saying is not exactly true. She has neglected Fania in the last year. How shameful of me, she thinks, how disloyal.

"I don't blame you," Fania shrugs. "I would do the same, if there were someone in my life I could pay attention to."

The avenue is quiet, empty and dark except for the blaze of light from the windows of the notorious Auberge du Clou at the end of the street.

"Maybe you're better off," Nina says in a somber voice.

"Maybe," Fania says, but her tone is cold, uninviting of confidences and Nina would like very much to confide in her.

"I hate walking down this street at night." Nina mimes a shiver.

"You get used to it," Fania says. "I walk alone all the time."

Nina sighs. She thinks how enclosed her life has been, how protected.

Fania kicks a small object with the point of her shoe. It is the cork from a bottle of beer and it rolls soundlessly into the gutter.

Two young men in short jackets and bright neck scarves, foreheads plastered with pomaded curls, totter through the swinging doors of the brightly lit Auberge du Clou. The odor of beer, fried grease, and vomit rolls out onto the street. The young men circle Nina and Fania. The smaller one, beardless and not much older than Yudel, removes his beret with exaggerated politeness and presses it against his heart. "Coffee, lovely ladies? Or beer, if you prefer? We can buy you champagne, too. What do you say?"

Nina grabs Fania by the sleeve of her jacket. She can hear the riotous noise coming from the Auberge, but here on the Avenue, they are alone. "Ignore them," she whispers to Fania. "Just walk away."

"Go on," Fania says, waving her hand at them. "Why aren't you boys in bed at this hour?"

The taller one bursts out laughing. He uncorks a bottle of beer, letting the cork drop to the pavement. The foam rises and spills over his hand. He waves the bottle in the air.

"You are right, beautiful lady. This one here is nothing but a child. I'm more your man. Try me." He swings one arm around Fania's waist and with the other grabs the edge of Nina's shawl. Nina screams.

"You're a nuisance," Fania says and kicks the young man sharply in the shins. The shorter boy, defending his friend, shoves Fania into Nina. Nina's knees buckle under her.

"Now stop that," Fania says as she helps a trembling Nina to her feet. "Go away. Leave us alone. Are you all right, Ninotchka?" she asks as Nina, shaken, dusts off her skirt. "What idiots," Fania says as the young men, braying like donkeys, let them pass. "Stupid apaches. I wish I had a stick to beat them off with." Nina, her heart still pounding, holds tightly to Fania's arm. In her mind's eye, she had seen her fate and Fania's sealed by these absinthe drinkers, opium eaters, inhalers of ether, white slavers. She follows with relief the unsteady silhouettes staggering down the street. But it will take a moment to calm herself.

"Those pests," Fania says. "Men just make me mad."

Nina would like to agree, but she is breathless. It is neither proper nor safe for young women to be walking down the Avenue alone on a dark, lonely night. And Nina thinks, her hand gripping Fania's arm, that nothing like this would have happened if Abraham had been there.

Fania continues as she straightens her shawl and pins loose strands of hair under her hat, "I'm so tired of the life I lead. You can't imagine how lucky you are. I'm twenty-seven now and the only men who look at me are those apaches on the street or that bastard boss of mine, Yankelovich, who pinches my bottom and other places, too, whenever he can. And I can't slap him, because he'll dock me."

Nina gasps.

"Yes, that's right." Something bitter has been unleashed in Fania. "And he's married too. Where am I going to meet a suitable man? At the Jewish Union Hall? Every man there has a wife in some town in Poland and children he doesn't want to think about. Do you think anyone respects me?"

"I'm sorry," Nina says. "I respect you."

"Yes, but can you make that nice widower appear, the one with two sweet children, so that I don't have to be treated like a . . . Never mind, tell me about you and Abraham."

"Well," Nina starts. She is about to tell Fania how Abraham has said unforgivable things to her and then how he brought her tarts and tickets to the theater, and even turned up with a small Persian rug he bought for her parents in Berlin as if he could buy forgiveness with his gifts. But she decides not to. It's too complicated, she tells herself. It would not be fair to Fania. And it seems to her, walking where the gaslights still flicker uncertainly along the empty Avenue, that perhaps she should forgive Abraham after all. He has apologized enough with those tarts and tickets and presents for her parents. He has not walked away from her, in spite of his protests. And she doesn't want, cannot imagine a life like Fania's for herself. Or like her spinster teacher Mademoiselle Chambon, so full of poison and recriminations. Abraham's persistence must mean something. And so she thinks she might accept the next offer of theater tickets, the next invitation to a ball at the Jewish Union Hall, to a lecture at the Russian University after all.

"So, when are you getting married?" Fania asks.

"Oh, we never discuss marriage," Nina says, her jaw set, her back ramrod straight.

Fania examines her friend from under half-closed lids and thinks how evenly matched they are, Nina and Abraham, each as self-righteous and proud as the other.

NINA AND ABRAHAM ARE walking along the Boulevard Haussmann. She is wearing a fringed cashmere shawl over an outfit of brown wool, a long jacket, tucked in at the waist and a skirt with two wide pleats starting at the knees. She is gloved and hatted as befits a young lady strolling with a young man on a Sunday afternoon. Abraham is also wearing brown, a brown suit and a brown hat with a low crown. He is using his cane, but his walk is jaunty this morning as if the soft air promised not just spring, but the blessings of good health.

February has been an unusually warm month. Although the trees are black and bare and the sky a pale wintry gray, there is a softness in the air and the contrast between bare trees and mild air is exhilarating. Women have abandoned their muffs and men their woolen scarves. Motorists lean out of the windows of motorcars, inhaling whiffs of spring-like air above the gasoline fumes. Ragged boys in short pants sail wooden hulls along the rivulets in the gutters where only two weeks before there had been ice. On the Boulevard Haussmann, newly paved with asphalt, carriages clatter, elegant Victorias, ordinary hackney cabs mingle with smoky motorcars. Traffic is dense and noisy; sidewalks are crowded.

Nina is happy too. It is pleasant to be counted among the couples who amble along the Boulevard enjoying the unseasonably fine weather. Although it would be nice if Abraham would stop in front of the shop windows and admire with her the rolls of wallpaper in designs of vines and entwined flowers, the lampshades of iridescent glass, the riding habits for men and women, or the display of straw hats that make her yearn for spring. But Abraham does not like to stop and start. When he walks, he walks, and there's an end to it. That is in part because it is hard for him to stand still on his bad leg, in part because he does not like to do more than one thing at a time, as Nina has come to know well. Still, Nina is determined not to think complaining thoughts. It is Sunday; the day is a gift.

The building that houses the Galeries Lafayette looms ahead of them. The huge store, which began as a small shop carrying ladies' notions, gloves, buttons, trimmings for hats, lace, and ribbons, has become a five-story emporium, elegance at bargain prices. Even the exterior reflects a whimsical fantasy: giant daisies decorate the facade, a metal and glass overhang protects the window shopper from the elements; each display window is lit by a huge bulb of magical electricity. Inside, of course, the effect is spectacular: The cupola, thirty-three meters high and made of colored glass panes mounted into curving armatures, lets in the streaming sunlight; electric lights sparkle on every floor, the arches are painted, the balustrades gilded, the staircase has a curlicue railing designed to outdo anything found in nature. It is a grand palace of commerce where every weekday carriages wait outside to deliver the packages that no lady would think of carrying home herself.

But not today. Today the castle is closed; the magic is in the tantalizing windows, the display of articles that just might be within reach of the lady telephone operator, the salesgirl, the schoolteacher.

Abraham and Nina pause to take in the great building that has been Chaim and Abraham's first employer in Paris.

"I don't always think kind thoughts when I pass in front of the Galeries," Nina says. "I wonder whether stores like the Galeries and Printemps and Bon Marché will someday put my father out of business."

"Nonsense," Abraham answers. "Ladies will always want good-quality clothes that fit perfectly and are made to their specifications. Ready-to-wear is shoddy. I cannot imagine a self-respecting woman who will want to wear the same dress as everyone else. It's absurd."

"But look, how big the Galeries has become. Everyone shops there for something. The owners must make so much money."

"Capitalists," Abraham fumes. "Exploiting the workers—your father when he worked for them, the workers in Yankelovich's workshop. Yankelovich pays nothing because the Galeries pays him nothing. A hierarchy of exploitation that produces second-rate goods and makes everybody suffer. That's how the capitalist system works."

Nina is having trouble taking her eyes off the imitation Poiret gowns in the windows. Showy, vulgar, and poorly made, she thinks, on the backs of workers like her friend Fania. Still, there is something ravishing to the eye in that abundance of silk, beads, lace, and plumes.

"Nina," says Abraham. "Let us stop for tea."

"What is it? Are you tired?"

"No," Abraham says firmly. "But I am thirsty."

They have reached the salon de thé. It is a small establishment, quiet and curtained, with tables at which ladies can sit and sip tea after the rigors of shopping. This afternoon, because it is Sunday and the shops are closed, Abraham is not the only gentleman in the room. Several couples and a family of six whisper politely to one another across the tea things.

Abraham and Nina order tea and peach tarts from the pale young waitress who keeps touching her lace cap as if she were afraid it was about to fall off. Nina wonders if this is her first real job.

Nina removes her gloves and places them on the left of her plate. Abraham unfurls his napkin and spreads it methodically on his lap. When the tea comes, he drinks it through a cube of sugar. Nina, who has given up Russian habits in public, stirs the sugar in her tea.

"I have something to tell you," Abraham says when he has finished his first cup of tea. "I have lost my job with the Berlin magazine."

"Oh no," Nina says, alarmed. Abraham works freelance. He must have several employers to make ends meet. And then, she thinks, is it Abraham's fault? Has he done something wrong?

"They are changing the illustrations in the magazine from drawings to photographs. And they are going to use German photographers working in Berlin. So there is going to be less money now for a while."

"I am so sorry," Nina says and means it. Loss of income is something she understands well.

"Nina, we should get married," Abraham stares firmly above Nina's head as he says this. He might be looking at the waitress in her pretty starched apron or at the molding around the room, painted pale blue in imitation of English Wedgewood, but of course, he is not. He is only embarrassed. He has never asked anyone to marry him before.

Nina's hand shakes so the tea puddles in the saucer and drips on to the tablecloth.

"Oh dear," she says, "I'm making a mess." She stares at the cup as if she had just discovered an unusual substance floating on the surface of the tea.

"Well, what do you think?"

"I don't know." Nina dabs at the spilled tea with a corner of her napkin. She smiles apologetically.

"I thought you considered marriage a bourgeois institution," she says and lifts a quizzical eyebrow. She does not mean to be unkind; she is stalling. She needs time to compose herself, to think.

Abraham's face hardens.

"I will not be pushed," he says.

"Neither will I," Nina answers. And suddenly there is a silence between them, heavy with old hurts.

It is Abraham who relents. He leans toward Nina.

"In spite of everything, I have always considered us to be engaged," he says. "This may not seem like the right time. But I think it is an excellent opportunity. I will be changing my life now that I don't have to go to Berlin. I will work more in Paris. You can help me."

Nina frowns.

"I must finish my classes and get my diploma. The diploma will be very useful to me."

"Of course. We will work together. You can keep the books and type the letters," Abraham says.

"Certainly not. I do not want to be your secretary. I already do that for my father."

Abraham, retrieving some ancient memory of chivalry, takes Nina's hand in his and kisses it. "Nina, you will be my wife."

A jolt of heat radiates from the base of her stomach through her arms and legs. Is it the touch of Abraham's lips on her hand that leaves her breathless? Or the way he says "wife" with unusual tenderness.

"Say you will marry me, Nina. Please."

Nina allows Abraham to keep her hand captive. She knows she is on the verge of her future, final and unimaginable.

"Oh," she says. "Yes, I will."

The tea lies cold in the rosebud teapot, the peach tarts half eaten on the gilded dessert plates. Both Nina and Abraham are overwhelmed with the immensity of what they have agreed to. Marriage, an end and a beginning. It is hard to know which of them is more terrified, more uncertain, happier.

Abraham drops Nina's hand. His famous scowl has reappeared. He looks furious, as if something in this chatter-filled teahouse has offended him.

The young waitress asks if they would like to order anything else.

"No," growls Abraham.

"Yes," says Nina.

The waitress fingers her cap nervously.

"More tea, please," Nina says.

"Whatever the lady wants," Abraham mutters in his rough French. He is already conceding to Nina. This makes him nervous.

Nina's heart is beginning to thrum. Surprising joy floats through her limbs.

"Abraham," she says, her eyes brilliant and clear. "Are we really going to get married?"

"Why not? We should set a date."

"I am very happy," she says. And she means it. At this moment, she loves Abraham, her man. She loves her future husband; she loves the life she sees streaming out in front of her.

"June is a good month for weddings," she says. Abraham places both his fists on the table like a man who is just about to enjoy a good meal.

"Yes, I don't want a long engagement."

Nina wipes her mouth delicately with her napkin. Abraham drums on the table. "So you agree?" he asks. He is afraid she will go back on her word.

"Yes," says Nina, "I will tell my parents." She imagines Alta and Chaim and a prickle of apprehension mars her happiness.

The pale waitress has brought a fresh pot of tea in the rosebud teapot. It remains on the linen tablecloth untouched. Nina wants Abraham to take her hand again. She liked the warmth of his hand, the unfamiliar muscularity. Sasha's hands were long and narrow, his fingers elegant and tender. Abraham's hands are like him, blunt and solid.

"There is something I must tell you," Abraham says. And again, he looks beyond Nina, perhaps at the ecru lace curtains partly covering the window or the gentleman's top hat on the rack by the door. "I will not be married in a synagogue."

Nina's eyes, so clear and full of promise a moment ago, darken.

"I will sign whatever papers are required by the civil authorities. But in my view, marriage has nothing to do with religion."

Now Nina's eyes fill with tears. Her happiness, such a fragile membrane, is beginning to tear.

"My parents will be so hurt," she says. "My mother especially. My parents are not very religious people. But a wedding, Abraham. It will break my mother's heart not to have a Jewish wedding."

"We are not getting married to please your parents."

Nina drops her hands in her lap, her shoulders droop, her mouth draws unhappily down. Already, she glimpses the arc of her future life, how torn her loyalties will be; how she will have to cause pain to the people she loves most in order to give pleasure to Abraham. Why must this be so, she thinks? And she cannot answer because she is still a young woman and full of hope and promise and yearning for a happy future.

"I have always dreamed of wearing a white dress at my wedding," she says wistfully as if Abraham might ever be convinced by such an argument.

"You can wear white to the city hall," says Abraham. "I have no objections."

"Everyone knows you have principles, Abraham. No one asks you to give them up. But to step into a synagogue for a few hours. To make other people happy. Is that so much to ask?"

Every muscle of Abraham's face is taut. His eyes are fiercely bright.

"I said Kaddish for my mother when she died because I knew it would have made her happy. But what was the real point? She was already dead. She suffered until her last breath. I do not believe in God. I do not believe in being a Jew. I will never again enter a synagogue. We will have a legitimate marriage, with all the documents signed and sealed and, if that's what you want, all the fancy trappings of a wedding. I am not trying to get out of my obligations toward you, your family, or the state, but I will not be married in a synagogue. Now, if you want to break off this marriage, that is your prerogative."

Nina takes a deep breath. She shuts her eyes for a moment and when she opens them, they are still here, in the teashop, with the blue moldings and the watery aquarelles, and the murmur of voices and the pale nervous waitress. But her life has changed and what seemed only a few moments ago, to be blissful, now seems difficult and full of the auguries of loss. Does she want this?

"I understand what this means to you, Abraham. I do. Only it is very hard for me. I do not want to cause my parents any pain. They will be so happy to learn that we are getting married. It seems cruel to spoil their pleasure."

"Nina, I have never lied to you. I told you when we met that I was a Socialist, that I was against all forms of religion. I have not changed my mind or my politics. But you are a modern woman, Nina. An educated woman. You speak French. You read the news-papers. You know what is going on in the world. You are not a shtetl Jew. And so I ask you, why would any intelligent person hang on to such superstitious nonsense? Religion is obsolete. Marx said so. Your Frenchman Voltaire said so. All the great minds say so. And you, Nina Schavranski, who plays Chopin and Mozart, who has opin-ions about literature, who was smart enough to be admitted to the Russian High School in Yekaterinoslav, you still want to be mar-ried in a synagogue?"

Nina flattens out her napkin with the palm of her hand.

She looks very young and unhappy, like a schoolgirl scolded by a well-meaning teacher for not having done her best work. Abraham scowls at her. But he doesn't understand, doesn't know yet that he has found his best argument, the only one that can touch Nina. Unwittingly perhaps, unconsciously certainly, he has shown her his heart. Abraham thinks she is a modern woman, a smart woman, a woman who can think for herself. How can she refuse him anything now? Armed with this secret knowledge, she can do anything; she can face her parents.

"We will be married wherever you like, Abraham," Nina says, looking down at her lap. Then, she raises her head and, looking straight into Abraham's still fierce eyes, adds, because she cannot concede without a sharp reminder of the loyalties that exclude him, the loyalties he has just devalued, "My parents will agree because they love me and want me to be happy."

"Good," Abraham says. "Then it's settled." He smiles at Nina and once again, covers her small hand with his. He does not know how close he came to losing her; he does not understand what a powerful weapon he has just wielded.

As NINA SKIMS THE STAIRS TO her parent's second-floor-apartment, she feels as if she were carrying her happiness in her hands, a gift from Abraham. It is only at the top of the stairs that she experiences a weakness in her knees, a familiar light-headedness as if she hadn't eaten all day. Her hand trembles as she lets herself in with the long metal key.

She hesitates in the entrance hall, listening for familiar sounds, the whirr of the sewing machine, the rustle of newspapers, the low murmur of her parent's voices as they speak softly to each other. The silence gives Nina hope that perhaps no one is home. She slowly unbuttons her jacket, removes her hat, tucks her gloves into her purse, drawing out these actions as if she could hold back the moment when she has to face her parents.

She hears a noise in the dining room, something clatters and rolls on the floor. This is followed by a deep sigh. Alta has probably dropped a spool of thread. There is the scrape of a chair and the shuffle of someone's feet.

Alta is indeed in the dining room, on her knees beside a small table. The delinquent spool is under the table next to a pincushion that has also fallen. Without waiting for her mother to get up, Nina says, "I am going to marry Abraham. He asked me to this afternoon."

Alta slowly pushes herself up from the floor. When she stands, the expression in her eyes is veiled, cautious.

"Well," she says, "And what brought this on?"

"Is that all? Aren't you happy for me, Mama?"

Alta shakes invisible dust from the skirt of her black dress.

"Abraham has wanted to marry me for a long time. Only the moment wasn't right. Now it's right."

"I see. And what makes this the right moment?"

"His work. He no longer has to travel to Berlin. He can settle in Paris now."

"With you?"

"Yes, with me. Of course, with me."

"It has not always been clear to me that Abraham wanted to settle down or with whom."

Nina squeezes her eyes closed in pained exasperation. "Oh Mamatchka, be happy for me, please, please." She braids her hands together, like a supplicant.

"I am happy if you are happy. But for months you were in tears about him. Now you want to marry him. Is it enough for a man to want to marry you to make you change your mind? Are you sure he is the right man for you?"

There is little left to her happiness now, some shreds, remnants, a memory of her joy.

"He is a good man. Only sometimes a little hard. He will change, Mamatchka, I know it."

Alta lets out a long stream of air.

"Tell your papa the good news. See what he says."

Chaim parts the curtain separating the dining room from the other rooms in the apartment. He carries a piece of cloth draped over one arm.

"What?" he asks. "What news?" He looks anxiously into the tense faces before him.

"I am going to get married," Nina says and this time her voice is defeated.

Chaim looks at his wife and two little lines of strain show above his eyebrows.

"Is my little girl happy?"

"Oh yes, I am happy."

"See how mistaken we were, Chaim," Alta says. "It seems that Abraham has been a suitor for our daughter all along. Although he never came courting like a proper gentleman," she cannot resist saying and her voice rises with bitterness.

"Mama," Nina covers her ears like a child. "Stop." She drops her hands. "You are so unfair to Abraham. And to me. You are unfair to me."

"Oh my dear," says her father. "Do you think he will make you happy?"

"Yes," Nina says. "I am already happy." A new fierceness takes possession of her. It is not so hard to be happy, she thinks. I can do it.

"Well," Chaim says. "If that is what you want. Your mother and I will stand by you. If you are happy, we are happy too."

Alta advances toward Nina, her arms outstretched. She takes Nina's face in both hands. "Your father is right, my darling. You shall have the most beautiful wedding. We will ask the rabbi from the synagogue on the rue Buffault to marry you. I will make you a beautiful white silk dress. Chaim, do you have a nice bolt of silk for your daughter?" She presses Nina's face against her cheek and holds it there for what seems to Nina like a very long time. Only not long enough, because when Alta releases her and wipes her teary eyes with the back of a knuckle, Nina panics and flings her head on to her mother's shoulder, burrowing her face into the powdery folds of Alta's neck.

X

May 1912

To Nina's surprise and delight, Abraham has bought tickets for them for the Paris Opera, box seats on the left side of the orchestra. The tickets were a huge expense, twenty francs each, forty francs in all, equal to three weeks' salary. It is an extravagance that, Abraham has already warned Nina, he will not be able to repeat anytime soon, especially now that his Berlin employers have let him go. Nina is touched and impressed. Abraham, she knows, does not spend money easily. This, as with so much about Abraham, is a quality she approves of and occasionally resents.

Tonight, presented with this immoderate expense, Nina feels only gratitude. Who in their circle of mostly impoverished Jewish immigrants has set foot in the splendid opera house, symbol of everything Abraham condemns, luxury, opulence, showy displays of wealth created on the backs of the working classes? But Abraham is very fond of opera, although not so much of French opera. He prefers Wagner to the lightweight French composers Massenet, Charpentier, Gounod, Bizet, and Halévy, but he tolerates Berlioz. And Nina had read in the newspaper *Le Figaro* that the stage effects for Saint-Saëns' *Samson et Dalilah* were spectacular: battle scenes with chariots drawn by live horses, two hundred supernumeraries representing Hebrews and Pharisees, a ballet sequence so suggestive it was said to rival the notorious dancing in the café-concert, and of course Samson's collapse of the temple at the end of the third act. Only the other day, Nina and Abraham had passed a poster listing which operas were to be performed on Monday nights, opera night, and Nina, always eager to make conversation, had told him about the article in *Le Figaro*. At the time, Abraham had shrugged his indifference. But after work, he walked to the Place de l'Opéra and bought box seats, not the best seats in the house, those were in the orchestra, but respectable seats from which, he was told by the ticket seller, who peered at Abraham through his thick lenses, they would be sure to see the entire spectacle.

It is all very exciting and Nina's mood is festive. Even Abraham seems pleased. His gaze travels around the theater. There is so much to see: the ornate friezes above the columns, the nymphs and cherubs frolicking on the domed ceiling of the auditorium, the abundance of velvet fringe, gold leaf, and marble, and of course the electrical chandelier weighing six tons, which had already killed an unfortunate spectator when a counterweight had fallen on his head ten years earlier.

Abraham and Nina are alone in the box, although it seats six. Nina settles contentedly into her chair. How much has changed in her world since she first came to Paris, when Mademoiselle Chambon, her teacher at the night school for foreigners, invited her to see Sarah Bernhardt perform and she, still the dutiful daughter, had to refuse. Now she is in a box at the Paris Opera, cushioned in red velvet, curtained in red damask, with the man she is engaged to marry at her side. She has only to lean slightly over the velvet-covered balustrade to see the immense stage, only to stare across the auditorium to observe the ladies in glittering silks and ropes of pearls that glisten against powder-white bosoms and shoulders, sitting next to gentlemen in evening dress in boxes almost exactly like the one she is in with Abraham. How extraordinary, how democratic, that I should be here, Nina thinks, and then catches herself. No, this is only the democracy of money and Abraham and I don't belong here.

Abraham sinks back into his seat, less eager than Nina to be impressed with his surroundings. He is wearing his best suit, dark wool, with a new cream-colored shirt and a plain dark tie he bought in Berlin. Nina thinks he looks handsome. In this setting, his frown gives him an appropriately serious mien, like a man who knows what he likes. Nina has also taken great care with her appearance. She is wearing a pale gray satin dress with a bell-shaped overskirt and a flowing lace jabot. Nina chose the pattern from an illustration in *Le Journal des Dames et des Modes,* and Chaim, of course, made it for her. The fabric shimmers and rustles as she moves, and the clever cut of the bodice shows off her tiny waist, of which she is justifiably proud.

The curtain parts and the house lights dim. Nina is shocked. She has never been to a theater where the audience sits in the dark. At the Yiddish theaters she has attended with Abraham the plays are performed in bright light so that the spectators can see each other as well as the actors. But the dark and the hush in this great hall are thrilling. In the pit, the orchestra begins to play.

Nina leans against the railing. Abraham listens to the overture with his arms folded across his chest. Ten minutes into the first act, Abraham draws his chair closer to hers. He slips his arm around her waist, kisses the nape of her neck. A shiver of delight runs through her and then intense embarrassment.

"Not here," she whispers. "Everyone will see us."

"We can move back. There's no one else in this box."

"How will we see the opera from back there?" she asks.

"The view is perfectly good," Abraham lies. "Come."

With a gasp of excitement, Nina allows Abraham to move their chairs into the darkness at the back of the box. At first, she stiffens as he draws her mouth to his; the thrust of his tongue feels alien and muscular. The willful way he holds her, his hand on the small of her back, pressing her against his chest as if she were a rod he wanted to bend. But after a while, cushioned in the safety of the velvety darkness, she allows herself to enjoy the pressure of his lips under his mustache and the ardent feel of his tongue in her mouth. From time to time, she pulls away and makes a pretense of looking at the stage, but Abraham pulls her back and she collapses gratefully into his arms.

The curtain comes down and the houselights come on. Nina blinks against the bright light. Abraham beams at her.

"The *Figaro* critic said the first act was boring," Nina says with a sly smile. "I don't suppose we missed much."

Abraham clears his throat. "The music was pretty, but it isn't Wagner." And Nina, glowing with affection, thinks that Abraham's judgment is musically sound.

The first act of the opera is short and they spend the intermission discreetly holding hands in the yellow glow of their box. Occasionally, Nina points with her free hand to the spectacular decorations above the boxes opposite theirs, a nymph emerging from the folds of her draperies, the mask of tragedy facing away from his twin brother, comedy, a delicately carved spray of acanthus leaves. Abraham nods but, happily, does not release her hand.

The house lights go out, the stage manager knocks three times on the stage floor, and the curtain parts. Abraham wraps his arm around Nina and she nestles contentedly against him. Delilah sings her enticement of Samson, Abraham strokes Nina's shoulder and the side of her neck with his hand. "*Mon Coeur s'ouvre à ta voix*," Delilah sings and Nina is moved and troubled because she knows Delilah is false. Abraham kisses her behind the ear. Nina shudders with pleasure. "Listen, Abraham," she says. "The music is very beautiful." And the curtain falls just as Samson cries out that he has been betrayed.

This time when the houselights go on, Abraham and Nina are silent. Below them, the audience streams out for the second intermission. Abraham stretches out his good leg and stamps the other on the carpeted floor. He says he needs to get up and walk. Nina nods her head in agreement. The curtained and cushioned loge feels tight, claustrophobic. And indeed, once Abraham pulls open the door of the box and they step out into the Grand Foyer, Nina feels restored to herself. The spectacle is dazzling. Ladies draped in iridescent satin and beaded lace, some with feathers and some with flowers in their hair, carrying their trains in one white gloved hand while talking to pomaded gentlemen in frock coats or tails. Perfume, not the lavender or rose water she is used to, but complicated, exotic scents waft in the air and mingle with the odor of expensive cigarettes and a faint trace of sweat. Men and women glide along the marble floor, so animated, so knowing, so apparently at ease among the columns and caryatids, the arches decorated with marble marqueterie, the blazing electric lights. The forward movement of all these people pins Abraham and Nina against the wall. Abraham leans unsteadily on his cane.

Nina, undaunted, pushes herself away from the wall. She wants to see, to smell, to drink in the spectacle, and her need propels her a few feet into the crowd. A woman elbows past her. The woman's dress is coral silk and trimmed with an abundance of sequins, beads, and rhinestones. In her hair, she wears silk feathers dyed the same coral color as her dress. In one hand she holds her fishtail train, in the other a pair of gold opera glasses. The woman is young, Nina notices, and so is the pale-haired man who offers her his arm as they glide off. Nina's heart plunges. While it is amusing to see ladies decked in laces and pearls and gentlemen whose collars and cuffs are whiter than her mother's bleached bed linens, this young woman, who pushed Nina aside as if she were a piece of furniture, whose bare shoulders and bare arms make a mockery of decent behavior, this young woman makes Nina feel ugly. Her dress is suddenly drab, her hair badly done, the onyx brooch that holds her lacy collar down a dreary piece of ornament. She is a poor relation in her long-sleeved gray dress. A governess who has been allowed to come down to the glamorous party from her attic bedroom. Invisible. Or noticeable only because she is completely out of place. She turns back toward Abraham but the crowd has jostled her away from him. "Excuse me," she says, "Excuse me," and ducks her head as she passes.

"Where have you been?" Abraham says. "It's hot out here."

Abraham would never admit to being intimidated, but even he cannot ignore the contrast between himself and Nina and this display of wealth and privilege. He holds the door to the box open and Nina sinks quietly into her chair.

The stage manager knocks three times. Nina and Abraham settle into the protective darkness of the box.

The orchestra plays the opening bars of the third act. This time when Abraham slips his hand around Nina's waist and draws her to him, the gesture feels aggressive, desperate, as if he feared he had lost her to the opulence of the surroundings. Nina leans into him. She too has been shocked and now she wants to feel that they are protection for each other. It is when his hand rests against her breast, brushing her nipple, that she panics. There is an intense fluttering at the base of her stomach, a delirious loosening of all the muscles in her body. She has felt this before, with Sasha on that terrible afternoon. And sometimes just before falling asleep, when her hand strays between her legs and she rolls over onto her stomach, pressing the heel of her hand against that part of her body she never names, pressing through the material of her nightgown, as hard as she can, her hips digging into the mattress, in order to sustain the irritating, delicious feeling until she feels feverish, afraid, and embarrassed. It always surprises her, this current of feeling and it leaves her fragile and unsteady. She does not want to feel that way now, not in a public place, not because of Abraham's brazen exploratory hand, and so she gasps and removes his hand.

Abraham does not pull away from her. Instead, he keeps his mouth on hers and brings her hand to his lap. There he places it on the warm bulge she recognizes with horror. He holds her hand in place for an instant, then releases it. On stage, the dancing girls are pantomiming lustful enticement *en pointe*. Samson, chained to a post, sings his torment and his remorse. Abraham turns away from Nina and, leaning his elbows on the railing, appears to be suddenly enthralled by the music.

Nina huddles, arms across her chest, in the darkness of the box. Tears prick behind her eyelids. She is deeply offended. What has she done to provoke such a breech of decency? Is she some rouged and powdered and tarted-up girl who roams the boulevards at night? Even in the fraction of an instant she laid her hand on it she could feel his . . . his organ . . . alive with heat. It is difficult not to believe he didn't want to humiliate her, to put his wretched mark on the evening and on her, now that she is his. And yet, does Abraham know? Can he smell her secrets, her nighttime pleasure on her hands, her fingers? Is she as complicit as he in this awful business? Nina shivers with misery and confusion although the box is warm. She rummages in her reticule for a handkerchief. She blows her nose and wipes her eyes. Abraham continues to watch the spectacle, stony-faced. His hands grasp the velvet-covered railing, his elbows are tense, his head turned toward the stage.

Abraham is not listening to the opera. He is embarrassed and irritated. They are to be married soon. When will Nina understand how a man feels? Granted, it was a crude thing to do. But what does Nina think happens when a man and a woman kiss?

Samson, blind and shorn of his locks, calls on God's vengeance. Pieces of the scenery begin to tumble onto the stage, pillars, cornices, blocks of fake masonry. Smoke rises from the back of the stage. The music soars and crashes. The crowd applauds. It is what they have all come to see, the spectacular stage effect made possible by hundreds of pulleys, ladders, and trapdoors.

The curtain falls on the final act. "A ridiculous opera," Abraham says. "Not worth the money."

Nina wraps her cashmere shawl around her shoulders. Abraham, ready to leave, gathers his hat and cane.

Carriages, victorias, broughams, and elegant cabriolets are gathered in front of the Place de l'Opéra. Some have been standing there waiting for their owners since the beginning of the performance. Others are cabs for hire. The chauffeurs of a few motorcars have parked their machines away from the main entrance so as not to frighten the horses. It has been raining. The pavement glistens.

A young man in a top hat and black opera cape jostles Abraham off the curb. A woman in a dark velvet cloak streams toward the young man, the bracelets on her long black gloves catching the light from the street lamp. She is laughing. The young man helps her into the brougham, gets in, and pulls the door shut. The coachman snaps his whip. Although it is the same young man and woman Nina observed in the foyer of the opera house, she doesn't even notice them, so deep is she in her misery.

"We must catch the last omnibus," Abraham says. "Or we shall have to walk."

The omnibus clatters to a stop behind the opera house. Nina stepping up to the platform, lifts her skirt, revealing her stockinged ankle. Abraham barely notices. They settle into their seats. The ticket collector comes by to collect the fare.

The omnibus continues along the rue La Fayette. The ticket collector hangs on to the overhead strap, swaying with each jolt of the bus on the cobblestones.

Nina, sitting so close to Abraham, thinks she can smell the cloth of his suit, damp from the humid night air, mingled with the faint musky smell that is his odor. The smell is not unfamiliar or unpleasant, but tonight it carries a burden of intimacy that she refuses to accept. Abraham sits stiffly, his bad leg stretched out in front of him, the expression on his face as blank as any stranger's. Now he is angry, Nina thinks, and she feels her own anger coil back on itself in the presence of his. I have offended him. How easy it is to offend a man. It is unbearable. Any other woman would handle him better than I, she thinks. Nina's throat stings with the effort not to cry. Why is she doing this inexplicable thing, marrying this man?

"Perhaps you would be happier engaged to someone else," Nina says, bursting through the silence that is like a sheet of ice over turbulent waters.

"What?" Abraham growls under his breath. "What did you say?"

"I don't know why you even bother with me."

Abraham does not turn his head. "What are you talking about?"

"I know you've kissed other women the way you kissed me." Her voice is loud in the empty bus. The ticket collector stares, then turns away.

"Be quiet," Abraham snaps. "You are a crazy woman."

"If that is what you think, then why don't we break off our engagement," Nina says. "We have nothing in common. Nothing."

Abraham's skin has turned an angry pink. "If you don't want to marry me, you must tell me so right now."

"You should find another woman. Someone like Rosa. She's more your type."

"Rosa? What has she got to do with anything? Have I proposed to her, Nina? Am I going to marry her?"

"Perhaps you should."

"Yes, you're right. Perhaps I should."

At that moment, Nina hates Abraham. She wishes he were dead. Her hatred is so forceful it passes through her like a bolt of electricity, a flash of feeling so instantaneous she doesn't have time to be ashamed of it.

Abraham folds his arms across his chest. An elderly gentleman wearing a long overcoat totters up the central aisle of the bus. He gives Abraham a nasty look. "Mind your cane," he says. "Someone might trip over it." Abraham jerks the cane toward him and holds it firm between his knees.

Nina pinches the bridge of her nose. Unhappiness squeezes a band of pain across her forehead and along the back of her head. The beginning of a migraine. Abraham leans on his cane with both hands. The horse-drawn bus rocks along the cobblestones. It is turning into the rue de Maubeuge with its uneven, untarred pavement. Abraham stares ahead at the window opposite him. Nina sees their two heads, blurred and distorted in the glass, and she thinks how ugly they both look.

XI

May 1912

NINA LOOKS OUT INTO THE courtyard from the window in her bedroom. The courtyard glistens in the moonlight. The rain that seemed so threatening as she and Abraham were leaving the opera has stopped, and the sky is clear and starry. A surprising night breeze blows out the muslin curtains. Nina has prepared herself for bed. Her hair hangs in a long braid behind her back; she wears an old shift that leaves her arms bare instead of the long-sleeved night dress that is too warm for this late May night.

The cool breeze against her skin makes her shiver. She feels feverish, light-headed; her breath is shallow and painful, her limbs ache. Perhaps she is sick. Perhaps she caught a cold walking from the opera to the omnibus stop in the rain. Wouldn't it be ironic if she who has always been in good health should begin to cough blood just before her wedding? No one would expect her to go through with the ceremony then, would they? And she could waste away quietly, heroically in her parents' house where her father would braid her hair as he did when she was a little girl and her mother would feed her bits of herring. And Abraham would be free to marry Rosa, or anyone else he cared to marry. Melodrama, Nina thinks, hearing Alta's voice in her head. Do you or do you not want to marry this man?

A cat observes her from his perch on a windowsill across the yard. His stare is cold, assessing. My life is over, she thinks. Soon I shall no longer belong to myself. When she thinks of marriage to Abraham, she feels as if someone had placed a heavy hand or a bag of stones on her shoulders. Is that right? Should she feel this way?

The cat across the way cocks his head quizzically. She will not be afraid. What is there to be afraid of? From time immemorial, women have married men, different and unknowable creatures, and stepped blindly into an unknowable future. Is Abraham awake in the middle of the night, worrying about her? Certainly not. He is sleeping, the sleep of the reasonable, the unimaginative, the absurdly confident. It makes her angry to think of him this way. She would like it better if he were anguished, tormented, like her. Is that true? Then what does she want from him? Nina cups her hands to her face.

Beside Nina's bed there is a wooden chest. The lid is open. The scent of lavender wafts over the chest like a perfumed cloud. Inside, there are, in addition to four tablecloths and three tea cloths with embroidered napkins for eight, two complete changes of bed linen with pillow slips, a nightgown, two lingerie sets in satin. All these lovely things she and her mother have been collecting since Yekaterinoslav, a fantasy of happiness and domestic bliss, finely hemmed in Alta's adroit hand, perfectly laundered and folded, wrapped with ribbon, scented with lavender, a gift of herself to the man she will marry. But Abraham doesn't care about linens, and ribbons, and tea things. And does he even care for her?

Nina sinks to her knees beside the chest. Slowly she lifts the first set of sheets out of the chest, unties the ribbons and drops sheets and ribbons to the floor. Her hands shake, her fingers tingle. Then, one by one, she tosses the second set of sheets to the floor and the pillow slips, the tea cloths, the embroidered tablecloth from Russia until she is surrounded by a sea of white. She reaches deeper into the chest and with both hands, scoops up the underclothes, the night-gowns, the delicate chemise and flings them to the floor as well. She stands up and kicks the white crests made by the stiff linens; she stamps on the puddles of soft cloth. Her head pounds. It is full of loud and mean thoughts. Why hadn't they said, No, we will not let you marry our precious daughter. Go away, they could have said, we have taken her where you shall never find her. And now Nina feels teeth-grinding rage at her parents' betrayal. They have given her up so easily.

Her hands work fast. She tears the lacey neck of the peach-colored satin nightgown. She rips the lace around the tiny buttons. She tears the nightdress down the front. The cloth as it rips makes a sound like water rushing through a sluice. She flings the gown, sundered down the middle, away from her.

Suddenly spent, she contemplates what she has done. The gown is unwearable, the linens scattered and wrinkled. Shame, like a bloody stain on the back of her dress, spreads through her. She picks up a sheet, shakes it out, folds and flattens the wrinkles with the palm of her hand. She puts the sheet back in the bottom of the chest. She does the same with the other sheets, the tablecloths and the napkins, and the pretty underclothes. The brown tissue paper is unusable, but she can rub the sprigs of lavender between her fingers. Only the night-gown appears to be beyond saving. She clasps the gown and buries her face in it.

Nina gets up and removes a small wooden box from the top of her chest of drawers. Inside there is a collection of threads and needles of all sizes, a gift from her mother. She sits on the edge of her bed, threads a needle with thread as close to peach-colored as she can find and begins to sew the two sides of the gown together with the tiny, almost invisible stitches she learned from her mother. Time presses, she feels an urgent need to repair and restore the gown, the linens, her thoughts. How can she take the next step in her life with her thoughts all mangled and twisted? He is a good man, she thinks as she bends over her sewing, steadying her hand, tamping down her disorderly breathing. He loves me and I love him. I really do. I will marry him and we shall be happy forever.

Before

Yekaterinoslav
Ukraine Province

1885–1905

XII

MENACHEM FRIBURG, THE foremost Jewish tailor in Yekaterinoslav, fingers a bolt of blue serge in front of two young women. He is a short, animated redhead with a graying beard and blue eyes, one of which tends to drift as he speaks.

"Now this would be nice for the winter," Friburg says as he strokes the serge. Behind him rolls of cloth, like so many cannons about to be fired, line the walls. Swaths of wool, velvet, and taffeta lie stretched across a long wooden table. Gaslights flicker blue-green.

"Of course, you might like the taffeta. It is appropriate for every season. Or the gabardine. I can show you velvet, if you prefer. Anything you ladies want. In my workshop, we have the best fabrics in all the province," Friburg continues. "And the best workmanship. That I can guarantee."

As he talks, his drifting eye floats over the fabric. This is disconcerting to one of the young women, who is already in a state of resentful suspicion. She is Alta Perel Wolfovich, twenty years old, handsome in a forceful way with deep-set eyes, a strong, straight nose, and firm mouth. She wears her thick curly hair parted in the middle with a fringe of brown curls over her forehead that soften her face and bring out her brown, lively eyes. The outfit Menachem Friburg is about to make is not for her. It is for Alta's cousin Drina, and it is to Drina that Friburg is addressing his remarks. Drina's husband owns sawmills outside of Yekaterinoslav, one of the few enterprises allowed to Jews in this fertile region of the Ukraine. Yekaterinoslav is a town of some 120,000 inhabitants on the banks of the lower Dnieper river. It is a provincial town, not as lively and culturally rich as Kiev, not as open to new ideas as the port of Odessa, far from Moscow and St. Petersburg, but still not quite a backwater, certainly not a shtetl, although it has a substantial Jewish population. It is in the Pale of Settlement, the region established by the Empress Catherine in 1792 that includes Poland and parts of the Russian Empire where Jews have been allowed and encouraged to live.

The Kagans, Drina's husband's family and the Grinbergs, on her mother's side, are the leading families in Yekaterinoslav by virtue of their wealth and their piety. When the tailors of Yekat decided to build a new synagogue, they turned to the Kagans and the Grinbergs to help finance the splendid red brick building near the Potemkin gardens. Alta Wolfovich is only a poor relation. She has no husband and few prospects since she is an orphan. Her father died when she was five and her mother, impoverished by a bad second marriage, has been dead for four years. Now, although her grandfather was a rabbi and her father owned a successful distillery for making plum brandy and beer, Alta is penniless. She has had to learn a trade; she is a seamstress. She lives with her aunt Malie Grinberg, Drina's mother, and she is always conscious of her subordinate relation to the Grinbergs. This visit to Menachem Friburg's workshop is galling. Here she is with the skills, the experience, and yes, the taste, and no money for a new dress. In fact, she will be obliged, when Drina's dress is finished, to accept Drina's old one and, most probably, she will have to wear it for the Passover Seder.

"It's so hard to know what to do," Drina says with an apologetic giggle to the tailor whose darting smile and fluttery hands remind

Alta of a fish swimming in a transparent bowl. "My husband always complains that I take too long to make a decision. But really, it's impossible to know what's right. Menachem Friburg, you have given me too many fabrics to choose from." Drina, who is small, thin, and nervous, bobs her head under her dark wig. She wrings her hands. She seems truly anguished, which Alta finds absurd.

"What do you think, Alta dear? What would be best?"

Alta surveys the expanse of fabric on the table. She raises her head and gives the tailor a hard stare, but Friburg's smile is plastered to his lips.

"You can't go wrong," the tailor says. "Everything here is first quality. Here, feel the wool. So light, so soft."

"I know, I know," Drina says and her voice carries with it the torment of indecision.

Alta is annoyed. Drina lacks character. She has everything and yet she agonizes over frivolities.

"For Passover," Alta says. "I would choose the taffeta."

"Oh, do you think so? Yes, yes, I agree. Taffeta is lovely. But the wool gabardine? It can be cold at Passover and the wool, well, one can really wear wool all year, except during the summer, of course. I simply don't know."

Drina presses her hands prayerfully against her mouth. Alta sighs. The tailor continues to smile. His fingers rub against the taffeta as if he could lure Drina with the siren song of rustling fabric.

"Yes, the taffeta," Drina says finally in an exhausted voice.

At last, Alta thinks. She likes Drina, who is kind if scattered, yet she is always aware of how much she owes Drina's family. It is hard to be twenty, to be asked for your opinion when you cannot even consider a new dress for the holidays.

"If you are ready," Menachem Friburg executes a small bow. His red curls under his cap dangle in front of his ears. "I will call my new cloth cutter in. He is a young man, but a first-rate tailor. You'll see what a splendid job he does cutting and sewing. I am lucky to have stolen him away from Brodsky in Goroditche." Friburg rubs his hands together. "You'll see, you'll see."

Alta frowns. What is it about Menachem Friburg that distresses her? He has no dignity. All this bragging: everything he touches is the best, his fabrics, his workers; he probably boasts about his clients too. Drina Kagan came to my shop and ordered twelve yards of taffeta. Yes, Kagan, the rich miller's wife. Oh and there was a young lady with her. Undistinguished. I think a poor relation. And so Alta adds to her own misery and resentment.

"Chaim Yudelovich." Menachem Friburg snaps his fingers in the direction of an open door through which a crack of light suddenly appears. A young man enters the room carrying a kerosene lamp that he carefully places on a small table beside the bolts of cloth.

"My new man," says Friburg, "Chaim Yudelovich Schavranski."

The young man, who is tall and beardless, inclines his head toward the two women. He stands quietly, hands by his sides, his head angled slightly toward Friburg, waiting for instructions. In his dark suit and white collar that seems to glisten even in the dim light, Alta thinks he looks refined and distinguished, not at all like a tailor. And he is handsome. He has a long, narrow face, a small, delicate nose, and high cheekbones. His eyes are gentle, as far as she can tell. She immediately thinks there is a sweetness about him. Of course, such observations are foolish. What can she tell about a person she sees for the first time, in a poorly lit room, about whom she knows nothing? Alta, always practical, shakes herself out of her reverie.

Chaim, too, is struck by the young woman. He is twenty-two years old, away from Kiev and his family for the first time. He lives above Friburg's workshop and he is lonely. He takes his meals with the Friburg family, which helps of course, but is also a source of discom-

fort. Friburg has a daughter, Rochele, who is red-headed like her father, but plump and slow-moving, a languid contrast to Friburg's
hectic energy. Chaim worries that his employer has designs on him,
especially if he remains with the family for much longer. Chaim is
quietly ambitious and eager to set up shop on his own.

Alta hands Chaim a sheaf of brown papers. This is the pattern for
Drina's dress. Alta measured Drina at home and drew and cut out
the pattern herself. It would not have been proper for Friburg to take
the measurements of a married lady, and as for the young assistant
. . . the thought makes Alta smile and lower her eyes.

"WHAT?" SAYS AUNT MALIE Grinberg to Alta who has just announced
in her direct way that she will marry Chaim. "That penniless young
man? What are you thinking of, my dear? Marry a tailor? You, the
granddaughter of Rabbi Josef Tarnopolsky, of blessed memory? You
can't be serious."

Aunt Malie is a large woman in her fifties who exhibits the dignity that stoutness and money can bring when combined. She, Alta,
and cousin Drina are in Aunt Malie's sitting room, a room that once
took Alta's breath away with its abundance of Turkish carpets, velvet draperies, and heavy, ornate furniture.

"Why are you in such a hurry to marry?" Aunt Malie says. Alta
catches Aunt Malie smiling slyly at her daughter. This is not unusual.
Aunt Malie often looks as if she were in possession of a delicious
secret. Her mouth curls up, her eyelids curve down, her cheeks become as round as balls of hard wax. Ordinarily, Alta allows her aunt's
smug self-satisfaction to drift by her. It so rarely has to do with any
of Alta's concerns. But today, Alta, tense and nervous, imagines a
trap in Aunt Malie's every gesture, every change in facial expression
and so she presses her hands together in her lap until her fingers are
red and her knuckles white.

"Are you unhappy with us?" Aunt Malie continues through her half-closed lids. "Do we treat you badly? Why don't you wait? Someone more suitable will surely come along. You are a young handsome girl. There is no need to settle for less than you deserve. I will make a lovely match for you. I know all the young men in Yekat."

Alta takes a deep breath. She is about to stake her future on a notion that will undermine her aunt's authority, but that is so beautiful, so true it fills her with happiness even to her bones.

"That is kind of you, Aunt, but I have found the man I love."

Aunt Malie opens her eyes. They are small and sharp and dark with anger.

"I have nothing against love, Alta. Drina loved Naphtali when she married him, or maybe after, it makes no difference, isn't that so, my darling?"

Drina, who is always nervous in her mother's presence, manages a weak, but obliging smile.

"But love is not the best predictor of married happiness. That is why such matters are best decided by those who have had more experience with life. And you have not even bothered to consult me. That is the most painful of all."

Aunt Malie sighs theatrically and wags her head.

Alta hears her aunt out with steely calm. Every word her aunt utters now drops into a pocket of condemnation that Alta will draw on for the rest of her life. In the four years Alta has lived with her aunt and her aunt's family, Aunt Malie has never mentioned marriage to her, never invited anyone to tea for her, never asked the matchmaker to supply a list of eligible bachelors.

"It is because I have no mother," Alta says, "that I have had to find my own husband."

Alta waits for her aunt's rebuke. Ungratefulness is a serious matter. But Aunt Malie only knits her brow and slides her hands along the sculptured arms of the chair she is sitting on. "Tailoring is a respectable profession," Alta says. There is a tremor in her usually clear, bright voice. "It is you who encouraged me to become a seamstress. Now Chaim and I can carry on by ourselves."

"Phooey," Aunt Malie waves her hand as if she were brushing away bad air.

"You could at least have asked my mother's permission first," says Drina, who is horrified at Alta's brazen independence. "We knew nothing about this."

"That is because you chose not to know," Alta says, her hands locked in her lap, her back as straight as she can make it. Ever since she and Chaim agreed to marry (Chaim, bending toward her, his eyes full of delicate hesitation, saying, "Shall we marry? Do you agree?" as they strolled along the Prospekt, dodging nannies and children on a pretty spring day on one of Chaim's few afternoons off), she has dreaded this encounter with her aunt. Now she feels the frightening exhilaration that comes with defying not only her aunt but all the social constraints of her community. "It is true we have not known each other long," she says. "Three months. But how many marriages are made between people who have only met once or maybe twice? At least Chaim and I chose each other freely. And Chaim came to the house frequently. Drina, you invited him to the Seder, if I'm not mistaken. What did you think was going on?" Alta turns her fierce gaze on Drina, who shrinks into her chair.

"Enough," says Aunt Malie, sensing perhaps that she has lost the battle. Her face is dark. "If you insist on marrying this man, so be it. You must understand that although I love you tenderly, I cannot give my blessing to this marriage."

Alta squeezes her eyes shut. It is terrible not to have Aunt Malie's blessing, but she is prepared. It's just that the muscles of her jaw hurt and there is a sharp pain in her throat, a constriction, as if her throat were closing up with the effort not to cry.

"No one is obliged to come to my wedding if they don't want to," she says, in the steadiest voice she can manage. She fixes her gaze on the mirror in a gilt frame above the mantelpiece. "I certainly can't force anyone to come."

There is a silence as Aunt Malie slips a cube of sugar between her teeth and takes a sip of tea from her glass on the table beside her. When she is done, she asks, without lifting her eyes toward Alta, "And when is this wedding to take place?"

"Soon," Alta says. "Next Saturday." She does not know if this is true, but she does know that she wants to start her new life as soon as she can.

CHAIM IS KIND AND comforting when Alta tells him of her talk with Aunt Malie. They are sitting in the back of Menachem Friburg's workshop. Chaim is sewing by the feeble light of a candle. Friburg, always looking to economize, has turned off the gas for the night. Chaim's stitches are so tight and so neat and his hand is so quick, that Friburg does not encourage him to use the sewing machine, a brand-new Pfaff from Germany, with a foot treadle, a rotating bobbin, and a design of pink roses on the body of the machine.

The silk lining Chaim is sewing into a man's jacket drapes over his lap. Alta touches it. It is like touching Chaim, she thinks.

"After we are married, I will never set foot in my aunt's house," she says, her face frozen into hard lines.

Chaim continues to make his tiny, rapid stitches. He is a young man and his eyes are very good, but even he is squinting in the low light. He chews on his lower lip. A thread breaks.

"It is not that I want her to forgive me," Alta continues. "Not at all. In fact, I want nothing from her. Especially not her famous hospitality. All those balls and parties she gives to show off her gilded mirrors and her new carpets. If she thinks it is so degrading to marry a tailor, then she must also think that I have demeaned myself. And that is offensive to me."

Chaim threads the needle, turns the jacket so that he can work on the lining of the sleeve. He moves the candle closer to his eyes. Alta peers into his averted face.

"What am I saying? Forgive me, my dearest." She touches Chaim's sleeve. "I am so thoughtless. There is nothing degrading about hard work. Drina thinks it is beneath her to sew a button on little Yankele's jacket. She thinks only peasants work. Well, we shall be peasants then. Yes, that's it. We will work very, very hard and Aunt Malie will come to visit us in our home."

Alta's usually pale skin is tinged with pink. Her eyes are luminous. She is exalted by her vision of the future.

Chaim nods as he continues to sew. "Of course, you are right, my dear. We have the future ahead of us."

"We don't need anyone," Alta says. "We can manage by ourselves."

"Absolutely. Yekaterinoslav is a good place for Jews and a good place for tailors."

Chaim believes what he says. How could he not? What experience does he have of disappointment and displacement? And besides he has Alta. She is so amazing, fearless, energetic, determined. They will make a good team. He has already picked out a storefront where he will open his own workshop, with Friburg's help, God willing. If he is disturbed at the moment, it is because he knows he is marrying into a family where he is not wanted. Chaim cannot imagine not being liked. In his young life, he has never come up against opposition. He is the sixth child in a family of seven and all his life he has gotten what he wanted through the casual indifference of his overworked parents. His family will approve of Alta. But as he finishes stitching the lining of the sleeve, he wonders if her family will ever approve of him.

Alta touches his shoulder again.

"Someday my aunt will love you too, Chaim. She will love you for the good, kind man that you are. She will see that we are happy and that will make her happy. She is not a bad woman, you know. Somewhere, under all those layers of fat, she has a good heart."

And Chaim smiles and lifts up grateful eyes to Alta. That is what astonishes him most about her. That Alta knows not only her own mind, but sometimes his as well. That without a word from him, she seems to understand how his heart works, what his dreams are. And he thinks, as he puts down his sewing and reaches for Alta's slender hand, that this must be the best part of love, this communion, this understanding between two people who are not the same and yet who are.

XIII

CHAIM PULLS THE BRUSH through the tangled mass of Nina's unruly golden brown curls. Nina tries not to squirm. She stands between her father's legs, a sturdy three-year-old in brown lace-up shoes and long blue and white checked frock, her hands resting on Chaim's thighs and her small fingers digging occasionally into the fabric of his trousers.

When this happens, Chaim says, "Did I hurt you, Ninotchka?" and tries to catch his daughter's eye. Nina loves this time with her father and doesn't want to mind the way her scalp tugs and her head is thrown back when the brush hits a tangle in her hair. But it does hurt and so she winces and digs her chin into her shoulder.

Chaim says. "Brushing your hair is like walking in the forest, nothing but trees and bushes and rocks."

Nina frowns, ready to be hurt. "My hair is not a forest."

"Of course, it isn't," Chaim says and places a kiss on the top of her head.

Chaim brushes and combs Nina's hair every morning when Alta is sick. Alta suffers from mysterious collapses, nervous prostrations that sweep through her like fierce, but passing storms. It is hard for Chaim to accept these transformations in his energetic, determined wife, his helpmeet in the tailoring establishment they run as equal partners, except that Alta must also take care of the household and look after Nina and keep the books, and perhaps that is why she collapses, why she is prone to these bouts of debilitating exhaustion. The doctors at the Jewish hospital have pronounced her healthy but overworked. When she is sick, Chaim spoons tonic out for her three times a day.

Alta is in one of these collapses at the moment. She sits in bed, pale and hollow-eyed, propped up by pillows against the wooden headboard, her hair pulled into a long braid, and watches Chaim and Nina. She is happy that Chaim takes such good care of Nina, it is a relief not to have to worry about either of them, but the closeness between father and daughter, so apparent in the arch of his back, the sweep of his arms around Nina, the way the child leans into him, content and se-cure, causes her a familiar jab of pain. Nina is the heaven–sent bless-ing on her happy marriage, but after Nina was born Alta was confined to her bed for eighteen months, cared for by Chaim and a Ukrainian peasant women. When he could take time away from the workshop, Chaim took charge of Nina, bathed her, dressed her, played with her, taught her to drink from a cup and eat with a spoon, toddled after her when she took her first steps while Alta looked on, grieving the loss of her daughter. And it is this sense that Nina is his more than hers that besets Alta when she watches the two of them together.

"Don't make her braids too tight," Alta says from her bed as Chaim weaves a yellow ribbon between the strands of curly hair.

He ties a bow at the end of each braid, and releasing Nina, pushes her gently toward her mother. "Even if you are badly combed, you are the prettiest little girl in the world," he says, and Nina, certain that she is indeed the prettiest little girl in the world, climbs up on her parents' bed and snuggles into the space made by Alta's out-stretched and welcoming arm.

Alta and Chaim have been married for eight years. Just as Chaim predicted, Menachem Friburg was furious when his best tailor left to start an establishment of his own. Business is good, thanks to Aunt Malie, who, in spite of lingering resentment against her niece's willful marriage, switched her allegiance from Menachem to Chaim as a wedding gift to the young couple and encouraged her friends to do so as well. Chaim and Alta work at home, he at the Pfaff sewing machine Friburg sold him for a scandalous sum, behind the painted screen that divides the work area from the front room that serves as parlor and dining room. Alta measures the clients, all of whom are women, finishes the outfits with her tight hand stitching, and enters credits and payments in a black leather ledger, as a good Jewish wife should. It is a hard life, but satisfying with the promise of better times to come. It was only after Nina was born that Alta's health became troublesome, the eighteen months in bed, the frequent but minor illnesses, and now something else, bouts of fatigue that devastate the family. Chaim worries, Nina frets, the Ukrainian woman is asked back to take care of the house. Fortunately, Alta recovers quickly. After a few days, rarely a week, she is herself again and takes on with her customary intensity the chores she abandoned, the hems that need basting, the buttons that must be attached, the care of her beloved daughter. She tells Chaim, unprompted, and Cousin Drina too when she comes to visit, that she has everything she wants, a good husband, healthy, hardworking, affectionate, and a darling little girl. And yet something is missing in Alta's life. There is a worrisome absence, a failure not quite but almost shameful that preys on her mind and drains her energy. Her happiness is so nearly complete it feels selfish to want more. But she does.

Chaim tickles Nina's round baby belly.

"I'm better today," Alta says, as Nina wriggles happily on the bed beside her. "I'll get up tomorrow."

"Will you feel well enough to travel?" Chaim asks.

"Of course. Your sister is expecting us."

"She'll understand if you're too tired."

"Nonsense," Alta says, and there is that firmness in her voice that tells her husband that she is already on the mend.

NINA SITS SOLEMNLY BETWEEN her mother and her father on the backless bench of a horse-drawn cart that is taking the family to the outskirts of Smila. Smila, 250 kilometers north of Yekaterinoslav and twenty kilometers inland from the Dneiper River, is where Chaim's sister and brother-in-law run a small grocery store in the Jewish section of town. It is a daylong ride on the narrow-gauge railroad that runs from Yekat to Smila. Alta and Chaim undertake this journey only once a year, but with much preparation and fanfare. Alta brings gifts for everyone, a pretty dress for little Feiga, a lacy blouse for Frume, Chaim's sister, a hem-stitched neck scarf for brother-in law Isaac, a tiny cotton jacket for the baby. All of which, even a handkerchief embroidered by Alta, take on the exotic aura of the big city.

Smila is also where the Giter Yid, the good Jew, holds his court. This year, for the first time since they began coming to Smila, Alta and Chaim are going to consult the Giter Yid, much as their parents might have done twenty years before. And so on this chilly spring day, Alta, Chaim, and Nina have exchanged the warmth of the grocery store with its fragrance of spices and pickles for the muddy ruts and evil-smelling puddles on the road to the Giter Yid's house. Patches of dirty snow cling to the roots of trees, and in the fields, still bare, birds peck hungrily between the empty furrows.

"I want to go home," Nina says, each roll and pitch of the cart loosening the fur rug Alta tucked around Nina's legs as a precaution against the cold.

"Soon, soon," says Chaim and pats Nina's hand. Alta straightens the rug with a worried sigh. Nina is a sweet-natured child, not in the least troublesome, but anxious, alert to every disturbance in the air around her, quick to sense a change of mood or manner in her parents. Now she looks from Chaim to Alta; both parents seem distant and preoccupied. Nina thrusts her thumb in her mouth.

"Ninotchka, don't. You're a big girl now." Alta leans toward her daughter and gently pulls the thumb out of her mouth. Nina pouts, but she is grateful for her mother's attention.

The driver of the cart, whose thick black beard, side curls, and enormous hump swelling his sheepskin jacket alarm Nina, points his whip in the direction of an imposing wooden house. Nina huddles against her mother.

"You better have money ready," the driver says. "They won't let you see him unless you make a donation."

"Of course," says Chaim. It is insulting to be reminded of one's obligations. Alta keeps her lips pinched. She has deep misgivings about this journey.

The Giter Yid's house is a one-story wooden building with a portico above the entrance, flanked by bare trees that appear black against the sunless April sky. The Giter Yid lives with his wife and his acolytes, young men who spend their days reading and explaining the Talmud under the old man's scholarly tutelage. The mornings are spent in prayer and study; in the afternoon, the Giter Yid receives his visitors.

Alta and Chaim are not particularly pious; Alta does not shave her head or wear a wig. Her father, an enlightened man, taught her to read Hebrew, an unusual accomplishment for a girl. Chaim does not wear a yarmulka, a skullcap, although he covers his head when he goes to synagogue. Alta and Chaim observe the holidays and Alta does not mix meat and milk dishes. They think of themselves as good Jews, respectful but not fanatical. City Jews. They are going to see the Giter Yid at the suggestion of Chaim's sister; on their own, they would not have thought of it.

They were sitting around the dinner table after a meal of smoked herring and potatoes in dill when the matter came up. "How can it hurt? Maybe it will help," Chaim said when Frume, Chaim's plump, matronly older sister, made the suggestion. The room was invitingly warm and smelled sweetly of wood smoke. Nina was asleep on the bed she shared with her parents in the curtained alcove near the stove. "I don't like to say 'miracle.' But the counsel he gave me, it was like a miracle. And now, here's our Schmuli asleep in his crib," Frume said, wiping beads of perspiration from her forehead with the back of her hand. She rocked the wooden cradle with her foot. "Such a good man. So pious and scholarly. A man like that appears once in a hundred years. A thousand years. We are fortunate in Smila. Go tomorrow. You'll thank me." Isaac, Frume's husband, knocked his pipe against the table and winked at Chaim. Women's talk, he seemed to say. As if we counted for nothing. But Alta was reluctant; she doesn't like to plead, to ask for favors from anyone. She relented only when she saw the need in Chaim's eyes.

The driver reins in the old horse. Chaim steps down first, scoops Nina off the bench. Alta descends more carefully.

She asks, "How will we get back?"

"I won't wait, if that's what you want," the driver says. "It'll be hours before you see him."

"Go home then," Chaim says. "We'll find a ride."

"Hah, even the Giter Yid can't make drivers appear out of nowhere. If you like, I'll be back in three hours. If you're ready, good, if not I'll go home for dinner."

Chaim nods and takes a few coins out of his pocket. The driver counts them by pushing the pieces along the flat of his hand. When he is done, he tips his cap. Chaim has been generous, as always.

Chaim takes Nina by the hand. Alta secures her hat, jostled by the bumpy ride, with a long hat pin.

"Take my hand too," she says to Nina and Nina grips both her parents' hands tightly. A yellow dog on the front stoop opens one sleepy eye, then drops his head back onto his paws.

A young man with a wide expanse of brown beard, a long black coat, and round black hat ushers the Schavranskis into the front room. The air is colder here than outside; this part of the house, where there is no stove, holds in the winter air like a trap. The room is dimly lit by two smoking oil lamps. Seated on benches pressed against the wooden walls, the petitioners wait patiently, elderly women wrapped in plaid shawls, pale mothers with sickly children hunched on their laps, a young couple, she, round faced and bewildered, he fingering his wispy beard, at their feet, a chicken squawking in a wicker basket. A man with weeping pustules sits apart, head bent, arms across his chest. Two little boys, side curls dangling, roll marbles back and forth between their legs.

Alta slips into a space at the end of the bench. She is careful not to lean against the wall where countless heads have left a trail of dirt and grease. Nina rests her head in her mother's lap. Chaim, standing, leans against one of the supporting wooden pillars.

Alta strokes Nina's hair. The yellow ribbons on the end of her braids have come undone and Alta absently winds one of them around her finger. She has been of two minds about this expedition all along. And now she is plunged into doubt. They have no business with the Giter Yid, she thinks for a wild instant. It is tempting God's wrath to ask for favors. She anxiously searches Chaim's face and when he smiles his kind, encouraging smile, she can't keep a sprig of hope, like an early spring flower, from blooming in her heart.

A second young man in black approaches Chaim. "If you have something to ask the rabbi, please write it down on this piece of paper." Chaim inclines his head toward Alta and she takes the paper and pencil from the young man's hands. When she has finished writing, she drops the note into the small wicker basket he holds out.

"Now if you could make a donation for the orphans. We are building a new infirmary in Smila."

Chaim takes out his wallet and places two ten-ruble notes in the basket.

"Thank you, sir. Can you be a bit more generous? It has been a hard winter for the poor."

Chaim deposits another bill into the basket.

Nina's head droops. Alta resettles her on her lap. Nina's eyes close. When she wakes up, it is to feel her father gently shaking her shoulders. "Come on," he says. "It's our turn."

A blast of heat from an enormous enameled stove surprises the Schavranskis as they enter the Giter Yid's receiving room. It is a big room simply furnished, a long table, two wooden benches, ceramic oil lamps set on each end of the table. The windows, curtained in dingy white muslin, barely let in the thin gray April light. In the center, on a chair covered with a Persian rug, sits the Giter Yid. He is a small man with gossamer strands of white hair under a black cap, a beaked nose, and a beard like a collar of cotton. He is attended by several men in black coats and hats who pour him tea from the teapot on top of the samovar, plump the pillows behind him, straighten the blanket draped around his legs, dab a handkerchief at his watery eyes. His face is like the muddy road from Smila, lined with ruts and crevices, but he smiles benignly at Alta and Chaim.

"I am pleased to meet you at last," he says in a surprisingly strong voice. "I know your sister and her children well, Chaim Yudelovich."

"It is a privilege to be here," Chaim says.

The Giter Yid's chin trembles. "I am an old man. I do not know the answers to all the questions that are posed to me. Prayer and patience are what works miracles. Let me see what you have written." He slips a pair of rimless spectacles on his nose. He smiles. "Aha," he says when he has returned the paper to the wicker basket. "So this is your little daughter? A pretty, healthy child. How old is she?"

"Just turned three," Alta says.

"And her name?"

"Nechama," says Alta giving Nina her Hebrew name.

"Well, Nechama, I have something for you." He reaches back into the pocket of his long black coat. His arm trembles. Immediately, there is someone at his side, a young man who fumbles in the old man's pocket. The pocket jingles. Chaim guides Nina's hand upward. Nina casts an anxious glance at her mother. Alta nods. The old man drops a coin into Nina's curved hand. "If you are a good girl from now on, you will soon no longer be an only child."

"Faith and prayer, faith and prayer," the old man repeats, his splendid white head bobbing. "Be careful. It is easy to lose your soul in a big city. Teach Nechama to honor religion, to be respectful of traditions. Bring your children up to be good Jews." The old man manages a sly, knowing grin. "Children, young woman, children," he says, and Alta, embarrassed but pleased, lowers her eyes.

The driver of the cart is waiting outside. "So," he says, "I was right. Three hours. Did you get what you wanted from the old man?"

Chaim smiles and shrugs. Alta says, "We shall see."

"Can I keep it?" Nina's little hand is clamped around the coin.

"You must keep it," Alta says "Otherwise the prophecy will not come true." And the conviction with which she says this surprises her. "When we get home, I will sew a special bag for your coin."

"What's prophecy?" Nina wrinkles her nose. Alta and Chaim exchange mirthful glances and their smiles expand into bursts of hilarity. Nina grins too, baffled but pleased to see her parents laugh with such abandon.

"How do you feel, my dear?" Chaim asks Alta when the three of them have settled into the cart. "The trip hasn't tired you out?"

"Not at all," Alta tucks the fur rug around Nina who, exhausted, has stretched out on both their laps. "I really feel quite strong," she says. "We must thank Frume when we get back."

XIV

THE DNIEPER HAS FROZEN OVER and snow is banked high all along the Prospekt, the broadest and most elegant avenue in Yekaterinoslav. At one end of the Prospekt are the Potemkin Gardens, on this day a stark silhouette of leafless trees. It is four o'clock in the afternoon, the sky is already dark as night.

A bulky shape occupies a bench at the entrance to the Gardens. At close range, the shape dissolves into a man and a woman with a large bundle across both their laps. The man wears a fur hat and a dark cloth coat. The woman wears a dark coat as well, long enough to cover her skirt, and a shawl around her head and shoulders. The bundle is a child tightly swaddled in blankets and covered with a fur rug. The lower part of his face is hidden by a loosely woven scarf that his mother lifts from time to time. She wants to make sure he is breathing properly. Only his closed eyes are visible, the long fringe of lashes flutters occasionally. His sleep is not very deep, but it makes his parents happy. Chaim and Alta have been sitting outside, on this bench or on one just like it a few paces away, for the past three hours with their four-year-old son immobilized across their lap. Yudel is recovering from typhoid fever, and his doctors, there were nine of them at the height of the crisis—all the Jewish doctors in Yekaterinoslav—recommended that he spend three hours in the fresh air every day, every day, mind you, that is what the child needs to regain his strength. And so his parents sit in the cold, absenting themselves from their other obligations, the tailoring workshop, the household tasks, from Nina, who is almost nine years old and, thank God, doesn't need them nearly as much as Yudel, their darling boy, so long awaited and so recently snatched from the jaws of death.

"Chaim," Alta whispers. Her jaw hurts from the cold. It is painful to speak. The bone feels frozen. Chaim inclines his head to hear her. He too is suffering. His mustache is stiff; the hairs in his nose feel like so many tiny nails driven into his nostrils. "Don't you think we can go in now? It's almost four." Chaim nods. He curls and uncurls his toes in his boots, shudders his shoulders under the greatcoat. Very carefully releasing his grip on the boy, he slides off the bench. Alta holds Yudel's head. The child moans in his sleep.

"Maybe he won't wake up this time. Please be careful," Alta says. Chaim slips his arms under Yudel and lifts him off his mother. Yudel opens his eyes. "Mama," he says.

"Sleep, Idelka," says Chaim, using his son's Yiddish name. "Sleep."

Under the wrap of blankets, Chaim can feel Yudel's arms and legs beginning to tense into wakefulness. Alta adjusts the scarf around her son's head and mouth. By the time they have reached their apartment on Karaim Street, the child is awake and screaming.

Chaim jiggles the kicking bundle in his arms.

"Hush," he says. "Everyone will hear you. You don't want that, now, do you?"

"He hates being confined like this," says Alta. "Soon, soon, we'll be home and you can run around as much as you like."

Yudel continues to yell, full-throated ear-piercing yells, as his parents climb the two flights of stairs to their apartment.

Inside, Nina is waiting for them. She has prepared the samovar and set the table with poppyseed cakes and jam. Of course, she has heard the noise on the stairs. She's been listening for it all afternoon.

She always hopes her parents will be back before the three hours are up. Because that is what they say when they leave. We'll be home soon, soon. You won't even notice. But she does notice. She does not like to be alone in the big apartment. A lump of worry forms in her chest as soon as they leave and sits there until she hears Yudel screaming across the courtyard. Then the dreadful lump dissolves into a different sort of anxiety and she rushes to the balcony, struggles with the doors, flings them open, and waves to her parents until they disappear from her sight up the stairs. But even when everyone is home safely, there is still cause for concern. Is the boy cold? Is he hungry? Please God he hasn't caught something out there! Quick, Nina, the hot-water basin. May I dry his feet, Mama? May I rub his hands? Don't splash, Yudel. Don't hit me! There, he's dry. Does he want a piece of cake? I'll make him some tea. Let me do it, Mama. I can, I know how. Don't bite me, Yudel. I'll tell Mama. Yes, I will. No, I won't really because you are my darling baby brother.

When Yudel came down with the fever, he was moved out of the room he shared with Nina into his parents' bedroom, and Nina, used to the comfort of her little brother's nighttime noises, could not fall asleep alone. There were the anxious comings and goings of the grown-ups, what seemed to her like a continuous murmur of voices through the night, and in the morning no one came to wake her. She stopped going to school. It was still dark when she had breakfast alone with her father in the dining room. During the day, she read her school-books or drew maps of the ancient boundaries of Kievan Rus for her geography class. Mostly, she sat next to her mother at Yudel's bedside and watched over them both. She saw her brother's progress through Alta's eyes and read the changing lines of worry on her mother's face as she would have read a terrifying book she could not put down. Sometimes her mother's hand grabbed hers, the fingers clenched, the grip so hard, it seemed to Nina that she alone was her mother's anchor in the world and this, while it made her feel important, also frightened her. At other times, especially when Yudel slept quietly, Alta would sigh and then Nina would sidle up to her mother, flatten herself against her chest, and wait for Alta's arms to make a cave around her.

The night the doctors gave up on Yudel, Alta walked out of the apartment with only a thin shawl around her shoulders, although it was the middle of the winter. Chaim, already in mourning, slumped in a chair in the living room, his hands clasped between his knees. Nina stayed at her brother's side. She was afraid to take her eyes off him; something terrible might happen if she wasn't watching. Yudel's breathing was raspy, beads of perspiration trickled down his cheeks, his black hair lay damp against his forehead. He kept moving his arms and legs. "Stay still," she said. "Don't jiggle around so much." She held him down a little, not hard, just because it bothered her to see him wiggle and kick his feet all the time. How would he get better if he didn't rest? So she held his wrists to give him a little time to recover. When she looked up at his face, she noticed blood issue from his nose, a trickle at first and then a gush of red down his lips and chin. Yudel turned his head in his sleep; blood spread along the pillowcase making a red halo beneath his head.

"Papa," Nina screamed. "He's dying."

Chaim rushed into the room, the flaps of his black vest open. He lifted his son's head off the pillow.

"Idelka, Idelka. What is the matter?"

Yudel coughed and sputtered, blood spewed onto his nightshirt, his little hands were sticky with it. He cried out, "Mama, Mama."

"Hold him, Nina," said Chaim. "Take my handkerchief and pinch his nose."

Nina slipped one hand behind Yudel's head and with the other pinched his nostrils tight. The child beat his legs under the covers and flayed his arms. He gasped for air. Blood seeped between Nina's fingers. When she looked up, she saw that her father had taken out his pocketknife and flipped the blade open.

"Don't do anything bad to him!" she cried.

Chaim winced. "Just something cold to stop the blood," he said and he held the blade of the knife flat against the nape of Yudel's neck.

"I don't want him to die, Papa."

"Hold his head back."

Yudel was choking, the blood backing up in his throat. He spewed out a dark-red clot of blood, and mucus dribbled down his chin.

"Papa!" Nina cried.

"Cotton. Where is the cotton for his nose?" asked Chaim.

Nina jerked her head toward the bedside table. "Mama keeps it in the drawer."

Chaim pushed a small wad of cotton into Yudel's right nostril, then another into his left one. The cotton was quickly saturated. Chaim removed each bloody wad as carefully and as expertly as he cut cloth. He inserted fresh ones. Yudel thrashed in the bed.

"Hold still," said Nina. It seemed to her that all of Yudel's blood must be flowing out of him. There would be nothing left and he would die. Used cotton, red with blood, made a smeary pile at Chaim's feet.

"Now it's better," said Chaim. "Look, not so much blood."

Nina nodded. It was true. Yudel looked as if he had stuck red marbles up his nose, but at least there was no new blood. The child relaxed into Nina's arm. She kissed his damp forehead.

Chaim said, "We must change the pillowcase before Mama comes back. She'll be frightened when she sees all the blood."

"Where is Mama? Where did she go?"

Chaim lifted the pillow from behind Yudel's head and shook the pillow out of the bloody pillowcase. Blood had soaked through the pillowcase making brown stains on the ticking.

"I don't know where she went," says Chaim. "Maybe to the synagogue."

"The pillow is dirty," Nina says.

"Never mind," Chaim looked down at his son, who had fallen asleep with his mouth open. "I don't want to disturb him."

When Alta arrived three hours later, there was a new doctor with her. She had gone to fetch him at the other side of Yekat, where her Uncle Grinberg and her Aunt Malie lived. This doctor was a surgeon at the Jewish hospital and it was a measure of Uncle Grinberg's position in the Jewish community that such an important man would come to see the son of a tailor.

The doctor said, "This is the worst. If he lives through the night, he will recover."

Alta was too distraught to show the doctor to the door. She had not even removed her shawl. She slipped into the chair beside Yudel. Nina wanted to tell her about the terrible blood and how frightened she was when Chaim put the knife against Yudel's back but it was just to staunch the blood and how she was afraid Yudel would die anyway, how maybe she had provoked this nosebleed, by being annoyed at him when he wouldn't lie still, and holding him down, gently really gently, and please say it wasn't her fault, but she knows from her mother's attitude, head and back rigid, face white, that she would not receive any comfort from her tonight. That terrible night, the night of the crisis, she forgot to wash her hands and face before going to bed. In the morning, her hands were still sticky with blood.

But now Yudel has been well for three weeks. He is getting stronger every day. Alta and Chaim, and Nina too, are thrilled; look how color has come back to his cheeks, look how much energy he has. God be thanked. Still, something has changed. Today, for example. Here is Yudel, fresh from a nap in the cold air, freed from the hated wrappings and, as soon as his parents have placed him on his feet, he runs to his sister and pushes her hard against the dining-room table. Nina knocks her back and her right elbow on the edge of the table. Tears flood her eyes. Yudel pushes her again. His face is wrinkled with rage.

"Stop, Idelka," says his mother. "You have hurt your sister. You are making her cry."

"I'm not crying," says Nina as she rubs her elbow. "It doesn't hurt."

Chaim swoops the boy up. Yudel kicks his feet and beats his fists against his father's head and shoulders. Chaim presses the boy against his chest and begins to sing a tuneless song as he bounces the boy up and down. Alta sings too and Nina joins in, rubbing her hurt elbow. She will calm her brother down. Sometimes she is the only one who can. She hops on one foot and then on the other, she claps her hands and twirls on the tips of her toes, fans her skirt in front of her. She makes funny clown faces, sticks out her tongue, raises her eyebrows, blows out her cheeks. Yudel begins to smile.

"Aren't I the silliest person you've ever seen?" Nina says in the high-pitched voice she uses to make him laugh.

"Silly," says Yudel and beams at his sister. "Down," he commands. "I want to eat." The tantrum is over for the evening.

By spring, Yudel is well enough to go to the park. Nina continues to stay home from school so that she can entertain her brother. Nina misses school. She loves her gray-cotton school smock, her notebook with its neat pages of exercises, drawings, maps, poems. She loves her book bag with its long strap and leathery smell and the pen nibs she keeps in a separate leather pouch. She misses the orderliness of school, sitting in rows and standing when the teacher enters, the long lines of girls who walk through the halls with their hands behind their backs. The classes are held in Yiddish, but twice a week the Russian teacher comes to review the Cyrillic alphabet with the girls and to give them dictation in Russian. No one speaks Ukrainian. That is only for servants and peasants. There is not much time during the day to make friends with the other girls and besides, Nina is shy. At school, she is rewarded for being good: her notebooks are filled with "Excellent." "Very good work." "Always neat."—in her teacher's careful hand. At home only her father tells her what a good girl she is and what a help to her mother in this trying time. Alta is too distraught to notice her daughter. When she does, it is to wrap her arms around Nina, to press her to her chest so tightly, that Nina is only made more anxious, more aware of how much she must do to be really good. At school, it's easy. At home, it's not. So Nina longs to go back to school.

Yudel is increasingly tyrannical. He refuses to walk outside and must be carried to the park. He will not eat by himself. Nina, or Rosa Semyonovna, the elderly widow whom Alta has hired to take Nina and Yudel to the Potemkin Gardens every day, feed him his porridge and little bits of bread and butter. This Rosa Semyonovna has no teeth, and when she talks the bottom portion of her face collapses into her chin. She makes little clucking noises to Yudel that Nina thinks are disgusting.

In the gardens, Nina plays hopscotch on the dirt walk with a bit of rock. "Come play, Yudel," she says.

Yudel beats his legs against the bench. "No," he says. "I'm tired."

"You can't be tired. You've been sitting all morning."

"I'm tired. Rosa Semyonovna, tell her I'm tired." He casts a surly glance at his nurse who has been contentedly chewing her gums.

"My darling boy is tired. Leave him alone, Ninotchka." Nina pinches her lips with resentment. Yudel has grown during his illness and convalescence. He is now tall and sturdy for his age and, according to the doctors, completely well. And yet he will not bestir himself for anything or anyone, not even to play games. Alta says he will outgrow this stage. But Nina knows that her brother is the king of the house, and why should he give this up? As she hops across the hopscotch board and bends to pick up the stone she tossed on number six, she thinks to herself, I must not have bad thoughts about my brother. He is a good boy. And I will love him as much as Mama does. That way she will be happy with me too.

XV

ALTA, SEATED AT THE HEAD OF the long table, agreeably light-headed from the unaccustomed vodka, surveys her guests with a pleasant sense of accomplishment and relief. It is the third day of Chanukah and the Schavranskis' annual dinner party is, by all measures of hospitality, a success. The candles have been lit in the splendid silver menorah Chaim has recently bought to celebrate the holidays, the prayers have been said. Supper is over. The table is set with what was a starched white cloth but is now stained with food and drink: the dark flecks of the smoked duck breast Alta prepared for dinner, the smoked tongue, caviar, black olives, and the spilled vodka. There is pickled watermelon rind in a large bowl and smaller bowls filled with sunflower seeds. Alta's latkes, which must be eaten when they are hot, are all gone. As usual, Alta has baked, and the guests have eaten, several egg challahs, and for dessert two flaky strudels with apples, walnuts, and raisins.

IN THE JEWISH COMMUNITY OF Yekaterinoslav, the Schavranskis are known for their warmth and the generosity of their dinner table. Alta's breads and pastries, her pickled fruits and smoked fish, the beer in Chaim's cellar, as well as his tolerance for discussions of all sorts, political and religious, make this a friendly house. Many of the Schavranskis' friends are here tonight, the Rosovskys, the Etlins, and an assortment of young people, Moussia, Yudel's new tutor, Gasha and Rouia, two seamstresses who have worked for the Schavranskis' for years, Goldstein, the Polish deserter, and tonight, from Kiev, a new young worker in Chaim's workshop by the name of Sonya Scherle. Alta has cleverly placed the young children next to their parents, the Etlins' two boys, the Rosovskys' older daughter, Chane, and the little one, Rosa. Yudel, between his mother and Nina, made faces at the children throughout dinner. Only the Friedmans are missing. They have gone, with their son Sasha, a student at the University in Kiev, to spend the holiday with family in nearby Mykolajivka. Even Drina Kagan and her husband Naphtali are here, but not Aunt Malie. Although Aunt Malie keeps up her connection to her niece with invitations to the Seder and gifts for the children, Alta has not gone back on the promise she made before her marriage never to cross the threshold of her aunt's house. This is why neither Nina nor Yudel have ever seen the inside of Aunt Malie's house, although Drina has repeatedly tried to lure the children with visions of glass bowls filled with marzipan candies and Turkish delights and gilded mirrors that reflect your image three ways.

Chaim has set up the tables for cards. He is now a slender man of forty, not so straight and tall as he was as a young man, somewhat stooped perhaps from spending days hunched over a sewing machine. But he is still handsome, with thick brown hair, high cheekbones, and delicate features. Alta once said to Nina that she had fallen in love with Chaim because he had the eyelashes of a girl, and although Nina thought this was a lovely thing to say about her father, she wasn't sure her mother meant it as a compliment.

Tonight, Nina is wearing her best holiday frock, a plaid cotton dress in blue, yellow, and white, with a tight bodice, long sleeves, and, what Nina likes best, a big bow at the neck and a ruffle along the hem.

She has pinned her thick braids into circlets around her ears and on her feet she wears a new pair of blue leather shoes with a hint of a heel to match her dress. She likes the bow on her dress because it hides her breasts, about which she is still uncertain. Today she is particularly uncomfortable. She has been menstruating only for a few months and she is afraid of staining through the folds of the rags her mother has helped her pin to her underwear. The discomforts of being a woman are new to Nina, and on days like this she profoundly regrets not being a child anymore. She is thirteen years old.

Gasha and Rouia have begun clearing the dishes, but the guests seem reluctant to leave the table. The men are a bit tipsy from the unusual amount of vodka they have drunk, and the women, although pinched in their tight corsets after the meal, sigh in contentment.

"A lovely meal, Alta Perel, as always," says Avram Rosovsky, a portly man in a checkered waistcoat who manages a factory in Yekaterinoslav for making oil paints. "What a pleasure to be among good friends." He beams his large, round, oily face at Alta.

"Yes, indeed," says Lena Rosovsky, plump and even rosier than usual after an evening of good food. Her head continues to nod like a balloon on a string.

"To celebrate Chanukah in peace, that is a great blessing," says Chaim in his mild, soft voice.

A collective grunt of assent rises from the men. The women share understanding looks.

"We have much to be thankful for," says Alta, an eye on Gasha and Rouia as they scurry around the guests, lifting dishes off the table. The two young women are not really servants; they are seamstresses in the workshop, but good-hearted and helpful, especially since Alta always includes them at Friday night dinner. Alta has aged more than Chaim. Her hair is threaded with gray and her skin looks papery, withered. She has become an anxious woman; her feisty spirit drained, although her pride is undiminished. She works with Chaim in the workshop, supervises the workers, cooks, bakes, sews for her children, distributes food and clothing to the workers in Chaim's workshop. A privileged life, she insists, but several times a year, Alta collapses and takes to her bed for a week, alarming Nina and Chaim. Nina has begun to think of her mother as fragile.

"It has been a difficult year," Naphtali Kagan pats his thin lips with the edge of his napkin. "I was saying to Drina this morning," here he nods in the direction of his wife, who, compliant and fearful as always, nods back. "There is so much unrest everywhere. Not just in Petersburg or Moscow. Right here in Yekat. We nearly had a strike in the distillery. One of our men, a good worker who never made any trouble before, suddenly he's angry, suddenly he wants to be paid more for less work. And when I ask where he gets such ideas, he tells me he's been attending workers' meetings. Workers' meetings! Imagine. And half the distillery was ready to follow him. Isn't that right, Drina?"

Drina nods again, taking in the others at the table with her anxious eyes.

"What did you do?" Avram Rosovsky asks.

"I shut down the distillery for two days. With no back pay. Everyone came back to work after that, tails between their legs, believe me. This is not St. Petersburg here. We don't tolerate strikes." Naphtali leans his fists on the table, glowers at his audience as if they had suddenly become as obstructive as his workers.

"Well, you're a lucky man," says Rosovsky. "Our plant was closed for a week by strikers. It's the fault of outside agitators. There's a man, his name is Babushkin, he comes from Petersburg and he is a scoundrel of the first order." Rosovsky's voice rises. "One of those revolutionaries, they call themselves Social Democrats, here to make trouble. I am surprised the police haven't arrested him yet." He reaches across the table for a handful of sunflower seeds and begins mechanically to crack the hulls between his teeth.

"We have had no trouble in my workshop," says Chaim, in his mild voice. "I hope it is because we treat our workers fairly." He glances up at Gasha, who smiles but averts her eyes.

"We treat our workers perfectly fair too, Chaim Yudelovich. Don't think we don't. We pay good wages and the work is honorable, not dirty or dangerous like the workers in the Baku oil fields. Besides we give work to our own people. Do you know a Jew who works for the railroad? Let me tell you something, it is bosses like you who are making it difficult for us. People with so-called advanced ideas. Excuse me, Alta, my dear, I don't want to seem ungracious. This has been a delightful evening, and will continue to be delightful I'm sure, but your husband is too soft with his workers. It gives them ideas."

Alta's slight frame stiffens. Her eyes darken. Her voice is bright, charged with energy. "Dear Avram Moisevich, if we are kind to our workers, it is because we understand how much they suffer. Chaim and I have been almost as poor. Perhaps you didn't know us when we were struggling. But Drina remembers." Here, Alta casts a fierce look at her cousin and her cousin's husband. Drina cowers slightly under the glare, but Naphtali looks blank. Perhaps he has truly forgotten how much the family objected to the poor tailor, or perhaps Alta's marriage never meant anything to him, never distressed him more than, say, the marriage of his children's tutor. And now Chaim and Alta are almost his equals, not completely, of course, since Naphtali is a very rich man, but the Schavranskis are comfortably well off, enough so that Naphtali can enjoy their hospitality without reproaching himself or watching his consumption of food and vodka.

Alta continues. "Now that our life is better, I believe it is our duty, our obligation, to alleviate the suffering of those who are not as lucky as we are. That is why our workers work hard for us. They would never turn against us."

Rosovsky spits out a mouthful of sunflower hulls into his hand. "I hope you are right, my dear."

"And then there is that stupid war the Tsar is losing against the Japanese. Don't think that doesn't affect morale, especially among the Ukrainian workers. Those peasants." Naphtali honks his nose into a large handkerchief.

"Oh please," says Mrs. Rosovsky, fanning her hand in front of her rosy face. "Let's not talk about the war."

There is a pause as the guests exchange glances. Goldstein, the Polish deserter from the Russian army, seated between Yudel, who at eight years old has been allowed to stay up for the evening, and skinny Mrs. Etlin, looks down at his plate. Goldstein is a thin young man, with large ears like cabbage flowers and skin furrowed with pockmarks. He sports a narrow military mustache, the only vestige of his service for the Tsar. Goldstein has not said a word during dinner and now with all eyes upon him, he seems to shrink further into the large black jacket that once belonged to Chaim.

At the other end of the long dinner table, Nina observes Moussia, Yudel's tutor, and the new worker, Sonya Scherle as they sit in stern silence. Nina is acutely aware of their disapproval. Moussia is a Socialist, perhaps even a member of the Social Democratic Party in Yekaterinoslav. Chaim knows this and doesn't quite disapprove. Nina knows this too—it is a bond between father and daughter—but they have kept the information from Alta. It isn't socialism that frightens Alta, but radicalism of any kind can attract the attention of the authorities and Alta's task is to keep her family safe.

Moussia has been passing books to Nina, books like Karl Marx's *The Communist Manifesto*, Lenin's *What's to Be Done*, and pamphlets by Plekhanov, texts Nina cannot begin to understand but that she cherishes as acts of trust and affection. Not love, since she is not silly enough to think that handsome Moussia might be in love with a thirteen year old, but still, she keeps the books under her bed and takes them out at night, stroking the inky pages and trying to follow the text with her finger.

Moussia is eighteen years old and as long and narrow as a stalk of corn. His long blond hair falls across his forehead like a poet.

Next to Moussia, Sonya is a prickly thorn bush to his cornstalk. She has red hair and pale skin. She wears glasses and tugs nervously at wisps of unruly hair that escape from her tight bun.

"How does he know about Babushkin?" Sonya whispers to Moussia. "There must be a leak in the organization somewhere."

"We'll bring it up at the next council meeting," says Moussia.

"Too late. We must tell our comrades now." Sonya, who is small and thin, radiates fierceness.

So she is a socialist too, Nina thinks and her heartbeat quickens. Right here, at her parents' dinner table in the midst of the Chanukah celebration, there are two people who lead secret lives, conspirators who belong to outlaw organizations, who disagree in the most profound way with how the world is being run. It is almost unbearably thrilling. Moussia is so brave, but then it is fitting for a man to be brave. But a girl, Nina peers intently at the slight figure of Sonya. Is it possible for a girl to be brave? Not brave like her mother, who is not afraid to visit the dark smelly houses of her poor and sick workers, places that make Nina, even when she imagines them, shiver with distaste. But brave the way a man is brave? I hope Sonya will be my friend too, Nina thinks, and directs a bashful smile at Sonya, who is too preoccupied with her own thoughts to notice Nina at all.

"It is hard to be a Jew at a time like this," says Lena Rosovsky with a sigh. "Whenever there is unrest, you know who gets blamed. We're always waiting for the other shoe to drop."

"In Kiev, when the Railway Shop and South Russian Machine Works struck, it was the Podil, the Jewish district, that was destroyed by the Black Hundreds." Rosovsky spits out his words.

"And Kishinev. Remember Kishinev," says Naphtali. "We had relatives in Kishinev."

Silence, like a dense, surprising fog, envelops the dinner guests. Nina looks at her mother whose face has gone as white as paper.

Isaac Etlin, a thick-set man of medium height, with a florid face and a wide flat nose that is covered with raised bumps and always red, pulls his napkin off his neck. "Enough. All this talk upsets my digestion. My dear Alta, a most splendid repast. But now," he narrows his eyes conspiratorially at Nina. "Let us pass to the best part of the evening. A good game of whist."

Nina manages a thin polite smile. She does not like Isaac Etlin. Even in her childish experience of people, she senses that his elaborate courtesy is not sincere. He is not a nice man, she thinks. Not as nice as her father or as nice as Moussia.

"Not yet," says Alta. "There is plenty of time for cards. Ninotchka, would you like to recite something for our guests?"

The bumps on Etlin's nose grow darker with displeasure. He lets out a long audible groan.

Chaim beams at Nina. Nina always recites a poem between dinner and cards. And only Etlin protests. Perhaps that is another reason Nina dislikes him.

"Papa," says Nina. "Please. Not this time. I don't know what to recite."

"That lovely long poem in French," says Alta. "The one you recited in school."

Nina casts an embarrassed glance at Moussia, who is leaning against the back door, one foot crossed over the other in a most studiedly casual pose. Moussia leans over Sonya, whispers something in her ear. Sonya laughs and Nina feels a sharp pain as if she had been punched in the ribs.

"Come," says Alta. "The French poem."

"No," Nina whispers. "Please." She hates performing in front of all these people. And yet there is pleasure in having everyone's attention and the praise at the end, the approving looks—such precious recognition. She remembers the time her parents took her at her word when she said she wouldn't recite and she didn't. Immediately, she was disconsolate.

"Come now, young lady. We want to get on to the cards," says Etlin.

And so Nina straightens her back, presses her hands stiffly at both sides and begins to recite, in heavily accented French, LaFontaine's fable about the ant and the grasshopper. When she is done, there is polite applause from the audience and murmurs of "How nice. What a clever girl. You must be so proud of her."

Alta says, pulling Yudel's hands off his ears, "Nina is so good at school. I wish Yudel would give me as much satisfaction as she does." Yudel wrinkles his nose. He is not a good student. That is why he has a tutor. He did attend school for a while, but the schoolmaster complained that he could not teach Yudel so much as the alphabet. He is a lump of worry in his mother's heart. Alta, Nina, and Chaim are counting on Moussia.

Nina curtsies politely. In the crowd, she notices Chane, the Rosovsky's daughter, an ashen-faced girl who is a year ahead of Nina at the Progymnasia Klutch, the Jewish high school in Yekaterinoslav. Chane's eyes are dull with boredom; her mouth is set in a surly pout. Nina doesn't care what Chane thinks of her. Chane is a boring girl, stupid and narrow-minded. It is Moussia's opinion Nina cares about, and Moussia, so languid and romantic, standing much too close to the new woman, Sonya, doesn't seem terribly impressed with Nina's recitation in French. Sonya chews on her thumbnail. She clearly has not been listening. Nina smiles hopefully at both of them, but only Moussia smiles back although without enthusiasm.

The grown-ups settle themselves at the card tables. The children play at shooting nuts into a bowl on the floor. Nina does not join them. She helps the two young women, Gasha and Rouia, clear the table. From time to time, she glances back at Moussia and Sonya who lean against the wall, deep in conversation.

There is knocking on the door. Conversation stops. Something about that knock, the force and urgency of it, has alerted the card players, the children, and Alta's helpers. Catastrophe, like a rabid animal, can pounce at any time.

Chaim opens the door to David Broytman, the cantor of the synagogue.

"Gut yontif," says Chaim, warily.

"Gut yontif," responds Broytman. "There is trouble tonight. The hooligans are massing at the town square. There is a rumor that Jews are preparing to massacre the monks at the monastery before Christmas. A bad time to be outdoors. I suggest everyone stay in until it is over."

Alta's hands rise to her throat. The Rosovsky children huddle around their parents. Gasha and Rouia hug each other. Nina squeezes Yudel's hand. He looks at her with round, perplexed eyes. Broytman, a tall old man with an uneven beard, takes out his prayer book. His voice is deep and comforting. The words, incomprehensible to Nina but soothingly familiar, have a singsong quality that reminds her of the lullabies her father sang to her as a child.

Everyone is standing now with heads bowed. From time to time, those who know the prayer mumble the words. The men sway on their heels. Nina registers that neither Moussia nor Sonya pray. Moussia stares at the ceiling as if he were about to whistle, but Sonya's glare pierces through the back of everyone's head. It makes Nina uncomfortable.

"Now quickly," says Alta, when the prayers are over. "We must close the windows and cover them."

Gasha draws the draperies closed. Alta appears with piles of blankets against her chest and distributes them to the men. Chaim and the other men hang the blankets over the windows that do not have draperies. The gaslights are shut off. Only the candles on the dining-room table are allowed to burn. Broytman continues to pray.

"Boiling water," says Mr. Rosovsky. "That's what we need. Vats of boiling water."

"I have only so many pots," says Alta, plaintively.

"Well, fill them up. Use the wash basins. Use the vase here." He hands a delicate Meissen vase to Rouia, who gives Alta a horrified look. "We will fight off these hooligans with everything we have."

Moussia brings in a bucket of hot water from the kitchen. He places it carefully in front of the window.

"This is medieval," he whispers to Sonya, just loud enough for Nina to hear. "All we need now is boiling oil for a truly effective defense against men who carry guns."

"Cynicism is not a socialist strategy." Sonya's little mouth is pursed and tight "Lend us your muscles, Moussia, and keep your mouth shut."

"She's a tough one," Moussia shakes his head in mock admiration. The exchange disturbs Nina, but she doesn't have time to think about it. Alta grabs her by the wrist.

"Take the children into your room," she says. "Hide them under your bed if there's trouble."

Nina nods.

David Broytman continues to chant.

Alta pushes Yudel and the other children out of the dining room and into the hall.

Now Nina is truly frightened. Alone with the children in her room, she feels responsible and abandoned.

"Let's hide under the bed," Yudel grins at the younger children. "Come on. It's fun." The boys slip, giggling, under Nina's high bed.

Nina notices that Chane is not among them and she feels a pang of jealousy. Chane, big, dumb, slow-moving, remains with the adults while she, Nina, is a child among children.

Six-year-old Rosa slips her hand into Nina's and Nina grips it tightly.

In the parlor, the guests are huddled in small groups, some around the table, some around the fireplace where Moussia is keeping a small fire burning. Chaim and Etlin stand by the window; from time to time, Chaim lifts up a corner of the blanket. There is nothing to see, the snow-covered courtyard is quiet. In the kitchen, Alta fills all sorts of vessels, cooking pots, porcelain bowls, tin basins, even the chamber pots usually kept under the beds, with recently boiled water. Gasha, who is broad and muscular, carries the pots into the living room and places them in rows under the window. As soon as the water in a pot cools, one of the young women, Rouia or Gasha, carries it back into the kitchen to replace it with another pot. The air in the room becomes warm and steamy. A damp smell, of damp wool and damp walls, prickles the nostrils of several guests and makes them sneeze.

"Moussia, I don't think we need a fire in here anymore. It's so hot. The women are about to faint." Naphtali Kagan, his usually florid complexion the color of oysters, loosens his cravat.

Moussia stamps on the fire with his boot. Naphtali rocks on his heels and continues to murmur along with David Broytman. The women pray too, softly. The voices are tense, tinged with hysteria, hypnotic.

"You cannot know how much I hate this," Sonya says to Moussia.

"You're a funny one," Moussia says. "Does anyone enjoy a pogrom?"

"No, you don't understand. I hate being confined here when there is so much that is horrible outside."

"You would rather be in the street fighting the pogromschiki? With what? Your hands? Your teeth? A big stick? And the Cossacks, do you think they won't rape you because you're a Socialist."

"Stop it, Moussia. I know the dangers," Sonya says, narrowing her eyes behind her lenses.

"Well, then, don't be silly. Look at what we are doing here. Isn't that silly enough for you? Do you think for a minute that we can defend ourselves by pouring hot water on a crowd of enraged peasants and Cossacks with guns?"

"Then what do you propose?" Sonya says in a low, intense voice. "I thought you were a Socialist."

"Being a Socialist doesn't mean dying stupidly. I want to stay alive and then when this is over, we must organize, organize and educate. Assuming, of course, that I survive."

Sonya looks rebuked. She pinches her lips.

Someone is beginning to cry. It is Chane, big Chane, not so grown-up after all. She weeps in long, anguished moans.

"Hush, Chanele, be quiet, be quiet." Her mother places a hand over Chane's mouth. Chane stifles her sobs.

The apartment is dark and, except for the murmur of praying voices, quite still.

In the children's room, Nina sits on the floor with little Rosa's head in her lap. Her back hurts. She has no support for it. Yudel and the Etlin boys have fallen asleep under Yudel's bed. It is very much past their bedtime. Nina, of course, cannot sleep. At first, she thought her heart would crash against her ribs, the thumping was so strong. Now she is calmer. An empty, tired feeling has come over her. She lets her head drop against her chest. But that is not at all comfortable. Gently she lifts Rosa's head off her lap and slips down on the floor beside her, her arm around the little girl for comfort, hers and Rosa's.

It is morning. Alta, pale and disheveled, stands over Nina.

"My darling," she says. "It's over."

Nina, startled into wakefulness, sits bolt upright.

"What?"

"Nothing. Nothing, my dearest. We are going to be all right. Come and have something to eat."

Nina casts a quick glance at Rosa, who is still sleeping, her fist against her mouth. Alta raises a finger to her lips.

The guests are in the living room, to Nina's astonishment. Mr. and Mrs. Rosovsky and big baby Chane, Drina, Naphtali, Etlin and his wife, Sonya, and even darling Moussia. Nina understands that all these people have spent the night in her house. Everyone looks different, worn, untidy, bewildered.

In the center of the room stands Natimzef, the Gentile baker who lives in the building with his family. He is a young man with a round face and round eyes. Even his nose is round. Nina likes him because he often gives her and Yudel a freshly baked roll in the morning as they cross the courtyard on their way to school. His stock among the Jews in the building is very high, not only because he is a good baker, but because he speaks Yiddish to the older tenants for whom Russian, let alone Ukrainian, is a foreign tongue.

"Will you take a glass of tea, Natimzef?" Chaim asks the baker. "It is so kind of you to let us know what is happening out there."

"I must tell you that we were frightened too, when we heard the rumors about the monastery," Natimzef says, rubbing his pink hands, a rim of floury white under his nails. "We were sure they would come down the Prospekt. Everybody knows this is a Jewish house."

"How do you know the pogrom is over?" Mr. Etlin asks. To Nina, he seems darker and greasier than ever.

"There was no pogrom. It was just a rumor. According to my friend, Cherkassy, the baker down the street, the city was quiet last night. He didn't even know there was supposed to be a pogrom."

Drina sighs. The other guests mumble, shift their weight, shake their heads. Moussia raises and lowers his shoulders. Sonya passes her hand across her mouth.

"So you can all go home now," Natimzef says, looking a little embarrassed, as if it had been his fault that all these good people had to spend the night in terror.

"How can we be sure?" Etlin asks. "This may be a trap."

"You can trust our good friend, baker Natimzef," Chaim pats the baker's shoulder. "He looks after us very well."

Natimzef, who looked puzzled and hurt by Etlin's comment, now turns grateful eyes to Chaim.

"Tea for everyone," Alta says. "Stay for a glass of tea."

When the guests have left, Alta sinks into a chair.

"This is only the beginning," she says. "The beginning of bad times."

"Maybe not." Chaim tugs at his vest. Gasha and Rouia take down the blankets from the windows. Alta follows their movements with anxious eyes. "Broytman may have exaggerated," Chaim continues. "In this town, we have not been bothered for almost twenty years. Not since the assassination of Tsar Alexander."

Gasha pulls the draperies open and a gray morning light suffuses the room. Nina walks to the window and looks out into the courtyard. The early morning guests have left a trail of footprints in the snow.

"Well," Alta says as she receives the pile of blankets from Rouia's arms. "In my opinion, optimists may be happy, but pessimists are usually right."

Nina turns to look at Chaim. She wants her father to contradict her mother, to say that everything is going to be all right, because it has been so for as long as she can remember, but Chaim says nothing and then Nina suspects that Chaim, too, believes that Alta is right, as always.

XVI

NINA AND SONYA, LEANING OVER the balcony railing, look down into the courtyard of the Schavranskis' house, a complex of two-story buildings built around a rectangular courtyard. The Schavranski apartment faces the door to the street and is immediately noticeable as you enter the courtyard. Alta has planted seasonal flowers on the balcony, narcissi and lily-whites in the spring, roses and columbines in the summer, asters and chrysanthemums in the fall. The burst of color against the gray stone is an exhilarating vision to anyone who crosses the dingy courtyard. That is what Natimzef, the baker, says whenever he meets Alta in the courtyard. "Alta Schavranski, your balcony is a bower of beauty again this season," and Alta brushes away the compliment with a wave of her hand. But to Chaim she says Natimzef is a poet with flour under his nails.

On this sunny September day, the two young women on the balcony are framed by pots of late autumn blossoms: mums in yellow, orange, and red. Sonya is dressed in a maroon serge skirt with black braid along the hem. Her starched shirtwaist is blazing white in the sunlight and her dark gray tie tucked neatly into her shirt. Her short jacket is slung carelessly over the iron railing. Nina wears a gray schoolgirl smock that covers her navy-blue school dress. Her hair is in two long braids. Nina is fifteen years old and in the sunlight, her brown hair glints with gold, a summery reminder of her childhood. Sonya is twenty.

Moussia, Yudel's tutor, has left Yekaterinoslav. He has gone south to Odessa to work with the Bund organization there. Sonya, who is a committed Social Democrat, was horrified.

"If I had known what a shallow thinker your friend Moussia was, I wouldn't have wasted any time on him," she said to Nina when Moussia left. "Imagine, he has become a Zionist! What a fickle insubstantial person he is. And he claimed to want to organize the workers here in Yekat. Well, this tells me how little he understands about the real struggle, the struggle for all workers' rights, not just Jewish workers."

Nina was saddened by Moussia's defection. She loved the soft, blonde hair that fell over his eyes, the ironic manner that made her feel privileged to be his friend. She loved the shivery feeling that came over her when he smiled at her and called her Ninotchka.

But he is gone, and according to Sonya, he has betrayed the cause. Faulty analysis of the historical situation is the same as a character flaw. So Moussia is simply stupid. This is hard for Nina to accept, but Sonya is so ferocious about him that Nina must believe she is right. And at fifteen it is not too difficult to replace Moussia—who has betrayed his dear friends as well as the cause—with Sonya.

Now that Sonya is definitely Nina's friend, Nina has forgotten that she ever felt twinges of jealousy toward Moussia and her. Instead, she overflows with admiration. Sonya is so hard working; that is clear from the long hours she spends in Chaim's workshop. She is brave. It takes courage unimaginable to Nina to leave home. Sonya has beautiful ideals. She talks to Nina as if they were almost equals; she wants to guide her along the proper moral and intellectual paths. All this is irresistible to Nina's yearning heart. Even Sonya's appearance is praiseworthy. Her back is always straight, her white shirtwaist remains neatly tucked in at all times, she wears her red hair parted in the middle and caught in a bun at the nape of her neck, which Nina, who struggles with her unruly hair every day, also envies. Everything about Sonya is enviable except for a mole that nestles in the crease above her right nostril. Nina is sorry about this small defect in her otherwise perfect friend. Sonya doesn't seem to mind, and that is another wonderful thing about her. She doesn't worry about her appearance. She is a revolutionist.

As for Yudel, he misses Moussia hardly at all. He is ten years old now and he goes to Mr. Verchorine's school for boys, where he is as bad a student as he ever was. He thinks of Moussia only when Pavel Ossipovich hits him across the knuckles with the back of his ringed hand, and then Yudel remembers Moussia's soft, patient voice coaxing the right answer out of him.

The courtyard, usually empty at five in the afternoon, is swarming. The baker Natimzef and his good friend Achourkof, whose wife takes in laundry for the building, appear to be in serious conference, shoulder to shoulder, round belly to round belly, pipe to pipe, while their children, those that are visible at the moment, a girl of six and two boys of about nine or ten, race around their fathers playing tag. Their wives are seated on a bench beneath the plane tree that in September offers a green canopy of shade. The women are talking seriously, leaning their brightly kerchiefed heads into each other. David Broytman, the cantor, whose full white beard appears in the bright sunlight to be made up of the same cottony substance as the clouds in the sky, walks up to the two speakers and shakes each man's hand. As he does so, Natimzef and Achourkof delicately reposition themselves to allow Broytman to step into their confidential circle. Natimzef and Achourkof and their families are the only non-Jewish tenants in the complex of buildings, and although respectful of their neighbors, friendly even (the Achourkof and Natimzef children speak Yiddish), their business is usually with the Jewish women who are at home rather than the Jewish men. So it is all the more surprising to

Nina, observing the scene from the balcony, to see David Broytman, a respected member of the Jewish community, talking seriously with his neighbors and even allowing Natimzef, who is the more outgoing of the two friends, to touch him on the shoulder.

"Oh," says Nina. "Look, Sonya, how Natimzef and Broytman are talking to each other. Like friends."

"Well, why not? They're both capitalists," says Sonya, in her sensible voice.

"Oh," says Nina, disappointed. "Is that why?" She had hoped it meant something else, something about how unity was possible between Jews and Christians.

"Natimzef may be a baker, but owns his own business and he employs other workers. That makes him a capitalist."

Nina feels mildly rebuked. Sonya is teaching her to see the world and it is not always easy to keep up with her clear, sharp vision.

"Do you think the men down there are talking about the strikes?"

"Why not?" Sonya shrugs her thin shoulders. "Broytman owns a lumber yard just outside of town. He must be worried."

"Is the situation very bad?"

"Very bad or very good, depending on which side you are on."

"Will the strikes spread to Yekat? Will there be a revolution?"

Sonya fixes her blue eyes on her friend. She wears round lenses, which make her look stern and older than her years, but which Nina admires. She thinks Sonya's glasses are a badge of her intelligence. "Maybe."

"Sonya, you must tell me everything you know."

Nina takes her friend's hand in hers and presses it to her heart. Sonya manages a small smile. "I don't know anything yet. But I promise to tell you when the time comes. Now let's go inside. I can't bear the sight of those men plotting to keep their pennies in their pockets."

Nina laughs. "You are so hard on everyone, Sonya."

The two young women slip into the sitting room, which is still warm from the afternoon sun.

The round mahogany table, covered with a red damask cloth, is littered with Nina's schoolbooks. A snake plant has been pushed to the side to make room for the textbooks, the notebooks with pale paper covers, the inkwell, the penholder, and the two carefully sharpened nibs. Sonya seats herself on the edge of the horsehair sofa and Nina slips into a hard-back chair beside the table. There is a moment of quiet between them and then Nina, who cannot endure silence and who is in any case too excited to sit still for long, says, "What will you do when the Revolution comes?"

"I will dance in the streets."

"No, really."

"I will continue to work for the betterment of humanity. There will still be much to be done, in Russia and throughout the world."

Nina looks thoughtful. "Tell me, Sonya dearest, how did you come to be so brave? I want to be as brave as you are."

"Then you must have something to be brave for." Sonya's right foot in a black lace-up shoe taps the floor. Her hands, large-knuckled and raw from needle-pricks, knead each other mechanically. Even in repose, Sonya looks as if she is about to spring up. "One cannot be brave about nothing."

"I know. If I'm brave about reciting a poem in French in front of the class, it's not the same as when you're brave about speaking in front of people."

"That doesn't require bravery. You forget who you are when you have something important to say. A person who works for the people knows he is working for something bigger than himself."

Nina narrows her eyes in concentration. Tonight she will try to write down all the important things Sonya has said, if she can only remember them.

Sonya's right foot is quiet. She leans toward Nina and says, in a low intense voice that forces Nina to slide forward on her chair, "You have already been brave, Nina dear, distributing those pamphlets I gave you. You and your father came to our workers' circle meetings. You could be sent to Siberia for less."

Nina stares into Sonya's intense blue eyes behind her thick lenses. "Is that true?" she asks, half frightened, half pleased. "Are we on their list of radicals, do you think? My mother was so upset when we went to that meeting. She said my father was putting his family's life in danger."

"Oh, you are a selfish man, Chaim Schavranski, if you think that the Revolution is more important than we are," Alta had said. Nina remembers how startled she was by this remark of her mother's. Her father was not selfish, she knew that. But Sonya, was Sonya selfish when she left her family in Vilna to work for the rights of people she did not know? What kind of ungrateful daughter, Alta said, leaves her mother broken-hearted and worried? Was it selfish to put the rights of thousands of people you didn't know before the needs of the few you did? And what about her mother? Alta would never carry a banner down the streets of Yekaterinoslav. And yet every Wednesday she delivered basketfuls of food for her old people, her sick folks, for Boris, the young orphan she dressed and who celebrated every holiday with the family. And Goldstein, the Polish soldier who was sent so far away from home, was Alta wrong to serve him dinner every Friday and Saturday night? Charity, Sonya said with contempt, charity perpetuates the status quo. Who was right? It was so confusing.

"What do you think, Sonya? What is more important, your family or your ideals?"

"That is something everyone must decide for himself," Sonya says solemnly. "But I will tell you this, little Nina," she breaks into a smile. "If you are on their list of radicals, it won't take much for them to swoop down on you and take you away."

"Don't talk to me as if I were a child, Sonya. I know there are important decisions I will have to make." How can she feel grown-up under Sonya's stern and critical gaze? "But you, are you on their list?"

"I am an organizer. I believe in the struggle. It will be impossible to overthrow the Tsar without an armed uprising, and an armed uprising is impossible without organized workers educated in revolutionary theory. That is why I am here. That is why I work at your father's shop. To organize and educate the workers.

"Here in Russia," Sonya continues, "our proletariat is not developed enough to take on the armed uprising alone. We must be their teachers." Sonya pushes herself off the sofa. She wraps her arms around her chest as if she were suddenly cold.

"In our circle, we discuss this problem all the time. Who is to lead the Revolution? The bourgeoisie or the proletariat? Those who patronize the workers or those who believe in them? I believe it is the proletariat, the workers, the people who will effect a real change in our system. Yes, I believe this." Now Sonya is pacing. Her hands are thrust into the pockets of her maroon skirt, her movements across the room propelled by some inner fuel.

Nina loves Sonya, loves her fierce intelligence, her dramatic life. She loves the Revolution, too, but when Sonya's voice begins to rise, when the sounds in her mouth are like the sounds of a person talking to a crowd, then Nina feels herself wilt like one of her mother's balcony plants on a hot, sunny day.

Now she observes her friend with a touch of irritation. She has heard these arguments before, although she doesn't quite understand them. They bore her a little but they also frighten her. When her father took her to the meeting of the tailors' working circle to which Sonya had invited him, there was such disagreement among the speakers—men, women, everyone seemed to speak at once, waving arms, raising voices, stamping on the floor, hitting the table to make a point. Even Sonya spoke in her loudest "soapbox" voice. At first it was thrilling to listen—the words that floated in the air were so inspiring: "the struggle," "uprising," "together," "freedom," "equality," "higher wages," "comradeship," "brotherhood." These words she understood, and whenever she caught one she smiled and nodded at her father. He, on the other hand, seemed pale and troubled. He leaned forward, hands on knees, squinting attentively at the speakers and only occasionally acknowledged his daughter with a nod and, when his hand was free, a squeeze of her fingers. Her father's anxiety alarmed her. On the way home, Nina asked, "Why were they arguing so much, Papa?" And Chaim, turning up the collar of his jacket although it was not a cold night, replied, "I don't know what they want of me. I am not a radical. I own a tailor shop, that is all. This talk of armed uprising makes me nervous."

And here is Sonya talking passionately about a possibility that alarms and frightens her father. As she listens to Sonya rant about trade unions, Nina feels dismay. Maybe she is more like Chaim than she thinks, not quite ready to follow Sonya into that complicated, demanding, and sacrificial world. She desperately wants to change the subject.

"Of course, we all know Goldstein is in love with you," she hears herself say.

Sonya whirls around, her skirt slapping the leg of the mahogany dining table.

"What are you talking about?"

"Goldstein, the soldier, he follows you around like a puppy. You could marry him and then the two of you could work together for the people." Nina giggles into her hand. Sonya, in a good mood, likes to be silly.

"What?" Sonya snaps. Nina drops her hands into her lap, startled into nursery room attentiveness.

"Nina," Sonya's voice is low and emphatic. She has ceased to pace and stands in front of Nina, arms folded across her neatly pressed shirt. Nina lowers her eyes. That is the best thing to do to avoid a scolding. "What has this got to do with our struggle? What can you be thinking of? What is going through that empty head of yours?" Nina gasps. "Do you think you will always have . . ." Sonya's arm sweeps across the room. "Your piano . . . your velvet-lined draperies . . . your bubbling samovar . . . your pretty school frocks. Your privileges will not last forever. The people will rise up and strike you and your kind down. You have told me often enough that you want to be part of our struggle. That you want to fight with us for equality and justice, for a better world." Sonya's voice breaks as she catches her breath. "And yet you say these idiotic things, report these ridiculous empty rumors about nothing—about me and a stupid illiterate soldier with no political consciousness who deserted the Tsar's army just to save his life. Marriage to a man like that—for a woman like me? Nina, how can you be so shallow?"

Nina feels bitter tears pricking behind her eyelids. Her nose is suddenly so tightly clogged she can hardly breathe. Sonya executes an angry turn and faces the fireplace, her back to Nina. She places her hands on the mantelpiece as if to steady herself.

"I cannot believe you are that simple-minded," Sonya says to the wall in front of her.

"I am not simple-minded," Nina says, her voice choked and throaty. "I thought maybe you liked him too."

"That's exactly what I mean," Sonya says, unrelenting. "Even when I was your age, I didn't think like you. You will never be a real revolutionary."

Blackness as black as the ink in her inkwell flows through Nina. She has just proved to her friend that she is a foolish creature, profoundly bourgeoise, unworthy of Sonya's esteem. It is a terrible thing to have bad thoughts. Bad thinking leads to bad action, she knows that from Sonya herself. And Nina looks through her tears at the stern set of Sonya's shoulders and she feels a familiar desolation. There is something about Sonya at this moment that is just like her mother when she is angry and makes Nina feel small and unloved.

"I'm sorry," Nina says.

"Oh, what has sorry to do with anything?" Sonya waves her hands in mock helplessness. "Sorry is such a bourgeois notion. I'm sorry about exploiting the workers—I'm sorry about being mean and greedy and small-minded. Please! Don't ever use that word with me."

In the silence that follows, Nina, aswirl in humiliation, longing, and the helplessness that comes from not knowing how to please, collects her books and papers and moves toward the door of the sitting room.

As Nina turns the doorknob, Sonya says to the mirror over the mantelpiece. "I only want you to learn to look at the world properly. Come back. There is something I must tell you."

"No. Why should I?" Nina says, and her voice cracks with self-pity. "You don't think I'm worthy."

"Really, Nina, you are full of the most absurd ideas. Pride, too, is a bourgeois notion. So come, what I have to tell you is important." Reluctantly, Nina releases the doorknob and walks toward the fireplace. She stands very straight as Sonya directs a stern gaze toward her. "Don't pout, what I said is for your own good." She takes the books from Nina's arms, places them on the table, and motions Nina to sit on the sofa. Nina, submissive, but wary, arranges her skirt around her knees.

"What I'm going to tell you is not a secret," says Sonya, slipping on to the sofa beside Nina. "But it is not something everybody knows either." Nina feels a pinch of interest, an imp of curiosity doing his dance inside her.

Sonya takes Nina's hand. "When I was about your age, maybe a year older, I joined the Socialist circle in Vilna. Why? I don't know. Perhaps there are some souls who are more easily touched by the misery of others, people who feel injustice in their bones. Oh, I know about your mother." Sonya waves her hand dismissively. "She's a charitable woman. But I wasn't interested in charity, I wanted to take action against injustice. At the high school in Vilna, where I was one of only two Jewish girls in the whole school, there was a Russian girl, Varvara, and she was like me, interested in social problems. Varvara brought me into the circle. I knew right away that this was going to be my life's work. Right away, not like you, you little silly," Sonya smiles at Nina, but Nina, still stricken, does not smile back. "I did not tell my parents, of course. My family was not rich, but not poor either. We spoke Yiddish at home, but my father knew Russian, he read Hebrew. He was an enlightened man. He encouraged me to learn Hebrew, like my brothers and against my mother's wishes. However, although he believed in education for women, he was not a political man."

"Just like my father," Nina says. "My father is like that too."

Sonya nods. Nina knows Sonya likes her father and this both pleases and worries her. Sonya does not like Nina's mother, which pleases and worries Nina as well.

Sonya continues. "It became very difficult to hide my political activities from my family. Although I believed in freedom and equality for women, I was not free myself. I belonged to my parents. Do you understand?"

"Yes," says Nina. "I understand." She thinks of her father holding her hand, her mother slipping an apple into her schoolbag "for later." How could she ever want not to belong to her family?

"At the circle, I met a man. He was German. Not Russian. I could never have married a Russian."

"You married him? Oh, Sonya!" Nina is disappointed and baffled (Sonya married is not the same Sonya, not her Sonya). "Is he a nice man?" she asks.

"There you go again," Sonya shakes her head, "thinking like a reader of romantic novels. I married this German so that I could be legally free of my family. Whether he was a nice man or not is totally beside the point."

"Do you have any children?" Nina asks. It is the only question she can think of asking a married lady.

"Nina," Sonya's voice carries a warning. "Stop that. After we were married, this German went to Berlin to work with the Social Democrats and I came to Yekaterinoslav."

"Oh," says Nina. "So you aren't really married. Not like married people are married."

Sonya laughs, her freckled nose wrinkling. "That depends on what you mean, little bird. He is my legal husband and I am his wife."

Nina nods, hoping she looks thoughtful and understanding. But in fact, she is troubled. To be married and not married. To give up the greatest good in a woman's life for politics, is this a wonderful thing or an appalling sacrifice? Would she, Nina, do that? Could she? Sonya's hands are working, kneading imaginary dough. "I shall probably never see him again." Nina, moved by the regret she thinks she hears in her friend's voice, reaches for Sonya's hands.

"Don't worry. I have the best of both worlds," Sonya says, pulling her hands away from Nina's tight, small ones. "I can do my work without anyone's consent. No one has power over me. Not my family and not my husband. I am married and yet I am free."

Nina nods again. "I suppose that is best."

Sonya pushes herself away from the sofa. She moves toward the balcony and stands there, her small, fierce figure framed by the balcony door. Shoulders squared, hands behind her back, she looks solitary, unapproachable in the mild September light. Nina would like to put her arms around her, but she knows Sonya does not need or want comforting. She is magnificent, but her words are hard. And Nina, who cannot bear the distance between them, draws closer to the balcony. Yet when Sonya turns her head toward Nina, her eyes are expressionless as if they were still focused on a point somewhere beyond Nina's imagination.

XVII

IN THE SCHAVRANSKIS' PARLOR, the fringed velvet draperies have been drawn tight over the windows and the balcony doors. The room, usually so sunny, feels muted, hushed, turned in on itself. Chaim stands by the cast-iron stove in which a fire has not yet been lit, although it is a chilly October morning. Sonya is a few feet in front of him and behind her Moiche and Benjy Kotov, two cloth cutters from the Schavranski workshop, wait by the door, heads bowed.

"Look, Alta, a delegation," Chaim says with a small smile that is meant to reassure his wife. Alta, whose pale face is a study in barely controlled panic, tugs at the drapery pulleys until not a sliver of light penetrates the room.

Sonya faces her employers, feet apart, hands behind her back, torso thrust forward. Her face, already narrow, appears to have lengthened and her chin sharpened to an aggressive point.

Chaim holds a printed flyer in his hand. He is very pale. He looks up at the young woman in front of him, his eyes dark with distress. Nina, who has just come into the room, ready for school, feels her heart thrumming anxiously against her ribs.

Alta has already put on the black apron she wears to protect her clothes from the dirt and dust of the workshop. There are patches of red on her face as if she had scrubbed her cheeks hard with the hemp washcloth she uses to soften the skin on her elbows.

"But Sonya," Chaim says. "These demands." Here he slaps the paper with his hand. "I have already given the workers of my own free will. Better working conditions? My workshop is known for the kindness we extend to everyone who works for us. My wife bakes bread for the workers' families and our table is set on Friday night for anyone who wants to join us. Some of our workers, the Lithuanian Arsimov and his daughter, you know them, were homeless when they came here. Now they sleep in the workroom, on the bales of cotton we prepared for them. I pay fair wages to everyone, everyone. It makes no sense to strike against me."

Sonya lifts her chin a little higher, avoiding her employer's baffled, pained eyes. She wants to be unsentimental and to the point. She stares hard at the elaborate molding on the wall above Chaim's head.

Nina thinks Sonya looks very proud and strong, yet her friend's defiance is unsettling. She doesn't like to see her parents, especially her father, pained in any way.

"Chaim Yudelovich, sir, please excuse me," Sonya says in a clear voice, "but your workers are not complaining about you. See," Sonya waves her right hand toward Benjy and Moiche, who still huddle in the doorway to the parlor, a look of wary expectation on their faces. They wear black vests over their long-sleeved shirts and skullcaps. The fringes of their tallises are matted with cotton dust.

"See," Sonya repeats, "they are happy here." The two men nod and yet, to Nina, they seem more fearful than reassured. Benjy, the sly one, tugs at his beard. Moiche, who is the quieter of the two and shyer, looks down at his boots. "But we must show solidarity with those who toil under dreadful conditions and earn wages barely enough to live on. Solidarity with all the workers across Russia who are being . . ." here Sonya pauses for breath and closes her eyes. When she opens them again, they glisten with excitement. "Exploited," she says. "The workers who are being exploited."

"But we do not exploit our workers," says Alta. She has been quiet up to now. She speaks Yiddish to Sonya, although her Russian is excellent. Nina remembers with a pang that her mother has never liked Sonya. A troublemaker, an unnatural daughter who left her family, a good, loving family not so different from the Schavranskis, to come to Yekaterinoslav to stir up hard-working people. "We take care of our workers; they are like family," Alta says.

"All over Russia," Sonya continues in Russian, as if she hadn't heard Alta, "workers are striking. The size of this movement has never before been equaled in the history of any country in the world. Everywhere, from Petersburg to Odessa. Even the pickpockets in Moscow want a trade union." Sonya laughs.

"All this activity is illegal," says Chaim. He wipes his long hands nervously on his trousers. "Strikes, trade unions. It's against the law."

"I know." Sonya exults. "Isn't it wonderful?"

Chaim shakes his head. "I am a peaceful man. I do not love the Tsar. How can I? I am a Jew. But I am law-abiding and, I hope, honest and fair. Should I be punished for that?"

A smile stretches Sonya's lips. She knits her fingers in front of her waist like a schoolteacher about to bestow first prize on her best student.

"You have misunderstood, Chaim Yudelovich, sir. What your workers want is for you to represent them before the council of workers."

"Ah," says Chaim. He turns his head toward the two men. Behind them is Goldstein, the soldier who defected and is now one of his workers. "Ah." He closes his eyes and the long lashes flutter against his cheeks. Color comes back to his face. "But I am not one of them," he says in a mild voice. "I am not a worker any longer, although I have shared all their troubles in my life."

"We know." Sonya switches from Russian to Yiddish. She is appealing to him now, not as an owner, a proprietor, an enemy of the class struggle, but as a fellow Jew and sufferer. "We know you are a virtuous man."

"Then why are you doing this to us?" says Alta. "This strike is a terrible disruption. How will we fill our orders? How will we pay our workers? How will we feed and clothe these people, because that is what we do. Moiche's eleven children with six pairs of shoes between them and maybe now without food. Benjy's new baby without milk. You will drive these folks to the poorhouse with your socialism."

Alta has stepped up to Sonya, obscuring her husband who fingers his beard. Now she is talking into Sonya's face.

"Maybe, in your opinion, this has been a good year, but to my mind, it has been a terrible year. Nothing but strikes and demonstrations, starting with that priest in St. Petersburg last January. Then strikes, strikes, and more strikes. And the mutiny of sailors in Odessa. You cannot tell me that was the fault of the Jews. And yet who pays? If there's trouble, here come the Cossacks and the police. We are quiet people; we mind our own business. You must leave us alone." Alta places her hand on her chest as if she could still her racing heart. She has never said so much to that dreadful girl.

Sonya looks grim, arms crossed over her chest. She has had a great deal of experience facing angry women. Her own mother cursed her and her politics. She will not be intimidated by someone as firmly entrenched in bourgeois thinking as her employer's wife.

Nina winces. In her anxiety, she has bitten the inside of her cheek.

"Now then, now then," says Chaim to his wife. He puts a hand on Alta's arm.

"No," says Alta. "This is outrageous. I won't have it. Our workers cannot strike."

"This is not up to you," says Sonya. "Your workers have already agreed to join the strikes. Just like the railroad workers in Moscow.

And the mill workers in Petersburg. Everywhere the workers are asking for their rights. Jews and Christians," says Sonya, her voice bell-like and passionate. "Jews and Christians together."

"Hah," Alta says. "There will never be Jews and Christians together. There is no such world. You," she looks into Sonya's face, "are simply encouraging our workers to be ungrateful. Ungrateful." She waves one hand in the direction of Benjy and Moiche, who look even more uneasy than before.

"Hush," says Chaim. "Don't say that. Our workers are good people. We will try to support them. We will do our best."

"Thank you," Sonya says. She stretches out her hand. Chaim takes it and places his on top of hers.

Alta moans. "Moiche, Benjy, have we not been good to you?" Her voice cracks. She takes a handkerchief out of the pocket of her apron and blows her nose. "What will happen to us?" she says. "This is terrible."

"Maybe not," says Chaim. "It is the beginning of something new. Maybe even something good."

"We will be made to pay. That's all I know." Alta sniffs into her handkerchief.

"We will close the workshop for the time being," says Chaim. "And then we'll see." He nods toward the door where Benjy leans against the jamb, fingering his curls nervously. Moiche keeps his head bent and his eyes lowered.

Nina's heart has stopped pounding quite so furiously. But now her head throbs. She would like to hold her father's hand and her mother's and Sonya's too. We are all on the same side, she thinks. Her eyes drift toward Alta's suffering face and she feels a terrible tug of guilt.

Sonya gathers her large leather bag, the one in which she carries the pamphlets and tracts she distributes in the streets of Yekaterino-slav, and slings it over her shoulder.

"Where are you going?" asks Nina, clutching her friend's sleeve.

"To a meeting," says Sonya. "We are organizing a trade union. All the workers in the tailoring workshops, the cloth cutters, the seamstresses, the tailors, the women who iron the clothes, even the delivery boys. Everyone will belong and this will make us strong. Oh, Nina," Sonya says suddenly, carelessly daring in front of her employers. "This is what I have been working for these past two years."

Nina's head feels about to burst. Sonya's passion, her words are so invigorating, like drinking cup after cup of strong tea. How can she love Sonya and still be a good daughter?

Sonya adjusts her satchel and turns to kiss Nina good-bye, but as she leans toward Nina, Sonya seems to collapse. Her head wobbles against Nina's as if it had come detached from the support of her neck. Her bag slides off her shoulder. Nina throws her arms around Sonya's waist.

"Sonya, what's the matter?"

"Exhaustion," Sonya says. "I haven't slept in days." She throws back her head, blinks, and draws in her breath. She leans one arm for support on Nina's shoulders.

"What are you doing?" Alta rushes up to Sonya. "Do not touch my daughter. Take your hands off her. We are not on the same side, you and I. Remember that. Now get out of my house."

"My dear, do not be so severe," Chaim stammers, as he places himself between Sonya and Alta. "Sonya is a good girl and maybe not so wrong as all that."

Alta whirls away from her husband. Nina recognizes the angry arch of her mother's back and knows her mother feels betrayed. "Mama," she says. "Don't worry. It will be all right."

Alta responds in a pinched voice. "You'll be late for school, Nina."

Nina gives her father an anguished look. Chaim blinks and signals a nod. Alta keeps her back turned.

"Come on, I'll walk with you," Sonya takes Nina by the arm. Nina feels Sonya's will like a strong, purposeful wind in her back. She shrugs into her coat and slips her school bag over her shoulder.

The streets are crowded. People walk in the middle of the street as well as on the sidewalks, blocking the traffic of carts and carriages. Along the Prospekt, many shops are shuttered. The owners of the shops that are open have posted themselves in front of their doors, their wares safely inside. They look anxious or defiant depending, Nina suspects, on their assessment of the situation. In this predominantly Jewish neighborhood, people are wary. There are policemen in gray capes and polished boots stationed along the Prospekt but who can trust them?

When the girls reach the Progymnasia Klutch, the Jewish high school near the School of Mines on the Prospekt, the school guard, an old fellow with a white beard and a soiled blue cap too large for his head, tells them that all the classes have been canceled.

"Oh no," says Nina. "That can't be. This is not a pogrom. Classes are only canceled in case of a pogrom." She looks anxiously at Sonya, whose narrow face has acquired the same defiant look it had when she was talking to Nina's parents.

"The administration says that all you young ladies should stay home with your families. I'm waiting until nine o'clock and then I'm going home too," the guard says. "It's dangerous out here."

"Nonsense," says Sonya, planting herself firmly in front of the guard. "The Jewish school should not be closed. What are you all so afraid of?"

"Repercussions, little lady." The guard lifts a finger like a rabbi commenting on a passage in the Talmud to an unruly scholar. "Repercussions."

"Why is everything always about the Jews?" Sonya asks, irritated. "Don't you think the Christian workers have been mistreated, exploited? Look at you, old man. How much does the administration pay you? And I don't believe you are a Jew."

"I'm Ukrainian and loyal to my bishop." The old man squints at her with watery eyes. "And you? Are you a Socialist?"

"Yes," says Sonya. "I am. I belong to the Social Democratic party of Mr. Lenin." Nina feels something buoyant fill her lungs, like sharp, fresh air in the country.

"Never heard of him," says the guard. He turns toward Nina, "But you, little lady, I know you. You're a nice girl. You shouldn't keep company with crazy people."

"Oh, I'm one of them, too," Nina lies. "Oh yes, I believe in . . ." she struggles for a moment, "everything she believes in."

Sonya laughs and her laugh makes Nina happy. "We are all the same now," Nina says. "Christians and Jews. Workers and owners. School guards and schoolgirls." She smiles at the guard, delighted at her own boldness.

Sonya grabs the guard by the sleeve of his soiled blue jacket. "Come, you must walk with us. You are a worker too."

The guard's face shuts down. "Foolishness. Foolishness," he mutters. "Go home."

Sonya drops the guard's arm and shrugs her shoulders. "I don't have time for foolishness either. I have a meeting to attend."

"Sonya," Nina says. "May I come with you? Will Babushkin be there? I would like to hear him speak."

"No. Not today. Maybe next time. And you can bring your father." Sonya reaches into her leather bag and takes out a stack of pamphlets printed on cheap newsprint. "On your way home, distribute these to anyone you find. Be careful the ink doesn't get all over your nice school clothes."

"I don't care about that," says Nina, her back as straight as she can make it.

"Maybe not. But your mother does."

"Oh Sonya," Nina says and shoves the pamphlets under her arm, pressing her arm hard against her chest. "Today, what do I care what my mother thinks!"

"What a little socialist," Sonya says and Nina smiles, although she cannot tell for sure whether or not her friend is making fun.

Nina waits until Sonya's energetic figure, bright red head arched forward, leather bag swinging vigorously, rounds a corner street and disappears off the Prospekt. Then she turns around, and begins the walk home.

"A little socialist," she thinks as she adjusts the flyers under her arm. Yes, that is what she is, what she will become. Like Sonya, someone who works for the good of all the people, not just Jews or Russians or Ukrainians, but everyone all over the world. Nina's head rings with excitement and purpose.

"Here," she hands a flyer to a woman walking toward her holding a little boy by the hand. "You must read this. It's important."

The woman, who carries a basket under one arm and appears to be dressed for shopping, stops and puzzles over the already smudged flyer.

"What does it say?" she says. "Is it about the new dry goods store?"

"Oh, no," Nina says and then realizes with dismay that she hasn't read the flyer herself. "It's about how to make the world a better place."

The woman looks at Nina blankly. Her little boy is sucking his thumb. He looks both forlorn and content. "That's very nice," says the woman as she hands the flyer back to Nina. "Do you know where the new Einhorn's is? I need buttons and more thread. This one wears out his clothes so quickly."

Nina looks down at the child who has wrapped himself in his mother's skirt. He gives her a baleful stare.

"No, I'm sorry. I don't," she says.

"Well, never mind," says the woman and tugs her boy's thumb out of his mouth.

Nina rests her book bag and flyers on the ground against an iron fence mounted on a low concrete wall. She leans against the iron spokes and reads the flyer: "Workers! Join in solidarity with other workers all over Russia! The time has come! Together we are powerful; alone we are nothing! Come to a meeting tonight at 7 p.m. 31 Tsverskaya Street near the Town Hall! Join us!"

Reading the flyer, Nina's heart pounds, her breath comes fast. She is almost dizzy with the anxiety of happiness. She does notice that the flyer says nothing about a strike or about a revolution, nothing that you can be sent to Siberia for. She thinks that is very smart of Sonya, because she assumes that her friend has had a hand in preparing these smudgy pieces of paper.

She thrusts the flyers under her arm again and straps the book bag across her back. A man is coming toward her. He has a woolen cap pulled over his eyes, his shoes are brown and muddy; even his hands, she notices, are splattered with paint. A worker, she thinks, and thrusts a flyer at him. The man glances suspiciously at her under thick eyebrows, but he takes the paper and walks away. He may not be able to read, she thinks. I must be more careful. I can't afford to waste these flyers. An elderly man takes a flyer, a young woman, a student in his student cap and double-breasted jacket. (Nina manages a shy smile. Students are our best hope, Sonya said. And besides, this one has nice eyes.) A couple refuse, an old woman shakes her fist at her.

It is then that Nina becomes frightened. She feels quite suddenly that she has strayed too far, opened herself up to too many dangers. She feels unprotected without the strength of Sonya's fierce will by her side. She begins to walk faster, clutching her book bag to her chest, and counting the steps to her parents' apartment on Karaim Street.

The following day, October 13, all of Yekaterinoslav is out on the streets or so it seems to Nina, to judge from the ruckus on the other side of the courtyard. The stamp of clogs and boots, a drum roll in the distance, whistles, and the roiling thrum of voices. What has happened? The workers have shut down the distilleries, the sugar refinery, the wine warehouses, the lumberyards, many of which belong to Jews. The printmakers have walked out of their shops; so have the workers in the tailoring workshops, the pharmacy employees, the clerks and office workers, the hairdressers, the bakers' assistants, the carpenters' apprentices, the cooks, the maids, the household servants. The railway workers are on strike across the empire. And the demands. Not just higher wages and better working conditions. But for political freedom. For universal suffrage. For human rights. For the creation of a parliament elected by the people. For—can it be said?—more just and humane government. Oh, it is too much to take in, Nina thinks, as she peers at the stream of joyous humanity from the safety of the half-open courtyard door.

"Come with us, Nina." Gasha and Rouia, the two young seamstresses from Chaim's workshop, each slip an arm through Nina's and attempt to push her past the door.

"I can't. My mother won't let me."

"Of course, she will. Ma'am," yells Rouia to the woman on the balcony, "Let our Ninotchka come with us. It's perfectly safe. We'll take good care of her."

Nina casts a worried glance back up at the balcony, where Alta and Yudel glower down at the young women, Yudel sulking because he is too young to join the fun, and Alta hiding her anxiety behind a facade of icy calm. She thinks marching against the Tsar is a benighted scheme, a willful stupidity that will bring calamities to rain upon the Jews far worse than the Biblical plagues. But the sight of Nina's excited and hopeful face moves her. Nina is her father's daughter, an enthusiast, an idealist. She tightens her grip on Yudel's wrist and barely nods her consent.

"I'll be careful," Nina says. "Don't worry." Alta waves dispiritedly. She pulls Yudel in by the hand and shuts the balcony doors behind her as if she could keep turmoil out as easily as bad weather.

"Did you see my father? He left so early this morning." It seems to Nina that she cannot possibly join the marchers without her father's blessing.

"He is well, miss. We walked him to the workshop where he will be safe all day. Everyone knows he is a good man. Nothing will happen to him. He is on our side," says Rouia. Gasha nods her head. Each young woman has tied a red kerchief around her neck, which surprises Nina. They are always so docile at home, so tractable and unthinking. Have they been secret revolutionaries all along?

"Come," says Rouia again, "or we'll miss the fun."

"Yes," says Gasha. "No one is working today. It's like a holiday. Only better."

Still Nina resists. "Where is Sonya?"

"Oh that one, she was probably out all night recruiting the workers, making preparations, printing leaflets. You know how she is."

It seems to Nina that neither Rouia nor Gasha has the proper revolutionary seriousness, despite their red neckkerchiefs.

"Surely we'll run into her," says Gasha seeing Nina's frown and lightly trembling lips. She is the more sensitive of the two seamstresses and feels a certain responsibility for her employer's daughter.

"Come on," says Rouia. "I don't want to miss any of this."

And indeed, out on the street it does feel like a holiday. Here are the railwaymen in boots and blue tunics, the factory girls in long cloth coats over their flowered skirts, bright-colored scarves tied around the chin, the apothecaries' assistants in dark jackets over their white coats, the hairdressers showing off their brilliantly pomaded hair, waiters in baggy trousers and white shirts carrying the insignia of their professions, a silk sash and a purse of black patent leather tucked into their sashes. There are high school students in black-belted gray uniforms, and university students in military jackets and peaked caps. And distillery workers, smelling of hops and fermented grain, and tanners, smelling of tannin and uncured skins. Even army officers with red ribbons in their buttonholes. And placards shifting in the October breezes. Some mild and informative: "Distillery Workers of Yekaterinoslav." "South Russian Railroad Workers." Others are more radical and incendiary: "Workers Unite!" "Down with the Tsar!" "Needs are Rights! Owners, stop exploiting the workers!" "Land and Liberty!" "Up with the Revolutionary Councils of Workers!" "We demand universal and direct suffrage!" These are usually carried by the high school students and the students from the university. There must be tailors in here too, Nina thinks, and Jews among the crowd. And indeed, she spots, two workers from Menachem Friburg's tailoring establishment, now practically a factory for turning out fashionable women's clothing, wearing skullcaps and ringlets and incongruous red kerchiefs around the neck.

"What a mess," says Gasha, "This is not at all what I expected. Stop pushing," she says to a man wearing an apothecary's tunic under his long coat and sporting a narrow English-style mustache.

"Well, move along," says the man. "At this rate, the snows will have melted in Moscow before we get there."

"My, my," says Rouia, turning her brightly kerchiefed head to the man. "Aren't we in a hurry? And just where are we all supposed to be heading?"

"To the Potemkin Gardens. There's going to be a demonstration there. Don't you girls know anything?"

Rouia narrows her eyes. "We know more than you do." She winks at Nina. "We know the Potemkin Gardens are only a few streets away. So there's no need to push." Her voice rises; she jerks her chin aggressively. The man shrugs his shoulders and maneuvers around the three women, elbows out, head down.

"He thinks we smell bad," Rouia laughs. But Nina is unhappy. She hates confrontations and especially public ones. Rouia is not a trustworthy companion; she makes scenes in the street. Where are the real revolutionaries? Nina scans the leather coats in front of her, the headscarves, hats, shawls, but no Sonya. No one who even resembles Sonya.

A chill fall breeze causes Gasha to turn up the collar of her short jacket. "It's getting cold," she shivers. "Are you cold, Ninotchka?"

Nina shakes her head. It is wonderful to be part of this crowd, and she is not at all cold. She is exhilarated. She feels buoyed along in a great sea of purpose. This may be the beginning of what Sonya has been talking about for the last two years. A more equal society, a society free of the cruel and constricting differences between owners and workers, rich and poor, between intellectuals and peasants, between Christians and Jews. She is part of the revolution, something bigger than she is. Something bigger even than being a Jew.

Gasha slips her arm into Nina's. "We can have some tea from the vendor," she says.

The vendor of warm drinks, an enormous copper samovar lurching on his wheelbarrow, a garland of bread rolls strung around his neck, the pockets of his apron clattering with tin cups, walks alongside the crowd. He pauses from time to time, to serve a bearded railway man or a shop assistant a cup of tea.

Again Nina shakes her head. Alta would disapprove.

"Well then, here," Gasha says. "Chewing these will keep you warm." She offers Nina a handful of sunflower seeds from a pouch attached to her belt. Nina refuses these, too, although she is hungry. Eating should be done at home, not in the street, says Alta's condemning voice. When she looks down at her feet, she notices that the pavement, usually swept clean by the street sweeper, is covered with the hulls of small black sunflower seeds as if it were a carpet of crushed insects.

"Look," Rouia says. "Mushrooms." And indeed, there, in front of a greengrocer, are barrels of pickled cabbage and salted cucumbers and casks of brine where gherkins float among fennel branches and currant leaves. Rouia pulls at Gasha's arm and the two women stop to admire the baskets of white, yellow, and brown mushrooms, the crates of chick peas and lentils, of Smyrna figs and dried apricots.

"We could buy some for Alta Schavranski," Rouia says. "Let's see how much they are."

"Stop, Rouia. This is not a shopping expedition," says Gasha, casting a embarrassed look about her as if she were afraid someone would accuse her of an excess of frivolity. The crowd pushes behind them. Schoolboys, restless on their day off, play at keeping their balance along the tram tracks. Today, the tram has been shut down to prevent its being taken over by strikers. From time to time, the boys toss pebbles at the strings of birds, sparrows and occasionally a crow, perched on the roofs of the two-story houses that line the Prospekt.

Nina, Rouia, and Gasha follow the crowd down the Prospekt toward the Potemkin Gardens. They pass the School of Mines, where Professor Lebedev, the director of the school, who has often come to dinner at the Schavranskis with his Jewish wife, teaches engineering. The school has been shut down by the authorities because of the student strikes. They pass the Scheidische Shul, the new synagogue that is only as old as Nina, without averting their eyes. On this day, it is possible to be a Jew without terror. We are all brothers and sisters, Nina thinks, that is the blessing of socialism, and joy fills her lungs like pure, fresh air.

At the corner of the Prospekt and the Potemkin Gardens, policemen, stationed there to control the crowd, fall into line to form a barrier. A rumble of discontent rises from the crowd. It travels like the wake of a steamboat toward Nina and the two seamstresses.

"Why are they stopping us?" asks Rouia. "We haven't done any-thing wrong. What is the problem?" she asks a worker in a short coat and flat cap.

The worker frowns. "I think it's the Tsar."

"Is he dead?" says Rouia. "Oh my God, the Tsar is dead." She grabs Nina's hand and squeezes it, from fear or delight it is impossible for Nina to say. A small crowd has gathered around them.

An old man points to a university student in a smart military jacket. "He says the Tsar has just issued a declaration."

"What's that?" asks Gasha.

"A declaration," the old man begins uncertainly and then shrugs his shoulders. "Tell them what you told me." He points to the uni-versity student. The young man, who is tall and wears his tunic but-toned to the neck, says in a voice hoarse with feeling, "I can only tell you what I have heard. Martial law has been declared across the empire. We are all, everyone of us, participating in illegal acts." He lets out a laugh, like air from a bellows and slaps the old man on the back. "You and I," he says, "and these three young ladies, are out-side the law. So is everyone on the streets. All of us, outlaws. Martial law is the best thing that can happen to us. It means that the Tsar is scared. He sees that we are mighty and united. He knows that we will win. There is panic in the Winter Palace. It is magnificent."

"If you say so," says the old man, but he looks dubious. "What do you think, my darling?" he says to Nina. "You're young, you under-stand these things."

But Nina does not understand. Without Sonya to explain the world to her, she feels adrift and in danger. The university student laughs again, showing large yellow teeth. "What a day," he says.

Nina threads her arm through Gasha's. "Where is my father? We should go to him. Maybe he is in danger."

"Oh, I don't think so," says Rouia, who is smiling brashly at the student.

"Leave him alone," Gasha tugs roughly at her friend's coat sleeve. "Come on. I don't like this anymore."

Rouia snarls. "What a spoilsport you are." But the university student has a friend among the strikers and signals happily to him over Rouia's head, and so she turns and follows Nina and Gasha as they push their way out of the crowd.

CHAIM'S WORKSHOP IS IN AN old section of the city where the rambling wooden houses seem to lean toward each other for support. Stone archways join one side of the street to the other. Tinsmiths and water carriers, peddlers and lottery ticket vendors compete for space on the sloppy cobblestones, while housewives, wrapped in plaid shawls, thread their way among the puddles and horse droppings. This is the poor Jewish section of Yekaterinoslav, and Nina feels uncomfortable, out of place here. She watches her feet and avoids grazing the walls with the side of her skirt. Mold grows like ivy along these walls, and wizened mushrooms appear in the damp cracks. The smell is of cooked cabbage and turnips and sometimes urine and, of course, horse droppings. How does my father stand walking through here every day, she thinks. And Sonya too. And my mother, with her Wednesday basket of bread and shoes for our workers. Determined to be as good and as brave as the others, Nina squares her shoulders and quickens her step, while Gasha and Rouia, perfectly at ease in this neighborhood, chat companionably behind her.

The workshop door is bolted from the inside. Nina knocks and waits. She hears Chaim's solid gait on the stone floor, the rasp of the latch as he pulls it open. But she is not prepared for Chaim, who holds out his arms to her as if there had been a death in the family. He looks, she thinks, old and sad and tired. "Papa," she says and drops into his arms. Chaim presses her head against him as if she needed consolation and she does, although she doesn't know why. It is such a relief to burrow into her father's chest. His shirt smells of sweat and starch and the bluing Alta uses to keep his shirt white. She begins to cry.

"What have they done to the workshop?" Rouia asks as she surveys the long, narrow room.

"It is over," Chaim says, as he cradles Nina's head. "The workshop is closed."

The room is empty. Benjy, Moiche, the soldier Goldstein, Arsimov and his daughter, Raya, who presses the garments, Dora, who sews the buttons and tightens the seams, all the workers are gone. The machines are quiet. The table and benches are lined up neatly against the wall. The three enormous gas lamps that usually give off so much heat are cold. Even the blankets have been removed from the bales of cotton that serve as beds for Arsimov and his daughter. What is most striking is how empty the workroom is of anything personal, any sign that workers have been here at all. The caps are gone, the jackets, the occasional bowl or glass of tea left over from the night before. The bolts of cloth are stacked up neatly against the wall. Some unfinished items, a man's suit, a lady's evening dress, some skirts, a few blouses, an overcoat hang from the overhead pipes like abandoned scarecrows.

"Why is it like this?" asks Gasha. "Where is everybody?"

"I imagine they have gone home. Or perhaps they are out walking with their comrades."

"You mean they have gone on strike too." Gasha casts a pained look at Chaim.

"Exactly, dear Gasha. No one turned up for work today."

"But Papa, Sonya said they wanted you to represent them before the Council of Workers."

Chaim nods sadly. "Perhaps they did, once. But now they are gone."

"But will you open the workshop again when this is over?"

186 • MYRIAM CHAPMAN

"When this is over? This? If I knew what this was, I could give you an answer."

"Well," says Rouia who is always practical. "You cannot remain here, Chaim Yudelovich, sir. You will catch your death of cold in this place. Come home with us. Your wife will be so worried. Martial law has been declared, have you heard? I don't know what that means, but it doesn't sound good. I'd rather be home in these times, wouldn't you?"

Chaim releases Nina, whose skin is puckered with the shape of the buttons on Chaim's shirt.

"Come, Ninotchka. I will lock up and we'll go home for lunch," he says softly, and tugs at her braids.

"I hope you have a sturdy lock on the door," says Rouia. "There are too many hooligans about these days."

Chaim sighs. Rouia, thinking of lunch and a hot soup, pushes him vigorously out the door.

XVIII

CHAIM, ALTA, NINA, AND YUDEL are seated at the dining-room table, which is set as always with the faded and fringed red damask cloth. It is midday. There has been no school for either Nina or Yudel since the imposition of martial law. With the workshop closed, Gasha and Rouia have retreated to a shared room in a rooming house in the poor Jewish quarter, for which Chaim is paying. The other workers are home with their families. Chaim has been paying them too, but the funds are running out. There will be no new orders for clothing in the foreseeable future. Yekaterinoslav has come to a standstill. The university remains closed, as does the Russian high school. The tram, a possible target of militants because its cars are so easily overturned, is no longer running along the Prospekt. It is not possible to leave the city by rail since railroad workers continue to strike across the empire from Moscow to Odessa. A few shops are open: green gro-cers, dry-good shops, but none of the Jewish-owned shops or the Jewish-owned businesses, many of which continue to be struck by their Jewish workers.

Alta is serving her family potato soup seasoned with dill. A bottle of beer has been brought up from the cellar for Chaim, and there is sweet cider for the children. This is fare not so different from the meals the family took before the events of October, although Alta has not had the heart or the white flour to bake her bread. The bread on the table is as black and as sour as peasant bread. The baker Natimzef apologized for its poor quality, but Alta was glad to have any bread at all. Chaim remains optimistic.

"Good will come of this, you'll see, when all the dust has settled," he says, as Alta spoons soup into his plate. "We mustn't worry too much." He smiles encouragingly at his children.

Alta looks grim. She is tired of hearing about the wondrous changes that the nationwide strikes will bring about. At night, she sleeps badly. Huddled under the goose-down cover on the high hard bed, she lies stiff with the effort not to wake her husband. But doom crouches in a corner. What will happen to them? Their small savings dribbled away. Everywhere strikes and terrible reprisals. Pogroms in Zhytomyr, in Kiev, in Odessa. Not in Yekaterinoslav yet, thank God, but who knows? And now martial law! Alta feels untethered. And meanwhile Chaim sleeps the sleep of the just. Is she the only one to understand that calamities loom ahead?

"Moiche Friedman has sent his wife and children away." Alta sounds angry, almost resentful. "They're going to France and maybe to America. Did you know this, Chaim?"

Chaim shakes his head. "I think he is making a foolish mistake."

"Sasha is gone?" Nina asks. Sasha, three years older than Nina, has been studying at the university in Kiev. He is said to be a good student, and a good son, but his father complains that he has developed dangerous political ideas. Nina would like to talk to Sasha now that they are both grown up. She remembers how kind he was about her piano playing when he came to visit during the summer. "I suppose we won't see Sasha again for a long time," she says.

Alta gives Nina a long searching look. Then, turning to Chaim, she says, "Moiche Friedman thinks there is going to be trouble."

Nina is silent. Alta's anxieties stream through her like shared blood. She is worried about Sonya too, whom she hasn't seen since the strikes started. And her father's optimism seems forced even to her. So she says nothing.

"I don't want any soup," Yudel lifts his spoon full of soup and dribbles it back on to his plate. Yudel is a sallow-faced ten-year-old, tall for his age, but thin and listless, a boy who still does not wash his own face or lace up his own boots. "I'm tired of potato soup. I'm tired of herring. Why can't we have boiled beef like we used to. I like boiled beef."

He looks at Alta as if it were her fault that there is no boiled beef. He continues to dribble his soup.

"Don't play with your food," says Nina. "It's not polite."

Yudel jerks his chin at his sister.

"Children," says Chaim, "Stop." He pushes himself away from the table and begins to pace. He walks the length of the dining-room table, chewing on the skin around his thumbnail.

"See what you've done. You've upset your father, you two," says Alta. "Behave yourselves."

Chaim makes a placating gesture with his hand, but Nina knows that it is not their misbehavior that upsets her father. They are all on edge.

There is a forceful banging on the door, which, left unlocked, swings open. Sonya stands in the doorway, flushed with excitement.

"You cannot imagine where I've been."

She opens her arms, taking in the surprised faces.

"A demonstration. In front of the City Hall. Thousands of people. That half-wit in the Winter Palace has issued a manifesto."

"What's a manifesto?" asks Yudel, looking from Chaim to Alta.

Chaim eyes Sonya doubtfully. "Is that a good thing?"

"Listen," Sonya says. "There is to be a constituent assembly, a Duma elected democratically with delegates from all over the Empire. But it solves nothing of course," she continues with ill-contained glee. "It is only another sign of the government's stupidity. As for us, the Social

Democrats," her back straightens, her jaw tightens. "We shall continue to work for real justice. The Soviet in St. Petersburg has agreed to continue striking. The struggle will go on. And we shall prevail."

She pauses. Around her, faces are blank or suspicious, or gently encouraging. Nina doesn't know what to think. She is happy to see her friend safe but she will need Sonya to explain it all to her in private, in safety, away from her parents and their conflicting opinions.

"Well," Sonya says. "Whatever happens now, we know how the people feel. They are with us. You should have seen the crowds, spilling out into the side streets like a fat lady in a corset." Sonya puts her hand to her mouth and giggles. "And the singing. Everyone sang "La Marseillaise." And the red flags everywhere. Even army men with red ribbons in their buttonholes. Lots of good speakers, too. Schlikhter from Kiev, the leader of the railway workers, and people from the Bund also. And Babushkin came out of hiding. That was brave of him. He talked about continuing the struggle against the Tsar and for socialism. And, do you know, there were many there who agreed with him. People who were not in our workers' circles. Outsiders, ready to be moved by the spirit of revolution. A worker from the sugar refinery got up to read his own poetry. Imagine. Such a happy, joyful crowd. Oh, it was so moving. Never in my life have I felt such excitement, such enthusiasm. Oh it was wonderful, wonderful, wonderful."

"Why did you leave if it was so wonderful?" Yudel asks.

"Why, I came to get you all to come with me!" Sonya says, her eyes darting at the rather solemn faces. "You must come, Chaim Yudelovich. It will do your heart good. You too, Ninotchka. You've wanted to be a part of our movement. This is the moment."

"Never. I forbid you to go, Nina," says Alta, rising from her seat. Her hands shake. Her voice trembles.

"Calm down, Sonyatchka. Sit, have some food," says Chaim. He does not want to leave the house. Sonya's glittery enthusiasm feels alien. All that joyous optimism, all that hopeful energy. He feels old, all of a sudden. "Maybe later, we'll go and have a look."

"Chaim," Alta warns.

"There is no danger," Chaim says slowly. "Sonya says so herself. Everyone is calm and happy. Isn't that so?"

Sonya doesn't answer. She rubs her hands together as if she could start a fire between her palms.

"If you go, we'll all go," says Alta. "We will not be separated."

"Good," says Chaim. "We'll make it a family outing." But his shoulders droop and his voice is wan.

Nina walks around the table to where Sonya stands and slips her arm around her friend's waist. Sonya pats her hand.

"A constituent assembly," Nina says. "That is a very good thing. Like in a democracy where everyone is equal." She is a good student. She has learned her lessons well. If only Sonya could be pleased with her, too. But Sonya's foot taps restlessly on the carpet.

"It's getting late. Let's go."

"No. Not yet." Alta's voice crackles with anxiety. "We have not finished our meal. Yudel, there's still soup in your plate. Nina, you haven't eaten a thing."

"Alta Schavranski, when will you stop!" Sonya whirls to face Alta. "This is intolerable! Absolutely intolerable! All you think about is food. Nina, come with me now!"

Suddenly, Nina feels she cannot move. A panic of indecision roots her to the spot. She looks beseechingly from Alta to Sonya, clutches the back of her father's chair, her fingers digging into the elaborate curves.

"Schavranski. Schavranski!" A voice, muffled by the thick draperies, calls from the courtyard.

Chaim rushes to the balcony doors, pushes apart the folds of velvet, and throws the doors open. Below him, a tiny lady, not much taller than Nina, in a fur coat and hat, waves her muff at him.

"Schavranski. Come down. Come down immediately."

"What is it?" says Chaim.

"They have started shooting at the City Hall," she says. "The police and the Cossacks are shooting the demonstrators. The pogromschiki are looking for Jews. There is no time to waste. Come home with me." It is Mrs. Lebedev, the wife of the director of the School of Mines.

"What is it? What is it?" Alta has moved to the door.

"A pogrom," says Chaim in a sepulchral voice.

"I knew it," Alta says, her hand on her heart. "Dear God."

"What?" says Sonya. "A pogrom?" She forces herself between Chaim and Alta and peers down at the woman in the courtyard. "It's not possible, I have just come from the City Hall. Everything was calm. You are mistaken," she yells. "Don't believe these rumors."

"Hush, Sonya," says Chaim. "Come away."

Sonya leans over the balcony railing, her clenched hands white.

"No," says Sonya. "No! It's not true."

Windows open into the courtyard. Faces, curious, frightened, perplexed, appear and then disappear. In the courtyard, some families have already begun to assemble. Women in long coats and headscarves, men in fur hats, children swaddled in blankets.

"They are going down to the cellar," says Chaim. "It's hardly safe there. Everyone knows this is a Jewish house. We're better off at the Lebedevs'. If we can get there in time."

"No," Sonya says. "I'm not going with you."

"Don't be ridiculous." And now it's Alta's turn to be forceful. In an emergency she can be forgiving. Sonya is only a child. "You are our responsibility. Our worker. You come with us."

"No," Sonya trembles. "Never."

"My pillow," Nina says. It is suddenly imperative that she find her goose-down pillow. She rushes into her bedroom, crouches for a moment beside her bed to catch her breath and tears the pillow from under the coverlet.

In the dining room Sonya remains standing by the table. Alta buttons Yudel into his jacket and jams a fur hat on his head. He does not protest. Sonya also doesn't move, a figure of such transcendent grief that Chaim is moved to put his arm around her thin shoulders.

"Come, my girl," and he pushes the sorrowful young woman gently toward the door.

Alta grabs Yudel and Sonya by the hand as if they were both her children. Chaim waits for his daughter.

"Hurry," screams Mrs. Lebedev from the courtyard. "Hurry."

In the courtyard, Natimzef the baker is herding stricken tenants into the cellar.

"Are you coming?" he says to Chaim.

"No, we are going with this lady."

Natimzef gives Mrs. Lebedev a narrow, suspicious stare, then shrugs. "God bless you," he says.

"We will take the side streets," says Mrs. Lebedev in a voice that is surprisingly commanding for such a slight, elegant lady. "The Prospekt is not safe." In the distance, Nina hears shutters being lowered on the Prospekt. It is a sickening sound, recognized by all the Jewish families in the area, a signal that an action against the Jews is about to begin. Nina digs her nails into her fists.

Yudel walks between his parents, shocked into silence. They are walking quickly ahead of Nina, but not so quickly as Mrs. Lebedev, who is sweeping the sidewalk with the skirt of her long fur coat.

The side streets are quiet and empty as if all of Yekat had been warned to keep off the streets. Windows are shuttered or heavily curtained like so many eyes shut tight. A horse tethered to a pole munches calmly on a bag of oats. Behind him a cart, abandoned, lurches on its side. The midday smells of boiled cabbage and wood fire linger in the air, although there is no smoke issuing from any chimney. Clearly, all the telltale fires have been extinguished in the houses belonging to Jews. Once a workman in a cap passes them with his head down, and then a peasant woman carrying a shopping basket darts an assessing glance at the group, but no one stops them.

Sonya is crying. Surprising tears flow down her cheeks.

"You'll be safe with us," Nina says and squeezes her friend's hand.

Sonya shakes her head and continues to weep silently, her glasses steamed with tears.

Nina says, "I'm sorry." And she is. If being sorry could make everything all right for her friend and her dream of revolution, Nina would be happily sorry forever.

The cobblestone streets open up on to the broad lanes of the Prospekt. The pogromschiki have not yet reached the main thoroughfare, but someone has set small fires at intervals along the street and broken glass crackles under Nina's feet. All the Jewish shops are shuttered, Einhorn's dry goods shop, Lazarof, who makes and sells high-quality shoes. Davidovich, the greengrocer, has retired his barrels from the front of the store. The windows of the Scheidische synagogue are dark; behind the portico with its four majestic columns, the door is bolted with a huge padlock. A horse-drawn wagon passes them. A young man holding the reins spits out, "Jews! Death to them and their dirty, smelly asses. Long life to the Tsar." He flicks his whip at Chaim. It grazes Chaim's back.

Yudel looks up at his father in alarm.

"It's all right, Idelka. It didn't hurt."

The wagon clatters down the avenue; the driver hunched over, whip slicing the air.

"Ah, your coat's ripped," Alta wails. And indeed there is a slash along the back of Chaim's black coat.

Yudel begins to cry.

"Sha, sha, Idelka. Crying doesn't help. Let's walk a little faster."

"How did he know we were Jews?" Nina asks her father.

"Who else would be walking the streets? Do we look like pogromschiki?" Chaim says.

They pass the dark and shuttered School of Mines and stop at a two-story house with an iron gate. "Hurry," Mrs. Lebedev says, as she holds the gate open. The family and Sonya file through the courtyard in silence. Yudel, clinging to his mother's hand, is not reprimanded when he stumbles on the cobblestones. Professor Lebedev is at the top of a flight of concrete steps. He is a portly man, older than his wife, with a generous white beard. He leans on a gold-tipped cane and greets his visitors with a grave, silent nod.

"What is that noise?" Alta asks. Instinctively, she pulls Yudel toward her and claps a hand over his left ear. Yudel pulls away.

Everyone pauses on the stone landing to listen. Bursts of gunfire puncture the silence, and so do the clang of hooves on cobblestones and human voices, not so distant any more, and a peculiar thwacking noise, like iron being hit against wood.

"Come inside now," says Lebedev.

The Lebedevs' parlor is dark. The gaslights have been turned down, the curtains drawn. To Nina, it already looks like a house in mourning.

"I am sorry I did not come to get you myself," Lebedev says to Chaim. "My legs are not so strong anymore. Gout. Please, forgive me."

"You are kind to do this for us," says Chaim. He is out of breath. He would gladly sit down, if he could.

"We have enjoyed your hospitality so often. Now you will have to enjoy ours." Professor Lebedev tilts his large head. He smiles a small, sad smile. "You will be safe here. Dr. Schneider and his family are already in the basement. Everything is ready." After a pause, he adds, "My wife is Jewish."

"Ah, yes," says Chaim, and Nina can see that this reminder puts her father at ease.

Mrs. Lebedev has disappeared into the kitchen. Now she returns carrying two kerosene lamps. "Take these please," she says. "I will bring two more."

"Professor!" Nina turns to see a young woman in a starched cap and apron, her gaze fastened intently on the professor and his wife.

"There are some men at the front gate. They say they want the Jews who have just arrived to be handed over to them."

Alta lets out a moan. Yudel stares anxiously at his mother.

"Tell them to go away. There are no Jews here," says the professor to the little governess who is wide-eyed with terror.

"They are very angry," she says in a quavering voice. "They say they will burn down the School of Mines."

"Drunken hooligans," says the professor. "I will speak to them myself."

"No." Chaim clamps a restraining hand on Lebedev's arm. "We cannot let you take such a risk. We will leave. What can they do to us? We will promise to give them money. That is what they usually want."

"Nonsense." Lebedev shrugs off Chaim's arm. "I will not be bullied by thugs and petty criminals." His wife, who Nina can now see is much younger than her husband, wrings her hands nervously. "Don't go, my dear, think of your leg." But the professor lumbers out of the room.

"A good man, a very brave man," says Chaim to Alta. "We owe him our lives." Alta nods weakly. She is very pale under her black shawl.

"They are gone," the professor says upon returning moments later. "I told them to go home. We are all patriots here, I said. We love the Tsar. They wanted vodka, but they settled for my gold watch. A lot of good it will do them. Drunken cowards." He shakes his large frame like a dog shaking off water. "Now into the cellar."

Nina takes Sonya's hand as they step carefully down the wooden stairs, not to steady herself so much as to guide her friend who seems

to have lost all will, all judgment. It is alarming to see Sonya so be-
reft. The bones in Sonya's hand appear to Nina as thin and break-
able as matchsticks.

The cellar is damp, moldy, and cluttered with the detritus of the
lives above—disemboweled chairs, books without bindings, a piano
stool that no longer turns, scraps of old clothing. The walls of uneven rock appear to sweat to the touch. Trails of green mold give off
a pungent, earthy smell like the darkest part of a forest. Overhead
pipes crisscross the ceiling and gurgle ominously.

A table, on which the remains of a meal—bread, salami, a samovar, glasses are waiting to be removed—has been set up at one end of
the cellar, and chairs, four of them, placed in odd corners among the
household debris, one near the table, another against the wall, two
beside a crate on which a chess set totters precariously. A worn Persian carpet is spread not too close to the wall, and some pillows, a
quilt, and two woolen blankets have been placed on its threadbare
surface.

"It may be a long siege," says the professor. "Three days is not
unusual."

"Well, we have tried to make you comfortable," says Mrs. Lebedev
with a shy smile.

Nina feels a tightening in her chest. Her heart races, her breath
catches. She gasps as the latch on the cellar door snaps shut behind her. Three days in this horrible place! Three days without air
or natural light. Three days without clean water, without toilets.
She knows it is foolish of her to feel this way when above ground
people are being beaten to death, but still, three days without a
change of clothing. She will smell like a peasant. She casts an anxious glance at her friend. But Sonya's face has shut down in her
private sorrow.

A set of kerosene lamps, one hanging from a beam under the stairs,
another on the table, give off a smoky glow. Particles of dust appear

suspended on the beams of light. There is a smell of damp and sweat and something else, a smell that Nina recognizes from her visits to her uncle Isaac's house in Smila, the odor of dead animals trapped in the walls. Nina thinks they will die too, trapped like animals in this airless space.

A tall, stooped man with spectacles and tufts of brown whiskers steps forward to greet them. Dr. Schneider, amiable Dr. Schneider, who treated Yudel when he was sick. Nina is relieved to see him.

Dr. Schneider clamps his arms around Chaim. "My dear fellow," he says. "My dear fellow." Chaim, caught in the embrace, nods his head like a rabbi in prayer.

In a dark corner of the room, a woman sits with her back against the wall, a child on her knees and another one at her feet. Dr. Schneider jerks his head toward them. "My wife is speechless. The children cannot cry. It happened so suddenly. We have brought nothing with us. I do not know how we will survive."

"Ach," Alta shakes her head and moves into the shadows. She encircles the seated woman with her arms. For a moment, they merge into one gray sorrowful shape. Then Alta picks up the child on Mrs. Schneider's lap and Nina can hear her mother's murmuring, reassuring voice. The tightness in her chest loosens a bit.

Yudel tugs at his father's sleeve.

"Papa, how long do we have to stay here. It smells."

"Not long," Chaim whispers, bending over his son. "A day or two."

"A day? A whole day? I don't want to stay here a whole day." Yudel's voice clatters in the silence like coins dropped on a stone floor.

"Hush," says Chaim in his light voice. "A day is not so long."

Yudel slams against his father's leg with the side of his boot. Chaim ignores his son's small act of defiance.

Dr. Schneider says, "In 1903, it was three days in Kiev and three days in Odessa. After three days the authorities decide the Jews have been taught enough of a lesson. I can't imagine they've changed the rules since then."

Sonya has secured a corner of a wall for herself and sits, knees to her chest, arms grasping her knees, as if, by making herself into the smallest possible presence, she could deny the fact that she is here at all. Nina looks about her, uncertain what to do. Chaim has slipped onto a chair with Yudel beside him. Yudel's head rests on his father's knee. With one hand, he attempts to twirl a small coin on the stone floor. Alta jiggles the Schneider baby in her arms. Dr. Schneider paces in front of his wife, pausing from time to time to ruffle his son's hair. Schloima, who must be about five, chews on the front of his white collarless shirt, which has become as wet and as wrinkled as an old rag. Nina thinks she would like to be helpful like her mother, but the dusty air is suffocating and she cannot breathe properly. There is still something pressing on her chest. She decides to sit on the floor beside Sonya. The cold seeps through the fabric of her school skirt, her petticoat, and her bloomers. She does not lean against the wall because, unlike Sonya who appears to be heroically impervious to any discomfort, she worries about the creatures that may be creeping along its damp surface. She clutches her pillow in her lap.

Nina leans toward Sonya, who hides her face in her hands. "What is it, Niunia?"

Sonya shakes her head.

"Tell me. You promised to tell me everything."

Nina slips her arm around Sonya's shoulders. Sonya shudders Nina's arm away. She looks up, distraught. "How could this happen? We had everything planned, everything, the demonstrations, the strikes, the petitions. We were going forward. So many people were on our side. And now we have been stopped in our tracks not because we are Socialists and revolutionaries, but because we are Jews! It is so humiliating."

"But at least you're safe." Nina links her arm through Sonya's and pats her hand. "That's good, isn't it?"

"Oh safety," says Sonya, bitterly. "Yes, I am safe. Safe and useless, useless."

"Is it my fault?" Nina asks in a tiny voice. "Because I am glad that you are here with us."

Nina drops her head on to Sonya's shoulder. Tears sting behind her eyelids.

"I can bear this if you can, Sonya. I can be as brave as you are. You are my dearest friend. Only I don't want you to be unhappy."

Sonya does not reply. Nina feels a contraction of hurt in her chest. Sometimes, Sonya, marching ahead, does not seem to see Nina.

"What is going on out there? It is intolerable not to know. We have family scattered all over the city." Dr. Schneider, seated on a stool, presses his hands between his legs and sways back and forth, as if he were praying.

"So do we," says Chaim. "My wife's family. They own the distillery that's been on strike. I'm sure the hooligans have ripped through it."

"I have heard of rich Jews who kissed the Tsar's portrait on their knees," Dr. Schneider says. "They were beaten to death anyway."

"My workshop," says Chaim. "It could be right in the path of the pogromschiki." He shakes his head sorrowfully and sees in his mind's eye the corpses of his dead machines, wires pulled, treadles smashed, holes punctured in the walls by flying metal, and torn clothing, arms and legs strewn across the floor, linings ripped out of coats and jackets gutted like the insides of a cat. The wreck of his life's work.

"And my workers," says Alta, hands clasped, the arch of her eyebrows raised in worry. "What is happening to them? Oh dear God. I hope they are safe. It breaks my heart. You know," she says, bending over Mrs. Schneider, whose features seem carved into permanent misery. "Benjy's wife has arthritis. She cannot walk. Raya is pregnant with her eighth child. And little Alma, only fourteen years old and about to be married.

"Why do they do this to us?" Alta wails suddenly, her voice shockingly strong. "Let them plunder. Let them loot. We're used to that. But why do they shoot? Why do they kill? Where is their Christian God, this Christ about whom we are always being reproached?"

There is a melancholy silence in the room.

Alta draws her black shawl over her head.

A disembodied voice begins to drone. It is Dr. Schneider, reciting the Shema Yisrael. Alta's thin murmur joins his, and finally Chaim too mutters the prayer. The cellar echoes with mournful humming.

Nina listens. After a time, Sonya whispers, "What good is it to pray? Do you know what Marx says? Anti-Semitism is an error that will be corrected when society reaches socialist apotheosis. Do you think anyone here understands this?" Her words come out in bursts, as if she had trouble breathing. "Oh Nina, what am I doing here? I'm trapped. I should be out there. Fighting."

She turns her back to Nina and folds herself on her side, wrapping her skirt around her ankles.

The hours underground pass slowly. Unease settles over everyone like a coating of dust. There is nothing to do. No one has brought anything to pass the time, no playing cards, no books, nothing to do with one's hands, embroidery or knitting. Occasionally, Chaim moves a chess piece from the board on the wooden box. Dr. Schneider paces, and from time to time, after a glance at the chessboard, moves a piece. Mrs. Schneider's little girl sucks on her two middle fingers and rests her cheek on her mother's chest. She does not cry, which is strange. Her mother coughs, a timid cough, more like a whimper than a real cough. Alta wraps her black shawl around Mrs. Schneider's shoulders. Schloima plays worriedly with the hem of his mother's skirt. There are two large chamber pots under the stairs and the Lebedevs have considerately hung a sheet to provide a bit of privacy, "especially for the ladies." Once, Yudel, in his little boy urgency, pisses into the chamber pot, making a sound that, in the silence of the cellar, startles with its clarity and specificity. Now a faint odor of urine rises and mingles with the smell of rot.

No one talks. It reminds Nina of her visit to her grandfather's sickbed years ago, when no one mentioned the horror of the old man dying for fear of making it real. It is the same now. Silence keeps horror in check.

Dr. Schneider consults his watch from time to time. He announces that it is four in the afternoon and then seven o'clock at night. At nine Mrs. Lebedev comes down with a new tray. Vegetable soup and herring. Fresh water for the samovar. But no one is hungry and the news is very bad. The pogromschiki have ransacked all the Jewish-owned stores on the Prospekt. There is broken glass and blood all over that lovely, elegant street. They are going into the houses too, looting and clubbing old people, women, and children. Fires burn hungrily in the alleys of the Jewish section. Mrs. Schneider begins to weep.

Mrs. Lebedev continues rapidly as if she feels the need to unburden herself of so many horrors. "Natasha, our governess, went out into the street and what she saw terrified even her, although I suspect she is no friend to Jews. Boys, little fellows not more than fourteen, carrying sticks and clubs like weapons, throwing stones through the windows of Jewish shops, grinning with excitement, and right behind them the hooligans, so drunk, many couldn't stand up by themselves, laughing and shouting, "Beat the Jews and the Democrats." And the horrible old women, already out on the streets, picking up what the hooligans haven't been able to stuff into their leather bags. Natasha saw one with three pairs of old shoes tied around her neck. You wouldn't think there were so many old hags in Yekat."

Mrs. Lebedev sighs as she pours hot water into the samovar. "They are spreading the usual rumors," she continues. "They say this pogrom is to prevent the Jews from murdering the monks at the monastery. Who puts these horrors into people's heads?" She hands Yudel a slice of thick bread and butter. Yudel tears into the bread with the side of his mouth.

"As usual, the authorities are behind this," Dr. Schneider says in a loud voice that has lost its amiable tone. "As soon as anything goes wrong, a war, strikes, a minister is assassinated, it's a signal for the police, the Cossacks, and the Black Hundreds to turn on the Jews. It keeps the people's minds occupied."

"The international socialist movement is the only answer," Sonya says from her dark corner. Her voice is blunt and reverberates loudly against the stone walls.

"Maybe. But in the meantime," Dr. Schneider wheels around to face Sonya who is hunched over her knees in the dusty light of the kerosene lamp, "it is because of you radicals that we are here today."

"That is not true." The light from the lamp glitters against Sonya's glasses. "We are the excuse, not the cause of these troubles." With her jaw thrust forward and clenched fists she looks fierce to Nina, defiant, heroic. "Besides you cannot stop the march of history. Dialectics tell us that."

"We should not squabble over politics," says Chaim, a melancholy cast to his voice. "We are really all in agreement."

"Not so," says Dr. Schneider. "I do not agree with this young lady. The Tsar has initiated a number of important democratic reforms in this manifesto. Things will get better slowly, slowly. That's my motto. Little by little. But this young lady wants a revolution." Dr. Schneider glowers at Sonya crouched in her corner.

"Then you are a foolish, nearsighted man," says Sonya, her fists digging into her sides. "And you will be swept away when the revolution comes."

"Oh," says Dr. Schneider. "How dare you, young lady. You see how she only proves my point." He turns to Chaim who is chewing nervously on his mustache.

"Stop. You must not fight," says Chaim. "Please, Sonya, please."

Nina would like to put her hands over her ears. Raised voices make her want to cry. She can feel her chest rise and fall with anxiety. How can she be a revolutionary when even the slightest disagreement makes her unhappy?

Mrs. Lebedev says to Alta, "I will bring you some more bedding."

"Thank you. We are very grateful to you." Alta's voice trails off. She is exhausted. Not enough sleep for days, and now the strain of keeping terror at bay. She feels this as a responsibility toward everyone in the cellar. "You are so kind."

"Please," says Mrs. Lebedev. "I will also bring a wash basin for the children."

Nina wonders if she is included among the children. Her hands feel crusty with dirt, but she will not wash if Sonya doesn't. That is the least she can do to show solidarity.

Yudel curls up on a blanket on the Persian carpet and immediately falls asleep.

"Ninotchka," says Alta. "Come. Lie here next to your brother." She pats a space on the worn carpet.

Nina throws a quick glance at Sonya whose face is still averted and whose back, even with her knees pressed to her chest, is straight as a chalkboard. "I am not at all sleepy, Mother. How can one sleep in a place where it is impossible to tell day from night. And please," her words stream out like water from a pump that has just been primed, "do not tell me that tomorrow is another day and that I must prepare for school and get up early and brush my teeth and have my clothes ready and do my homework because we are in the cellar of some professor's house for I don't know how long and there is no toilet here and no water and out there on the streets they are killing Jews every minute so what does it matter if I sleep or not." She catches her breath. Sonya rolls around and looks at her friend as if from a great and amused distance.

Chaim says, "Ninotchka, what has come over you? Talking to your mother like that." Alta's face has lost some of its color, but she is silent.

"Nothing," Nina says. "Only I hate it here."

She shrinks into the space next to Sonya. She wants desperately to urinate. Alta, whose face has gone as stony as the edge of a cliff, moves to the back of the room where she begins to coax sugar water from a spoon into Mrs. Schneider's little girl.

"There is the problem of the natural functions," says Dr. Schneider as if he had read Nina's mind. "As a physician, I must tell you that it is not healthy to keep a full bladder. Not relieving yourself can cause severe damage to the kidneys as well as much discomfort. We cannot now be overly modest. Fortunately, the Lebedevs have provided two large chamber pots and an extra pail. That should do for all of us."

Nina giggles. Sonya, for the first time since they entered the cellar, laughs too. "What a pompous ass," she says.

The men use the chamber pot first and after them Sonya, who strides in her determined fashion and makes many rustling noises from behind the sheet. Mrs. Schneider leans on her husband's arm. She appears almost too weak to walk. Dr. Schneider pulls the sheet over her and stands aside averting his eyes modestly. Then it is Nina's turn and she is very glad, although it is a mortifying experience, in front of strangers, making that unavoidable and very particular noise. Still, when it is over, she feels remarkably better. Only Alta does not move from her chair. "I am all right," Alta says when her husband questions her with raised eyebrows.

"Come, Nina, lie down next to me," says Sonya. "We will keep each other warm." Sonya steps out of her maroon serge skirt and spreads it on the floor. Nina watches. How fearless her friend is and yet how practical. Still, Sonya's white cotton shift under her shirtwaist is badly soiled along the hem and Nina wonders, just in passing, when it was last washed.

The night passes. Nina dozes and wakes, startled by an invisible presence as if the demon of fear had lodged himself beside her. There is always a grown-up awake in the dusty light of the kerosene lamp. Her father, his back against the wall, legs stretched out and crossed at the ankles, smiles at her whenever she looks up. Her mother dozes, her head falling heavily on her chest. She too seems to sense when Nina wakens and nods sleepily at her daughter. Once a watery noise breaks through Nina's sleep. When she opens her eyes, her mother is not in her usual place and the sheet over the staircase has billowed out to cover someone's ample skirt.

At some point in the night Sonya whispers in a strangled voice, "Nina, I can't breathe."

"What?"

"I can't breathe. This place, it's like a tomb. I'm suffocating." Sonya sits up. "There's no air here. I must have air. Nina, help me."

Nina, baffled and frightened, reaches for her friend's hand. "What can I do?" Sonya's hand is damp. She clutches Nina's fingers.

"Help me get out."

"I can't."

"Oh," Sonya groans, and drops Nina's hand.

Nina wraps her arm around Sonya's shoulders.

She says, with Alta's voice in her head, "It will be better in the morning. The morning makes everything better."

"There is no morning here."

"Lie down, Niunia," Nina murmurs. "Here take my pillow. Put it under your head. I'll hold your hand." And gently she coaxes Sonya to the ground. In the dim light of the cellar, she can barely make out her friend's features but she places her hand on Sonya's forehead, as she has seen and felt her mother do countless times. Sonya's forehead is wet, strands of moist hair cling to the skin. Her breathing is fast and shallow.

"There, there," Nina murmurs. And for a moment, she is calm watching over Sonya, calmer than she has been since she came into the cellar, as if Alta, the caretaker, had taken hold of her body. Sonya's little mouth, usually so stern and straight, trembles and a soft whimper passes her lips. "There, there," Nina says again and stretches out beside her friend. The two young women lie, side by side, clutching hands.

But the calm feeling does not last. Terror creeps in as Nina listens to Sonya's uneven breathing. Overhead, the crosshatch of pipes creates menacing patterns in the semidarkness. The air is thick with the pungent odor that humans give off in a confined space. Sonya will be herself in the morning, Nina thinks. Sonya is always brave. She turns her onto her side. Through half-closed lids she searches for her mother's shape and seeing Alta hunched over, her head bobbing with sleep, feels a wave of comfort such as she felt when, waking as a child from a nightmare, she remembered that her parents were asleep in the next room. "There, there," she repeats as much to herself as to Sonya and then, curled on her side, hands between her knees, falls asleep, like a child.

When she awakes, it is to the sound of someone coming down the stairs. Mrs. Lebedev in her morning dress carries a tray with pickled watermelon and bread and butter. And a basin with a pitcher of water. Her blond hair is tacked up carelessly and the skin around her eyes is puckered and discolored as if she had not slept much. Professor Lebedev stands at the head of the stairs, a crimson silk robe tied around his ample waist and an embroidered fez tacking on his head.

Sonya is sitting up, her back against the wall. She looks haggard without her glasses. Her thin face seems to have acquired sharper planes and angles during the night. Nina scrambles to her feet. Disoriented and confused, she steadies herself with one hand against the damp wall. The cold wet stone jars her awake. Sonya reaches for her glasses. Sonya's skirt, on which both girls have slept, is so creased it no longer hangs properly around her waist, but Sonya does not seem to notice.

She walks to the table where Mrs. Lebedev is setting up the breakfast tray. "I cannot stay here any longer," she says, "I must leave."

"You can't leave now," says Mrs. Lebedev, as she arranges the bread on a plate. "All night I heard windows being shattered. Screams too. They're hurling rocks at everything they think belongs to a Jew."

"I am not a Jew," Sonya says in a low voice. She is standing very close to Mrs. Lebedev. "I stopped being a Jew years ago. I am a Socialist."

In the stillness of the cellar, everyone has heard Sonya. Alta draws Yudel, sleepy-eyed and confused, between the folds of her skirt and covers his ears with her hands. "Don't listen," she says.

"Then perhaps you do not belong here." Mrs. Lebedev's voice is soft, measured and very firm, like a schoolteacher's. She pours the hot water into the samovar.

"You're right. I do not. I do not." Sonya leans against the table. "I must leave." Her glance skims off the faces of the others, past Nina whose eyes are dark with desolation.

"You can't go," Nina says. "It's too dangerous. Please don't go."

Dr. Schneider slips on the waistcoat he must have removed the night before. "The child is right," he says. "And besides you may be putting us all in danger."

Sonya whirls around. "How will I put you in danger? Do you think I will run straight into the arms of those hooligans and tell them that there are Jews hiding in the professor's cellar. What a base thought, Dr. Schneider." Dr. Schneider opens and shuts his mouth, a fish in a crowded aquarium.

"Sonya, please be calm," Chaim ventures, from one of the dark corners of the cellar. He gets up slowly, as if he had acquired old bones overnight. "We are all in a state of nerves."

"But I have work to do."

"What work can you possibly do in the middle of a pogrom? And besides," he says. "I am responsible for you, my dear, I cannot let you harm yourself."

Sonya turns at the sound of Chaim's voice. The bright, hard glare of her eyes softens behind her little spectacles. She leans toward him and her voice lowers to an intense, private pitch.

"This may be the moment. Everywhere the edifice of our corrupt government is crumbling. Oh, Chaim Yudelovich, you of all people must understand how I feel."

Chaim looks sadly at Sonya. He shakes his head and his gaze drifts toward some indefinite place above Sonya's head.

"If there is going to be a revolution," Dr. Schneider continues in his loud, irritating voice, tugging at the points of his waistcoat, "it will not fail because you are not there. You flatter yourself if you think you are indispensable. I have read enough history to know that much."

Sonya looks at Chaim and it seems to Nina as if all the strength of her friend's anguish is concentrated in that look, but Chaim turns his head away.

"Oh," she says. "How can I make you see the truth?" Sonya clamps her hands across her mouth. She begins to weep. Spasms roil her thin shoulders. Mrs. Lebedev holds out a cup of tea.

"Talk to your friend," says Chaim to Nina, "Make her see reason."

Sonya leans her head against the rock wall. Nina places a tentative hand on Sonya's back. She can feel the protrusions that are Sonya's vertebrae under her fingers. Wherever she touches Sonya, she has the impression of fragile, unprotected bones beneath the skin. It makes her want to cry too.

"Well," says Alta, "the children must eat." She walks to the table and hands Yudel and little Schloima a slice of watermelon on a thick china plate. Over the green arc of the melon, both boys look forlorn as if eating were a chore undertaken to please their parents, like using a toothbrush or practicing the violin.

Sonya has stopped crying. She lifts her head off the wall. Her eyes have a dry glazed look, but her shoulders are straight and the line of her jaw is firm, as if she has settled an argument with herself. "Now then," she says. "I'm sure the children would like to play a game. Who wants to play with me?"

"Come, Yudel," Sonya says sternly. "Let's play." Yudel, a slash of red juice across his upper lip, gives Sonya a belligerent stare. "Schloima too. Come, little one." Sonya nods her head at the younger boy, who having left his mother's side, now follows Yudel with adoring eyes.

"What shall we play?" Sonya asks. She sinks to the floor, her skirt forming a pillow around her.

"I don't want to play," says Yudel. "It's stupid. I want to go home."

"We mustn't think about home. We must think like soldiers." Sonya's voice sounds tired and falsely brave, like a teacher at the end of the day. "Don't you play with soldiers, Yudel?"

Yudel shrugs.

Suddenly Nina is annoyed. Irritation fills her mouth with the taste of dirty water. "You're so rude," she says to her brother. "Don't be like that." And then, by way of explanation to Sonya, whose shoulders sag and whose eyes have closed, "Yudel never plays with anything. Even his teacher complains that he's too lazy to play at games."

"That's not true," says Yudel. He screws his face up, lunges toward his sister and pinches her arm.

Nina yelps and flails her arms at Yudel who tumbles backward, tripping over Schloima's outstretched legs. The little boy screams in pain.

"Stop that," Sonya shouts. "Stop all this right now." She jumps up and shakes both fists at the children. "You are impossible. Impossible. How can anyone do anything with you? You fight all the time!"

Alta is suddenly beside Sonya. Her face is hard with rage. "What have you done to these children?" she says. "You stir everyone up. You make trouble. Look at these little ones, they're all in tears. My poor Nina, even she is crying. Yudel, stop kicking your sister. Dr. Schneider, please take your son away."

There are footsteps on the stairs. Professor Lebedev, now in a proper waistcoat and trousers, attends cautiously to his feet as he descends the creaking steps. The door to the cellar remains open behind him.

Sonya makes a dash toward him. "Professor," she says. "I am leaving now. Don't try to stop me." The professor looks amazed. His generous girth bars Sonya's flight up the stairs.

"Dearest Sonya," says Chaim, "You must not do this. Do not put your life in danger."

"Stop her. Stop her," says Mrs. Schneider, in her tinny, high-pitched voice.

"Enough. Enough," Sonya says, shaking her head. "I will go mad if I stay here a moment longer." The professor looks worried. His eyes roam the room as if he could intercept a signal from the others.

"Let her go," says Alta. "She is a dangerous woman. A selfish woman. A troublemaker. She has poisoned my daughter's mind."

"Mama," Nina says. Her limbs feel hollow and shaky. Her head throbs. "That is not true."

"Not true?" Alta clamps her hands to her chest. "Who gave you those leaflets I found under your bed? Who gave you that socialist propaganda? You'll be sent to Siberia. You, an innocent child!"

"How can we be sure she won't betray us?" asks Dr. Schneider. "She's a Socialist. She admitted it. She said herself she didn't care about the Jews."

"Oh," Sonya says, gripping the banister and facing with delirious eyes the broad, suddenly reddened countenance of Professor Lebedev. "You are all terrible people. Terrible people I trusted with my life!

Mean people, small-minded people. Oh, I cannot breathe the same air as you. I am suffocating."

"Lev Isaacovich," Chaim places a trembling hand on Dr. Schneider's arm. His face is as stern as Nina has ever seen it. "I have known Sonya for two years now. She is a good girl and a good worker. It demeans us all to think she would betray us to the pogromschiki or the authorities. Besides, she may be right, who knows? A revolution will be good for everyone."

Sonya releases a long, slow column of air as if she had been unable to let out the air in her lungs until then.

"Thank you, Chaim Yudelovich." There is a softness in her voice that creates a fleeting pain under Nina's ribs. "You are the only one who understands. The only one who can see beyond your narrow self-interest. Unlike him." Sonya points to Dr. Schneider. Her finger trembles. "You see, Ninotchka, your father believes, the way I do. True believers will change the world. I hope you will be one of us forever, Chaim Yudelovich."

"And me?" Nina says. "I understand also. I believe too."

There is anguish in her voice, but Sonya doesn't notice. Her eyes are glowing with new vision. "I have no interest in betraying anyone," she says. "That is an absurd and hateful assumption. There has been nothing but humiliation for me here. Please, Professor Lebedev, let me pass."

"Miss, do not do this," he says, in a sorrowful voice.

"Let me go, please."

"This is madness."

"I'm going," Sonya says. "You cannot stop me."

Frowning and shaking his head, Lebedev presses his back against the banister. Sonya rushes past him, arms outstretched, her skirt flapping around her legs like a sail that has just caught a fresh breeze.

"Stay here, Sonya," Nina cries and finds that tears are flowing down her cheeks. "Stay here with me."

Alta throws her arm around Nina's waist. Nina feels her mother's arm like the laces on a corset, intricate, binding, breath-denying. Sonya flies up the stairs and pushes open the door that the professor had left unlatched.

Nina strains toward the door but her mother holds her back. She drops her head to her chest. Alta turns her daughter around gently, places both hands on her cheeks, and lifts Nina's head.

"Mama," Nina cries, her voice small and childlike. "Mama."

"There, there," Alta says. "There, there."

XIX

THE CELLAR DOOR SWINGS OPEN.

"It is over." Professor Lebedev thumps down the stairs, one hand on the railing. "As I predicted. Three days exactly.

"Come now," he says, when no one in the cellar reacts to his announcement. "Come now. I will find some transportation for you. You can go home, Chaim Yudelovich. Lev Isaacovich, you can take your wife and children home. It is safe now."

"It is over?" Chaim lifts his head toward Lebedev. He has been sitting on a chair close to the wall, occasionally dropping his head against his chest and dozing. Now he blinks at the older man and makes an effort to focus his eyes. "Is it morning or night?"

"Noon," says the professor.

His broad, florid face reddens with the effort he makes to bend over Chaim. He places a large hand on his shoulder. "I know, I know," he says quietly. "It has been very hard. But, come, the worst is over. At least for now. The mayor has given the official signal. Anyone caught looting will be shot. A laughable order when you consider what has happened."

A tremor passes through Chaim. "Thank you," he says. "Thank you for your kindness. We will leave right now. We don't want to impose any longer than we have to."

"Nonsense, that is not what I meant at all. Take your time. Take all the time you need."

There is a rustle of skirts behind the two men. Alta rises from her chair. She totters toward Lebedev, then seems to fall. She braces herself on the table and lifts her head.

"Many thanks, Professor," she says and extends a shaky hand. "Many thanks."

Lebedev pulls his head into his shoulders, his white beard fanning out over his waistcoat.

"Not at all," he says. "Not at all."

Nina also rises from her place in the corner. She thinks of it as Sonya's corner, a wedge of damp wall in the darkest part of the cellar. She would never have chosen this spot for herself, it is too unpleasant to sit so close to the wall. But the discomfort connects her to her friend, a connection that is also a reproach. Swathed in cold and darkness, she imagined Sonya roaming the streets of Yekaterinoslav, head high, and hated her for loving the revolution more than she loved anything, more than she loved Nina. In the space where Sonya had been, a hard shell of resentment has been growing in Nina's heart.

Now relief floods through her. Fresh air, blue sky, maybe a bath, a change of clothes, and her own bed. She promises to be grateful for all those pleasures she took for granted once she is out of this hateful cellar. She shakes out her skirt, tucks her shirtwaist in. She pats the front of her braided hair. Her head itches. Since entering the cellar, she has not combed her hair and it is knotted and thick with dirt. She longs for a comb and a mirror. Her mouth feels clotted, as if dirt had penetrated there too.

Alta scrubs Yudel's face with a cloth she dips into the washbasin. Yudel does not wiggle or protest and it is the sight of her brother, usually so defiant, so resistant to cleanliness, that jolts Nina out of herself. Yudel has been so good, so quiet, so compliant since that first night in the cellar. What else will be different now? Chaim, as fastidious about his appearance as his daughter, is rumpled and dirty and gray. Alta's bun became undone hours, or was it days, ago? Now it hangs behind her in a braid as if she had just risen from bed and didn't care. There is something careless about her movements too, the half-hearted way she wipes Yudel's face with a towel and doesn't bother to smooth his hair. Please, Nina prays, let everything be the same as it was.

There is a bustle in the cellar now. The children are hastily dusted off, waistcoats adjusted, legs tested against the stone floor. But no one speaks. They are like travelers silently gathering their belongings after a long wait, relieved to be moving but apprehensive about the journey.

Outside in the fresh air and with daylight streaming into her face, Nina is light-headed. Putting one foot in front of the other seems perilous and strange. She tests the steps with the tips of her shoes and nearly topples over a cat that had been sunning himself on the warm stone. Alta, behind her, hangs on to Chaim's arm. Yudel, looking solemn, holds his father's free hand.

"Good-bye. God's blessing on you," says Mrs. Lebedev, from her perch on the stairs. Behind her, Dr. Schneider peers anxiously into the courtyard. Nina opens the gate. Alta disengages herself and jackknifes her body into the street. With a gasp, she draws back and throws her shawl over Yudel's head. Chaim presses the boy against him. Yudel, covered in his mother's black shawl, does not protest.

An open wagon fitted with wooden benches waits for them on the curb. The driver, a Ukrainian, in flat cap and sheepskin jacket, cracks the whip. Yudel, about to climb into the wagon, pulls the shawl off his head. Chaim lets out a warning cry, but it is too late. Yudel stares, his mouth open. The Prospekt is littered with torn and broken objects, clothing, skirts, shoes, kitchen utensils, furniture, shards of glass from smashed windows. Shutters dangle precariously from wooden beams. There are smears of blood along the walls, bloody puddles on the sidewalk. Among the looted storefronts, the Christian stores stand intact.

"Don't look," says Chaim as he pulls Yudel up.

The wagon clatters down the Prospekt. It runs over something foul, dark, and bloody on the cobblestones. Yudel leans over the side of the wagon and stares, wordlessly. The sound of the horses' shoes on the paving stones goes down Nina's spine like a long shiver. Why do they hate us so much, she thinks. I hate them too. I do.

The house on Karaim Street is intact. In the courtyard, in front of the exterior staircase that runs up to their apartment, the baker Natimzef emerges from his shop, slipping his good jacket over his flour-dusted arms.

"Chaim Yudelovich. We waited for news of you everyday."

"How was it here?" asks Chaim, his voice strained.

Natimzef shakes his head. He continues in Yiddish, not his language, but the one he uses to show his sympathy for the Jewish tenants of the building.

"They came one night with sticks and flaming torches. They were drunk. We said, Achourkof and I, there are no Jews living here. This is a good Christian house, we said. Russians and Ukrainians only. They shouted for a while. We gave them vodka and then they left. After that, we were afraid they would come back. But they didn't."

Chaim looks up. The balcony doors of the apartment are open, just as the family had left them. Innocent windows with nothing to hide. No Jews here. He smiles at Natimzef and shakes the baker's hand. Alta nods weakly.

Upstairs in the apartment, a cold wind from the open window has blown an empty vase off a table. It lies on its side like an outgrown toy. Otherwise, everything is the same. The gray horsehair sofa, the green velvet drapes, the woolen carpet. In the dining room, there is still bread on the table, rock-hard. What was left of the potato soup in the tureen is blotchy with mold. Napkins, dropped in haste, are puddles of white on the floor. They had been having lunch when Mrs. Lebedev appeared at the door, warning them that the rally for the October Manifesto was over and Jews were being beaten on the main square. Nina remembers how her breath felt like ice in her chest.

Alta rushes to the open windows. She slams them shut.

"Help me, Ninotchka. Quickly." Nina pulls the draperies, and the room, so harshly bright when she entered it, is shrouded in gray. Alta rushes from room to room, pulling curtains, locking shutters until the apartment is tightly sealed, like a cocoon. Nina follows her anxiously.

"Mama, it's like the cellar in here now. Why must we do this?"

Alta gives her a stricken look but does not answer. She takes her daughter's hand in hers and silently kisses it. Nina nestles her head on her mother's shoulder. She is taller than her mother now, and the position feels awkward, not comforting as it did when she was a little girl. Alta pats her daughter's cheek with a sigh.

"Mama," Nina says. "What are we going to do?"

"Come," says Alta. "Let's find your father."

Chaim is pacing through the rooms. He thumps the walls, examines the ceilings, peels off cracks of loose paint. He is looking for invisible damage as if the pogrom might have leaked noxious, treacherous substances into the walls.

"We must leave," says Alta. "We must leave immediately."

"Leave?" says Chaim. "What do you mean? We have only just arrived."

"We must leave Yekat before it is too late."

Alta's voice is firm.

Nina's heart leaps. Leave Yekaterinoslav? Could her life take such an unforeseen, unimaginable turn? Could they, she and Alta and Chaim and Yudel, could they have a different, blurred but tantalizing future somewhere other than Yekat? Paris, she thinks and she remembers Sasha. Why not?

Chaim says. "That is not such a simple thing to do."

"Why isn't it?" says Alta. "We will sell everything. The furnishings, the workshop, everything. It can all be sold."

"Alta, what are you thinking of? Where shall we go?"

"To Switzerland," says Alta in the same firm voice. "We will start over someplace safe."

Chaim does not respond. He chews his lip.

"The Rosovskys are in Switzerland," Alta says. "They have been urging us to visit them."

"Visiting is different from moving. Why give up a loaf of bread to go looking for crumbs? That is all we can hope for in another country. Crumbs and misery."

"We will be miserable here too," says Alta "More miserable. I cannot go through another pogrom. Next time we may not be so lucky."

"There is my workshop," says Chaim, sadly. "How I can leave it? How can you leave your workers, Alta? It is too hard."

Alta fingers the arm of a blue cloth jacket lying on the worktable. She straightens the fabric with the palm of her hand. The seam rips. "Look," she says. "This sleeve is not right. It will have to be done over."

"Benjy will take care of it," Chaim puts his hand over Alta's. "Don't worry."

Suddenly, Alta collapses on a wooden chair, her hands clasped in front of her.

"Do you know what Nina has in her suitcase and under her bed? Tracts, Socialist pamphlets. What if they come for her, she will die in Siberia."

"Alta, Alta, you exaggerate." Chaim looks at his daughter. "Let us think about this sensibly," he says.

"Why are they sending Nina to Siberia?" asks Yudel, who has crept on to his mother's lap and drapes his long limbs awkwardly over her knees. He blinks his eyes nervously several times. It is a tic he has developed since leaving the cellar.

"No one is sending me anywhere," says Nina. "It's just nonsense." But to leave Yekat for a new life, the thought brings heat to her face.

"I think I have a fever," she says.

"Dear God," says Alta pushing Yudel off her lap. She places the back of her hand on Nina's forehead. "Don't get sick now." Yudel squints and blinks his eyes.

That evening, after dinner, Alta takes up the subject again.

"The Aronofs want to leave. Mrs. Kellerman, too, with her children. Everybody wants to leave this place."

"How can you not want to save your daughter's life?" Alta, in her anxiety, overturns her glass of tea on the lace doily that covers the top of the table beside her.

"Mama," says Nina and rushes to mop up the spill with her handkerchief.

"It doesn't matter," Alta says. "What does it matter now?" The sadness of a lifetime of dusting and polishing are concentrated in her voice.

Chaim rests his elbows on his knees. His head is bent, the arch of his back signals misery.

Nina, a speculative expression on her face, looks at her mother. What is going on? There is a shift, a change in the air. Something has passed between her parents, some shared assumption, some vision of the future. Perhaps it is the same as hers.

"Your mother is not wrong," says Chaim. "We should leave."

THEY SELL THEIR FURNISHINGS. Moiche Friedman, Sasha's father, who owns a furniture store, buys most of the important pieces: the mahogany dining-room table, the chandelier with its brass arms and tinkling glass, the deep wool carpet, the glass-fronted cabinet. Alta's most cherished objects, twelve crystal glasses with saucers and handles in chiseled silver and the velvet draperies embroidered in satin that she made herself, go to Aunt Malie for a pittance. (Aunt Malie, affronted once again by her niece's willfulness, refuses to encourage the Schavranskis' departure.) The basket of artificial flowers the workers in Chaim's workshop had given Nina for her fifteenth birthday must be left behind as well as most of her books. (Nina dusts the little orphans reverentially as she stacks each one in a wooden box that will be given to Natimzef to dispose of.) But she will not abandon Moussia's copy of *Fathers and Sons* or *Le Père Goriot*, given to her by her French teacher as a good-bye present. Although she cannot read it yet, she thinks of it as a harbinger of her future life.

Only when the moving man straps her little spinet to his back do tears cloud Nina's vision. It too is going to Moiche Friedman. Alta is dry-eyed.

"Don't cry, my darling," she says. "God does not want us to be weighed down with possessions." But Nina knows that her mother does not mean what she says. Alta acquired with a sharp practiced eye all the objects Nina is suddenly sentimental about. Alta, so house-proud, how can she now be so proudly house poor? And Nina vows that she will never become attached to anything she cannot carry with her ever again.

"Come with me to say good-bye to Benjy and Moiche. I don't know what they will do without us," says Alta. And Nina is glad to have this excuse to leave the house.

Unfortunately, as soon as they have completed the sale of their house and everything in it, there is a general strike of the railroads, and Nina, her parents, and Yudel have to move into a hotel until the strike is over.

Chaim says a Jew rarely leaves home alone. In order to prove to himself that he is doing the right thing, he has to persuade others to join him. Chaim cannot decide if Alta has been persuaded or is the persuader. In the end, nineteen people leave Yekaterinoslav on the same train as the Schavranskis. Nineteen people and their bundles, because, of course, they have no suitcases or trunks, not because they are poor but because they have never traveled anywhere before. Nineteen people wrapped in all the clothing they can fit themselves into, layers of overskirts and jackets, shawls for the women, long coats for the men, the children bundled as if still in swaddling clothes, not to mention all the household goods. As soon as the strike is over, nineteen people board the first train out of Yekaterinoslav to Switzerland and to freedom.

XX

Late November 1905

NINA IN HER WINTER OVERCOAT, fur hat, warm gloves, sits by the
frost-covered window of a second-class railway carriage, looking out
at the flat desolate wintry landscape. She is happy. That is her secret. At the station in Yekaterinoslav, she and her mother wept in
each other's arms, Alta comforting Nina with whispered words and
closely held hugs. But once the train had barreled out of the station,
Nina was so excited that she threw her arms around her mother and
only just restrained herself from laughing out loud when she saw Alta's
still mournful face.

Now Nina notices the fields covered with ice, the long expanse of
gray sky, the occasional hut with a thatched roof and a lone, skinny
cow, a wisp of thin smoke issuing from the chimney, or a peasant
wrapped in a blanket crossing a field spotted with spikes of frozen
hay. It is all new and all wonderful. Nina has never left Yekaterinoslav
before. It is true that when she was little her parents took her to Smila,
where her Aunt Frume and Uncle Isaac lived with their children, but
that was a long time ago. Maybe that is Smila, Nina thinks as she
clears frost from the train window with the back of her glove and
sees in the distance the clustered houses of a small village without
the onion dome of a church. Maybe that is where the Giter Yid still
lives, the saintly old Jew who predicted that her mother would be

blessed with a second child. Does she remember the old, beak-nosed man with the white beard? Not really. She was only three then. Does it matter? Not really. She has heard the story so often that her heart swells with the mystery of connection as if it were a golden thread attaching her to her young parents.

The train lurches to a stop. Nina cranes her neck to see through the little patch of clear glass she has created in the window. There is nothing here but another expanse of flat, snow-covered land and in the distance a ribbon of dark trees. The train often stops like this, willfully it seems to her. Nina has never heard such noises as this train makes, clatters and squeaks, grinding of metal on metal, and the whistle that goes off whenever there is a bend in the tracks. Perhaps to scare off the cows or sheep who may be wandering across the tracks. It is hard to think, hard to know who you are when all your senses are being jolted, bounced around, loosening the brains in your head. And Nina wants to think. She feels she is embarked on a momentous journey and if this journey is as important as she thinks it is, then she must remember the past as well as imagine the future. Although she would not admit it to anyone, Nina has begun to think of herself as the heroine of a novel, the novel of her new life.

Many bad things have happened since the pogrom. Sonya has disappeared. No one knows where she is. Chaim made inquiries among the workers, but no one had anything to say. One young man, a student organizer from Kiev, said he had heard that she had left the country, that she was in Germany, helping to build up the party. Perhaps she has gone back to her husband. Perhaps she is doing good work somewhere, organizing the workers, promoting the revolution. Perhaps she is dead.

When Chaim reports this story to Nina and Alta, Alta said, "Good riddance."

"Be charitable," said Chaim.

"I reserve my charity for those who really need it."

And Nina does not defend Sonya. She feels a pain in the area just below her ribs, on the left where her heart is. Perhaps her heart is broken.

"Is Sonya still your best friend?" Yudel asks her one morning at breakfast, and Nina, who thinks her brother's question is sly and meant to tease, says, "Of course, she's my friend." But she thinks with some black satisfaction, as she slathers a piece of egg bread with chicken fat, that if Sonya ever came back to Yekat, she, Nina, would not be so foolish as to love her so completely again.

The landscape from the window of the train is monotonous. Another village of snow-covered huts. More frozen fields, frozen ponds, a sledge gliding across the fields behind a small dark horse. Telegraph poles slide past Nina's eyes. The frosted windows frame patches of white and foggy earth. The Steppes, flat and richly agricultural in the summer, stretch out mercilessly barren before her.

At Zhmerynka, all the passengers must change trains. The station house, a low wooden building with a towering water tank that supplies the steam engines, is crowded. There are men in uniform everywhere: policemen, soldiers, railway men, students dressed in military tunics. A railway man, in baggy trousers and black boots, his nose red from vodka and the cold, lowers the suitcases of a well-dressed couple on to the platform. The gentleman, having just stepped out of the blue first-class car, reaches into the pocket of his long fur coat and drops a coin into the railwayman's hand. But when Chaim signals to the railwayman, he turns away and mutters, "I'm not a porter. Carry your own bags." And so the Schavranskis and their friends must hoist their own bundles and baskets out of the windows and doors.

Nina surveys the platform without letting her gaze fix too closely on anyone. Some of the young students walking up and down the platform and casually smoking cigarettes are good-looking in their neat jackets and braided caps. Nina's eyes wander over their heads.

She is looking one last time, before leaving Russia, for Sonya in the crowd. A cap of red hair, a pair of eyeglasses on a pale, freckled face, a determined walk, and Nina's heart leaps up. But it is not Sonya, never Sonya, and after a while Nina gives up. A student doffs his cap as he passes her and she lowers her head with pleasure.

The station house gate is opened by a woman with a round, weather-beaten face, her head covered with a kerchief, felt boots on her feet, and a horn slung around her shoulder. Inside the building, there is a steaming samovar from which another old woman is pouring tea in mugs of dubious cleanliness.

Chaim accepts a cup of tea. Alta settles herself on a wooden bench next to Mrs. Aronof, who is eight months pregnant. Nina talks to one of the girls whose name she discovers is Nechama, and like her, is called Nina. Yudel draws a few marbles from a leather pouch in his pocket and displays their glistening beauty to Mrs. Kellerman's admiring boys.

The next train arrives a half hour later. There is another bustle of anxious preparation, another rounding-up of stray children. The bundles and baskets are now covered with a light dusting of snow since they were left outside the station house. No porter would move all this wretched stuff inside and in the end it does make it easier to load the train from the platform.

Mrs. Kellerman, a large woman with a round face furrowed with fat, is traveling with her two sons and her daughter.

"My Isaac should be here," she complains to Nina, who has heard the same lament many times since they left Yekaterinoslav together. "Why he had to stay in town and mind the stupid store I shall never know. Yekat is finished for Jews. In the meantime, who is going to help me with the children?"

"Please," Nina says. "I am here. I'll help."

Mrs. Kellerman nods absently. "Mendl, Lazar," she calls her sons, quiet creatures with dark, anxious eyes and ears that stick prominently out of their caps. "Go to Nina and stay with her. Now where is my daughter?" she says to no one in particular. "Have you seen Feiga? That impossible child."

The first bell has already rung. Now the second bell rings and there is only ten minutes left before the train leaves the station.

"She's probably on the train. I saw her with Mrs. Aronof," says Nina, watching Chaim, Alta, and Yudel disappear into the yellow second-class car. "Everyone is on board. We should hurry."

Mrs. Kellerman heaves a sigh as loud as the station woman's horn. Nina pushes the two boys up the steps behind their mother and into the train.

Mrs. Kellerman pokes her head into the first compartment.

"Is my Feiga with you?"

Mrs. Aronof looks blank.

"Alta Schavranski, is Feiga with you?" Alta, wide-eyed, shakes her head.

"Oh my God," says Mrs. Kellerman. "Where is Feiga? My Feiga. She's not here." She pushes past the railwayman and the surprised attendants, stumbles over the bundles in the hall. "Nina Chaimovna, this is your fault," she screams. "Let me off. Let me off this train." Her sons watch their mother totter off the train, their eyes round with terror. "Keep the boys," she shouts to Alta from the platform. "I must find Feiga. Oh my heart, my heart!"

The third bell rings. The gatekeeper blows her horn. The train pulls out of Zhmerynka. Mrs. Kellerman disappears into the station house in a flurry of snow.

Alta wraps her shawl around the two little boys. "How can a mother lose her own child?" she asks.

"It's my fault," says Nina. "I thought Feiga was on the train."

Alta looks at her daughter reproachfully, then turning to Yudel says, "You must never do that to me." Yudel, swathed in a long over-coat buttoned from top to toe, shrugs as if to say that getting lost would hardly be worth the effort. But his eyes keep blinking as the Zhmerynka station disappears from view.

Nina, guilt-stricken, chews on her fingernails, then reaches for the goose-down pillow, retrieved from the Lebedev's cellar and stuffed into her satchel with her other prized possessions, Moussia's copy of *Fathers and Sons* and her school copy of *Le Père Goriot*. She hugs the pillow tightly to her chest.

MIDNIGHT. PAD VOLOCHISK, Galicia, the frontier between Poland and Russia. A field of snow glistening with moonlight. A velvety sky studded with stars. In the distance a wooden house with a pointed roof and scalloped fretwork. The snow crackles under Nina's boots.

The travelers have changed trains again, this time because of the difference in gauges. Russian trains have the widest gauge in all of Europe, says the railwayman explaining the change at the Volochisk station. That way no one can invade us. But Chaim says it is idiotic and typically Russian to make life more difficult for everyone. Nina doesn't care. She is tired. They have been on one train or another for three days.

There is only one inn at Volochisk, hardly an inn at all but a large room in which peasants in felt boots and rich travelers in polished leather must share space. There are no accommodations for sleeping, although it is possible to obtain vodka or beer and of course tea for an outrageous sum. Here the barnyard smell of wet fur and dirty clothes mingles with the acrid odor of cigarettes. Wooden benches line the walls blackened with smoke from the single pot-bellied stove. There is only one gas lamp and it is barely enough to light the room. There is a constant stream of new, strange-looking arrivals, Polish soldiers in ragged uniforms, Jews in long black coats, their women wrapped in plaid shawls against the cold, sullen gypsy families with dark shy children, drunken peddlers, and an occasional lone traveler.

Nina sits on one of the benches, her back to the sooty wall. Yudel is beside her, nervously pouring marbles from one hand to the other. The clack of the marbles against each other annoys Nina.

"Stop that," she whispers. "You're making too much noise."

"I don't care," Yudel whispers back. "I don't like it here. You said the trip was going to be fun."

"Well, I was wrong."

"You don't think it's fun either?" Yudel seems disappointed.

"No. It's horrible. Horrible and boring." She remembers with shame her part in little Feiga's disappearance.

"I'm not scared though," says Yudel, not very convincingly.

"Well, of course not. There's nothing to be frightened of here," Nina says as she shoots an uneasy glance at the sinister shadows cast on the wall by the only gas lamp.

"Idelka," says Alta. "Are you warm enough? You mustn't catch cold." In the semi-darkness she looms in front of her children, carrying a fur rug under her arm. She tucks the rug around Yudel's legs, which he accepts with tranquil indifference. "You'll make sure he stays warm, Ninotchka, my darling," she says. Nina mumbles yes and sinks back against the sooty wall.

There is a soft buzz of voices. Occasionally, someone gets up and takes a lighted candle into another mysterious room. Then the voices stop and a dark silence settles over the travelers.

In the middle of the night, someone removes the iron bar that bolts the door shut. A group of new arrivals appears, shrugging and shivering and stamping off the snow. Among them, peering anxiously from under the brim of her fur hat, is Mrs. Kellerman. She holds a young girl by the hand.

Alta is the first to go to her. "Ah," she presses her warm cheek against Mrs. Kellerman's cold one. "You're here. What a relief."

"Can you believe it?" says Mrs. Kellerman. "This child was asleep behind a column. We could have left her there. What a horror! You must never ever do that again, Feiga."

Feiga, who is ten and whose nose is red from weeping and the cold, looks sullenly down at the puddle of snow at her feet.

"Come kiss Mrs. Kellerman," says Alta to Nina. "Nina was so upset. Look at her fingernails. She chewed them to the quick. Isn't that so, my darling?"

Nina, mortified, jams her hands into her pocket.

Mendl and Lazar cling into their mother's wide skirt. "We are very relieved you are here," says Chaim, in his measured way. "Now we can cross the frontier together. Tomorrow morning we shall be in Poland."

"Imagine!" says Alta, pressing her hands together. "Out of Russia. What happiness."

Yudel leans an elbow on Nina's shoulder. She squirms a little under the unaccustomed weight, although she is pleased. It's rare for Yudel to make a gesture of affection. He continues with a grin, "When we cross the frontier, I think we should all shout hooray and kiss each other and slap each other on the back and jump up and down."

"Now, Idelka," says Chaim. "As a Jew, you must remember not to call too much attention to yourself when you travel."

"Why? We'll be in Poland where nobody cares what you do!"

Surprisingly, Nina agrees with her brother. She pulls Yudel's cap down over his ears and plants a wet kiss on his nose. Yudel, for once, does not blink.

NINA'S NECK HURTS FROM sleeping upright all night at the inn at Volochisk. The jarring motion of the train sends sharp pains up her spine. Soot spews through the top of the window, which has been left open at Mrs. Kellerman's instructions. Mrs. Kellerman believes, and it is probably true, that the air in the train is unhealthy, carrying with it miasmas that will kill them all, but especially the children. So the window has been open all day and Nina is covered, hands, face, and the front of her coat, with flecks of black. She looks out of the window and sees, not far from the tracks, a cluster of wooden houses, leafless trees circling a low wooden building, roads rutted with ice and mud. A village, she thinks. Perhaps we are going to stop. That is a good sign, because when the train stops in a village, the villagers come out with cheese and bread or dumplings and sometimes milk from a cow or a goat to sell to the passengers. Although Alta remains suspicious of these vendors, Chaim always buys bread and sometimes a salami from them. He says these people are poor and need the money as much as he needs to eat. It is a transaction that profits them both.

The train grinds to a halt. The peasants are there, a woman wrapped in a shawl and two men wearing leggings and wide jackets. Chaim signals to the woman. She lifts her basket to the window and pulls away a piece of cloth to reveal a small, round bread with a dark crust. The woman smiles, she is young, her eyes are sharp and lively, but she has only two teeth in her mouth and her swollen hands are encrusted with dirt. Nina, who is as fastidious as her mother, shakes her head. But Chaim stretches his arm, drops a coin into the woman's basket and picks up the bread, carefully using only his thumb and third finger.

"Come, come, Ninotchka," says Chaim. "Don't be difficult. Your mother will cut you a piece of cheese and you can have some bread. Not a bad breakfast."

"She is dirty," Nina says. "Her hands are filthy." She mimics a shiver.

Chaim wipes the bread with his handkerchief. "There," he says. "Clean as your mother's best egg bread."

"Chaim," says Alta. "It is Friday."

"I know. We must talk to the others."

"I don't think we should postpone our journey," Alta says. Her jaw is set in that straight stubborn line that Nina knows so well. Two depressions like furrows in a newly plowed field appear between her eyebrows. "We cannot afford to stop."

"Let me see what the others want." Chaim dusts off his black jacket with the back of his hand. He steps over the bundles that are piled one on top of the other in the small area beneath their feet. Yudel lifts his head. He has been sleeping on one of the bundles, covered with Alta's fur rug. Chaim picks his way through the aisle.

"Mama," Nina worries. "How are we going to celebrate the Sabbath on the train?"

"God will forgive us," says Alta with a sigh. "In our position, we cannot afford to be good Jews."

Nina is silent. If her mother, so pious, so good, can dismiss a sacred obligation, then, very occasionally of course, can there be something greater, more urgent than service to God? The idea, frightening and exhilarating, makes Nina want to wrap her arms around her mother, to thank her for this unexpected gift.

Now there are hills instead of the flat dismal fields, sturdy wooden houses instead of huts, the spires of a church, a different landscape, another country. This is Poland, not the Russian Empire, and even the trees look different. Nina finds it all so interesting.

Chaim comes back. He looks relieved.

"They are all in agreement," he says. "We should not get off the train. Soon we shall be in Vienna. We will pray there in the proper way."

Alta nods. She removes her hat and rests her head against the wooden back of the seat. She closes her eyes. Wisps of graying hair spill out from the bun in the back of her neck. The skin under her eyes is dark, as lined as a piece of rumpled silk. Nina thinks she looks old. This is a shock. When has her mother become so fragile? Nina turns her head away. Everything is different, she thinks, as she surveys the wooded hills. Am I different? The thought makes her smile, a shiver of pleasure dances up her arm. Who will she be when she gets to her new life?

At two in the afternoon, the train pulls into Lvov. There will be a wait at the Lvov station as the train takes on water for the engine. Three men board the train. They are dressed in long black coats that graze the ground, black hats edged with brown fur. They have long beards and ringlets around their ears. They are speaking loudly to each other in Yiddish.

Nina cranes her neck to see them better. Of course, she knows what they are. She has heard about such people from the Polish soldier, Goldstein. Jews from Poland, very pious. Even more pious than the Giter Yid and his followers. To her, these men look like fancy-dress puppets and she dislikes them immediately. In Yekaterinoslav, Jews do not dress in this foolish fashion. In Yekaterinoslav, it is important, here she catches her own thought, it *was* important to appear to be like everyone else. Except on the Sabbath and holidays, of course. Then Chaim wore his yarmulka and Alta covered her head. And Alta doesn't wear a wig, either. Never has, to Aunt Malie's horror. But then Alta's behavior has always horrified Aunt Malie. Alta even reads Hebrew like a man. My mother is a modern woman, Nina thinks with a jolt of pride. Yes, that's it, that's what we are, modern Jews. She sits a little straighter on the wooden bench and strains to hear the conversation.

"What are they doing here? What do they want?" she asks Alta. Alta shrugs. "I have heard," says Mrs. Kellerman, "that they get on the train when it stops and go looking for Jews. Then they take them by force to their villages. They are like the pogromschiki, only in reverse."

Alta frowns.

There is a commotion at the other end of the car. The men in black clothing are waving their arms, beards nodding, hats bobbing. A short, balding man in his early thirties, Leon Bolin, one of the traveling party, is talking to them. He looks perplexed and then irritated. He signals his helplessness to Chaim. Chaim with his erect bearing, refined good looks and well-tailored suit, is an impressive figure, even here. Besides, Chaim has some experience talking with people beyond his family and friends. He was, after all, asked to represent his employees at the union meetings during the strike. It is natural, thinks Nina, as she watches Chaim make his way to the back of the car, that he should be called on to represent this traveling party as well.

Chaim nods solemnly as he passes the others and makes a calming gesture with the flat of his hand.

"What is the matter?" he says to Bolin. He leans one hand against the compartment door to steady himself.

"They want us to get off the train. They say we are bad Jews."

An older man, beard reaching to the middle of his chest, eyebrows protruding like ledges, says in Polish Yiddish, "You must come with us. You can spend the Sabbath in our village. It is not far from Cracow. There is room for all of you. Sunday you can resume your trip."

"Thank you," says Chaim, in his mildest voice. "But we cannot. We are on our way to Switzerland and we must stay on this train."

The older man spits through his teeth. His eyes narrow behind his spectacles.

"You defy the Law? What are you? Heathens? Soulless pagans?"

The old man's voice is strong and loud. He is used to making pronouncements, and now he has cursed the travelers. Leon Bolin's voice quakes. "We will pray here, on the train, rabbi. We will light candles, won't we?" he says, turning his pale face to Chaim. A sudden and unexpected lurch of the train makes him stumble and he grabs Chaim's arm.

"That is impossible," says the old man. "You must pray in the synagogue, in a consecrated place. Not this filthy train."

"We are good Jews," says Chaim, disengaging himself from Bolin's hand. "We obey the Torah. But we have no money. We cannot pay you for your hospitality and we aren't beggars."

"Are you too proud to be good? Too proud to observe the Sabbath as it should be?" A younger man's voice quivers with rage. "It is too bad the pogroms didn't exterminate such bad Jews. You don't deserve to live."

A chorus of gasps is heard from the women. Alta makes a protective gesture toward Yudel. Yudel blinks.

"That is enough," Chaim says sternly. "Please leave us alone."

"God will not leave you alone," says the older man. "He will punish you for your bad behavior."

"We are not behaving badly," says Chaim, his voice rising now, too. "We are travelers."

"You are no better than animals," says the old man. He turns his back to Chaim. His followers also turn around. They pull up the collars of their black coats. Nina notices that they all wear leather straps around their left wrists. One of the younger men suddenly turns and shakes his fist at the group. The old man mutters something Nina cannot hear. A curse, she thinks and she sinks her chin deep into the goose-down pillow she has been hugging for comfort.

The first warning bell rings.

"Stop, don't go," Mrs. Aronof says, her belly round as a watermelon. She staggers up from her seat. "I want to go with you," she says. "Take me with you."

"Malka, what are you saying?" Her husband grips her by the shoulders.

"The baby," says Mrs. Aronof. "The baby will be cursed. I must get off the train." She pushes her husband away and stumbles over the bundles that line the aisle. "My baby will die. I know it. Oh please, let me go with you." Mrs. Aronof exhibits amazing dexterity for someone in her condition. The strength of her desire propels her over the obstacles, the packages, the hands stretched out to block her passage. She sinks to her knees when she reaches Chaim and the old rabbi.

"Dear lady," says Chaim. "Please get up."

Her husband has caught up with her. He pulls her to her feet. The train is about to leave. The second bell has sounded.

One of the young men tugs at Mrs. Aronof's arm. "Good. Good. Come with us," he says.

"I forbid it," her husband yells. "Malka, you cannot leave me and the child." Mrs. Aronof turns around. Her face is ashen. Her brown eyes enormous and panic-stricken under eyebrows arched with fear. Her mouth is open. She fixes her husband with wild eyes. Then her gaze wanders from him to the figure of a small child who faces her from the arms of an older woman. His black eyes are pinpricks of terror.

"Dovid," says Mrs. Aronof and pulls away from the angry grip of the young Jew. She holds out her arms and the older woman lifts the child into Mrs. Aronof's embrace. The child begins to scream.

"Leave us," says Chaim to the Polish Jews. "Go!"

The third bell sounds. The rabbi and his followers, shoulders hunched, heads bowed under their wide-brimmed hats, step hurriedly off the train.

"Let me have the child," says Mr. Aronof, and Mrs. Aronof hands the screaming boy to her husband. She collapses on the edge of the bench and pulls her headscarf completely over her face. She weeps into her hands. The older woman, her mother-in-law, rubs her back and whispers comforting words Mrs. Aronof does not seem to hear.

A gray pall settles over the travelers. No one speaks. Mr. Aronof bounces his whimpering son against his chest.

"It is her condition," says his mother, leaning toward him. "It is her condition that makes her do such things."

Mr. Aronof sighs angrily. He does not look forgiving. He closes his eyes.

Leon Bolin follows Chaim to his seat. He is very pale and his chin quivers. Spittle forms at the corner of his mouth as he speaks.

"We need the blessing of the old man," says Bolin, "and all we have is his curse."

"If he were a truly good man, he would give us his blessing," says Chaim. "He would understand our position today."

"He said such terrible things," says Mrs. Kellerman. "I have never heard a rabbi say such terrible things to other Jews."

Alta fingers the fringe of her woolen shawl.

"I am a religious woman," she says. "But I do not believe God is angry with me. He knows I would rather be in synagogue tonight than here on this train. It is absurd to accuse us of such awful crimes." Her voice rises. Her words crash in the air like waves against a pier. "Haven't we suffered enough? We have done nothing. Yet we live in constant fear. Isn't it enough to be victims of the Tsar and his terrible policies? Do we have to endure such abuse from our own people?"

Alta looks about her with angry eyes. Chaim, for once, does not try to calm his wife.

"Do we need to prove that we are good Jews to anyone but God?" she asks.

Chaim, stricken, stares out of the window. Yudel huddles on his seat, his knees pulled up to his chest. The train pulls out of the station.

A mantle of distress descends on Nina's shoulders. It is not going to be so easy to be modern. Alta has her armor-like convictions to sustain her and Chaim is the voice of reason, but how is she, Nina, going to live in a world where it is possible to make so many different kinds of people angry?

It is almost night. The train passes not far from Cracow. In the streaming glow of the setting sun, the four-story houses seem elegant and imposing, the lights in the windows brilliant, the double spires of a church glimpsed in what must be the center of town, gracefully tall and slender. Nina imagines dining rooms not unlike the one she left behind, with mahogany sideboards, soft carpets under foot, parents and children living their lives in the quiet security of unchanged circumstances, blessed with lives of order and tranquility. But of course, these people are not Jews. They have not been hounded out of their country by the authorities and cursed for desecrating the Sabbath by their own people. Nina hugs her pillow and wishes she could close the window, in spite of Mrs. Kellerman.

In Vienna, the traveling party must change trains again. A bus, drawn by a team of powerful-looking horses, takes them all from the Sudbahnhof to the Westbahnhof. There is no time to see the city, but Nina, even in her groggy confusion, admires the elegant women crossing the street in their tight skirts and elaborate hats, arms linked, unaware of their good fortune. Although the stores are closed, the lights are on, blindingly bright, and the store windows display a variety of goods such as Nina has never seen before. Mannequins fully dressed in fashionable clothing, furniture gilded and overstuffed, vases, lamps, wallpaper, and bakeries and coffee shops. She thinks she would gladly stay here in Vienna. How can any place be better than this brightly lit city, so noisy, so elegant, so well-tended. She leans her head against the spotless glass of the bus window and dreams, not about the past, but about the future.

Paris

1906–1908

XXI

December 1905

NINA IS WALKING CHAIM TO HIS job at Mischa Krasnopolsky's tailoring establishment on the Boulevard Haussmann. The Schavranskis have been in Paris since the beginning of October after spending a year in Geneva. Chaim is fortunate to have found work as a cloth cutter with Krasnopolsky. It is a blustery morning. The wind whips through the bare trees, around the streetlights, into the alleys that open on to the broad Boulevard. Pedestrians, walking by at a brisk clip, tilt their collars up, clasp their overcoats tightly, pull their hats over their ears. Winter in Paris is not dramatic, not like Yekaterinoslav, with its snow-covered roofs and fur-covered population. In Yekat, you accepted the winter and prepared for it. In October you began to look forward to the sun-glistened snow, the icy blue sky, the dry cold that prickled your cheeks and turned them pink. You were eager to snuggle into your fur muff and your fur hat and drink hot tea after school. The winter in Paris is a sad, gray business. It doesn't snow and the sun barely shines. The wind is bitter and the air coming off the Seine is damp, penetrating. Nina has developed chilblains, and her skin is horribly cracked. At night, she rubs a mixture of glycerin and rosewater into her hands; she soaks her feet in warm water and wraps them in woolen rags heated on the coal-burning stove.

Chaim has just turned forty-two. He has not lost his distinctive looks, the delicate features, slender artistic hands. But he is stooped now and almost gaunt, his hair and his mustache are flecked with white. Work has strained his eyes. They wear an expression of perpetual bemusement. Nina is walking Chaim to work because Chaim does not speak French, and she and Alta are afraid he will get lost. Chaim does not object. In Yekaterinoslav, Alta insisted that a young workman walk with Chaim whenever he had to make deliveries to the far side of town. Then it was for fear that Chaim would be waylaid and beaten, a trespassing Jew. Of course this would not happen in Paris, but fear, like everything else, can become a habit and so it has for Alta and Chaim.

The Schavranskis were also fortunate to have found a small lodging on the rue du Grenier Saint-Lazare, a stub of a street linking the rue Saint-Martin with the rue Beaubourg, in a section of the Marais known to be hospitable to Jews. The Pletzl, as the Jewish immigrants call it, resembles nothing the Schavranskis have known in Yekaterinoslav or in Geneva. It is an area of condensed Jewish life, of immigrant artisans from Russia, Poland, Romania, from every part of the Pale of Settlement. It is an area of large pious families and small workshops, of clothworkers, capmakers, leathergoods workers, of pale, dutiful children with rheumy eyes. Chaim feels degraded in the Pletzl. He was, after all, one of the premier tailors in Yekat, and even in Geneva he served a clientele of Russian emigrés, ladies and gentlemen who had brought with them the sophistication of towns. He is not a shtetl Jew; he is a city man transported to a shtetl in the depth of a foreign country. So he feels his alienness as a double hardship: he is a foreigner in France and a displaced person in a neighborhood from which he aspires to leave as soon as he can.

Nina has so much less of a past to regret. She does sometimes think, in Yekat this or in Yekat that, but it is not necessarily because she yearns for Yekaterinoslav; rather, she is busy making comparisons and gathering impressions. She is constructing a life for herself in her head, and it is a life in which hardship and disappointment are temporary and the future is a large, open space.

Nina's French is far superior to her parents. The nine months they spent in Geneva have helped her achieve a workable command of the language. So she is Chaim's guide and translator. Alta stays home, cutting and sewing fabric for the contractor from the Galeries Lafayette, who employs immigrants in the Pletzl as homeworkers. She too feels the degradation of her position. Not that she minds the work; Alta has always worked, in Yekat, in Geneva, so why not in Paris? But it is degrading to be paid so little. And Alta, who would not support the strikers in Yekat, does not feel solidarity with the immigrants in the Pletzl either. She keeps her distance from the women who marvel at the array of meats in the kosher shops and bless the cold-water tap on the landing. Better than drawing water from a well, eh, Alta Schavranski? To which Alta only smiles and nods and thinks bitterly of the excellent plumbing she had in Yekat.

As for Yudel, he is enrolled in a Jewish school for boys on the rue Turgot. This school for immigrant children is run by the Alliance Universelle Israelite, and here, too, Alta feels shame, although Yudel does not. He simply does not want to go to school. He is ten years old. He does not want to learn Hebrew, does not want to hear Bible stories, is indifferent to the geography of the Holy Land, or the geography of France, for that matter. But he does like arithmetic. Numbers have a clarity that excites him; when he does his sums or solves one of those silly word problems involving the rate at which water drips out of a faucet, he can feel his mind hovering over the problem like a great bird with outstretched wings. The bird darts swiftly and unerringly for a fish in the water and hop! there's the answer to the problem. No one knows Yudel can do this because between the moment he knows the answer and the act of imparting the answer to others, there is so much indifference and boredom that he often neglects to mark the answer on his paper or to raise his hand.

Nina loves this walk with her father. The distance from the rue du Grenier Saint-Lazare to Krasnopolski's workshop is just long enough for father and daughter to chat companionably together. And to marvel, for it is still marvelous, at the opulence of the city and the freedom of the streets. Since the family's arrival at the Gard de l'Est, the Schavranskis have hardly left their neighborhood except to cross east toward the Grands Boulevards and perhaps a bit north toward Montmartre. Even so there is much to see: buildings that are routinely six stories high, so different from the two-story stucco houses of Yekaterinoslav, shops that are never empty of goods or customers, carriages open and closed that never cease to negotiate the broad avenues or the narrow streets, motorcars, bicycles, omnibuses with two decks, and people, so many people at all hours of the day, housewives in shawls, baskets resting against a hip, gentlemen in hats that they hold against the wind with a well-gloved hand, and ladies wrapped in fur, secretaries, shopgirls, schoolchildren, all these people and vehicles crossing the Boulevard Haussmann at once, it's a wonder someone doesn't get hurt, and some people must, the confusion is so great.

"Papa," says Nina, "Do you like it better here or in Geneva?"

Chaim shrugs. "We had many friends in Geneva. Your mother and I, we enjoyed their company," he says. "Aie, Ninotchka, I would have stayed there if I could have made a decent living. Paris is too big and noisy."

Nina considers this, and although she does not agree, as she thinks the noise and size of the city are among its chief attractions, she cannot help but fall in with her father's mood. It is an old and comforting habit. She squeezes his hand and says, "We had fun in Geneva, didn't we?"

"Well, you must have had fun. What was the name of that young man who wanted to marry you?"

"Nobody wanted to marry me, Papa."

"Come now, your mother told me about a young man who asked for your hand in marriage."

"Oh, Jacob, Jacob Tavrovski," Nina blushes under her hat. She is pleased and embarrassed that her father remembers. "He was very kind," she says.

"Oh yes, kind and ugly. Is that why you refused him?" Chaim smiles at his daughter, a twinkle of mischief in his usually sad eyes.

"I never got to refuse him. He asked Mama for permission . . ." Nina catches herself. It is hard to discuss love and marriage, let alone say the words, to the only man she truly loves.

"To declare himself?" says Chaim.

"It never occurred to me. Really. Mama was surprised, too. She said I was much too young."

"She was quite right," Chaim's voice is so filled with secret laughter that Nina has to frown.

"I didn't think it was funny," she says as she clutches the sides of her coat. The wind is fierce now, and she has to duck her head into it.

"Now, now," Chaim says. "Even if you are badly combed, you are the prettiest girl in the world."

Nina allows a small smile to form on her lips. Chaim's words are a secret signal between them. It is what he used to say when he brushed her hair as a child, when Alta, ailing, fretful, or distracted, could not take care of her. When Yudel was sick, when Raya's little boy had the mumps, when Benjy, the cloth cutter's mother died and Alta had to arrange the funeral, when Alta, overwhelmed by the claims of others, took to her bed, then Chaim would braid Nina's hair, tie her sash, and bring her to Alta's bedside to be kissed and petted before school.

When they reach Krasnopolski's establishment in the eighth arrondissement, Nina kisses her father and hands him the basket Alta has prepared for his lunch. Smoked tongue and pickled beets in a jar, and several slices of black bread from the baker on the rue Ferdinand Duval.

From the Boulevard Haussmann to the Passage Brady in the tenth arrondissement is a distance of about two kilometers. Nina must be at work on time. Mr. Etlin's shop opens at eight in the morning and does not close until eight at night, although there is a break between one and three. Mr. Etlin is the same corpulent complainer from Yekaterinoslav, the avid and impatient whist player who often dined at Alta's table. Not a nice man, according to the thirteen-year-old Nina, and yet now, in Paris, at fifteen, she works for Mr. Etlin in his card shop. There he sells cards of all sorts, views of Paris, birthday cards, anniversary cards, albums for mounting photographs and souvenirs of Paris, miniature Eiffel Towers and Arches of Triumph, models of Napoleon's tomb, of the obelisk on the Place de la Concorde, tiny reproductions of the enormous ferris wheel that was the hit of the exposition of 1900, though these no longer sell as well as they did. These articles are a specialty of the Jewish immigrants who produce them, not in the Pletzl, but in the small foundries of the thirteenth arrondissement. Nina is Mr. Etlin's assistant. She is happy to have the work at a salary of three francs a month. It is a pitiful salary and she knows it, yet she is grateful to be able to supplement the family income with some money of her own.

Mr. Etlin is a hard employer, not one for praise or encouragement. Sometimes Nina thinks he takes pleasure in making her life difficult. He so hated to listen to her little girl recitations of French poetry in Yekat.

It is Nina's job to make sales and to enter each transaction into a large black notebook. This she does with pleasure, amiably—at least she assumes the customers like her—and conscientiously. But what she likes best is to organize the cards and display them in ways she thinks of as tasteful and artistic. The cards are arranged in boxes on the counter or on a revolving stand. There are boxes for black and white cards, for cards in sepia and in color. Nina loves the views of Parisian life—horseracing at Longchamps, boaters on the lake in the Bois de Boulogne, the guignol in the Tuileries garden, crossing the Seine on the Pont Neuf, descending into a metro station with its decorative iron-work—all done in tiny dots of vivid color that look like nothing in nature. She loves the birthday cards with their treacly sentiments and pretty ladies surrounded by flying cherubs. It is all so lovely and so evocative of another life, not hers at the moment, but one that could be hers when she has a life of her own. She thinks how sweet it must feel to send a postcard. *Paris is a beautiful city. I wish you were here with me. I'll be back soon. I miss you.* But of course, one must have someone to send a postcard to and that Nina doesn't have.

Nina has become so familiar with Etlin's merchandise that she can recite the number of each card and the name of the publishing house that produces it. She is a walking catalog. Each card is sold for five centimes, and fifty centimes for a dozen. In between sales, she has plenty of time to dream.

Today, Etlin is waiting for her in the doorway to the small room behind the counter and he is angry.

"Well, miss. You're late."

"I'm sorry. I had to walk my father to work."

"I know all about that nonsense. It is time your father took care of himself. You and your mother baby him."

Nina wishes she had the courage to glare at Etlin. Instead she purses her lips and looks above the man's head at the old clock on the wall.

"Well, never mind that." Etlin wipes his hands on his faded black jacket. He has not changed much since Yekaterinoslav. He is still a short, pudgy man with pomaded hair and his shirt cuffs are still dirty. Only the bumps on his nose seem redder and angrier and the look in his eyes is shiftier. "I have something more important to say to you."

Etlin removes the black notebook in which all the transactions are recorded, from the shelf under the counter.

"See here," he points a large-jointed and greasy finger on the last column. "Read this."

Nina leans toward Etlin so that she can see the writing on the paper. Etlin smells of sweat and unwashed clothes. "Add up that right-hand column," he says. "What do you come up with?"

Nina dutifully, but apprehensively, adds up the figures. She is good at this. It is a skill she has just discovered and is proud of.

"Twelve francs," she says. "For yesterday, you made twelve francs."

"And where are those twelve francs, my little lady? When I counted the money last night there were only ten."

Nina feels a constriction in her chest.

"I write everything down," she says. "Then I put the money in the register."

"Well, it isn't there now, is it?" Etlin opens the cash register drawer and dribbles fifty centimes pieces through his fingers.

"Now you see how things are. And I had faith in you, little Miss Nina." Etlin slams the register drawer. The machine, bought secondhand at the flea market, shakes like an old woman. "But Osip Davidovich, sir," Nina says in Russian, the language she uses with all the adults in her life who are not members of her family. "Yesterday, I said we were missing two francs. I told you so." Tears prickle behind her eyelids. She wants very much not to cry in front of Mr. Etlin. "I can't imagine what happened. I suppose I was careless."

"You suppose," says Etlin. "I suppose also." There is a note of malicious pleasure behind the anger in his voice.

Nina takes out a handkerchief from the pocket of her skirt. Her nose has suddenly begun to run while the held-back tears stream down her cheeks. It is as if nose and eyes have made common cause to humiliate her.

"Well," Etlin says. "Let us see what happens today." And he turns away.

The day passes painfully. Every coin she drops into the register is a reminder of her ineptitude. She wonders whether she will ever be good at anything in her life. And to make things worse, she has given Mr. Etlin another reason not to like her.

At one o'clock Nina walks home to have lunch with her mother.

"I lost two francs of Mr. Etlin's money yesterday. I don't know how it happened. He was so angry."

"Two francs, that is a lot of money," says Alta as she spears a thin strip of boiled beef onto Nina's plate and covers it with cabbage soup. "Almost as much as you make in a month. It is hard to feel sorry for Etlin, but he must be very upset."

"Mama, I'm very upset. I'm the one who lost the money," Nina blows out a stream of air. "Etlin never liked me. Now he must really hate me."

"Etlin is a hard man. I never liked him in Yekat. Always grumbling. Always thinking only of himself. Selfish, very selfish." Alta clanks the soupspoon down on the wooden table. "Your father and I, we are not happy that you have to work for such an unpleasant man."

"Well, I'm not such a bargain as an employee, am I?"

"Two francs!" Alta shakes her head. "How did this happen?"

"I don't know. I don't know." Nina pushes away her plate. "Mama, I can't eat."

Alta claps her hands together and presses them prayerfully against her mouth.

"We will have to repay him."

"Yes."

"We are not so poor we can't do the honorable thing."

Alta walks to the only bedroom in the apartment and returns with a small brown leather purse. "Here," she says. "Give him five francs. That will teach him to be more generous."

All afternoon, as Nina talks to the customers, directs them to the newest cards, carefully enters each transaction into the register, she is aware of the five-franc piece in her pocket. It is like an amulet against Etlin's anger. She imagines dangling it in front of him like a bone before a dog, or better yet slamming it down on the counter at some crucial moment. But Etlin is calm this afternoon and does not once mention the incident.

It is eight o'clock and Mr. Etlin is putting up the "Closed" sign on the door. Nina takes a deep breath.

"Osip Davidovich," she says in as firm a voice as she can muster. "I would like . . ." she stammers as Etlin looks at her from under his matted eyebrows. "Here is five francs to make up for the money I lost."

"Well, " Etlin manages a thin smile. "So you would like me to give you change of five francs?"

"No. Keep the whole amount."

"Indeed? And just where did you get so much money, my rich young lady. Let me tell you something. I don't want your five francs, or your two francs for that matter. Because I never lost that money. But you almost lost your job. I watched you yesterday. When a client gave you two francs, you left them on the counter instead of putting them in the register. So I slipped the coins into my pocket and kept the money. Just to see what you would do. And you never noticed it. Here are your wandering two francs." He picks two one-franc pieces out of his pocket and rolls them on the counter. The money clatters in front of Nina. "That should be a lesson to you, Nina Chaimovna. I need someone I can trust with my establishment, not an absentminded dreamer."

"Oh," Nina says. Her heart beats with incredulous anger she can barely keep out of her voice. "Then I shall take my five francs back. I'm sure you will not miss them either." Etlin shoots her a sly look, full of sardonic amusement.

At dinner, Nina says, "And the worst part of this story is, that I saw Osip Davidovich put the money in his pocket, but I didn't dare say anything to him. I thought he must have a reason. And then this morning, when he accused me, I got so flustered I forgot what I had seen."

"What a heartless, awful man," says Alta. "Playing a joke like that on a child."

"I'm not a child, Mama. I'm a working woman."

Alta glares at Chaim across the table. "What do you think? I think she should quit after being so badly treated."

Chaim sighs. "If she is a working woman, then the decision must be hers."

Nina loves to hear her father talk like that. Everything about her, down to her bones, feels stronger when he does.

"No, I want to work. I will continue to work for Osip Davidovich Etlin and I will be the very best assistant he ever had. Even if he hates me for it."

Chaim tries to catch Alta's eye. He thinks his daughter reminds him of her, the fierce, prideful Alta who refused to set foot in her Aunt Malie's house, whose energy and determination kept them both from despairing during the hard, early years in Yekaterinoslav. He would like to share this moment of parental intimacy, because he admires Alta and it pleases him to see how like her Nina is turning out to be, but Alta is frowning at her hands, all her energy fused these days into worry, and he is suddenly saddened at the transformation in his wife.

XXII

Mid–February 1906

ON THE RUE MILTON, THERE IS a four-story building that houses what Nina thinks of as her point of escape from dreariness. The ground floor is given over to the offices of Maître Allard, solicitor, and to a tiny shop that sells writing implements. Nina lingers at the window of the closed shop on the evenings that she attends the language school for immigrant women, mostly Russian and Polish Jews, on the second floor. She admires but does not yearn for the elaborate penholders and display of nibs, the colored pencils, blotting paper, notebooks designed for practicing penmanship, "Methode d'écriture" printed on the covers. Nina's writing tools are simple, a plain wooden holder and a box of cheap nibs. She has a notebook, which she cherishes, a blotter, and a bottle of ink, sufficient to unlock the secrets of the language she is so eager to learn well.

It is eight thirty and Nina has walked from her home on the rue du Grenier Saint-Lazare, to the rue Milton a good half-hour walk in the dark. A freezing rain batters her umbrella. Water soaks through the tightly knotted scarf around her neck. She waits impatiently for the concierge to unlatch the gate. Next to her are two classmates, plump, matronly looking young women who speak Yiddish to each

other and pointedly exclude Nina from their conversation. They wear
headscarves over their coarse horsehair wigs. They have kept the old-
country habit of wrapping large plaid shawls over their coats. In contrast, Nina is fashionably dressed. Her mother makes her skirts and
her shirtwaists. Her father cuts and sews her jackets. Today, she wears
a navy blue woolen coat that was made for her in Geneva. She keeps
her hair, darker brown now that she is older, but still as shiny as young
hair can be, piled on top of her head like a lady, although she is only
sixteen. That is because she works in a store and must present herself as older than she is.

Nina and the two women cross the courtyard and climb the stairs
to the second floor. On the landing, a curtained glass door opens onto
a narrow foyer. There Nina hangs her dripping overcoat on a peg and
leans her umbrella against a wooden umbrella stand already full. She
shivers and rubs her hands together. The tips of her fingers are red
and itchy. She takes out a small bottle of glycerin and rosewater she
keeps in her satchel and rubs a few drops on her hands. She hopes
the cast-iron stove in the classroom has been lit. Often it is not. This
night school is a public establishment, as are most schools in Paris,
but it does not cater to rich students. And while the government will
provide education for the immigrants, it does not feel obliged to provide heat as well. Tonight, the classroom smells of wet wool and a
faint trace of garlic.

Nina carries her notebook and her pen in a leather satchel. She
loves the pale green notebook she has chosen for herself. There is
such a choice here in France, covers in dark or light colors, pages in
smooth or rough paper, lines in blue or red ink. She loves the thrill
of the empty page, the possibilities inherent in blank paper. What
will she write there, what will she learn?

Nina slips into one of the wooden desks, runs her hand lovingly
over a new page, dips her pen into the ink bottle and writes at the

top of the page in a spiky hand quite unlike the small even hand of her teacher Mademoiselle Laure Chambon, the date, 17 February 1906. She blots the date with the green blotting paper, already stained in many places since she practices her French spelling diligently at home as well as in school.

She is ready. She looks around the poorly lit room at her classmates. They are all women, mostly older than she, tired-looking, dispirited. Many of them, Nina knows, have never been to a real school before, and she regards them with pity. She, Nina, has had the benefit of a serious education in Yekaterinoslav, was, in fact admitted to the Russian High School for Girls under the Jewish quota of two percent, an honor and a personal triumph. Although she was never allowed to go. Alta and Chaim argued that she would be better off, safer, in a Jewish school. Had Yudel been a good student, would they have let him go, Nina sometimes wonders with a residue of bitterness. In any case, history disrupted her education. And now among these women who have not read the books she has read or been educated in socialism as she has, she feels superior and a bit lonely. In class, she gives her complete attention to her teacher, Mademoiselle Laure Chambon, who speaks such elegant French and declaims lines from Racine, which Nina doesn't always understand, as if she were the great Sarah Bernhardt herself.

Today, Nina is anxious. She must say something to Mademoiselle Chambon, which, Nina knows, will make her angry. There is a rustle of paper, a clatter of pens, a low murmur of voices in a range of tones that do not resemble the music of French.

Mademoiselle Chambon enters with a quick step. She is a young woman, not much more than twenty-five, certainly under thirty, with obedient dark hair parted in the middle and pulled back over her ears. To Nina, she looks very French. Her profile is sharp, her nose straight and long, her mouth pouty in that way that Nina associates with the ability to make those difficult French sounds.

No one but Nina, holding her pen as delicately as if she were holding butterfly wings, looks up as Mademoiselle Chambon in her starched shirtwaist and dark skirt mounts the platform in front of the rows of desks and writes the day's maxim on the board. Mademoiselle regularly copies the maxims from a leather-bound book she keeps open on her desk—"Laziness is the mother of all vices." "Time is money." "Clothes do not make the monk."—and asks the students to explain.

Nina mouths the words as they appear on the chalkboard. Her hand is always the first one up.

Of course, she knows more French than her classmates. And, as she pointed out to Mademoiselle on the first day of class, she has recited LaFontaine in French and Heine in German. She did not say that this was in a Jewish high school in a provincial Russian town, of fewer inhabitants than some Paris arrondissements. Still Mademoiselle smiled in an interested fashion, and after class she walked down the stairs with Nina and asked her pleasant questions about how long she had been in Paris and where she lived. Nina's heart sang. The following evening, when class was over, Nina packed her satchel slowly, giving Mademoiselle time to wipe the board and gather her papers. So that, quite by accident, she should find herself next to Mademoiselle as she locked the classroom door.

"How nice to meet a foreigner who knows something of our culture," said Mademoiselle, buttoning her cape and drawing on her gloves. "It does not happen very often here. Our pupils are quite ignorant, as you may have noticed."

Nina was flattered.

"In Russia, we often spoke French at home," Nina lied. After all, hadn't she recited French in front of all those people year after year and didn't that count? "And I have spent a year in Geneva."

"Geneva," sniffed Mademoiselle Chambon. "A pretty town but quite a backwater, don't you think?"

"Oh indeed," said Nina. "Very provincial."

The next time the class met, on a Thursday evening, Mademoiselle Laure smiled at Nina as the other students were filing out. They walked together along the Avenue Trudaine. Mademoiselle pointed out the prestigious Lycée Rollin for boys.

"That is where you should be, Mademoiselle Nina, if you want a good French education. Of course, you and I suffer from the same disadvantage. Even today, in our advanced country, it is harder for a woman to be well educated. And once she has an education, what can she do with it? Teach in a night school for foreigners!" Mademoiselle Laure tossed her head and, lifting the veil of her black hat, looked hard into Nina's eyes. "Well," she said. "I am glad to find someone who has an interest in French culture in this desert where I spend my days. Would you allow me to use you to sprinkle a little water on this arid life of mine?"

"What do you mean, Mademoiselle?"

"Take you under my wing. Introduce you to the best French minds. That would make me happy. Would you like that?" Mademoiselle's eyebrows formed a seductive, inquiring arch.

"Oh Mademoiselle, if you could, I would consider myself the luckiest girl in the world."

"Then it's decided." Mademoiselle cocked her head to one side without taking her eyes from Nina's. "If I had a sister, I would wish her to be like you." Nina blushed, but her fate was sealed. Mademoiselle would open all those tightly locked doors for her; the world that every French schoolchild took for granted. She and Mademoiselle would be like sisters, clear-eyed and knowledgeable. What a wonderful country, where it is possible for a woman to be well read, articulate, to have opinions that went beyond politics. She thought of Sonya for an instant with a flutter of remorse.

At the intersection of the Avenue Trudaine and the rue de Rochechouart, Mademoiselle Laure shook Nina's hand firmly and boarded a bus home.

Nina now had a special seat at a desk in the front row, which, she noticed, the other students left free. She suspected her classmates disliked her for being the teacher's pet, but she didn't care. Long tendrils of adoration connected her to Mademoiselle Laure, who gave her the poetry of Hugo and Lamartine to read, the plays of Corneille, whom Mademoiselle praised for the grandeur of his themes, and Racine, for his passion and plain language. Nothing contemporary, no Zola, a degenerate writer, no Anatole France, no Eugene Sue. Only the truly great, the classics, she said to Nina, and Nina dutifully deciphered Corneille's "Horace" word for word without making any sense of it. Mademoiselle also recommended Charles Péguy, whom she claimed was the finest Catholic poet who had ever lived, although he was a Dreyfusard.

"A what?" said Nina.

"Never mind," said Mademoiselle Chambon. "Péguy's politics are misguided, but his poetry is splendid."

Eventually Nina learned some things about Mademoiselle herself. She was from a village near Nancy, in that part of Lorraine that had not been annexed by Germany after the Franco-Prussian War. Her father was a schoolteacher, and she had two brothers, but no family at all in Paris. When Nina asked her why she had left Véselise, Mademoiselle shrugged. "A village can be such a nasty place. Everyone knows everything about everybody else," she said. "I felt the need for broader horizons."

"Oh yes," said Nina. "I do understand so completely."

One evening, Mademoiselle invited Nina to have coffee with her at the café on the intersection of the Avenue Trudaine and the rue de Dunkerque.

"I'm so sorry. I can't. I must get home or my parents will worry," Nina said.

"Of course," Mademoiselle brushed her gloved hand across Nina's forehead as if to push away a stray hair. "You are a sweet child and always such a good girl."

"But I will ask my mother. Perhaps she will give me permission if she knows in advance where I'll be."

"Next time, then, little sister," said Mademoiselle and her lips lingered delicately as she kissed Nina on both cheeks.

Alta objected violently to Nina's staying out at night with someone the family did not know.

"Let us meet her," said Chaim. "She sounds like a nice young woman. Bring her here."

But Nina did not want to bring Mademoiselle Laure Chambon, who could quote Corneille and Racine, who loved opera, "*le grand Monsieur Wagner*," in particular, to the shabby, barely furnished, dark and smelly two-room apartment on the rue du Grenier Saint-Lazare, in the Marais, a district with some of the oldest, most sordid, tumbledown houses of Paris, and by the way, not far from the rue des Rosiers, the unmistakably Jewish section of Paris. And from whose streets emanated an odor of boiled leather and rotting meat as if the butchers, tripe dealers, tanners, and skinners who lived and worked there in the Middle Ages had bequeathed the smell of their filthy occupations to the old walls for all eternity.

Last week, Mademoiselle lent Nina her copy of Edmond Rostand's play, *L'Aiglon*, bound in white leather with tissue-paper thin pages. Nina is still reading it. At home, after class, she sat at the kitchen table under the blue flame of the gas lamp and tried to make sense of the plot and the odd versification. It was peculiar. She felt as if she understood every word but could not discern the meaning of a sentence. The plot escaped her. She will not give up, however. Mademoiselle promised to take her to the same theater where Sarah Bernhardt once played Napoleon's unfortunate son. Now Bernhardt is taking Paris by storm in a play by Catulle-Mendès, in which she plays Saint Theresa. "A Jewish actress in a play about a Catholic saint! Imagine! What could be more quaint," said Mademoiselle. "Still, they say she is worth seeing."

"I am Jewish, too," said Nina, who wanted to say this to Mademoiselle for some time.

"Yes, my dear. I know that. But you are an intelligent creature. Not like your rather thick classmates. And unlike any other Jew I have known."

"Have you known many Jews?" Nina said, interested in the cross-over points between one world and the other.

"Not many, but some. In Lorraine, they were always the richest families and they kept to themselves."

"We are not rich," said Nina.

"I said you are not like the others." Mademoiselle let her hand glide hand down Nina's cheek. "I like you, Nina. And I promised to make you better than what you are, didn't I?"

Nina told Alta about Mademoiselle's offer.

"Very nice," said Alta. "But don't count on it. Why should this Mademoiselle be so good to you?"

"Oh Mama," said Nina. "You don't trust anyone. This is France. All kinds of people can make friends here. Just because you don't know any real French people doesn't mean that I shouldn't. And besides, Mademoiselle is an educated woman. You do want me to meet educated people, don't you?"

Alta dropped her chin into her chest. "Education isn't everything. Besides, I don't think your father would like you to go to the theater with someone we have never met."

"There's no talking to you, Mama. You don't understand."

What Alta does not understand is that Nina has, once again, fallen in love.

Today, Nina must tell Mademoiselle that she cannot go to the theater with her after all. Chaim, giving in to his wife's anxieties, has said no. It is a crushing disappointment. To give up seeing the divine Sarah (Mademoiselle has told her that is what Bernhardt is called) perform in her own theater, is like having a brilliant light flashed on something precious and unique just long enough to desire it—and then have it extinguished. She is in a fury at the injustice of it all. And yet she submits. She knows she would have to invite Mademoiselle Chambon to meet her parents at home to get their permission and that she cannot bring herself to do.

The anxiety of disappointing Mademoiselle prompts Nina to make a decision she will regret.

She gets up from her seat and mounts the platform on which Mademoiselle has her desk and her podium. Mademoiselle gives Nina a censoring look. This is a breach of etiquette, a bad beginning, Nina realizes.

"May I speak to you," Nina says softly. She lowers her head. "I would so much like to go with you to the theater. But my father says I can't."

"What is this?" says Mademoiselle, in an angry whisper, which, Nina is certain, can be heard by the students who sit passive and indifferent at their desks. Mademoiselle empties her briefcase on the table. A newspaper tumbles out and then a notebook, papers. She pushes the heap away roughly. "What does your father think I am going to do to you? Lead you into a life of depravity through the theater? Seduce you? Oh, the viciousness of people. Everywhere it is the same thing. Narrow-minded, stupid people. When will you get away from them, Nina? Do you want to be like your father?"

Nina flinches at this tirade. Mademoiselle should not be so angry. Mademoiselle should not attack her father.

"My father is not a vicious person, Mademoiselle. He comes from another country and he is not used to French ways."

"Yes, that is exactly what I mean. All you Jews are the same. Now I must start class." Mademoiselle picks up her chalk and writes the maxim she has prepared for today.

"Learn that every flatterer lives at the flattered listener's expense," she writes in her small round hand. "Jean de La Fontaine."

"Who can explain what this means?" says Mademoiselle.

There is the usual silence and Nina's hand, still hopeful, shoots up. Mademoiselle looks right past her.

"It's from 'The Fox and the Crow,' Mademoiselle. I learned it in school," Nina says breaking the heavy silence.

"Did you?" says Mademoiselle. She smiles at Nina, but her smile is pinched, unpleasant.

"I'm sure you could tell us exactly what La Fontaine meant, Mademoiselle Nina. But we must give the other students a chance to learn something, mustn't we? You cannot always be the star."

A pink flush floods Nina's face. She lowers her head. She breathes hard to hold back the tears she feels are beginning to seep at the corners of her eyes.

"Henriette, what do you think about what I've written on the board?"

Henriette, large and sluggish, lifts her head from the desk. She blinks away sleep.

"Well, can you read it at least?" Mademoiselle's voice has taken on that impatient edge she often uses with her students, but not with Nina—not ever with Nina.

Henriette squints at the board and shakes her head.

"Mademoiselle Etta," says Mademoiselle, her voice rising. "Please read what I have written."

Etta, a thin pale girl with wispy hair the color of weak tea, looks helplessly at Nina. But Nina focuses her attention on the blank notebook page before her. Etta attempts to read. She struggles with the French sounds. Her mouth contorts around the unaccustomed shapes.

"I do not have all day," says Mademoiselle. "It is not my job to teach you Yids how to read." She slams down the chalk. "I have never had such uneducated, lazy, good-for-nothing students. You should all go back where you came from. Stupid Yids," she mutters under her breath but loud enough for Nina to hear.

262 • MYRIAM CHAPMAN

Nina raises her head. Her eyes are dry. So it is always the same. The language may be different in Paris, but not the feeling behind the words. "Gidorka, Gidorka," she hears the boys call as she walks home from school. "Dirty Yid!" as twigs slash across her calves, pebbles rain on her head and shoulders. She breaks into a run, her heart pounding against her ribs, her book bag held high over her head for protection.

At the end of class, Nina walks right by Mademoiselle Laure's desk. She will not wait for her today or ever. She has peered into Mademoiselle's soul and seen a familiar and unforgivable ugliness. Mademoiselle is still at her desk, her fists clenched on the table, her tight part so straight and neat, bowed over an open newspaper. Nina catches the name of the paper, *La Libre Parole*, out of the corner of her eye. She thinks, what a nice name for a newspaper, "Free Speech." And then her eye trails down to the blazing headline "The traitor Dreyfus pardoned by President Loubet. Jew to receive the Legion of Honor." And, even in her misery and confusion, she thinks, Dreyfus, where have I heard that name?

XXIII

April 1906

THE PARLOR OF THE Schavranskis' new apartment on the rue de Montholon is an improvement over the lodgings on the rue du Grenier Saint-Lazare. There are three small rooms opening into each other, a cold water faucet in the kitchen unlike the apartment on the rue du Grenier Saint-Lazare, which had a tap on the landing. And there is talk of gas coming soon for cooking and lighting, although Alta hopes they will be gone long before any modern conveniences are installed. Equally important, it is in a neighborhood much less exclusively Jewish, more working class, more, as Nina puts it to herself, French.

Nina sits on the sofa, her hands folded on her lap, an open schoolbook covering her hands. Sasha Friedman sits next to her. His legs are crossed at the knees, one arm is draped across the back of the sofa, one hand dangling just close enough to touch Nina's shoulder. With his other hand he is pointing to a page in the book.

Sasha Friedman is in Paris! He is nineteen years old now, a tall young man with a small head that never seems to sit comfortably on his long neck and slender frame. He resembles, Nina sometimes thinks uncharitably, one of those sea birds she has seen in books with darting heads and skinny legs. But she also thinks he is handsome. He has abundant black hair, a small nose, a kind, childlike smile, and dimples that appear when he smiles. He never finished at the university in Kiev and now he works in his uncle Friedman's shop where Chaim works too, not as a cloth cutter as he did for Krasnopolsky, but appropriately as a tailor. Moiche Friedman, Sasha's father, left Yekaterinoslav soon after he bought the Schavranskis' furniture and joined his wife and daughters in America. Sasha, to his father's dismay, chose to stay in France where he said the political climate was ripe for change. Sasha considers himself an anarchist.

"Show me where Devil's Island is," Nina says and Sasha thumbs through the pages of Yudel's geography book, where the maps are printed in colors so pale it is as if the printer had been unwilling to waste ink on the task.

"Here," he says pointing to a dot off the coast of South America. "This is where the French send their most dangerous criminals."

"The way the Tsar sends convicts to Siberia," says Nina.

"Exactly. Only Devil's Island is warmer."

Nina smiles at the hand on the page. The space Sasha has created with his body, the arm almost around her shoulders, the thigh almost pressing against the fabric of her dress, his head almost touching hers is like an embrace. There is a flush in Nina's cheeks that would give Sasha great pleasure to see if only he were not listening so closely to the pounding of his heart.

"More than ten years later they have finally given poor Dreyfus the Legion of Honor," Sasha says. "Can you imagine the level of hypocrisy? In the country that invented the Rights of Man? In the land of liberty, equality, fraternity?"

"But Sasha," Nina says in her most earnest voice. She wants to be fair to her new country as well as enlightened about it. "In Russia Dreyfus could never have been anything more than a private in the army. Here he was a captain, wasn't he?"

"Such distinctions are meaningless," Sashas says, shaking his head. "What was exposed in the affair was the corruption and hatred of the Jews at the core of the government and the army."

"How do you know all this?" she asks. She does not think she is in love with Sasha. She has never thought much about love. But she would like to stay in that encircling space Sasha has created for her, where she can almost feel her skin, the fine hairs at the side of her neck, the shape of her arms under her tight sleeves. The space defines her in a new womanly way.

"I read the papers," says Sasha.

"The French papers?"

"No, the Yiddish papers. They are full of the story. How did you miss it?"

Nina sighs. Nina does not read newspapers in French or Yiddish anymore. There is no time. Besides, trying to read the French papers is like reading the copy of *L'Aiglon* Mademoiselle Chambon gave her. The words are familiar but she has no frame in which to put them. She reads French without meaning, without sense, without much pleasure. She longs for a window into the larger world, but this window is still too hard to open.

As an anarchist, the misadventures of governments fill Sasha with glee.

He makes pronouncements that Nina, always a conscientious student, records in her notebook at night sitting on her bed by the light of the smoky oil lamp, as she did in Yekat when Sonya was her guide to the world:

"1. All governments are made up of equal parts hypocrisy and cruelty. 2. A government, like the law, is interested only in maintaining itself. 3. The army is the most malicious of governmental institutions. 4. The French army is cruel, hypocritical, malicious, and anti-Semitic. This, of course, is true of all armies in any country."

Does Nina agree with Sasha? Certainly. Nothing in her experience contradicts what he thinks. It is only that she believes in the possibility of a more perfect world. Sonya has left her this lingering inheritance.

"My teacher at the night school did not like Jews," she says.

"Why should that surprise you? She was probably a Catholic and reactionary, maybe even a monarchist. So her dislike of Jews follows naturally. Did you say she came from the provinces?"

"Yes," Nina whispers with her head bowed. Whenever she thinks of Mademoiselle Chambon, embarrassment floods her. She feels hoodwinked by Mademoiselle who preyed on her confidence, her affections. Who sold her a bill of goods. Only the other day, she bought a roll of gray gabardine from a street peddler on the rue des Rosiers. The fabric was so soft, the gray so deep, and the price so inviting—only seventy-five centimes for the whole roll. She bought it with one of the francs she had earned from Mr. Etlin, only to discover, when Chaim unrolled it, that the fabric was ripped right through as if a cat had sharpened her claws on it. Chaim forgave her, of course, but the flush of humiliation and the anger she felt was very much like the sense she still has of having been duped by Mademoiselle.

"You are too ready to believe the best of everyone," says Sasha, drily.

"That's not true. I only believe the best of people who deserve it," Nina says, in what she hopes is a voice full of indignation, but when she raises her eyes to Sasha's face she feels as if she's made a brazen confession and quickly lowers her eyes. (She does not care what Sasha has to say about Mademoiselle Chambon. She does not care about politics or the fate of the Jews. She would like to stay in that lovely space Sasha has made for her, her bones as solid as rock, her skin pleasantly taut over her bones, her clothes covering her body so lightly she does not feel them at all.)

The door to the living room is flung open. Yudel comes in tucking his shirt into his short trousers. He wears long gray woolen socks that barely cover his calves, a gray sweater buttoned to the collar and black shoes that lace up above his ankles. He is eleven now and nearly as tall as Chaim.

Nina's face reddens. Oh, she is not ashamed to be seen on the sofa with Sasha, Sasha is a good friend. He has every right to be sitting beside her, every right to be instructing her about the world. But Yudel has a gift for turning up where he is not wanted and making his presence felt, trailing dog-like behind them when Sasha walks her back from night school in the evening, or kicking pebbles at the back of her shoes when she sits with Sasha on a bench in the Square de Montholon or making animal noises and dancing like a fool to get Sasha's attention. "Go away," she wants to say to her brother in the same loud voice she uses to chase away the neighbor's obnoxious dog when he sniffs around her skirt in the courtyard. "Go away."

She inches away from Sasha. The magic enclosure, that lovely space has been destroyed. She tucks her skirt neatly around her legs. Sasha too looks uncomfortable. He removes his arm from the back of the sofa and uncrosses his legs. His boyish face assumes a serious, businesslike expression.

"Good morning, young man," he says, rather more loudly than he should. "And how are you this morning?"

Yudel shrugs.

"Yudel," says Nina. She smiles brightly at her brother. "Sasha has been telling me about Alfred Dreyfus. Do you know who Dreyfus is?"

Yudel looks blank.

Nina points her finger at the book on her lap. "See this tiny black mark on the map. This is where Alfred Dreyfus, a Jewish man, an officer in the French army, was kept in jail for a crime he did not commit. The real culprit was a Frenchman who was a spy for the Germans." Nina tilts her head toward Sasha. He nods approvingly.

"Can you imagine?" she continues. "Even here, in France, there is anti-Semitism in high places in the government." Yudel casts a bored look at his sister and at Sasha, sitting stiffly on the sofa.

"Why are you looking through my geography book?" he says. "That's my book."

"Well," says Nina. "When do you look at it? Here, take it back." She slams the book shut.

"I don't want it." Yudel drops into a chair. He has long legs now and a long body, all the parts of which appear at times to move independently. His head is long too and his eyes mournful as if life were a steady disappointment. "You can keep it."

"What should we do with him?" Nina asks in a falsely bright voice. "Why is he so impossible?"

Yudel stares out of the window. He is used to having people talk about him this way in his presence.

"You will have to exert yourself more," Sasha says to Yudel in his most professorial manner, "if you want to pass your grammar school exam."

Yudel doesn't answer. The day outside the window is gray, the sky leaden, the view much the same as the day before and probably the day after.

"I really don't care. I hate school. It's boring."

Nina adjusts the pins in her hair, pats a stray wisp around her ear. Yudel is so irritating. "Well, little brother," she says. "I don't see how you're going to get along in life without an education. Do you, Sasha?"

Sasha leans forward, elbows on his knees, hands clasped. He looks earnest, concerned. This also irritates Nina.

"Do you know," she finds herself saying, "I spoke to his teacher, to ask him to give Yudel private lessons so he could prepare for his grammar school diploma. But he refused. He said it was impossible to do anything for Yudel. He said he had never seen such a case in his life. He refuses to work." Nina catches her breath. She had never meant to go so far, to tell so much that is private and a little shameful. But the arch of Sasha's back as he leans toward Yudel shuts her out and she cannot bear being shut out from Sasha's attention.

Sasha says, not unkindly. "Is that true?"

Yudel scowls at his sister.

"Why did you talk to my teacher? What business is it of yours?"

"I was trying to help you. You know mother and father don't speak French well enough to talk to your teacher."

"Since when has taking care of me become your job?"

"It's always been my job, little brother," Nina says. "You've always been my responsibility. As far as I can remember. I took care of you. And now . . . And now . . . Sasha, you understand, don't you?"

Sasha has not changed his pose.

"You're always such a good girl," Yudel sneers. He digs his chin into his neck, his shoulders ride up to his ears, hands clasped between his knees.

Nina sets her jaw. She looks like her mother, stern, self-righteous. "Well, I worry about you. We all do. Mother and Father worry a lot."

"Why? Don't you make them happy enough?"

"Stop, Yudel," says Sasha in a voice that is surprisingly forceful. Nina thinks of the schoolmaster he might have become in Yekat. Then more calmly, he says, "You should not provoke him, Nina. That is not kind."

Nina feels the rebuke like a blow. And from Sasha, the sweetest of men. She is now even angrier at her brother. She turns her head and glares at the wallpaper across the room.

"Many great men have not liked school," Sasha says, all reasonableness.

"I don't believe that," Yudel slides deeper into the chair, his shoulders forward, his head tucked into his neck, turtle-like. "And anyway, who cares about great men. I'll never be a great man."

Yudel's declaration reminds Nina that her brother is unhappy in Paris. He doesn't seem to do what boys do, the jolly pranks, the mischief; he never talks about his school friends—perhaps he hasn't any. He is passive and sullen and lives too much in his head. Still, why can't he make the effort to be civil? He doesn't even try to find the world interesting in any way. Alta continues to cluck over him, although he is almost twelve. She worries that his nervous blinking is a sign of some graver, more debilitating weakness. She is always afraid of losing him. And Chaim pats him absently on the head whenever Yudel has a tantrum about school, which is often. At least in Nina's life there is night school and the customers in Etlin's shop; there are books to read and the piano to play, although she has few opportunities for that these days. And if she has not yet been to the great museum that was once a king's palace, she knows it exists; she has seen postcards in Etlin's shop of the lady with the mysterious smile and the Greek statue without arms. She will someday visit the Palace and the Cathedral and the Tower and the Gardens where ladies and gentlemen stroll along the leafy alleyways, of that she is absolutely confident. Only right now, there isn't much time for diversions. She has to keep her yearnings tucked away. What makes it bearable? Hope. And Sasha. When she thinks of Sasha, she feels a lovely warmth suffuse her.

"How do you know you can't be a great man? There are many ways to be great. You've only just begun, Idelka," Sasha says. At the sound of Sasha's voice, cajoling and tender, using Yudel's Yiddish nickname, Nina is riven with jealousy. A ribbon of feeling extends back into her childhood, before irritation, before annoyance, before the complexity of thought, to a moment when Alta, bent over Yudel's crib, allows the baby to play with the rope of brown hair that dangles over her shoulder while she murmurs "Idelka, Idelka."

A flush of pleasure spreads across Yudel's face. He sits up straighter in his chair. "If great men don't need to go to school, why do mother and father pay you to work with me?"

"Yudel," Nina says. "You are just bad."

This time Sasha looks hurt. Talk about money is humiliating. He pushes himself up from the sofa.

"I will tell your parents you no longer want my help."

"No, no," Yudel almost leaps up from his chair. He throws his arms around Sasha and clings to him the way he used to cling to Chaim when he was a child, only he is almost as tall as Sasha and nearly knocks him down. "We're friends, aren't we? We'll always be friends. Isn't that so?" And then to his sister, "Isn't that true, Nina?" Yudel eyes blink uncontrollably.

Nina, who has been watching with a mixture of annoyance and envy, has to restrain herself from throwing her arms around Sasha too. But she doesn't, and when, above Yudel's head, Sasha smiles his dimpled smile at her, including her in a private embrace, she feels she can finally be generous. She and Yudel are both attached to Sasha and neither of them must give him cause to leave ever. But Sasha is her friend first and he loves her best. She knows it from the tenderness in his eyes and the softness of his smile. After that, whatever is left of Sasha's love can go to her brother.

XXIV

March 1908

IT IS TEN THIRTY IN THE evening and Nina is tired. It has been a long day. She started in Etlin's store at eight o'clock this morning and now it is almost eleven. Sasha has come to pick her up at the Ecole Commerciale on the Avenue Trudaine and walk her back to the rue de Montholon as he has been doing every night this spring. It is easy to spot him, not only because he is the only man in a sea of women, but because he is so tall and striking-looking. He is letting his beard grow and his small round chin sprouts a covering of curly black hair that makes him look fierce and, Nina thinks a little sadly, like a real anarchist.

Nina is happy to see him at his post. She thinks of Sasha all day, or rather she tries not to think of Sasha during the day, but she is aware of an anticipation of happiness she doesn't dare dwell on, in case he is detained, forgets about her, doesn't bother to show up this time. But he is always there. And the students who gather around the doorway for one last chat or goodnight embrace before scattering in many directions see him too, and this, Nina admits, pleases her.

Etta, one of the girls from Mademoiselle Chambon's class, who, like Nina, graduated to the business school over a year ago, passes beneath the streetlight. She keeps her head down under her tight bonnet, but Nina knows that Etta, who is shy and very proper, is only pretending not to notice that Nina is walking down the street in the company of a young man. She sometimes wishes Mademoiselle could see her with Sasha, but Mademoiselle has long been gone and there is no one but Etta left to be impressed.

"Ninotchka," Sasha says breathlessly. "Gershuni is dead. He died yesterday morning. In Zurich. There is to be a cortege in his honor. We must be there."

"Who is Gershuni?" Nina asks after she has brushed her cheek against Sasha's wiry beard.

"A great man, an artist in assassination, the leader of the terrorist wing of the Social Revolutionary Party."

"Oh, Sasha, how can you admire an assassin?"

"What? He killed Sipiagin, that reactionary bastard. Anyway, he was arrested and sent to Siberia. Then he was smuggled out of prison in a barrel of sauerkraut and that's why he was called 'Mr. Cabbage.' In America, he met the famous Emma Goldman. Can you imagine? What a life!"

"He does not sound like a good man."

"Nina, you are not sufficiently evolved politically. We anarchists are in a battle against tyranny and oppression."

"Stop, Sasha. Do not tell me that I am not right thinking. I will not stand for that anymore." She thinks of Sonya and Mademoiselle Chambon. "I don't want to be battered by anybody's politics, left or right."

"Sorry." Sasha tilts his head toward her. He looks genuinely repentant. "Only Gershuni was an important figure in the party and now he is dead."

Nina sighs. Sasha, woebegone and penitent, is more than she can resist. She glances over her shoulder. Two of her classmates huddle on the sidewalk, giggling into their hands. She makes an effort to smile. She doesn't want them to think she and Sasha are quarreling.

"I would like to see who turns up at the cortege. Vladimir Ilyich Lenin himself might come. You never know. Some of my comrades may be there too."

Nina feels her will turn to liquid. She would like to do something amusing, light-hearted. She is tired of politics and earnestness and the kind of right thinking that leads nowhere. She blows out a stream of air.

"Please, Nina. The procession will go through Montmartre. And we can go to the fête on the Butte right after the cortege. That might be fun, wouldn't it?"

Nina shrugs her assent. But she is not at all grateful. She doesn't want to go to the funeral of this Gershuni, whoever he is, and she doesn't like being bribed, as if she were a child. But she hasn't the heart, or the will, to distress Sasha. And of course, when he smiles at her through his beard, the shivery feeling that runs through her leaves her speechless and compliant, if somewhat annoyed.

The following day is Saturday and it is raining lightly. Sasha has asked his uncle for the afternoon off. Etlin, who has become more religious in Paris than he was in Yekaterinoslav, closes his shop on Saturday, so Nina is free too. They join the cortege for Grigori Gershuni that began at one thirty near the Gare du Nord and ambled up the rue de Rochechouart where Nina and Sasha joined the marchers. It is a sparse, if somber procession. There aren't more than fifty marchers, mostly men and a handful of women, immigrant workmen in caps, short jackets, loose grimy trousers, and boots that have lost their shine, the women in smocks over their dresses and bare heads to show their solidarity with the workers. Some marchers, more prosperous or simply more respectful of the dead, wear black suits, shiny with age. There is a scattering of soft felt hats and long worn overcoats. The faces are grim, gaunt, and suspicious. This is not Yekat's holiday crowd on strike. These people are not hopeful. Their expressions are fierce, defiant, as if at any moment they expected to be shot.

And indeed, a handful of gendarmes follow the cortege like a shadow procession, turning down every street, pushing back passersby who have wandered idly into the gutter, blowing whistles as if to alert the neighborhood to the passage of lepers.

"There are only Russians here." Nina, who is carrying an umbrella against the light rain, turns to Sasha.

"Of course, who else cares about a man who organized the assassinations of Obolenski and Bogdanovich. Do you think the French are interested in what happens in Russia?"

Nina raises her eyebrows in half-hearted agreement. She doesn't care much about Russia either anymore.

The cortege proceeds up the steep hill of the rue de Dunkerque, past the tin ware dangling from loops of rope at the hardware store, past the second-hand shoe store that must be run by pious Jews, since it is closed on this the busiest and most commercially profitable day of the week, past the Hôtel des Familles, with its intricate iron work grill and dirty windows, past the little café at the top of the street with its half-dozen tables and chairs lining the sidewalk, onto the Square d'Anvers at the top of the hill. Here the cortege turns to the right.

Across the Place d'Anvers, the curious Byzantine domes of the Sacré Coeur still under construction after all these years, and ringed with scaffolding, remind Nina of the basilicas and onion domes of the Russian churches in Yekaterinoslav. The view has been in her vision since she arrived in Paris three years ago, but she has never ventured to the top of the Butte Montmartre. What reason could she have given for going so far out of her way? Who would she have gone with? Her world has been confined to the area between the Square de Montholon, the Passage Brady, and the Avenue Trudaine, family, work, and school. And so she is doubly pleased to be facing the great white church at the top of the steep streets with Sasha, even if it has to be for a funeral, even if it means walking side by side with the police.

"See that man over there. The short man walking with crutches. I've seen him before. He is a terrible ruffian. An anarchist to the core. He goes by the name of Albert Libertad. No one knows his real name."

Sasha's voice is puffed up with admiration and wonder. Nina jack-knifes around Sasha. She sees a powerful body on short, distorted legs, a huge head framed with a black beard, a face with fine regular features and an avid, exalted expression.

"Is he mad?" she asks.

"Maybe. He has half a dozen children he will not have registered by the state. He is against the oppression of the family."

"You can't possibly admire him for that."

"We are all oppressed by our families, don't you think?"

Nina pauses to think. Could she survive without Alta and Chaim, without Yudel? And yet she knows what Sasha means. Sometimes Alta's anguished face feels like an oppression. She says, "I love my parents."

"Of course. I do too. But I believe there is a strong element of tyranny in the bourgeois family structure."

"Oh dear," she says. "Why must you use such harsh language?" But she knows this must be how Sasha truly feels. He sends most of the money his uncle pays him to his family in New York.

Sasha says, "That is why I am an anarchist, a follower of Kropotkin. I hate oppression in all its forms. I believe in the freedom of the individual and in the comradeship of all men. Everything else can go to blazes."

"Oh, Sasha," Nina shakes her head. "I don't believe you. You are just a book anarchist. It's all nonsense. You would never blow anything up."

Sasha pauses in his walk. He frowns at the air. A pigeon swoops by him, fluttering its iridescent wings until it lands with an ungraceful lurch at Sasha's feet.

"I suppose not. I don't know if I have the courage to be an anarchist in life."

"How would your mother and your poor sisters feel? To have a terrorist in the family. Really, Sasha, you must think of them."

"I do. I do."

"Of course, you do," Nina says. She feels giddy with certainty. "That is because you are a respectable, kind person. And not crazy, like this Gershuni."

"Sometimes I wish I were crazier."

"That is pure silliness."

"Are you accusing me of silliness, Nina Chaimovna? Me, your brother's tutor and the most serious person you have ever met?"

"Yes," she says with a coy smile. "I am."

It is often like this talking to Sasha, sweet to be able to tease him, delicious to say what is on her mind without any fear of offending.

"Then I suppose you must be right." Sasha shrugs and gives her a smile that tints his face pink above his dark beard.

In the Square d'Anvers, with its lattice-work pergola and winged angel on a pedestal, mothers are pushing perambulators, children are rolling hoops on the sandy walks, an old gentleman is pushed in a wicker wheelchair by his nurse, a troop of young boys in caps and short pants are absorbed in a game of marbles. They glance at the marchers with untroubled eyes and return quickly to their game.

The procession continues past the Place d'Anvers across the Boulevard de Rochechouart and up the rue de Steinkerque without attracting much attention. When they reach the Parvis du Sacré Coeur, Nina is out of breath. The funicular that leads up to the curious white buildings has been functioning for eight years now. It is a fixture of the Paris landscape, but not for Nina. She has never been up this far. She would like to board one of the cars that travel up and down the hill but she knows it costs money, and besides they would have to abandon the cortege. The procession continues the climb into the village of Montmartre. Here the landscape changes drastically. The streets are narrow and twisty, the houses smaller, shabbier, and encrusted with mildew. There are vineyards here, dormant at this time of the year, which give the Butte the look of a village in the country. Geese amble across the street. The windmills are still. Flour is no longer milled in Montmartre, and the mills have been converted into inns and café-concerts. Housewives carry pails of water and shoo children away from the geese and the wheels of rolling carts. This Nina is accustomed to, as it is not so different from what street life was in Yekat. But in Yekaterinoslav you would not see a man in a broad-brimmed hat, a guitar slung across his back. You would not come across a painter at his easel staring not at the landscape ahead of him but at his canvas, covered in splotches of paint. You would not hear a burst of song from the open doors of the café-concerts or see perched on a flowery balcony a four-piece orchestra playing for only two couples, disreputable couples to be sure, women without hats and men in blue smocks, who are dancing with abandon in the middle of the afternoon.

"Oh please," Nina says. "Let's not go any further. Please, let's stay here. Look, there's a little bit of blue in the sky. It's stopped raining. Haven't we paid enough respect to Gershuni? Where are they going, anyway?"

"I don't know," Sasha says. "I think there is a hall in Belleville where the Social Revolutionary Party holds its meetings. I think they are going there."

"But that's so far away. You weren't planning on walking all that way. I couldn't. Not in these shoes."

Sasha looks glum. He would have liked to follow the procession to the end, to mark his commitment to anarchism with one final act of martyrdom. A small martyrdom to be sure, but one that would have been hard on his shoes, of which he only has one pair and these must last until he gets to New York. Because Sasha knows something he cannot bring himself to tell Nina. He will have to leave Paris soon. Yesterday, his uncle handed him a letter from his mother. Reading it, he was shame-faced and unhappy. Nina is right, he is not an anarchist; he is a good son first.

"All right," he says. "Gershuni is dead. And if he is counting the mourners at his funeral, he will have to settle for two less."

Sasha makes a helpless gesture with his arm. Nina follows his long, narrow hand. She notices how the bones of his wrist and the wreath of dark hairs just below his wrist escape from the too-short sleeve of his jacket. Fascinated, she has stopped listening to his words.

As they linger, a gendarme walks up to them.

"Where are you going, young lady and gentleman?" His red moustache droops imposingly to below the collar of his uniform.

Sasha turns to Nina. His French is not good enough to confront an agent of the law.

"We are going home," Nina says. "We are Socialists, not anarchists or terrorists. This parade does not interest us."

"Glad to hear it," says the gendarme. "Two nice young people like you should be dancing at the café-concert instead of marching on a Saturday afternoon. Leave these foreign gentlemen to us."

"Thank you, sir," says Nina. "You are quite right." And she beams at him, proud of her French, proud of her defiance, proud of her quick wit and only sorry that she has to translate for Sasha who looks suspicious and unhappy.

"I don't trust the police," says Sasha. "Here or in Russia."

"Look, I'll wave," Nina says. But the gendarme does not wave back. He is jabbing the last marchers forward with his nightstick.

"Where are we going?" Sasha blinks.

"Come," Nina says. "Don't you hear the music?"

She grabs Sasha's wrist lightly and tugs him to the left. It is a sisterly gesture, but it feels intimate and she is delighted at her own boldness. She and Sasha are walking away from the ambiguous safety of the procession into the unknown alleys of the city and it is entirely her doing. She is light-headed with daring.

To the left of the Sacré Coeur, the street opens into a leafy plaza, the Place du Tertre. The houses that line the plaza are low and countrified. Lilac are beginning to bloom, geraniums in boxes sprout at the base of the walls, a family of geese, proud and orderly, cross the plaza, undisturbed. The cafés, doors open to invite a late-afternoon public, exude a vinegary darkness. It is Saturday and the plaza is empty, except for the elderly domino players under the shade of a great chestnut tree and three cyclists who share a bottle of wine while their bicycles rest against the wall of a house with the number 21 inscribed on a small plaque. The music Nina heard issued from the pipes of a worn barrel organ, which is quiet now as the organist, looking melancholy, squats next to his instrument. Behind Nina and Sasha, the Church of Saint Pierre looms.

"Oh Sasha," says Nina, "Isn't this wonderful?" She is in a state of happiness that seems altogether natural, the way the world should be.

A barkeeper in a soiled apron steps out of his bistro and sets up a stand in front of his door. He places a barrel of beer on a shaky table and wipes the spigot with his apron. The spigot continues to drip steadily on to the stones beneath it. He brings out bottles of country cider, presumably for children and ladies who don't touch alcohol. Now the smell of hot grease wafts toward Nina and Sasha and mingles with the pungent aroma of malt and hops. The barkeeper's wife is frying potatoes in a deep kettle over a gas burner. Clearly, preparations are being made for the evening patrons.

"Smell the fried potatoes," Nina says. "Oh my goodness, I didn't realize I was so hungry."

"Nina, I don't have the money."

"Yes, of course," says Nina, humbled. Under the oak tree, a domino player curses and knocks his pipe angrily against the table.

"I don't have any money," Sasha says. "I don't have any money for anything. I cannot even buy you a cup of tea."

"It doesn't matter. I can have tea at home. We don't need money to enjoy ourselves. We shouldn't be foolish with our money."

"If I had money, I would . . ."

"What?"

"Do everything differently. I hate being poor."

"Well, we were richer once. That will have to be enough for us for a while."

"How practical and good-natured you are, Nina. I wish I could be like you."

"Oh Sasha, you are sweet. But you mustn't suffer so about money. It is degrading—especially for an anarchist." She laughs. Nothing dampens her pleasure today. The domino players look up at them with blank, preoccupied eyes and return to their game.

"I'm not a real anarchist either. Albert Libertad doesn't mind being poor. Oh, what am I saying? It's all nonsense anyway."

"Look." She wants more than anything to distract Sasha from his misery. "There's a house with a plaque on it. Come."

Reluctantly, Sasha follows Nina across the square. They stop at a small unimposing house with a brass plaque that reads "Commune Libre de Montmartre." Nina frowns. "What does it mean?" she asks.

"Free Commune of Montmartre." Sasha shrugs. "Perhaps it has something to do with the Paris Commune of 1870 that Marx wrote about."

"I don't know, but it sounds political. Perhaps there are Socialists living in this house. Or anarchists," Nina adds, gaily. "There, you see, we are still with Gershuni in spirit."

Sasha hoists his eyebrows. He is not convinced.

There is a low concrete wall behind the Place du Tertre. A chestnut tree spreads its branches over a bent old man drawing on his pipe. A young mother nurses her baby as she keeps an eye on an older child pushing a wooden hoop. Sasha and Nina find an empty spot to sit on along the wall.

Sasha drops his head into his hands. Nina sits quietly, her hands in her lap. She turns her head. For an instant, she is startled by the shape he makes as he leans forward. The slope of his back, the pull of his thighs against his trousers, his long hands with the thumbs pressing against the side of his face move her in an unaccustomed way. She thinks she has never seen anyone so clearly— or so lovingly.

"Nina, I have something to tell you," Sasha says.

He sits up, takes her gloved hand, folds the fingers, covers her hand with his. Nina has stopped breathing.

"It's nothing," he says. "I have no right."

Nina cannot speak. She cannot encourage him to say what she would like him to say. *I love you, I love you. You are the woman of my life and will always be.*

"I am very fond of your family," Sasha says. "Yudel is a good boy. Your parents are good people."

Nina waits, her breath suspended in her chest.

"Has your father thought of going to America? Life is so hard for him here in Paris."

Nina breathes out. This is not what she wants to hear. "Yes, once. When we lived in Geneva. He considered it when our friends were going to America. And then it seemed too difficult, too far away."

"Are you sorry?"

"How can I tell? I don't know what I am missing. Do you want to go to America?"

"No," he says firmly. And he isn't lying. He does not want to go to America. He never wants to leave Paris; he never wants to move from under this tree that is just beginning to bud in the mild March weather.

"Good. I'm glad you feel that way. I never want to leave France either." She is full of a happy certainty. When she smiles at Sasha she feels she is opening her heart to him.

Sasha bounds off the wall.

"Let's go to the bistro over there," he says. "I must have a couple of francs somewhere." He reaches into his pocket.

"Oh, no. Don't spend your money frivolously."

"I don't care. It's too stupid to worry about money now. It's too stupid to hoard twenty-five centimes that will never add up to much anyway. We are young. We should be piling up memories instead of money."

Sasha pats his jacket pocket. The absence of a future makes him reckless.

"Come," he says, extending his hand. She takes it and allows him to pull her up. They cross the Place to the bistro.

"Please, may I have a beer," Sasha asks in his overly courteous French. The barkeeper takes a glass, gives it a casual wipe with his apron and, turning on the spigot, pours out a glass of beer that is more foam than liquid.

"Five centimes," says the barman. "And for the lady?"

"Nothing," Nina says although she is very hungry.

"An order of potatoes, please," Sasha mumbles.

"Are you sure?" Nina asks in Russian.

The barkeeper stares at them with a new hostility. "Potatoes for the foreign lady and gentleman," he says to his wife, who throws a handful of air-browned potatoes into the boiling oil. When they are done, she wraps them in a paper cone made from a page of Jean Jaures' Socialist paper, *L'Humanité*.

"Five centimes," says the barkeeper.

"At the Gare du Nord, the potatoes are only three centimes," Nina says brashly.

"So they are," says the barkeeper, wiping his mustache with the back of his hand. "But here on the Butte Montmartre, in my establishment, they are five centimes. We don't work for nothing here."

"Never mind," Sasha hands the man a ten-centime piece.

Nina is tipsy with excitement and the thrill of rebellion. Beer and potatoes, eating on the street, walking out alone with Sasha. She has never done anything so unchartered, so completely without a compass.

Sasha wipes the rim of the glass with his pocket handkerchief and hands it to Nina. "Here, you must have some too." Nina hesitates, then takes the glass with both hands and tips it to her mouth. The liquid is thick and harsh tasting, but it slips quickly down her throat.

"I don't think your parents would approve of your drinking beer in public. Or in private."

"Probably not," Nina says and giggles. Then she adds, because she doesn't want Sasha to think badly of her, "In Yekat, we always had beer in our cellar. My father drank beer and my mother too, on special occasions."

"Well, this is certainly a special occasion," Sasha says. "Shall we drink to Gershuni?"

"No." Nina frowns.

"To Paris, then. To us." And he lifts the glass to his lips. Nina watches as he drinks with avid intensity. He passes the glass to Nina.

"Finish it," he says. And she does.

"Now let's finish the potatoes," says Sasha and hands her the paper cone. Nina, who would not drink tea from the tea man in Yekat, who refused to eat sunflower seeds in the street, accepts the fried potatoes greedily.

"It's amazing how thirsty I am. It must be the potatoes," says Sasha. "Let's have another beer."

"Can we afford it? I must have some centimes here in my purse."

"I can afford anything. I have never been so rich."

Sasha orders another glass of beer. He is smiling like a schoolboy.

Once again, he offers Nina the glass, which she takes with both hands. Instead of a dainty sip, she takes a long swallow. By now, there is a looseness in her limbs, a fuzziness in her perceptions as if a scrim had come up between herself and the world. They walk back across the Place du Tertre to the wall under the plane tree.

Sasha sits down beside her and slips his arm around her waist. Suddenly he places his lips on the back of her neck. A shiver runs through Nina. It is the most exquisite sensation. She holds her breath. He runs his hand over her forehead, pushing strands of hair off her face. She turns her face toward him. He is looking at her intently, gravely. She would like to tell him how happy she is, but she cannot speak. She allows her head to drop on his shoulder.

"Good," he says. "I like it when your head is on my shoulder."

She sits very still afraid to disturb the sensations that stream through her.

"We are making a spectacle of ourselves," she whispers. Why does she want to giggle?

"Why not? Who cares? You worry too much, Ninotchka. Rest your head."

And Nina closes her eyes. Images of the afternoon float on her consciousness and, at one point, she slips into a dream, then wakes herself up with a start.

"Come," says Sasha. "Let's walk a little." They get up and cross the Place du Tertre once again. In front of the bistro Sasha says, "Wait. I want another beer. The effects of this one are beginning to wear off. I'm not drunk enough."

"Sasha, you're not really drunk, are you?"

"No. I'm only pretending—to scare you." And he pays for a third beer with the last of his centimes.

"Let me have some too."

Now Sasha sounds a cautious note. "Are you sure? Ladies shouldn't drink too much beer. It can go to their head."

"Oh I'm fine," says Nina. "Just sleepy." I want to be drunk too, she thinks. Why shouldn't I? And Sasha, wary, passes her the glass.

They walk around the back of the Sacré Coeur and descend the rue du Chevalier de la Barre. Sasha's arm is wrapped around Nina's waist. They stagger hip to hip over the cobblestones, avoiding the horse droppings and the watery gutters. A housewife, going up the street, chuckles into her chin as she passes them. Nina feels a golden gratitude toward the woman. Never in her life has she been so happy. Never before has she felt so free of herself.

Sasha kisses her on the lips. His breath tastes of beer and cooking oil but to Nina his kiss is like a blessing on her womanliness. She arches her back and allows him to kiss her again. She is dizzy and hollow-limbed and very sleepy.

"I can hardly stand," she says. "My knees are shaking."

"Here, this is where I live," Sasha leans suddenly against a weathered door. "On the top floor, unfortunately. But I can carry you up."

"Oh no," she says. "That's impossible. I can't do that."

"Why not? Why can't we do something impossible?" He leans against the door, trapping her between his two arms. "Just to rest. You're so sleepy."

His face is very close to hers. She feels the sweet pull of his eyes, the memory of his lips. Please, she says to some unknown but terrible presence, give me permission to do this.

Sasha searches in his pocket for the key. He too is feeling the depth of his daring, although his imagination carries him only up the stairs to the landing, Nina recumbent on his arm. "I will make you tea," he says, "from my mother's samovar."

"All right," she says, and a wave of nausea sweeps over her.

The staircase is tight and winding and creaks under their feet. The smell of old cooking fat adds to Nina's nausea. A cat crosses the first-floor landing ahead of them.

Sasha's room is under the eaves. A garret window looks out onto the sloping roofs of Montmartre. The Sacré Coeur, brilliantly white in the late afternoon sunshine, looms above the winding streets and alleys.

Sasha's bed, a narrow unmade cot, rests against a white-washed wall stained with the prints of countless hands. Nina looks questioningly at Sasha. There is only one chair, on which rests a pile of tipsy, dusty books. Sasha smiles apologetically.

"I am not very neat," he says. "As you can see. Here, sit here." He pulls the cover over the bed and pats a place for Nina. Nina sinks onto the cot. Her umbrella drops to the floor. She lets it lie there, uncertain whether to remove her gloves, to unpin her hat. Alta disapproves of sitting on an unmade bed in one's street clothes. But then, Alta would disapprove of everything her daughter is doing. If only she were not so dizzy, so weak in the knees, she could think more clearly. She smiles uncertainly at Sasha who bends toward her. She extends her hand forward as if to steady herself against an invisible wall, but touches the front of his jacket instead. As she does so, Sasha catches her hand and brings it to his lips. Pleasure, familiar only in her dreams, shoots through her.

"Nina," Sasha's voice is hoarse as he slides onto the cot beside her. "Nina," he says again and takes her face in his hands. He tilts her head and gently brings her mouth to his. Nina closes her eyes and in her groggy happiness, lets him slide his hands along her neck, her shoulders, her breasts. Now Sasha searches her mouth with his tongue and with his hands makes avid, urgent circles around her breasts. It is nothing she has ever felt before, this delirious dissolving pleasure, unimaginable, nothing like the feverish, anxious warmth she sometimes feels at night between her legs. She draws on his tongue, rapaciously.

"Stop," Sasha says. "We must stop." He pulls away from her. Startled, Nina drops her hands by her sides. The pleasure begins to subside, leaving her shaky. Sasha stands up, his back to her.

"I'll make tea," he says in a throaty, unnatural voice.

Nina strains to watch as he lights the coals under the samovar. The room swims a little; she is afraid she will pitch forward with nausea. A twinge of disappointment hovers at the edge of her consciousness.

When Sasha, breathless, turns to hand her a porcelain cup, Nina is asleep, curled up on his bed like a child.

Sasha sits on the edge of the cot, staring at her. After some moments, he places his hand on her shoulder and gently shakes her.

"Was I asleep?" she asks drowsily.

"Yes," he says, still staring hard as if the answer to an important question were written across her forehead.

The sun has begun to set. The room glows with orange light.

"I must go home," Nina bolts herself upright "Everyone will worry."

"I have been sitting here looking at you. You are beautiful when you sleep."

Sasha's brown eyes are mournful. "Will we ever have an afternoon like this again?"

"Why not?" she says, a little defiantly, brushing away something uncomfortable in his voice. And then, because he has frightened her, "You are confusing me."

She looks around the bare room and it feels sad to her, like a space that has already been abandoned. She wants Sasha to take her in his arms and kiss her again.

"Nina, I must take you home. Right now. We shouldn't stay here a moment longer."

"Oh," she says. She is desolate. "I haven't finished my tea."

"It doesn't matter,"

Sasha stands up slowly. He doesn't take his eyes off Nina, which frightens her. "Come," he says gruffly. "Let's go."

On the landing, Nina shivers with misery. What has she done? What terrible mistake has she made? She should never have come to Sasha's room, and yet she wishes she were still there, in that exquisite, forbidden embrace. Only a sign, a gift from Sasha will steady her. Does he love her? Sasha, leaning against the balustrade, extends his hand to her, and she, on an impulse born of desire and fear of loss, throws her arms around him and presses her body against his.

Sasha holds her. He thinks there will never again be a moment as sweet or as sad as this in his life. Nina lifts her head.

"I don't know why I'm so sad," she says. "There's nothing to be sad about, is there? It's been such a wonderful afternoon."

Sasha looks down the dark staircase, no longer lit by the tepid beams of the March sun. He says, "We should be going home. Your parents will worry." And he vows to tell Nina the bad news later, at some other time, in a future as remote as possible.

XXV

IT IS EARLY EVENING IN THE Square d'Anvers. The weather is mild. In the fading light, it is still possible to discern the tulips blooming in military rows of pink, white, and red around the pergola. Bursts of yellow forsythia frame the benches, and neat alleys of purple and white pansies line the freshly raked gravel walks. Sasha has asked Nina to walk with him around the Square. Sasha said it was a fine evening for a walk, although Nina thinks it is a bit chilly. They have completed a turn around the pedestal of the winged angel in silence, Nina rigid with the effort to tamp down her excitement and her apprehension. This is the first time she and Sasha have been alone together since the afternoon they followed Gershuni's cortege up the hill of Montmartre and ended, glorious, troubling memory, in Sasha's room. Sasha has not once come to the Ecole Commerciale at night as he used to. Why has he avoided her? And now this request for a private conversation at an unusual time. Nina doesn't dare think what it can mean. Still, as they walk along the gravel paths, she catches herself smiling a small, secret giddy smile of happiness.

Sasha says, "The workers are shamefully exploited in this country." Sasha has shed his winter overcoat. He walks with his hands behind his back and his soft hat tilted forward. Nina wears a new spring hat, a navy blue straw boater with a grosgrain ribbon of the same color.

"Yes, that's true," Nina says, warily. She hopes Sasha does not want to talk for too long about the workers, or politics, or the state of the world. Aren't there truly important things they must say to each other? A small boy in a wide collar and short pants runs along the gravel path kicking up clouds of yellow dirt. Nina shakes out her skirt.

"You, for example," Sasha says fiercely. "How can you continue to work for that beast Etlin at three francs a month? That is not even enough to live on for a week."

Nina's heart sinks. This is not the conversation she wants.

"And yet you continue to turn up at his shop at eight in the morning like a good girl, ready to work until your fingers blister from the cold."

"It doesn't matter," Nina says. "I don't mind."

"You should mind. It is an outrage." Sasha's face darkens.

"Well, what else can I do? Even those few francs are a help."

"Exactly. Exactly. And your father! Such a good tailor in Yekat and now a nobody working for centimes for my capitalist uncles."

"My father is not a nobody, Sasha," Nina remonstrates quietly.

"No, I'm sorry. Of course not, that's not what I meant at all." He removes his hat and scores his hair with his fingernails.

"Well, what do you mean?" Nina says a little impatiently. The little boy is running in circles, making whooping noises. She wishes he would stop.

"Life is too difficult in Paris. There is no hope for any of us here."

"No hope?" Nina is stricken. She believes with all her heart in the possibility of improvement. Even now, at this very moment, she hopes for something more from Sasha, a touch, a kindness, a connection. "What are you saying? Is anything wrong?"

Sasha doesn't answer. On the Avenue Trudaine, a fire wagon gallops by; the siren blares its ear-jangling two-note song. Nina makes a face and covers her ears. Children look up from their games; nannies rock wailing babies in their prams. The old people follow the wagon with suspicious rheumy eyes.

"I cannot stay here forever," Sasha says, his voice rising above the noise. "My mother has written to me again from New York. She wants me to come as soon as I can."

"What?" Nina removes her hands from her ears.

"I must go to New York," he says. The air is quite still now that the fire truck has passed. "New York. I have to go to New York."

Nina's breath catches in her throat.

"But I thought. You said. We agreed." A stroll through the great museum hand in hand, the pleasure of a piano recital at the Salle Pleyel, the future rolling out before them like an intricate Persian carpet, roses and birds and a young prince with a falcon on his wrist, how can that not happen?

"Oh no, you can't. You can't go." She grips Sasha's sleeve. She feels as if her insides have been removed and in the hollow space there is a violent pounding: Why don't you love me enough to stay? A desire to fasten herself to him, to meld into him, arms and legs, stomach to stomach seizes her. She whispers, "Take me with you. Don't leave me here."

Sasha seeing her agonized face under the straw hat, says, "Don't cry, Ninotchka. You will break my heart if you cry."

He has not heard her. Thank goodness. She cannot say it again, or ever. It was a moment of weakness and disloyalty.

But he has heard her and he is stricken with his own helplessness.

"I'm not leaving soon. I promise. We will still be together."

But it is too late. Nina swallows her tears, squints shakily up at the sky, as if she were passionately interested in tracking the passage of the sun. A wagon rattles by, jangling barrels of beer. The horse's hooves clang against the cobblestones, his tail swishes behind him like a housewife's dirty rag.

"Have you bought your ticket?" she asks.

"My uncle is paying my passage."

"So you already have your ticket?"

"Yes."

"You have known about this for some time."

"Yes."

"What you said before about being together, it wasn't true."

"I don't know."

Nina turns away. The sun has set and a gray-blue light suffuses the sky. The pergola casts a shadow over the tulips and the pansies. A lamplighter is lighting the streetlights one by one with his long pole.

"Will I ever see you again?"

"Come to America. You don't need to stay here."

"How can I leave my parents?"

"They should come too."

Nina says. "Yes, but they won't. My mother will never move again."

"Then you come."

"Just like that?"

"Why not?"

Nina looks into Sasha's earnest face and she sees how simple it is for him to leave. And she understands how hard it will be for her if she stays—and she will. She and Sasha are both such good children.

"We will meet again, Nina. I'm sure of it." Sasha takes her hands in his. But Nina does not believe him. In her experience, when people leave, they leave for good.

CHAIM AND ALTA ARE WAITING for Nina and Sasha in the tiny dining room–workroom. Yudel is supposedly resting on his cot. Actually he is playing solitaire on the floor. He is a great hand with cards and loves to practice fancy shuffling tricks. The oil lamps are lit and the room, dim enough during the day, already has a cavernous grayness in the early evening. Chaim wears spectacles as he bends over the second-hand Thimmonier sewing machine he has just bought. Chaim often works at home at night, doing piecework for the Friedman brothers, Sasha's uncles. Alta is sewing too. She is especially good at the delicate details of women's clothing. Tonight she is working on a child's dress, pulling threads to make the gathers that will decorate the front of the dress. Both Chaim and Alta look tired. Still, they smile when Nina enters, bringing with her a breath of cool, mild air. Sasha is behind her, stroking his new beard.

"Ah, Sashenka! Thank you for bringing our daughter home," says Chaim. "We have come to count on you. Perhaps we shouldn't. It is an imposition on a man who has to get up early to go to work."

Sasha removes his hat, which he holds against his chest. "I told Nina she should never go anywhere without me and I meant it."

Nina turns her head away, toward the window that opens out into a narrow airshaft. Liar, she thinks, how can he lie like that? Alta casts a grave look at the two young people. She tears a piece of thread between her teeth.

"Here, for you." Sasha pulls a newspaper out of his back pocket. It is the Jewish paper, *Der Idischer Arbeiter*, a four-page publication printed on paper so thin and brittle it has already begun to tear at the folds. He has been carrying it in his pocket all day.

"Many thanks. Now sit, sit," says Chaim. "Have a glass of tea." The dented samovar on the three-legged table has traveled from Yekaterinoslav to Paris. Its copper spigot needs polish and the copper teapot at the top tips precariously, battered by its long journey. Charcoal keeps the water at a low boil at all times.

Sasha slides into a chair.

Alta prepares a glass of tea for him. She places the glass on a saucer with a long-handled teaspoon and two cubes of pale brown sugar. Nina, watching her mother, remembers with resentment that the silver-filigree tea holders that Alta prized in Yekaterinoslav were sold a long time ago to Sasha's father.

There is silence as Sasha stirs his tea. He has abandoned the Russian habit of drinking through a sugar cube. He takes a sip. When he puts the glass down, Chaim says, "So, how is your life?"

"I have no life," Sasha says.

Chaim makes a sucking noise through his teeth. He tugs the needle through the cloth.

"A young man like you, what sort of thing is that to say?"

Nina stands by the window directing her gaze at the courtyard where nothing moves, not even the leaves of the plane tree.

"I don't understand," Chaim continues. His voice is gentle, placid. "Who persecutes you here? Are you in fear of your life? Will you be sent to Siberia for the way you think? For the things you say? Come now, be reasonable, Sashenka. Life is hard in France. But not impossible. Isn't that so?" Chaim lifts his head toward his wife. But Alta remains solemn. She directs a dry steady gaze at her daughter and Sasha.

"I cannot approve of such a discouraging attitude. Do you think life will be better somewhere else?"

"Maybe."

"Ah?" Chaim smiles as if anticipating a joke. "Just where may that wonderful place be?"

"America." Sasha darts a glance at Nina but she will not turn her head toward him.

"What a dreamer you are."

Alta leans over her sewing.

"We cannot go to America," she says, looking gravely at Sasha. "We thought of it when we were in Geneva. But everyone discouraged us. It is too far away."

"I would certainly not take my family there now," Chaim says, shaking his head. "Although I did once consider it."

"But you work too hard. Your wife works too hard. Your daughter works too hard." Sasha's voice rises. "Besides nothing in this country changes. It is too old, too riddled with anti-Semitism and bourgeois prejudice. You will always be a foreigner here, you will always be despised and exploited. And Nina could be doing something far worthier of her than working in a card store. It is unbearable." Sasha raises his glass and finishes the tea in one gulp.

Nina keeps her face turned toward the window. It is not fair of Sasha to talk like this when everything has already been decided. America, she thinks bitterly, if her parents had not been so fearful, they might have gone to New York instead of Paris. And she remembers with anguish that moment of disloyalty and panic when she asked Sasha to take her with him. At that moment, she would have gone anywhere, to Timbuktu, if only he had insisted. But she knows that it would have taken someone less good, less kind, less like Sasha to sweep her away and she would not have loved him the way she loves Sasha.

"It was Nina's decision to continue working for Etlin. We have often told her she could stop." Alta holds up the child's dress, pulls the gathers straight.

"Yes, yes. Of course, I know."

"Besides, Nina goes to school. She is learning to write on a machine and to keep books. In a few years, she will have her commercial diploma. And she likes her classes. Am I not right, Nina?"

"Please, Mama. Sasha knows everything about my life. Why are you telling him these things?"

"Can you propose a better life for our daughter?" Alta asks looking Sasha in the eyes.

Nina flushes. "Do not ask Sasha such a question, Mama. You are embarrassing him and me."

Sasha frowns. He drops his hands between his knees in silence. Then he raises his head as if he were gathering strength to himself.

"I have nothing to offer Nina. Not now anyway."

"Please tell us exactly what is on your mind." Alta's voice is measured, calm as ice on a lake.

"Have you heard from your mother?" she says after a silence.

"Yes."

"What does she say?"

"My uncle and his wife are leaving Paris the day after tomorrow. She wants me to leave with them. She says I have been in Paris long enough."

Alta turns toward Chaim, whose eyes meet hers. They are in agreement about something that has already passed between them, long before this evening, perhaps in bed late at night when they discuss the children. They have been making plans. And now Sasha is leaving. She is ashamed for them and angry.

Yudel appears in the doorway, squinting into the light.

"I am sorry," says Sasha. "I shall miss you all. Yudel too." He nods to the doleful boy. "I hope he gets on with his studies."

Nina cannot think what to say. She looks down at her hands. They seem alien to her, and useless.

"I am leaving you all my books, Nina. I will bring them to you tomorrow. You must read them and write to me and tell me what you think."

She nods. She feels like a child being offered candy to keep her quiet. But I am not a child, she thinks at once, and this is a poor exchange.

"You have been very kind to me," Sasha says to Chaim. "Like a second family."

"No need to go on like that, young man." Chaim puts down his work, folds the jacket neatly on to a stool beside him. "You have been kind to us too." He manages a weak smile. "How are we going to keep up with the world without you? Who will tell us what is going on in this country?"

Nina wants to run to her room. She wants to claw at her bedcovers, pound her mattress, vomit up the clump of misery that lodges in her chest.

"I will be back tomorrow night. With a pile of books for Nina and Yudel. I haven't forgotten you, my boy."

Yudel moves to his mother's side, looking bewildered.

Sasha turns to Nina who keeps her eyes on the bleak view outside the window. "I will leave my Kropotkin for you. *Mutual Aid*. It is a beautiful book, full of ways to make the world better. You will like it, Nina. It is about cooperation, not violence. Kropotkin is not Gershuni." He gives Nina a hopeful smile as if sharing a memory was all that was needed for forgiveness. "I hope you will accept it."

For a moment, there is perfect quiet in the room.

"Thank you," Nina says. Her shoulders shake but she does not turn her head toward Sasha.

"Till tomorrow, then," Sasha says. He disengages himself unsteadily from the chair he has been sitting in as if he were just recovering the use of his limbs. He nods quickly to Alta and Chaim, opens the door into the dark stairwell and is gone.

NINA AND YUDEL HAVE LEFT Sasha at the Gare St. Lazare to catch the boat train to Dieppe. Sasha's Uncle Samuel and his uncle's wife were there, so it was not a very sentimental good-bye. Sasha embraced Yudel who braced himself stiffly in Sasha's arms, although his eyes were filmy with tears. Sasha took Nina's hands in his and said softly in Russian. "I'll see you in New York or in Paris. Nothing will keep us apart, believe me." Nina nodded, holding back her tears, although her throat ached. The station was very crowded. The porter, in blue cloth cap and blue smock, stood beside the trunks and wicker baskets waiting for his tip. A party of American travelers, lean and elegant in their linen traveling costumes, made impatient noises in their nasal language. Sasha and his group were blocking the entrance to the coach. It was a gray day. Pale light filtered through the tall glass panes of the recently built station. Still, there was an air of bustle, children shouting, passengers shaking hands and pressing cheeks, a general pushing and shoving that made Nina feel isolated in her unhappiness. She was almost glad when the train pulled out of the station and Sasha's hand waving good-bye disappeared in the smoke.

Now she and Yudel are walking back to the rue de Montholon. Nina has taken the morning off from Etlin's store, Yudel is playing truant, not so unusual for him.

Yudel kicks pebbles along the pavement. They roll with a clatter into the gutter running with dirty water. He swings his school bag over his shoulder.

"I'm glad Sasha is gone," he says, wiping his eyes with the back of his hand and sniffing noisily. "Now maybe mother and father will leave me alone about school. What do I have to go to school for anyway? Even Sasha said I didn't. Someday I'll make more money than all of you, without any help."

Nina continues to walk in silence, her shoes tapping against the pavement. She does not want to console Yudel whose forced jauntiness only irritates her. She does not want to be consoled by her father or admonished by her mother. There is no one in the world she wants to talk to but Sasha and he is gone. The knot of misery that clotted her chest in the last two days has dissipated somewhat, carried away with the soot and the smoke and the clatter of iron wheels. In the empty place where she had been unhappy, something else is growing, a new bitterness and a new yearning. She is eighteen years old now. She has been in France three years and she knows no one. Only her parents' friends and a few casual acquaintances from school, no one she can have a conversation with.

At the corner of the Square d'Orléans, a peddler is selling string beans from a cart. The beans are bright and fresh looking. Nina thinks for a moment of stopping to buy some for dinner. She looks in her purse for a few centimes, then pulls the closing string tight. She does not want to think of dinner, she does not want to be helpful and kind and good and thoughtful. Today, she wants. Oh, it is so hard to know what she wants, but it has something to do with the emptiness inside her. Then it comes to her in words, like a voice from the emptiness itself. When will she have something of her own? Just for herself, something that belongs to her, that she doesn't have to share with her brother or her parents. She is such a good girl, she cannot frame the word *love* even to herself. But that is what she wants. She wants to be loved. By someone who is not attached to her by blood or the fragile tendrils of friendship. Quite simple. Quite ordinary. Isn't it time?

XXVI

CHAIM, AFTER MUCH SEARCHING, has had the good luck to find an affordable space to set up his tailor shop on the rue Victor Massé in the ninth arrondissement. This establishment is not, and never will be, the well-appointed and well-run workshop he owned in Yekaterinoslav with its whir of sewing machines, great tiled furnace for heating the irons, three enormous gas lamps that radiated so much heat the workers worked throughout the year without their jackets, plumes of steam rising from the irons pressed against wet fabric, the slightly sour smell of damp wool, the murmur of voices speaking in Yiddish and occasionally in Russian. At night when Chaim lies on the poorly tufted mattress he shares with Alta, the memory of his former life seizes him like a cramp. What does he miss most? Not the money, not the comforts. He and Alta have always worked hard. What he misses is who he was. Politics and pogroms, those twin thieves of Jewish history, have stolen his best years. He feels the burden of being himself like a disappointment, as though he had failed to live up to the expectations of others. He is too old to reinvent himself in a foreign country. And yet he must. Alta worries about money; it keeps her alive with anxiety. They have been in Paris for five years and only now do they have a decent place to live, a four-room apartment on the rue de Bellefond. Chaim has given up worrying; he takes what he is given. And right now, he has been given a place to work he can call his own.

There is no sign yet either over the shop door or on the glass front itself, but from the bolts of cloth piled neatly one on top of the other in the window, the illustrations, mounted on cardboard, taken from fashion magazines or the catalog of the *Manufacture de France*, one can tell, says Chaim to reassure Alta, that this is a tailor's shop. Eventually, the words *Tailor/Dressmaker* will be etched in gold paint over the door, but right now there are too many and far more necessary expenses to be undertaken.

A handwritten sign hanging on the inside doorknob says "Open" on one side and "Closed" on the other. Today, an unusually warm day, the door has been left slightly ajar. Inside, the front room is small, dark, and clean. The walls have just been repainted, the counters varnished. A not unpleasant odor permeates the room: the store was a pharmacy owned by a Romanian Jew before Chaim bought it, and the hot weather has released the fragrant oils trapped in the wood. Eucalyptus mingles with the smell of paint, menthol and camphor with varnish, and a trace, if one bends carefully over the drawers aligned along the back wall, of oil of lavender and attar of roses.

Bolts of cloth lie on the windowsill and in cubbies along the wall. Most of the fabric is wool, either serge or gabardine, in solid colors, black, shades of blue, brown, and purple. There are also bolts of corduroy, popular with working men, although Chaim does not do much work for them, and some wool fabric in stripes and tweed. For the summer, Chaim has stocked muslin and cotton in light colors, linen in beige and cream, and a few bolts of silk, in green and red taffeta and a beautiful shade of rose organdy that Nina covets, oh not for herself, at least not right now, but someday, that would make a lovely summer evening dress. Nina is the principal and only salesgirl in her father's shop. It is an unpaid position, of course, but it saves her parents from having to pay a salary to a stranger.

Piled along the counter are catalogs and fashion magazines from which the customers can chose their patterns. Chaim is such an able tailor that he can make a dress or a suit from an illustration that will fit his customer like a charm. That is what Madame Kamenchikoff says and she is Chaim's most enthusiastic client.

The bell over the door tinkles and Madame Kamenchikoff herself sweeps into the shop. Madame Kamenchikoff is an improbable follower of fashion. She is a short woman, with untidy brown hair escaping from her broad-brimmed and flower-decked hat, large of shoulder and bust, whose son Maurice was Yudel's study partner in the hopeful days when there was still the possibility that Yudel might pass his grammar school exams. Madame Kamenchikoff's husband owns a furniture store on the rue de Dunkerque and does quite well, thank you, as his wife will point out without being asked. France has been good to the Jews, she says, good to us anyway, in spite of the troubles with that man Dreyfus, and she beams, her apple cheeks pink with satisfaction.

"Ninotchka, my dear," says Madame Kamenchikoff," Look what I have brought you. There, this picture shows you exactly what's being done. Look at that." She opens the *Journal des Dames et des Modes* to a drawing of a woman wearing a tailored suit in watered silk, with a long jacket and a narrow skirt, and thrusts it in front of Nina. "Isn't that lovely," she says excitedly. "So simple and elegant. Look at the flared cuffs here and the way the collar is held back with those little tiny buttons. Wouldn't that look good on me? Slimming too. I could use a little help there." She laughs coyly the way women do when they expect to be politely contradicted. But Nina only frowns and tilts her head as if she were giving Madame Kamenchikoff's words serious consideration. Madame Kamenchikoff, undaunted, points to the skirt and the long button boots that are visible under the hem. "The skirt is at least four inches off the ground. Isn't that daring? Oh Ninotchka, do you think your father could make something like that for me?"

Nina slips off her stool. She studies the picture. "Would you like it in silk like this or a sturdier fabric? Something you could wear all year long?"

"You are right again, my dearest. A nice soft blue wool for everyday. But keep the velvet trim and the buttons on the cuffs and that band of velvet around the bottom of the skirt. Narrow skirts are the latest thing. I saw them on the mannequins in the window of the Galeries Lafayette."

Mention of the big department store makes Nina wince. Chaim gave up his piecework there when they found the shop on the rue Victor Massé, and the Galeries remains their biggest competitor. All the department stores, Bon Marché, Printemps, la Samaritaine, now provide cheap clothing for just the kinds of people who could be Chaim's customers. Middle-class housewives, clerks and secretaries, telephone operators, teachers, women who like fashion and have a little money to spend on themselves. But for quality work, for clothing that will last, that fits properly and looks good, there is nothing like a good tailor. Irreplaceable, is Chaim Schavranski, says Madame Kamenchikoff, and she is never wrong.

"Please, Nina, show this picture to your father and let me know what he can do. Will you do that for me? Yes?" Madame Kamenchikoff looks about to pinch Nina's cheek, then pulls back her hand. "How is you mother? Feeling any better?"

Nina shakes her head. "Not really. She is still in bed."

"All this moving and painting and ordering and keeping track of the books. My goodness, I don't know how she does all that." Madame Kamenchikoff clasps her hands across her capacious bosom. "I know a little of what her life is like. When I have to spend time in my husband's store, not often, you understand, but sometimes when he is short-handed, I am exhausted at the end of the day. Exhausted. I have to take to my bed for three days."

Nina raises her eyebrows in acknowledgment.

She does not tell Madame Kamenchikoff, who is a stranger, after all, about Alta's sufferings, the shooting pains all over her body, the heart palpitations, the weakness, the dizziness. That would be a betrayal, but she does find Madame Kamenchikoff's robust looks suddenly offensive.

"Has your father called in a doctor?"

"Dr. Lichtenstein examined her yesterday. He recommended ocean baths." She does not say that the doctor diagnosed nerves brought on by overwork. She does not say how useless and hopeless his recommendations made her feel.

"Baths in the ocean! How horrifying! I hadn't realized she was so sick. My dear, I am so sorry."

Nina manages a small smile and a shake of her shoulders. "We couldn't afford to go to a bathing station anyway."

"I can't imagine bathing in the ocean." Madame Kamenchikoff mimics a shiver. But Nina can imagine the ocean, although she has never seen it. An expanse of blue above her head, and at her feet water lapping, a sea breeze prickling her skin, a languorous stretch of beach.

"You know, a tonic is probably what she needs. There are several on the market. I'll find a good one for you. And by the way, I am going to send you my friend, Madame Rabinovich. I told her all about your father. Don't look so glum, my dear. Everything will be all right. There, I'll be back tomorrow. If your father agrees, we can choose a nice fabric together."

At the door to the shop, Madame Kamenchikoff turns and asks "And how is Yudel? Is he happy working for the Epsteins? My Maurice is in a lycée now. In his second year I want him to pass his baccalaureate, like a real Frenchman. Anyway, love to all," and she flutters out of the shop.

Nina turns back the fashion magazine to the page with Madame Kamenchikoff's illustration. She should bring the picture into the back room where Chaim is working. Instead, she lingers over the illustration. She notes the unnatural sinuousness of the model's pose, the coy face surrounded by blond curls peeking under the brim of a broad-brimmed hat topped with a white dove. Madame Kamenchikoff will never look like this. But she, Nina, might. She is young enough and slender enough and yes, although she will never admit this to anyone, pretty enough to wear nice clothes and to see the ocean just for the pleasure of it. Nina closes the magazine and taking the long way around the counter, enters the back room.

Here the walls smell of mold, the floor is stone, a small high window opens onto the courtyard. Chaim works by the light of a kerosene lamp, the gas not having yet been piped into the second room. Only the front room has been made attractive for the customers, and as this was the case in the pharmacy, it is also true in Chaim's new shop.

"Papa," says Nina. "Madame Kamenchikoff was here. Why didn't you come out to see her?"

"I heard her," says Chaim without lifting his head from the black fabric that is being jabbed into shape under the sewing machine. "She makes too much noise. She wears me out."

"What would you do if I weren't there to take care of the customers?" Nina says in a voice she forces to make cheerful. Her father's shape in that damp and dark room, hunched, concentrated, and solitary, always fills her with pity. He works so hard and he has so few connections to the outside world. She would like to press her cheek against his for his comfort and hers.

She squints at the black fabric. "Is that Kippelstein's jacket?"

Chaim grunts.

"Will you be finished soon?"

"Soon."

Nina sighs.

"Madame Kamenchikoff wants to know if you can make her this suit." Nina places the open magazine next to Chaim. He nods absently.

"Of course." The sewing machine whirs.

"But Papa, don't you think she'll look silly in such a tight jacket? How can she walk in that narrow skirt? She's a little fat lady. It's ridiculous."

This time, Chaim peers at the illustration through his eyeglasses. Nina waits for him to smile, to acknowledge the absurdity of Madame Kamenchikoff's pretensions to fashionableness as he often has in the past. But Chaim says, in a flat voice, "She wants narrow and tight, that's what I'll give her."

Nina turns away. She walks to the window and looks out at the courtyard. The cobblestones are covered with slippery lichen, and along the gutters that run at the base of the building standing water has collected, runoff from the night buckets emptied into the yard by the tenants. Once a week, the concierge washes the courtyard down with soapy water, but until that time comes the smell is unspeakable. Nina closes the shutters.

"Until what time should we stay open today?" she says. "It's past seven o'clock. No one is going to come anymore."

"Go home, Nina, Tell your mother I'll be home by ten. I have to finish Kippelstein and then there is Madame Korn's skirt to shorten."

"But it's late."

Chaim lifts his head from the machine and looks sadly at his daughter. "We have to be grateful for the work. Go take care of your mother."

IT IS NOT FAR FROM THE RUE Victor Massé to the rue de Bellefond. The sun is just beginning to set. A soft orange light streaks the sky that, just above the rooftops, is a pale, lingering blue. Most shops

are still open and the narrow sidewalks are cluttered with the merchandise owners display on the street. Ladies boots and men's shoes
hang like strings of sausages from a narrow rod over the window of
the shoe store. A disconcerting row of headless torsos wearing
women's corsets blocks the pedestrian's path. As Nina brushes past
them, the owner comes out of his shop and waves a feather duster
over the undergarments in lace and cotton that have acquired a coat
of soot during the day. In the cap vendor's shop the caps are arranged
to look like the gears on a bicycle, in homage to that newly fashionable and popular sport, and Nina's favorite, the wigmaker, displays
ladies wigs and men's toupees on coyly smiling heads. Nina is almost
tempted to buy herself an ice cream from the vendor who sits beside
his cart peaceably smoking a pipe, but it is too close to dinner time,
and besides five centimes is a lot to spend on a selfish pleasure. At
dusk the lamplighter will come by with his long pole to turn on the
streetlights, but until then the streets are suffused with a pink summer glow that usually makes Nina happy, but not tonight. She barely
notices the balmy weather and the pretty sky. But she doesn't want
to go home either. She wants, what? Impossible to say, only that she
is discontented and restless.

Sometimes during these walks home she lets herself think of Sasha.
Not as often now as when he left two years ago. Then, her heart
thumped uncontrollably when the concierge riffled through the
skimpy packet of letters the postman left with her. Nothing today.
Maybe tomorrow. Occasionally, she still hopes for a letter. But if he
wrote, what would she say? Two years is a long time when you are
twenty years old. Her heart has hardened a bit. She had a fantasy
for a long time after he left: she is on the deck of a great ocean vessel
as it steams into the port of an American city. A young man, bearded,
with a thick head of hair and holding his hat in his hands, waits on
the pier. It is Sasha and Nina's heart leaps. In a moment she will fly
into his arms. Here the fantasy stops. Where will they go? What will

they do? It is enough to imagine the warmth of Sasha's body against hers, his kiss, the words he whispers into her ear. That is the fantasy that consoled her after a dreary day, that she called on at night as she lay on her stomach, hands between her legs, feverish with desire. But the fantasy has become mechanical, comforting but less weighted with feeling. She can consider it with a hard, cold eye. Would she go to America now? She could. Alta and Chaim are more settled, Yudel brings in some money. Would Sasha be the same? And what would it take to erase the hurt of the past two years? And so Sasha takes his place in her dreams, a memory of pleasure, perfect but slightly blurred, useful when she needs comfort, reassurance. But not real, not serious, not possible. And it is the real, the serious, and the possible that Nina yearns for now.

At the corner of the Square de Montholon and the rue Lafayette, before the staircase that leads to the rue de Bellefond, Nina stops to buy a Yiddish newspaper. The vendor, a short man with a drooping white moustache and a peaked Russian cap, sells only Yiddish papers that he carries in a sack around his neck. He knows Nina, who since Sasha's departure has been buying the papers for her parents every day.

"Here you are again, Miss," says the vendor and draws a copy of *Der Idischer Arbeiter* out of his bag.

Nina pays the five centimes, tucks the paper under her arm, and begins to walk away.

"Won't you say good-bye, Miss?" The old man makes a sucking noise with his teeth.

Nina turns on her heel.

"I'm so sorry. Good-bye, sir."

"Dreaming of young men again?" he says.

Nina doesn't answer. She doesn't want to be rude. She has been taught to be always polite, even to ugly old men with leering eyes. But in fact, yes, she has been dreaming.

"Good-bye," she says again in a firm voice.

Just before she reached the vendor, a poster on the window of the café Strasbourg caught her eye. It was an unusual poster for this neighborhood of petty artisans and shopkeepers and it made Nina dream. There in bold sinuous letters was the word *Royan* with the City Hall in the background and in the foreground a drawing of the beach where elegant women carrying parasols lingered to speak with men in straw hats and summer jackets and bold swimmers in bathing costumes paddled in the water. "*Bains de mer les plus frequentés*" said the poster. "The most popular bathing station, theaters, concerts, balls. Accessible by train." The ocean, Nina thought, it must be lovely. And for an instant, she allowed herself to be drawn into the picture, to hear the high lilting voices of the women, the splash of water, the shouts of the children rolling hoops along the boardwalk. What does the air smell like, she thought. Not like the courtyard of her father's shop, not like the streets with their cooking smells, and in the hot weather the smell of horse droppings. And perhaps in her ocean dream there might be a new young man walking beside her, taking her arm, looking into her eyes. Oh, what is keeping her from such simple happiness?

"Good-bye," she said again. But this time the vendor had turned away, looking for another customer.

By the time Nina has reached the Square de Montholon, she is hot and unhappy. The Square appears shady, green, and soothing. Nina chooses a bench under an acacia and near the splashing fountain. She thumbs through the Yiddish paper, looking for the announcement of lectures at the Russian University which she now regularly attends with her new friend, Fania Gomberg, a seamstress from Kiev recently arrived in Paris. The last lecture, the one at which Lunacharsky spoke, was quite interesting. Something vaguely disagreeable also happened at that lecture, but she can't remember what it was and brushes the thought aside. The next visiting lecturer will be Victor Chernov, and Nina makes a mental note to attend. She folds the paper. Today, lectures at the Russian University, educational and enlightening as they are, do not stir her soul. She gets up, opens and closes the gate to the Square and begins to climb the stairs that lead from the Square de Montholon to the rue de Bellefond.

The Schavranskis have made their fourth and last move to an apartment at number 28 rue de Bellefond. Four moves in five years, including a short stay on the rue de Rochechouart. Almost a move a year, that may be why Alta is so worn out. It must be hard to remain optimistic and cheerful through so many upheavals when one is already forty-five and middle aged.

Before she knocks on the concierge's window, Nina turns her head and sees one hundred paces behind her, as if he had been following her down the street, that man, Fania's friend, who attended the Lunacharsky lecture at the Russian University. She feels, for just an instant, surprised and off balance. The man was quite rude. His behavior toward Fania was insufferable. And then a wave of amused curiosity spreads over her. She doesn't remember his name, but his appearance, slightly lopsided, a high balding forehead, sad, serious eyes, and a fierce moustache, is distinctive enough to have imprinted itself in her memory.

She raises her gloved hand in a tentative greeting.

Abraham Podselver does not move. He remains where he is, leaning slightly on his cane, and tips his hat.

Nina, baffled, inclines her head.

She waits. Abraham lifts his hat again. Then he turns around and walks back up the street.

What a strange man, Nina thinks. What in the world did he want? But she is smiling as she knocks on the concierge's window and she is still smiling as she steps through the door.

Happiness

Paris
May–August 1912

XXVII

THEY WERE MARRIED ON JUNE 12 at the city hall of the ninth arrondissement, Nina in a blue silk suit and matching straw hat,
Abraham wearing the gray wool suit made for him by his uncle's tailor
in Vienna and a new gray fedora. There was no religious ceremony.
Alta and Chaim capitulated far more easily than Nina had imagined.
Perhaps they suspected all along that Abraham would never agree to
be married in a synagogue. Nina was relieved; she had expected a
scene and instead her parents were kind and reasonable. Still, she
felt a twinge of disappointment; she would have liked them to fight
harder for her.

The ceremony was quick and efficient, and when it was over fifteen
people repaired to Alta and Chaim's small apartment on the rue de
Bellefond for a luncheon Alta had insisted on preparing. Surely, she
said, Abraham could not object to good food on his wedding day.
Nina, numbly polite, remembers only a blur of well-wishers and a
sad, empty feeling. Alta fussed, Chaim's cheeks were pink with the
effort to appear jolly and hospitable, and Yudel smoked cigarette after
cigarette, in order, he said, to offset the boredom. Nina's friend Fania
flirted unsuccessfully with cousin Josef, who had come from Vienna
for the wedding. Abraham, anxious and ill at ease, was more officious
than usual, giving everyone instructions on where to sit. Abraham's

sister Rebecca was not there because, she wrote, her children's nanny was getting married too and she had no one to leave them with.

When lunch was over, Abraham returned to his rooms with cousin Josef, and Nina remained in her parents' apartment on the rue de Bellefond. It was a relief to postpone the wedding night until Josef left for Vienna. The prospect of a week of freedom made Nina feel as if she had managed to cheat the marriage fates of a little chunk of her life. One afternoon, two days after the ceremony, she took the rue Lafayette to the Opéra and from there the Avenue de l'Opéra to the Place du Palais Royal and along the river Seine to the Louvre. How bold she felt walking, parasol in hand, alone along the quays, protected only by the wedding band on her right hand. She had dreamed of visiting the great museum with Sasha; she hoped to visit it someday with Abraham too, but now she was going by herself and it was exhilarating to be so brave. As she strolled by the booksellers' stalls, it occurred to her that she could, if she cared to, riffle through the old magazines and out-of-print books that caught her eye. That was a privilege of marriage, she thought. She had, by marrying Abraham, bought bondage and freedom, security and independence. On this sunny afternoon in June, Nina was pleased with her bargain.

She had come to see the famous lady, the Joconde, in the Grande Galerie, but she was not there, stolen away two years earlier and not yet recovered. In its place, there was an empty space with the name of the painter and the painting and countless spectators, gawking, like her, at the heart-breaking absence. But she recognized with pleasure paintings she had seen in Etlin's card shop, pictures of the canals of Venice, canvases in which ladies and gentlemen in powdered wigs and luxurious silks pushed one another on swings or played musical instruments, a Madonna looking tenderly at the infant on her lap.

She wandered through room after room until she came to one off the Cour Carrée. There, surrounded by Greek and Roman statues looming in alabaster nakedness above her, she knew she was in an area of the museum where no lady should wander alone. But the statues drew her, in their beauty, their artfulness and their shocking undress. For the moment, there was no one in the room. Nina stared first at the toes, so beautifully modeled, then at the calves and thighs, finally at the lovingly rendered male member, shyly curved among the curling hairs, of a young Greek athlete. She made several turns around the statue, noting the rounded buttocks, the graceful line of the shoulders, the sinews of the back. It was discomfiting and yet she could not stop staring. She wanted to stroke, to touch all that round firmness. She stared at the women too, the high bosoms and modest draperies. She had seen the celebrated Venus de Milo and the armless and headless Victory of Samothrace, but nothing was like this abundance of flesh in stone. She told herself all this looking was instructive; she was about to live in intimacy with a man, shouldn't she know what he was like? But when she thought of Abraham, she could not make the leap.

In a corner of the room, perched on a three-legged portable stool, a man in an artist's smock copied the stone head of a young Greek with a band around his forehead. He worked quickly, his hand moving across the page of his sketchbook with sure strokes. Nina, coming up behind him, saw the head emerge, strong nose, full lips, curls framing the forehead and she thought how wonderful, what a gift. The artist turned his head. Nina, mortified, fled, but not before the man had caught a glimpse of her back and the swing of her skirt. As she hurried through the great rooms to the exit, Nina remembered the moment with embarrassment. Still, she was not for an instant sorry she had come.

Abraham came to claim his wife at the end of the week. Cousin Josef was back in Vienna and there was no reason for Nina to stay with her parents any longer. The wedding night, when it finally happened, was a shock and a disappointment. She had to get used to the crudeness, the astonishing physicality, Abraham's intense concentration that, she felt, excluded her. Although just recently, there had been, deep inside her a faint and surprising tremor of pleasure.

Three weeks after the wedding, Alta fell sick, heart palpitations, weakness in the legs, dizziness. A nervous collapse. Dr. Lichtenstein prescribed a tonic and bed rest, and Nina came every day to sponge her mother's forehead, to brew a cup of verbena, to assure Alta that she was happy, very happy, happier than she had ever been and that, no, if her eyes were sometimes red, it was only from irritation.

"You have not been crying, my darling," Alta said, a pale, veined hand raised above the sheets toward her daughter.

"No, no. I must rub my eyes too hard in the morning when I wash my face. That's all."

"You should be more careful." Alta leaned back into the pillows letting her head droop away from Nina. And Nina did not know if her mother believed her, and if she did, was Alta relieved or disappointed? Misery sometimes brought mother and daughter together, but happiness could only pull them apart.

Finally at the end of July Abraham received a letter from Rebecca inviting the newlyweds to visit her in Berlin. And Abraham, who preferred initiating requests to complying with them, replied that yes they would come but first they would go to Wittenberg and then to Bad Schmeideberg where Abraham would take the waters for his arthritic leg. And Nina, thrilled, saw herself traveling as she had always dreamed, not to escape from danger, not in search of a better life, but for the simple joy of moving one's body of one's own free will from one country to another, for the sheer pleasure of it. Marriage had granted her this wish.

THEY LEFT THIS MORNING FROM the Gare de l'Est, Nina wearing a dove gray suit Chaim had just finished hemming for her the night before, and a light blue veil fastened to her hair with a silver pin in the shape of a feather, a wedding gift from cousin Drina, all the way from Yekaterinoslav. Nina and Abraham had arrived together a little late, Abraham carrying two bags under one arm, real valises, made of sturdy leather, not the wicker baskets and cloth sacks the Schavranskis had traveled with from Yekaterinoslav, seven years earlier. Nina carried a small cardboard case and the tickets in her purse, along with their passports, their identity cards, and their marriage certificate. She and Abraham had agreed it was safer to carry all their documents with them, in case, for any reasons at all, the authorities stopped to question them.

Chaim and Alta and Yudel were already at the station, waiting by the great wrought-iron arch at the entrance to the platform. Behind them, the train loomed, like the backside of an enormous animal, metal plaques with *Paris–Berlin* stamped on the side of the carriages like brands. Nina, conscious of her dignity as a married lady walked stiffly in her little heels, but as she came closer to her mother and father, she began to run. Alta extended her arms to receive her.

"Mamatchka," Alta said, calling Nina by the most endearing term she knew, "little mother." She wrapped her arms around her daughter, "My arms are not long enough to hold you," she said, pressing Nina's cheek to hers.

"She's not going to America," said Yudel. "Why are we making such a fuss?"

Nina turned to her brother, who had been standing, arms crossed, hat tilted over his eyes in the slightly defiant pose he adopted whenever he found himself with his family. She raised herself on her toes to kiss him where the down of his unshaven cheek was still soft. Yudel had grown so that at seventeen he was taller than his father.

"Kiss me, little brother. I will send you a postcard from Bad Schmeideberg."

"What for?" Yudel said. And Nina noticed with surprise that her brother's eyes were glossy with tears. It occurred to her that her marriage to Abraham was hardest for Yudel. There was no one now between him and Alta and Chaim. He would have to bear the brunt of their clawing love just when he most wanted to get away.

"Be patient, little brother. Your turn will come," she whispered. But Yudel had lifted his head toward the skylight of the station where the smoke from steaming engines had left trails of gray along the glass.

"Don't make me cry, all of you." Nina said. "This is my honeymoon. Be happy for me."

Chaim said quickly. "We are glad for you. You are luckier than we were." And Nina, noticed how old her father and mother looked, as if age had dealt them a sudden blow, one night, as they slept.

"Abraham Podselver," Chaim said, "Allow me to help you with the bags."

Abraham shook his head. "We took the omnibus here without any trouble. We can make it to our carriage." Chaim raised his hands in a gesture of compliance. "Good-bye, my children," he said. "Write to us."

"Here, take this," Alta picked up a small wicker basket that had been at her feet. "I put some things in it for you. Who knows what the food is like on the train." She pressed the basket into Nina's hand. "There, now go."

Nina refused to look back once the train had left the station. It seemed to her that she had been a part of so many leave takings, always with an ache of misery, a terrible and fruitless yearning for those who would never stay. Now it was her turn, and although she was sad to leave her parents and Yudel, she understood how much simpler it was to be the one who was leaving, how the exhilaration of an unknown future made up for the sadness of saying good-bye and so, as the train pulled out of Paris, she forgave Sonya, and Sasha too.

They were settled into their compartment, side by side and facing a gentleman with a long face, spectacles, and whiskers, whose stiff-collared shirt, high-buttoned waistcoat, and black jacket proclaimed him a member of the prosperous bourgeoisie. Abraham took out his newspaper and began to read *Der Idischer Arbeiter*, and it embarrassed Nina. The gentleman was also reading a paper. Nina recognized it as *La Libre Parole*, the anti-Semitic newspaper that, many years before, her teacher, Mademoiselle Chambon had kept on her desk. The gentleman gazed at them over his spectacles in a bemused fashion. Perhaps he thinks we are Germans, Nina thought, perhaps he cannot tell the difference between Yiddish and German. She thought of the documents in her purse. There is nothing they can do to us. Jews are free and equal in France, under the law, even the Dreyfus affair could not change that, and she gave the gentleman a stony look. He went back to his paper.

Three hours later, the spires of the great cathedral of Reims loomed into view. The conductor, a young man with a scrappy blond beard, slid open the curtained door to the compartment and announced that the train would stop an hour in the station. The bespectacled gentleman got off. Abraham put down his paper.

"I am going out," he said. "My leg hurts."

He folded his paper and slipped it into his pocket.

"Please, Abraham, don't be long," Nina said. A vision swam before her eyes: Abraham abandoned on the platform. She put her hand to her mouth as if she had spoken an evil wish out loud. "I'll stay with the bags," she said.

From the window she followed Abraham, bobbing and weaving between the passengers, until he disappeared into the great hall of the station.

Half an hour passed, forty-five minutes. Nina standing at the window, hands pressed to the glass, felt her heart thrum against her ribs. The stationmaster blew the five-minute whistle. Abraham, his gait increasingly uneven in his haste, loped across the platform carrying a small package under his arm.

"Thank God," Nina said. "I was worried."

"Here, this is for you." And Abraham handed her the package wrapped in brown paper.

Nina sat down, her knees trembling from the anxiety of waiting and now the surprise of this gift. She unwrapped the package carefully. There on her lap, like a flower emerging from a burst of brown leaves, lay a small round box, decorated with white and gold puffs and "Coty" printed across the top. Gingerly, she removed the lid. A piece of netting stretched across the top of the box, and beneath it, Nina could see a mound of fine white powder.

"Rice powder," growled Abraham.

"Oh my dear," Nina said. "You went all the way to buy this for me."

Abraham lowered himself onto the bench, his bad leg stretched out in front of him. "I hope no one enters our compartment. I would like to travel in peace."

"Abraham, this is so sweet. I have never had face powder before."

"Well, now you do," said Abraham and, settling himself with his back against the bench, extracted three papers from his pocket. "The stalls at the station are very well stocked. Here is a German paper and a Yiddish paper from London. I will have plenty to keep me occupied."

Nina brushed her hand along the netting, rubbed the slippery, delicate powder between her fingers. Could she wear powder now that she was a married woman? Would she dare? She gazed over at Abraham, scowling into his newspaper, as if the paper itself could defend him against her. And she felt a wave of pity and affection toward this man who must have walked some way into a town he did not know, hurrying on his bad leg, stumbling over his bad French, to make her a gift he could not acknowledge. A gift of womanliness. Nina wrapped the box carefully back in its packaging.

The train traveled across the plains of Champagne, north through the flats of Belgium, at one point following the poplar-lined banks of the Meuse. And still, Abraham read, or dozed. They had finished Alta's basket of bread and salami before reaching Liege. At Cologne, Abraham bought her a sandwich.

AND NOW IT IS NIGHT. ABRAHAM is asleep beside her. He has slipped a little in his sleep so that his right thigh presses against hers and his right shoulder keeps nudging her further against the window. She doesn't mind. No, that's not true. She does mind, not the intimacy of his physical body, but his indifference to her comfort, to herself, even to the space she occupies. She wants to push him back, to straighten him, to put him in his place, but she can't. He is too heavy, too deeply asleep. His head lolls against his chest.

Nina has become extremely sensitive to smells in the past week and the odor in this second-class train compartment, a rank smell compounded of cigarette smoke and garlic that seems to rise from the fabric cushioning the benches, nauseates her. It is hot in the compartment and the curtained window can only be opened from the top. Since Nina will not sit back against the cushions, she presses her cheek to the glass pane, breathing in the air that comes in uneven gusts from the outside. It should be country air, night air, fragrant, fresh, redolent of honeysuckle and late summer blossoms. But Nina detects instead the coal vapors from the engine and the sharp, pungent odor of iron striking iron.

Outside, there are villages, mostly dark shapes against the blue of the night sky, an arc of light from a gas lamp, a trail of faint smoke from a chimney fire that has just been extinguished. There are stars in the sky, pinpoints of brightness, constellations she recognizes vaguely. The Pleiades, a bright cluster, the W of Cassiopeia, which Sasha once pointed out to her in a Russian book on astronomy. "Abraham," she says softly, "Wake up. Look at the stars." She shakes him but she is too gentle to wake him. "Abraham," she whispers, as

324 • MYRIAM CHAPMAN

if she had never said his name before, as if it were not his name, as if she could call forth another Abraham from his sleep. He stirs. She retreats back into her corner. She fingers the worn lace of the window curtains. The discomfort under her ribs worries her. What has she eaten that was so indigestible? So disagreeable? She can't remember. She places her hand in the hollow beneath her ribs. At some point, she will have to lie back against the smelly cushions and sleep, but not yet. She gets up slowly, carefully, and reaches for her cardboard case on the shelf above the seat. She snaps open the case and, from under the peach-colored nightgown with the tiny stitches so perfect no one would know it had ever been ripped apart, she extracts a small volume in Russian. It is Kropotkin's *Mutual Aid*, the book Sasha gave her before he left. *Mutual Aid*, the title strikes her, not for the first time, as touching, hopeful. She rereads the dedication: *To Nina, I know we shall meet again, in New York or in Paris. Always, Sasha.* She places her hand over the flyleaf and closes her eyes. She can hear Sasha's voice over the clatter of the train wheels. Dear faithless Sasha wishing her well in her new life. She replaces the book under the nightgown and snaps the case shut. If Abraham asks her why she has brought such a book on her honeymoon, she will say she has always been interested in anarchism and needs to improve her mind. He will not object. And so Nina adjusts her back against the bench, leans her head on the dubiously clean antimacassar, places one hand over her belly and the other so close to Abraham that she can feel the rough cloth of his jacket, and dreams, once again, of love.

AUTHOR'S NOTE

Several years ago, I discovered a manuscript my Russian grandmother had written in French about her childhood in Tsarist Russia and her life in Paris as a young émigré. After translating the manuscript into English for my own children, I wondered what my grandmother had not had the freedom to say about her life and decided to say it for her. In this novel I have attempted to re-create the world she described—the pogroms and strikes in Yekaterinoslav, the hardships endured in France, the courtship of the man who was to be her husband—by imagining what she left unsaid.